Welcome Reader!

Thank you for joining the crazy and entertaining world of Harry Strickland. Besides enjoying the story, we want to give each reader the opportunity to become totally involved in the novel's adventures. The one point of the plot I want to tell you about before you begin is that Harry hides away a great deal of money and jewels during the course of the story.

Your mission, if you want to be a part of the action, is to figure out where that secret location is. Clues are scattered throughout the book. If you can find them and do a little detective work on your part, you might be able to win or share in the cash prize. The reward money for figuring out the mystery starts at $5,000 and can rise to $500,000 depending on how many books sell.

Further details on the contest, how to enter, and the official rules are at the conclusion of the story in the back of the book. This information is also available at www.harryhidit.com. You can go there to follow the increase in prize money as more books are sold.

Enjoy the story. It was fun to write and I hope you thoroughly enjoy it!

Happy reading and happy hunting!

JJ McKeever
Author
June 1, 2016

Harry Hid It

But Where Is It?

Marie,

I hope you enjoy the story and have fun reading. Thank you for your support.

Love,
James

Harry Hid It

But Where Is It?

JJ McKeever

ISBN-10: 0-9966883-6-6

ISBN-13: 978-0-9966883-6-9

Freeze Time Media

Cover design by Janine Tusa

Author's photo by Megan Oates

To Billy, whose ideas and inspiration brought this story alive. Each member of Harry's Team knows you are the only reason we are here. Thank you!

"Suit your tactics to your enemy. When in a quarrel with a gentleman, the Queensberry rules apply. For everyone else, NO HOLDS BARRED..."

Col. M Hoare

Acknowledgments

Any book is the product of more than just the writer...and *Harry Hid It* proves that assertion more than most!

First, we have Tina Verderosa, the CEO of this enterprise. She was the person who first called me and asked me what I thought about writing a book where the reader could participate in the story by discovering the location of hidden money through clues in the book. Not only that, but they could win money if they nail the solution. I think I was silent for five seconds before blurting out, "What a great idea!"

Tina brought the team together behind the contest, marketing, and design aspects of *Harry Hid It*. Her excitement during the writing process was contagious and certainly affected every member of the team. It certainly makes working easier when you have such a positive and capable CEO.

Janine Tusa is the creative director of her own company and her skill and artistry is evident in the cover art of *Harry Hid It* along with all the designs used on the website and in promotional materials. Janine was able to capture the atmosphere and adventure of the story with her designs. For me, it is awe-inspiring to see someone take words and concepts and turn them into a rich visual presentation.

Jackie Weigel contributes a great deal of expertise and passion to the marketing aspects of *Harry Hid It*. I have told other authors embarking on their first book that there are three aspects to putting a book out to the public: writing, publishing, and marketing. I truly think the marketing is the hardest part and Jackie has brought her A game to this endeavor.

Di Freeze is the head of Freeze Time Media and publisher of Harry Hid It. Her attention to detail and guidance led to the finished product that you hold in your hands. By the way, that is also true if you are reading this as an e-book. She took care of all of those versions too!

These are all incredibly talented people who made all of this possible.

JJ McKeever

Chapter 1

HARRY STRICKLAND EYED THE tollbooth coming up. The sign cautioned him to approach at 15 mph. Harry glanced down and saw that he was only 80 miles an hour above that restriction. Looking quickly at the rearview mirror, he saw the red lights of the state trooper following him and trying to keep up. Instead of touching the brake, Harry stomped down on the gas pedal, straightened the car out so that he could smoothly enter the tollbooth area, and held his breath. He zipped past the tollbooth and concentrated on zigging in and out of traffic on the Meadowbrook Parkway. Looking behind him, he saw that the cop car had slowed down a little to negotiate the toll area. Harry had put a little distance between himself and the trooper. Figuring the cop had radioed ahead for help, Harry maneuvered the Mercedes C450 so he could access the parkway area and turn the car around.

It was a good thing he was driving a graphite gray model car and it was nighttime. When Harry was 100 feet from the turnaround, he shut down all the running lights of the car. He pulled the emergency brake up to slow the car down without his brake lights shining. As he came to the turnaround, he threw the car into low gear. The tachometer maxed out as he entered the turnaround and he yanked up on the emergency brake again. The Mercedes started to spin around. Halfway through the spin, Harry eased the brake back down and slammed the gas pedal to the floor. Now going in the opposite direction, he locked eyes with the trooper as the flashing red lights passed him on the other side of the concrete barrier. He gave a big grin since he figured he had now put at least a quarter mile between him and the trooper.

Harry kept up his speed to keep at least that distance between him and the cop car. When he came to the exit for Sunrise Highway, he took it heading east. He was moving pretty fast when he saw an Audi dealership on the right side of the street. He could see red lights coming down the exit ramp that he just left. He smoothly entered the drive for the dealership. The cars for sale were behind iron gates, but a few sat in front of the service bays. Harry slid next to one, shut off the Mercedes, and ducked down across the front seat.

Harry had to smile. Hiding behind the seat was a little silly since the windows of the car were tinted. The smile turned into a grin when he could tell that the flashing red lights had passed the entrance to the dealership and were heading away from him. He remembered as a kid reading Edgar Allan Poe's *The Purloined Letter* in school. Everybody in the story was looking for a particular letter, and it happened to be in plain sight with other letters. Sitting back up, Harry looked at the two Audis he was sitting between in front of the garage. Maybe a Mercedes was a class above these cars, but a foreign luxury car at night looked like any other luxury car. Besides, why would the cop think he was doing anything but keeping the pedal to the metal to get away?

Now that patting himself on the back was over, Harry wondered why the cop had followed him in the first place. Everything had pretty much gone according to plan. He went back over the last couple of hours to figure out what went wrong.

It had started a couple of days ago when Harry's cell phone rang while he was checking the landing gear of an Airbus A310. It was one of his many chores during a workday at Kennedy International Airport. Harry looked at his phone and raised his eyebrows at the name on the screen. Glancing around to ensure he was alone, he answered, "Hey, Tommy, what's up?"

Tommy Petrillo greeted him with, "You looking to make a little extra cash?"

"Always," responded Harry. "What do you have in mind?"

"I have a customer in need of two Mercedes C450s. I'll give you five grand apiece. Interested?"

Harry Hid It

Harry thought for a minute. "That's a hot car. Kind of a small piece of change, though, but I owe you, Tommy. When do you need them?"

"By Thursday night so I have time to make the necessary modifications," said Tommy.

Tommy's father taught and trained Harry back when he was only fifteen how to jack a car. Harry knew that the modifications included doctoring the vehicle identification number and some other changes to mask the identity of the automobile. Almost twenty years later, Harry really didn't like doing this type of work anymore, but the family had been a big help to him over the years. "Listen, Tommy, that's kind of short notice. How about an extra two thousand dollars per car for the delivery fee? You can pass the cost on to the customer."

Harry could almost hear Tommy smiling on the other end of the phone. "My dad trained you well, kid. You're on. Can you get them to our garage in Brooklyn? If you arrive by midnight, that would be great."

"Sure, Tommy. Anything else I can do for you?" asked Harry with a touch of sarcasm. "Special color, interior fabric, options?"

"Shut the hell up, Harry. I'll trust your discerning eye." With that, he hung up.

Harry put his phone away. As he thoroughly examined the landing gear, another part of his mind was plotting. He could bust his ass trying to find two cars like that on the street, either in Manhattan or one of the tonier towns here on Long Island. The other option was spiriting them out of a Mercedes dealership. Since Tommy wanted two cars, that would be a lot easier.

As Harry packed up his tools and headed back into the hangar, he knew exactly where to go. Harry loved cars. He had a few hobbies and passions, but cars were his biggest. Working on cars was his way to relax. Harry fixed his own cars and those of family and friends. Occasionally, he would find a good deal and "flip" it - fix it up so it was better than new and sell it. About six months ago, a cousin of his girlfriend, Sophia, brought him her old Mercedes that needed some work. Trying to find a certain part for the engine, Harry ended up at a Mercedes dealership off the Meadowbrook Parkway. Observing a place like the car lot was second nature to Harry. If he wasn't a mechanic, he could've been a security consultant.

Harry remembered that a solid fence surrounded the lot, but he only saw security cameras on the four corners of the parking area. He vaguely remembered seeing a half-open door as he walked back to the parts department that had monitors in it. Tonight he would check out the place and see if any security were on duty at night. If there were some guards there, he would figure out another way to do this.

The rest of the day went fast. Harry left work and went back home driving his restored 1968 Camaro convertible. He enjoyed the purr of the engine as he continued to think through the quickest way of getting what Tommy wanted. It really wasn't a lot of money, so the easier he could make the job, the better.

Pulling into the driveway of his little brick Cape Cod home, Harry heard a deep bark inside as he shut off the engine. Going around the back, he opened the door, and then quickly stood aside as a big mass of black hair went shooting past him. The Bouvier des Flandres quickly pivoted and came up to Harry. He stood on his hind paws, put his front ones on Harry's chest, and licked his face as Harry affectionately scratched behind his ears. At six feet two inches and a solid one hundred ninety pounds, Harry wasn't a small man. However, he knew from experience that if he didn't get out of the way when he arrived home, the dog could hit him with the force of a linebacker and knock him on his ass.

"Hey, Max, you protect the house today?" asked Harry. Max jumped up and down as if he was agreeing with his owner. "OK, you go do your business in the back. I'll let you back in soon." Harry went in while Max ran to the rear of the yard.

Harry Hid It

After switching on the radio in the kitchen, Harry cleaned up from work. He changed out of his work clothes into dark jeans and a plain gray sweatshirt. He let Max back in and fed both of them. While waiting for it to get a little darker outside, Harry thumbed through the contacts in his phone and chose the number for John Archer. The phone rang and Harry heard a lot of noise in the background as John said, "Yeah?"

"Geez," said Harry, "where the hell are you? It sounds like a friggin celebration there."

"I'm at Duffy's," shouted John. "It's happy hour."

Duffy's was a well-known bikers bar. Harry knew that John hanged with motorcycle gangs since he could walk. "Listen, you free on Thursday night? I have a couple cars I need to relocate."

"Relocate!" John laughed on the other end. "How much?"

"Three grand. I'll call you tomorrow with details."

"In other words, you have no idea what you need to do yet. Sure, bro, I'm free. Let me know what we're doing."

Harry clicked off his phone smiling. John was dependable and a good friend. The guy was a math genius who occasionally taught a course at Hofstra University. Harry always wanted to be sitting in the class the first time John came into the room with his straggly beard, ponytail, and biker vest. The students must think they time warped to a class in the 1970s.

Harry called for Max and together they went out to his Chevy Cruze. Harry opened the rear door and Max hopped in and sprawled out on the backseat. The dark blue Cruze wasn't Harry's usual ride, but he bought it because it was a solid, nondescript car. It was great for doing surveillance work and Max added to the normal appearance of it all. Besides, Max loved to go for rides.

When Harry got to the Mercedes dealership, he pulled into the parking lot of a CVS that was in a strip mall right across the street. He had a clear view of everything. His timing was good. The car place was shutting down and Harry watched as some lights went out and various employees left. Reaching into the glove department, he pulled out a small pair of Zeiss binoculars. Focusing in on the employee parking area, Harry watched a large man come out of the showroom building and lock the door. Getting into a small Mercedes, the man pulled out past the entrance. He got back out of the car and walked over to a keypad near the entrance. He punched numbers into it and a ten-foot gate slid across the driveway. The man went back into the lot through a door-sized gate built into the fence. Going around the back corner of the building, he soon came back out with two giant Rottweilers following him. As he got to the gate, he patted the dogs on the head, secured the gate with a padlock, and drove away in his car.

Harry sat there for an hour watching. Now and then, Max would stick his head between the two front seats for some petting. As near as Harry could tell, the dogs were the only live security the place had at night. Granted, the place was on a main drag and Harry lost count of the number of times a cop car came driving down past the dealership, but that shouldn't be a problem. With Max hanging over his shoulder, Harry started to formulate his plan.

Two nights later, Harry pulled up in front of a diner about two miles from the car dealership on the Meadowbrook Parkway. He parked his Camaro around the side of the building, got out, and perched on the front fender of his car. Tonight he wore black jeans, boots, and a hoodie. He took in a deep breath and looked up as he heard the low growl of a Harley motorcycle coming down the highway. It slowed down and he watched the bike turn into the diner and coast over to him. The driver hopped off and took off his helmet. John greeted Harry with, "I hope this goes quick. I have to get up early tomorrow." They fist bumped as John continued, "You have this all planned out, I suppose."

"Should be a piece of cake," replied Harry.

John rolled his eyes. "I've heard that before. Is it just us?"

"Nah, I got Ozzie helping us."

"Ozzie!" exclaimed John. "Look, Harry, the guys a pal and all, but he can be something of a loose cannon on these jobs."

"Who else was I going to get on such short notice?" Harry asked. "Frank?"

This brought a sincere snort of laughter out of John. "Frank could screw up a one-car funeral. You know he couldn't handle this. Besides, his wife would take a knife to your balls if she even sniffed you got Frank involved in something. You know Frank. He'd be the one bragging to Lisa that he helped you."

Harry smiled. "Yeah, that kinda sums it up. All Ozzie has to do is drop us off, pick us up when we drop the cars off in Brooklyn, and bring us back here. He's also bringing me two things we need to smoothly pull this off. What can he screw up?"

"You always were the optimist, Harry. I'm only doing this because there's a new bike I have my eyes on. The money for this job will be a big help. So what's the plan?"

"We're lifting two Mercedes C450s from that dealership down the road. The security is lax and we should be able to get into the building, lift the keys, and get out of there quickly. I was there right before closing pretending I was doing some car shopping. I think I prepped everything well. I even test drove one of the cars we're taking. I don't think the new owners will mind a few extra miles on their new car."

"That's your "P to the 7th" mantra?" asked John.

Harry said, "You know it. I got something out of that stupid management course I went through." In a previous job, Harry had to attend a three-day management course since he was supervising a few mechanics. The one thing that impressed him was when the instructor talked about P to the 7th. It simply meant that "Proper Prior Planning Prevents Pitiful Poor Performance." Harry liked that and he rarely walked into a situation half-cocked, not knowing what to expect. Things always went much better when he had the opportunity to look over the potential job.

"That's why I ride with you, Harry. These things usually go fine. There are too many idiots out there who are one step away from spending time in jail because they're so stupid."

"You can't teach stupid," said Harry. "You got your mask? There are cameras there."

"Right here." Out of his pocket, John pulled a ski mask with openings for the eyes and mouth. It was black and Harry nodded approvingly as it matched the black pants and sweater John was wearing.

"All we need now is Ozzie. The hardest part of this job is going to be driving through traffic to Brooklyn." As if on cue, a gray Ford F-150 pulled into the diner going a little too fast and stopped with a skid in front of Harry and John. The driver's door opened and a short, muscular man built like a bowling ball jumped out. You couldn't miss Ozzie Marco's black, curly hair. He gave a big grin and said, "You gents call for a taxi?"

Harry greeted him with, "Hey, Ozzie, did you get what I needed?"

Ozzie's grin faded slightly. "Sure, Harry, no problem." He indicated the back of his truck. "The plank is in the back. I picked it up from the construction site I worked at today. I didn't even touch it. Had a kid throw it in the back for me."

"Good man," said Harry. "Let's get this over with. The quicker we get there, the sooner we can be home in bed."

Harry opened the trunk of his Camaro, grabbed a heavy bag, and placed it in the pickup's bed. They piled into the truck and Harry instructed Ozzie where to drive. As they passed the Mercedes lot, he said, "OK, everything looks nice and quiet like it should. Here's the deal. John and I will scale the fence, get into the showroom, grab the keys, open the gate, and drive away. I wish I could close the gate behind us, but you can't have everything."

As they drove past, John eyed the eight-foot fence around the lot with a coil of barbed wire on top. "That's what the plank is for? To get over that stuff?" Harry nodded. "How we opening the gate? Just prying it apart?"

"Nothing so crass," said Harry. "When I was in there I saw a button clearly marked 'Front Gate.' I like when people make life easy for us. We press the button and we're out of there."

"You know the building is hooked up with alarms," said Ozzie.

"Took care of that before I left," said Harry. He quietly thought, "I hope."

As the truck left the dealership, Ozzie asked, "What do you want me to do now?"

"Do a U-turn and bring us back around. There's a bagel store right next to the car lot. Pull in behind that, we'll get out with our stuff, and you take off. Go hang out at the diner until I call you that we're on our way. Then take your time and meet us at the garage. I think we'll be in and out with the cars in ten minutes, tops."

"You're the boss," said Ozzie. He did a series of turns on the highway and was soon heading back in the direction of the car lot. He glided the truck into the driveway of the bagel shop and pulled around the building. Everything was closed and dark.

As he pulled to a stop, Harry asked, "Do you have the other thing I needed?"

Ozzie took a deep breath and reached under his seat. He pulled out two NY license plates. Harry looked at them and then glared at Ozzie. "You jerkoff, I said I needed two sets, not two plates."

"Sorry, Harry," Ozzie whined. "I was snatching them off cars at the mall. I got these and security started driving around. They seemed to take a particular interest in me. I slipped these under my jacket and walked into the mall. By the time I got out and back to the truck, time was running short. I know you would've been sore if I were late."

Not hiding his annoyance, Harry said, "Fine. We'll put these on the back of the cars and hope nobody notices the front." To John, he continued, "Let's put on our masks and get this over with."

Back in the Mercedes that was sitting between the two Audis, Harry smacked his forehead with his hand. That was it! The bloody cop was smart enough to realize that the two Mercedes cruising past him had the same license plate! Harry decided that when he delivered the car and got paid, he was going to dock Ozzie's cut for sheer stupidity.

Chapter 2

As it sunk into Harry why he was leading a cop car on a merry chase, he didn't know whether to laugh or scream at the idiocy of it all. "Time to get out of here," said Harry aloud. "I'll deal with Ozzie later.

He put his mask back over his face in case the cameras at this dealership were recording him. He quickly got out of the car. Reaching into his back pocket for a screwdriver, he took the license plate off his vehicle. He scampered over to the white Audi parked next to him and replaced the plate that got him in trouble with the one on the rear of the Audi. Deciding that he wanted to ensure no more police issues tonight, he went to the front of the Audi, took that plate also, and screwed it into the correct place on the front of the Mercedes.

Getting back in, Harry pressed the ignition button on the dash of the Mercedes and heard the quiet power of the engine start. He calmly backed up from where he parked and maneuvered the car back toward the street. Harry pulled into the light traffic and drove back to the Meadowbrook Parkway. No cop cars were in his vicinity and Harry pulled off his mask as he ascended the ramp and continued on his journey towards Brooklyn. He kept his speed at least five miles over the speed limit. In New York, doing the speed limit was as suspicious as going too fast.

Now that his adrenaline rush was over, he reviewed the rest of the theft as he drove. Except for the police chasing him, it had gone smoothly. Behind the bagel shop, John and Harry had put their ski masks on and jumped out of the truck. Grabbing the bag he had stuck in the truck's bed, Harry shoved it into John's arms and then grabbed the ten-foot two-by-six Ozzie brought. Harry banged on the side of the truck twice and Ozzie took off. The truck couldn't have been behind the store for more than fifteen seconds.

Harry and John jogged to the back corner of the lot. As they hurried in that direction, John looked at what he was carrying. "Harry, what the hell do we need cat food for?"

"Because the dog food bags were too big," Harry answered.

"Huh?" said John.

Harry ignored him as they continued. Reaching the corner of the bagel shop parking lot, they found themselves up against the fence to the dealership. Turning right, Harry led them along the fence so that they were walking away from the street. The Mercedes lot wasn't all that big, but the further away from the road, the better it was for them, Harry figured. He could see some type of small warehouse facility bordering the rear of the car lot. Reaching the far corner of the dealership, Harry angled the plank to the top of the fence so that it rested on top of the barbed wire. When the board made contact with the top of the fence, there was the sound of running paws as the two Rottweilers he observed two nights ago ran towards the two men. They were barking and barring their fangs. Despite the fence being between him and the dogs, John leaped back.

"Jesus, Harry, you didn't say anything about dogs. You know I'm not crazy about them, except for Max, of course."

"Don't worry about it," said Harry. "I have this covered. Give me that bag."

John handed it off and Harry crawled up the board keeping himself low. When he got to the top, he carefully made sure to avoid the barbed wire. The dogs were leaping and barking like Harry was a raw piece of meat they were waiting to devour. Harry took off the glove he had on his right hand and put two fingers in his mouth. He gave out a high, eerie whistle that made the dogs stop their jumping and snarling. Even John covered his ears and winced. The dogs both turned around in circles and lay down. They calmly looked up at Harry. He said, "Good dogs. Here you go." He ripped open the bag and poured out the cat food. "Sorry, guys. This is a low-budget job. No steaks. Eat." Louder, he once again commanded, "Eat!"

The dogs stood up, went to the food, and started munching on it. Harry jumped down. He looked at John. "C'mon. Time's a-wastin'. Kick the board back down to the ground when you jump."

John looked back at Harry. Uncertainty filled the eyes peering out from the holes in the mask. Harry sighed and went over to pet the dogs as they ate up the cat chow. "It's fine. Really."

With a gulp, John quickly reached the top of the plank. In a fluid motion, he leaped down while at the same time heaving the board backwards. It stood up on its end, poised straight up before it toppled over and away from the car lot.

After John landed and rolled, he stood up quickly. He was still looking fearfully at the Rottweilers. Harry grabbed his arm and said, "Let's go." They both started running to the back of the building.

"Damn, Harry, where did you learn to do that whistling thing with the dogs?"

"A few years ago I was doing some work with this Irish guy. He showed me that technique. He used to run guns for the IRA in Ireland and said it came in handy with places he had to break into. Max wasn't happy with me earlier because I hadn't done it in years and I practiced on him."

They reached the building and stood by a plain gray metal door without a handle. "Now what?" asked John. "The building must be wired."

"It is. When I was here earlier, I saw it has a basic alarm system. It's the kind that's activated on locked doors. The good news is that I didn't see any motion detectors so we should be fine once we get in."

"And how are we going to do that?"

Harry smiled. "On the other side of this door is a small hallway outside the restrooms. It's an emergency exit. I went to use the bathroom right before the place shut up for the evening. I balled up some paper towels, opened the door, and stuffed them into the door latch. Theoretically, the lock wouldn't engage so the alarm is, in essence, switched off for this door."

"Theoretically?" queried John.

"Yup. Time to see if I'm right." Harry took a screwdriver out of his rear pocket and slipped the flat end between the door and doorjamb. With a tiny prying motion, the door started moving out towards him. When enough of the edge showed, Harry put his gloved fingertips on it and pulled the door open about two feet. The two men crouched there listening.

"Nothing," said John. "Doesn't mean there isn't a silent alarm telling the cops we're here."

"True that. Let's hurry."

Before they could enter, they saw the flashing of red lights illuminating the front of the car lot. They heard two doors slam.

"Damn, that was fast," said John.

"Couldn't be from an alarm. We opened the door ten seconds ago. Quick, get inside."

John went in and Harry followed. He quietly let the door close behind him. Needing to know what was going on, Harry went to the front of the showroom. Crawling over to a desk by the double glass entrance doors, he peered around the corner and saw two local police cars in the street. Two cops were checking out the fence and talking. They were loud enough that the sound carried through to where Harry was on the floor.

"So the 911 call was from a cell phone. Somebody driving by thought they saw something funny here."

"Yeah," said the other cop. "That's all the dispatcher said. Something about climbing the fence, but I don't see anyone hung up on that wire."

"I was about to stop for some dinner too," said the first cop. "I guess we should at least walk around..." He let out a screech as the two dogs came out of the darkness and lunged against the fence. The cop who was speaking stumbled backwards and fell into a sitting position.

His colleague doubled over in laughter. "You...you...you should have seen your face." That was all he could get out as he kept laughing.

Harry had enough. He brought out his phone and punched a button. After two rings, Ozzie answered. "You guys in trouble?"

"Maybe. We're in, but we got a couple cops prowling around. Create a diversion. We need them to leave."

"I'm on it," said Ozzie, hanging up.

Harry focused back on the cops. The one who fell said, "If you're done acting like an ass, let's go around this thing and make sure things are secure."

"Really?" asked the other one. "Do those dogs that just scared the crap out of you act like there's anyone in there?"

"No, but we better make sure..." He stopped talking as their radios started chirping. They both listened. "Geez, some kind of break-in up the street. Let's go. You're right; those dogs would tear anyone apart in there. We need to see what this call is about. Is there a full moon out tonight?"

Harry couldn't hear what the other cop said as they jogged back to their cars. He finally breathed a sigh of relief as they hit the road with their sirens blaring and headed in the direction of the diner. Whatever Ozzie did, he did quickly. Harry gave him credit for that. Crawling back around the corner of the hallway, he stood back up and said, "They're gone. I'm ready to get out of here."

"Let's do it, man," agreed John.

Harry went over to a large board mounted to the back wall of the office. Turning on his phone's flashlight app, he shined the light on a carefully arranged collection of keys. Quickly scanning the keys, he found two sets tagged for C450s. The tags showed their location in the lot. They were right next to each other and one was the vehicle he drove earlier. They were not actually keys, but fobs. Harry knew you just needed to have the fob with you in the car to activate the ignition by pressing a button. He almost longed for the old days of hot-wiring a car. It could still be done on the new models, but it was a hell of a lot easier this way.

"Okay, John," Harry said, handing him a fob, "that's for a dark maroon car according to the tag. They should be out on the right side of the building. We'll spring the gate, get the cars, and roll."

"I'm good with that. Where's the switch for the fence?"

"Near the service counter. That's the next room on the other side of the hall." Harry suddenly stopped. John could see his eyes take on a thoughtful expression behind the mask. "Before we do that, though," continued Harry, "let's make one quick pit stop."

John followed Harry into the hallway. Before they had a chance to follow the sign directing them to the service area, Harry stopped at a door. He turned the knob and the door quietly opened. Looking over Harry's shoulder, John saw several TV screens. "This is the security office?" he asked in wonder.

"That's right. I think because this place is right on the highway, the owner didn't feel the need for a lot of high-tech security. That will probably change when he comes in tomorrow." Harry glanced around the equipment. "Geez, this stuff is almost as old as my Camaro. It's recording everything on videotape." He looked at John. "Take the license plates out of your bag and hold it open."

John had on a small black backpack. He slung it off his shoulder and fished out the plates. As he stood there with it wide open, Harry dashed around to the various videotape machines and ripped out the tape cartridges. He dropped them into the bag. "We can destroy them later. I'm OK not having anyone reviewing our entrance on film. I hate critics."

"Gee, Harry, they won't have any idea how we got in."

"A little mystery is good for the soul. Time to leave this candy store."

Harry went into the service area and punched the button for the gate. He looked out of the window for a second until he was satisfied it was rolling aside. He and John swiftly went back to the door they used to get inside the building. As they went out and John started to close the door, Harry stopped him. "Wait a minute." Harry gave a friendly whistle. The two Rottweilers trotted around the building and looked up at Harry expectantly. He opened the door wide and said, "In." The dogs looked at the opening and scampered inside. John looked oddly at Harry. He could see Harry smile behind the mask. "I don't want them running out on the highway and getting hurt," he explained.

John shook his head as Harry took the paper towels from where he had stuffed them into the latch and the door closed with a resounding click. As they headed off to where the cars were, Harry smiled at the idea of someone coming into the building and finding the guard dogs in it.

They found the cars in their respective parking spaces. John handed Harry one of the license plates and they screwed them onto the back of their vehicles. Harry instructed, "You go first. Watch your speed and all of that. No use doing something stupid at this point."

John gave a mock salute and got into his car. Harry did the same and started it up. He watched John pull away without putting his lights on. Harry followed suit and they slowly maneuvered themselves out of the lot. When John reached the road, he switched on his headlights and pulled out into traffic. Harry was a few seconds behind him and they started on the ride to Brooklyn.

Harry was enjoying the feel of the Mercedes. It wasn't really his type of car, but he could appreciate its design and ride. He thought his seat was almost as comfortable as his easy chair at home. He settled back and thought about trying out the radio when his rear-view mirror lit up with red lights. "Holy shit, what is it with cops tonight?" Harry said aloud. He glanced at his speed. It wasn't like he was speeding. It didn't matter; he couldn't afford to get pulled over.

He reached into his pocket and punched a button. After one ring, he heard John's voice. "Where the hell did he come from?"

17

"Have no clue," said Harry. "I'm not even sure why. Look, I'm going to slow down as if pulling over. Don't speed up too much, but get out of here. I'll meet you at the warehouse."

"OK, buddy. You got a plan?"

"Working on it," said Harry. "See you soon." He clicked off and stuffed the phone into his pocket. Flicking the turn signal, Harry slowed down and started to drift to the right to pull over on the side of the road. The cop stayed right on his tail. Harry weighed a couple of different options. He gave a grim smile as he decided what to do. He braked the Mercedes to a complete stop. Out of his side view mirror, he saw the cop get out of his car. He slowly walked towards Harry with his hand resting on the butt of his pistol. "Damn, it's a state trooper," Harry thought. Aloud he said, "I would've preferred a local. Those staties are pretty good drivers."

When the cop reached the back of the Mercedes, Harry stuck the car in gear and floored it. The German engine leaped at the touch and Harry shot forward. He swerved to miss a minivan on his left and started to zig in and out of traffic. Looking in the mirror, it wasn't long before Harry could detect the red lights gaining on him. He went as fast as he could while avoiding whatever vehicles were in his way.

After five more minutes of this, Harry saw the cop getting closer. He knew he didn't have a lot of time since this bozo must have radioed for help by now. That's when he saw the tollbooth ahead of him and pressed the accelerator to the floor. The combination of speeding through the toll area and quickly hiding the car was enough to throw the statie off his scent.

As Harry motored into Brooklyn, he knew cops would be looking for his car, but he hoped the new plates would throw everyone off until he got to his destination. He kept to the side streets and let out a long breath when he finally arrived at the warehouse. He drove up to the garage door and honked his horn. Slowly, the door rose up. Harry drove forward but had to stop quickly in front of another door. The one behind him closed. For a few seconds, it felt like he was in a tomb. Then the door in front of him opened and he was flooded with light. He moved forward and entered a huge, well-lit space with equipment all over the place. Harry drove the car forward until he parked next to the one John drove.

As he got out of the car, Harry heard someone clapping his hands. He turned and saw Tommy walking towards him with a big smile on his face. "Hey, the kid's still got it!"

Harry reached out and shook Tommy's hand. "As much as it pains me to say it, I'm not a kid anymore. And you're the only one I would do this for."

Tommy handed Harry a large envelope. "You got me out of a bind. There's an extra thousand in there above what we agreed on. John told me you ran into a bit a trouble. He and Ozzie are in the coffee room."

"Yeah, it got a little hairy. I have to say, though, a Mercedes moves! That's a sweet machine. You don't even have to worry about painting over any scratches."

"As professional as ever. You want a drink?"

"I could use one," agreed Harry.

They entered a room with tables, chairs, a soda machine, and a coffee maker. John and Ozzie were sitting there drinking a beer. Tommy went into a small refrigerator and pulled out a couple of Brooklyn Lagers. He opened them and gave one to Harry. Harry clinked bottles with Tommy and took a long swallow.

John said, "Thanks for taking the heat on that one. Did you have trouble losing him?"

"It took a little luck and a big chance, but he had no clue where I went."

"Why did he latch onto you?" asked John.

"Because of that jerkoff," Harry exclaimed, pointing his bottle at Ozzie.

Ozzie stopped with a beer halfway to his mouth. "What did I do?"

"The only thing I can figure out is that the cop saw two respectable Mercedes cruising by him well within the speed limit, until he saw that we both had the same exact license plate!" Harry's voice got louder as he got to the last few words.

"Harry, I'm sorry. Look, I got those other cops to move, didn't I?"

Harry calmed down a bit. "Yeah, how did you do that so quickly?"

"There was a little strip mall down the road from the diner," answered Ozzie. "It had a jewelry store in it. I drove over to it and shot out the window. I could hear the alarm blaring as I sped away."

Harry chuckled. "That was good. You're lucky. I was going to keep a piece of your share for stupidity. Let's get out of here. I'm tired and have to be at work in the morning." He drained the rest of his beer and said to Tommy, "Glad I could be of help. If you don't mind, though, I want to concentrate on bigger jobs from now on."

"I hear you, Harry," he said as they shook hands. "I was in a jam. You were all I could think of to do something like this so fast."

They said their goodbyes and the three men walked outside to Ozzie's truck for the drive back to Long Island.

Chapter 3

IT WAS NOW SATURDAY in the late afternoon and Harry was cruising in his Camaro to pick up Sophia. They had been going together for quite a long time now and after the week he had, Harry figured it was time to blow off some steam. Saturday was usually their date night, but this time he decided to use some of the money from Thursday's car adventure to treat his friends to a night on the town. Actually, it was going to be a night on the water. He had rented a party boat for the evening complete with booze and food.

Friday had been a struggle to get through work. Harry always felt a bit of a letdown after a job was finished. It had been extra difficult waking up for work on Friday morning. While the money from the job wasn't much, it certainly had been an adrenaline high with the police chase. If it weren't for Max pushing at him with his nose and paws to get up and let him outside, Harry probably would've rolled over, pulled the covers over his head, and called in sick. After a cup of coffee, he figured he might as well go in and earn his paycheck.

When he got home, Harry showered and put the big Bouvier des Flandres on a leash and headed out for a walk around the neighborhood. After a few blocks, he came to a tavern that simply said "Art's" on the sign. Harry and the dog walked in to a chorus of greetings. A cute little blonde barmaid came over, crouched down, and hugged Max. Harry held out his arms and said, "Don't I get the same treatment, Jeannie?"

The girl got up and punched Harry in the arm. "That's for telling that drunk lowlife that it was okay to pinch my ass last time you were in here. Geez, it's hard enough to put up with the octopus arms of some of these customers at one in the morning without you egging them on."

21

Harry rubbed his arm. For someone who probably weighed one hundred pounds soaking wet, the girl had some power. "Sophia gave me an earful about that when we got home. Sorry about that." He grinned. "It seemed like a good idea at the time."

"Jerk!" Jeannie said. "You want a table or you sitting at the bar?"

"Bar will work tonight. Can you bring me an order of chicken wings? And a hamburger, plain – no roll or anything."

"Sure can." With that, Jeannie headed through the swinging doors into the kitchen. Harry took an end seat at the large oak bar that stretched along the back wall of the tavern. Max flopped down next to the barstool. Harry looked around and could see the place was filling up for a Friday evening. He looked at the side-wall and saw that Jake was here with his wife sitting at a table. They nodded to each other. He was the man that he was hoping to see tonight.

Art, the owner, was behind the bar and strolled down to Harry. He was a big black man. It was easy to see him as someone who played reserve guard for two years with the New York Jets. When he blew out his knee, he used his carefully saved money and Notre Dame education to invest in this tavern. Maybe he wasn't making NFL money anymore, but his place thrived ever since he opened it. Harry marveled at how somebody his size could move with almost balletic grace. He placed a coaster in front of Harry and said, "What it be tonight? No Sophia?"

"Nah, she's going shopping or to the movies or something with her sister. We got tomorrow and Sunday together."

"Want any food?" asked Art.

"Already gave Jeannie my order," said Harry. "How about a vodka and cranberry tonight?"

"You got it."

At that moment, some guy in a suit came over to the bar and stumbled as he tried to avoid stepping on Max. Catching himself on the bar, he said, "That's a dog."

"You must have graduated at the top of your class," said Harry.

"What's a dog doing in here?" the man continued. He looked at Art, "Isn't that against code?"

Art looked thoughtfully at the man for a second. Slowly and deliberately, he said, "Max is a customer. A very valued customer. I'll have you know that I'm very particular about who I let in here." Art drew himself up to his full six foot five inches. "You understand that, right," he continued with a disarming smile that at the same time was full of menace.

"Yeah, yeah," said the man. Turning to Harry, he said, "Sorry, man, I didn't want to step on him. I love dogs."

"No harm, no foul," said Harry. "Max appreciates the concern."

The man looked uncomfortable as he bent down and petted Max. The dog took on the look of royalty as he held his head up and allowed the pat. Then the man hurried off to a table back along the far side of the tavern.

Harry and Art looked at each other and started to crack up. Art expertly mixed Harry's drink and set it down in front of him. Harry took an appreciative sip as Jeannie brought his food over. He cut up the hamburger into bite-size pieces. As he ate his wings, Harry would intermittently drop the meat down to Max. The dog cleanly snatched each piece out of the air before it hit the floor.

When he was finished, Harry ordered another drink. He picked it up and went over to where Jake and Sally were sitting. "Hey, I saw you guys were done eating," said Harry. "Can I join you for a few minutes?"

"Only if you bring Max over," said Sally. She was an attractive redhead who looked like she hit the gym every day. All three had grown up together. Sally was one of the smartest women he knew. Harry liked smart women. He knew Sally was completing her residency at one of the hospitals in Manhattan. After that, she was going to join a pediatric office as their newest doctor in the next town over. Jake always knew how to pick them!

Harry Hid It

Harry signaled for Max who was intently looking at him from his place by the bar. He obediently stood up and trotted over. Max went right over to Sally and plopped his head in her lap. Jake laughed as Harry said, "That dog knows where to go."

"He's no dummy," said Jake. "How's it going?"

"Couldn't be better," said Harry. "What about you? Getting around better?"

"You tell me," said Jake. He stuck his legs out from under the table. He had on jeans and sneaks. "Wouldn't know they weren't real, would you?"

Harry looked up and raised an eyebrow. "Nope. You moving around better on them?"

"Rehab every day. My goal is to run in the NY marathon next year. I have fifteen months to get ready." Jake saw Harry's look of surprise. Jake's legs had been blown off with an improvised explosive device (IED) hooked up to an abandoned car in Iraq. He had prosthetics that took the place of his legs from his thighs to his feet. Jake continued, "I'm not bullshitting you. My doc said that I can do it."

"That's great," said Harry. "You still working with the veterans group?"

"Yup. In fact, I'm going to become the new executive director. The money sucks and there are way too many guys and gals who need help after serving in that hellhole, but it's a real job." He indicated Sally with a smile. "I don't want the doctor to think I'm sponging off her."

"Not happening," said Sally as she continued to pet Max. "I'd be sending your butt to be a barista at a Starbucks if you didn't find something on your own." Her smile took any sting out of the barb.

"Listen, Jake, I want to make a donation to the group." Harry handed Jake an envelope. "There's five hundred dollars in there. I got a bonus at work and wanted to share it with a good cause. Can't think of one much better than our wounded warriors."

24

Harry Hid It

Jake smiled knowingly. "Bonus, huh?" He put the envelope in his jacket pocket. "Thanks, Harry. It's very much appreciated. We have too many people to help and no funds. This is great!"

"No problem, man. I'll let you folks go. Sally, Max can't go home with you."

"I know." She gave the black head another scratch behind the ears. "You be a good boy." Looking up at Harry, she said, "I would tell you that, but it would just be wasted words."

"Yeah, Sophia tells me the same thing." He hugged Sally. "You guys take care."

Harry picked up the leash and he and Max strolled out of the bar. He waved his goodbyes to Art and Jeannie. After wandering through the neighborhood for a couple of miles to exercise Max, they came back to the house. Harry gathered up his supplies for tomorrow and after watching some TV, went to bed.

Saturday morning dawned bright and beautiful. Harry grabbed his satchel of supplies, an easel, put Max in the car, and drove to the beach. Parking in a small deserted area that he knew about, Harry went to a hill and set up his canvas. Looking out at the seascape, he started drawing with a charcoal pencil. Soon he was able to bring out the paints and add color. Harry had always been good at drawing. Art class was his favorite time in school. His talent came in handy as a mechanic when he had to sketch out ideas for repairs or improvements for cars and other vehicles. Unbeknown to his friends, Harry enrolled in a couple night classes over a two-year period to cultivate his raw talent. For an adrenaline junkie who thought jumping out of a perfectly good airplane was fun, Harry had his moments when he loved the quiet and solitude of painting. He mainly did landscapes but recently started to practice sketching out objects and even a few portraits.

After sharing a few sandwiches with Max, Harry packed up at two o'clock and headed home. He cleaned up and dressed in cream-colored slacks and a black T-shirt. He grabbed a sport coat on his way out the door and headed over to Sophia's. She lived about fifteen minutes away and it wasn't long before he pulled up in front of the sprawling colonial. This was Harry's home away from home. Walking around to the back door, he rapped on it and walked in. He saw Sophia's father, Dan, sitting at the kitchen table. Dan was some kind of manager at the post office and he and his wife raised four daughters. It was his goal in life to get them all married and out of the house before he retired.

"So where are you two going today?" asked Dan in the way of greeting. "Or are you hanging around here today? We can put some steaks on the grill, open some wine."

"That's OK," said Harry. "We're heading out on the water today. Sophia ready?"

Dan snorted. "Your guess is as good as mine. I'll get her." Without moving from his seat, Dan bellowed, "Sophia! Harry's here."

Soon they heard steps above them, and then coming down the steps. Sophia burst into the room. She had long brown curly hair and in heels was a few inches shorter than Harry. She had a shape that she was proud of and dressed to accentuate her legs and ample cleavage. Today, she wore a red blouse that hugged her figure and black jeans with black sandals. The nails on her fingers and toes matched the color of the shirt. She went over and gave Harry a hug and a kiss. "You proud of me? I'm almost ready on time!"

Harry laughed. "Anytime you're ready within an hour of being picked up, I thank God. You got a jacket? We'll be out on the water and I don't want you to be complaining."

"You're so thoughtful," said Sophia sarcastically. "I'll get one." She retreated out of the kitchen and came back in with a lightweight leather jacket. She bent over and kissed Dan on the head. "I don't want you and Mom waiting up, Daddy. I'm a big girl now."

Harry heard Dan say as they left, "If you're so big, then why do you still live at home?" Harry had heard it all before. He held the car door open for Sophia and then they took off for the marina.

"You have a big night planned for us?" asked Sophia. "It's been a while since we went out on a boat."

"Yeah, it has," said Harry. "I rented us a party boat. We can all have dinner and some drinks. Maybe hit one of the clubs on the bay later."

With a warning note in her voice, Sophia asked, "Who do you mean by 'all' when you say that?"

"Just you and me, John and Julia, Frank and Lisa," he hesitated. "And Ozzie and whoever he's seeing now."

Sophia's hand came down hard on the car door. "Ozzie! You know I think he's dangerous and a jerk. He's going to get you killed."

"Come on, Soph, you know he's one of my best friends."

"Well, he's not one of mine." She looked at Harry suspiciously. "Are you guys chipping in for this ocean excursion?"

"Not exactly. I came into a little money and we hadn't done something like this in a while. We need a fun night out."

"Came into some money. How?" Sophia immediately cut herself off and waved her hands in the air. "Never mind, I don't want to know. But, Harry, please feel free not to invite Ozzie to everything we do."

Harry shut down the conversation by turning on the radio and playing it loud. He knew Sophia didn't care for Ozzie, but he couldn't invite the others and not Ozzie. They had been friends since middle school. He sighed. Sometimes life was too complicated when you had more than two people together. He glanced sideways at Sophia, who was trying to compose herself. Hell, two people together were complicated enough!

They drove into the marina and parked. Getting out of the car, they walked hand in hand toward the water. Harry soon saw the boat he hired. Her name was *Fun Times* and the owner made it available for parties and corporate outings. It was small as party boats go, but it had graceful lines and looked sleek with its white paint and red and blue trim. Crossing the gangplank, a pleasant man in his forties was there to greet him. "Mr. Strickland? I'm Captain Hannity."

They shook hands. "Call me Harry. We're in your hands tonight, then?"

"Yes, sir, just tell me where you want to go. You have me until two in the morning. I need to have the boat docked by then. There are two girls here to serve dinner, drinks, and anything else you need."

"For now, just motor us around for a couple of hours. Then we'll hit somewhere on the shore."

"Sounds like a plan," said the captain. "The rest of your group is aboard, so if you're ready, we'll shove off."

Harry nodded and he and Sophia walked to the back of the boat. A big round table that could sit at least ten was set up on the rear open deck. Arranged around the table were well-padded chairs. Other cushions and places to sit were all over the deck. Everybody yelled out greetings all at once. Harry and Sophia went around hugging and shaking hands with everyone.

Harry found out that the young woman's name that Ozzie was with was Donna. Harry tried not to look at the brunette's legs since her skirt barely reached her upper thigh. She certainly looked like an athletic woman, which was the type Ozzie usually went for. Harry knew Ozzie could find plenty of these girls if he flashed around enough cash. He only ever looked for a meaningful one-night relationship, nothing for the long haul.

John was different. He had been with Julia for a dozen years now. While John looked like a biker, Julia came across as a Wall Street lawyer, which she was. Like Sophia, she tolerated her man's extracurricular activities. She greeted Harry with a warm smile. "I thought this was a great idea. It's been ages since we got together."

"John keeps you hidden, so I needed to take the initiative and get you out of the house," said Harry. "I think he's embarrassed that he has such a fine-looking woman with his grungy appearance."

"I think he's just embarrassed that I'm a lawyer," said Julia. "Takes away his street cred."

Harry laughed. "He lives on the illusion of any street cred he used to have."

John came over and handed him a beer. He was in a white shirt, clean jeans, and black biker boots. "Stop flirting, pal. She knows she has it good."

Harry shook his head and turned. He stood face-to-face with Lisa and Frank. Where Julia's smile was congenial, Lisa's was neutral. Frank was a pal from way back. In school, he was always the hanger-on trying to get in the group. Through persistence, or the fact they could never get rid of him, Frank became part of the gang. He didn't help with any of their criminal activities, though he kept begging to be included. He was tall like Harry, but bald. He lost his hair very young, which was something his friends constantly ribbed him about. Lisa, on the other hand, was a foot shorter than Frank. She had extremely straight jet-black hair and a chest bigger than Sophia, and it was putting tremendous stress on the buttons of her blouse this evening. She liked Harry but wasn't fond of his dark side. She was certainly the boss in her relationship with Frank.

"Hi, Lisa, glad you could come tonight," said Harry. "How's life treating you?"

"We're doing fine, Harry. I wasn't sure what this was all about tonight."

"Chill out, Lisa. Have some fun. We haven't done anything like this for quite a while. Friends, food, some drink…what a great way to spend a beautiful Saturday evening on Long Island!"

Lisa's face softened a little. "You're right. I'm sorry. Thank you for inviting us."

"My pleasure," said Harry. He turned to hide the look on his face from Lisa and he walked to the back of the boat. It pulled away from the dock and slowly started to pick up speed. As he watched the mainland start to shrink behind them, Harry felt someone pluck his elbow. He turned and saw Frank.

"Hey, Harry, Ozzie told me what you guys did the other night. I wish you called me. I would've loved to help with that. I'm a very good driver."

"Sure, Rain Man," Harry said, referring to the Dustin Hoffman autistic character in the movie of the same name. Frank was a good friend, but Harry didn't think he had it in him to go the extra mile if things went wrong. That's why he never invited him along on any job. Besides, Lisa would kill both of them. "Don't even talk about that stuff tonight, Frank. Otherwise we'll be chumming for sharks later and you'll be the chum."

Harry went over to the table and said loudly, "Why don't we all sit down, break out some wine, and get started on the appetizers. We have a lot of food and booze here, and I think we should all enjoy it. You only live once!"

Chapter 4

EVERYBODY WAS HAVING A good time. "Even Lisa seems to be enjoying herself tonight," thought Harry. All of the food was superb. There had been steaks, crab cakes, and salad. The female servers passed around four or five plates of hors d'oeuvres in the beginning. Red and white wine flowed as well as beer and liquor. Everyone seemed to have a nice buzz on. Harry noticed with amusement that Sophia was talking with Ozzie and Donna. He also realized that he wasn't the only one sneaking glances at Donna's body. The girl was hot!

They had been motoring around for three hours now. They had watched the sun set and now it was getting dark. Lights from the shore indicated the different towns dotting this part of Long Island. Harry slowly made his way through the spacious cabin towards the control room. The party boat was tastefully and expensively decorated. It was nicer than any five-star hotel Harry had ever stayed in. He began to wonder what it was like to own something like this.

Harry seemed to have always been doing something on the outside of the law since he was a teen. Looking around the opulent boat, he realized it was all penny-ante stuff. He was getting tired of it. He knew he was good at planning and executing a strategy. However, he also knew he had been damn lucky at times not being caught. Harry was sort of proud that he had never been behind bars for even an hour. While Thursday night had been more of a favor than anything else, was the risk he took worth it? After all, no guts – no glory. Maybe it was time for him to up the game, do a few big jobs, and retire to Florida on a boat like this. He could rent it out and pilot drunken partiers around the south Atlantic.

Harry Hid It

He mulled this over as he knocked on the door leading into the control room. Captain Hannity opened the door and invited him in. Being around top-of-the-line airliners all day, Harry could appreciate the cleanliness and order of the room. He noticed radar and a laptop screen showing the weather. To his surprise, he saw that the captain didn't use a wheel to steer the boat. Instead, there was a small joystick sticking out of the console.

He pointed to it, "That steers this thing! Kind of a letdown for me. I expected to see a large silver steering wheel, or at least a wooden one with spokes."

Hannity laughed. "These new crafts are like playing a video game. If something happens to me, just find a twelve-year-old and he'll be able to figure all of this out in five minutes."

"Sums up where the world is headed," said Harry. "I came up to ask for a course change. There's a place called the Ocean Club. I think it's on the Intercoastal in Long Beach."

"I know it. Picked up a party from there once. They have a nice dock for berthing. If nobody else is docked there, we can pull right up."

"Let's head there then."

"Aye." Captain Hannity started typing on a keyboard and eased the controls to turn the boat. Harry shook his head at how the boat leaped at the captain's touch. He went back down to the group. He put his arm around Sophia's waist and asked the group, "Who wants to go dancing?" All of the women squealed with delight. The men weren't as thrilled but since nobody was feeling any pain from the drinking, they all went along with it. Soon he could see that the *Fun Times* was heading for a building bathed in Technicolor spotlights. An aqua colored neon sign advertised Ocean Club to the open water. Harry marveled at how the captain pulled up to the dock the same way that Harry would park his Camaro.

The boat was quickly tied up and the gangway extended to the dock. Laughing and joking, the four couples disembarked and went into the club. Loud music, multicolored lights, and women strutting around with their best look assaulted Harry's senses. There was a lot of flesh on display tonight. He saw that Sophia, Donna, and Julia were moving their hips to the music. Looking around, Harry called a waitress over and gave her a fifty-dollar bill. "Got a table that will fit us?"

She smiled when she saw the bill and stuffed it in her pocket. "This is your lucky night. One of my reserved tables just cancelled. You can have it."

She led them off to a corner table and they sat down. Harry handed the girl five hundred dollars and said, "Open the tab on that. Give them what they want. Let me know when you need more." She went around and took everyone's order. Then Sophia pulled Harry up from his chair and over to the dance floor. Harry knew Sophia loved to dance. He enjoyed it too but wasn't quite ready for all of the gyrating bodies in front of him. They found some space and got lost in the music and each other. After a few songs, Harry took Sophia's hand and they started back to the table.

"I need a drink after that!" Harry shouted above the music and noise.

Halfway back, they ran into Donna coming in their direction. She stopped them and said, "Ozzie isn't much for dancing, is he?"

Sophia started to say, "Ozzie isn't one who is much for any…" Then she caught Harry's eye. "No, he doesn't like to dance," she finished.

Donna took Sophia's arm. "Want to come back out with me? I miss dancing."

Sophia looked questioningly at Harry. "Sure," he said. "Have fun. I'll be back out there soon." He knew Sophia could dance all night if she could. She certainly looked good moving on the dance floor. He figured she and Donna would attract a lot of attention dancing together. He figured a quick drink and he would go watch them himself and join in.

Harry Hid It

He saw John and Julia on a corner of the dance floor. Harry knew John had to be half-drunk for Julia to get him out dancing. Back at the table, he saw Lisa and Frank drinking and talking. Ozzie was nowhere in sight. He wondered how long it would be before Frank passed out since he was way past his two-drink limit. The thought put a big smile on Harry's face.

Sitting down, he grabbed his glass and said, "You kids having fun?"

"Been a great time, Harry," Frank slurred. "This place is something else, isn't it?"

Harry had to agree. There was a lot of money invested in this place. It was big and colorful. It had the feel of no expense being spared to set it up and decorate it. With the size of the crowd, whoever put the bucks into the place was getting a good return on their investment tonight. Harry saw Lisa say something to Frank. She got up and walked off.

"She's going to the little girl's room," said Frank. "Listen, Harry, why don't you ever include me on any of your jobs? I have skills. I wouldn't mind a little extra cash here and there."

"Frank, you're like a brother to me. I just assume that whatever you do, you will screw it up. I can't let that happen. And I can't let you get hurt. Lisa will kill me if anything happens to you." Frank started to protest and Harry held up his hand. "Really, she will bloody well murder me. The woman scares me. No job is worth that much potential grief in my life. Besides, you and Spanky own your own construction company. You aren't doing badly." Spanky was another childhood friend. He and Frank had gone into business together and made it work.

Frank said, "Maybe. But it's terribly boring." He sat back pouting. "Tonight is fun at least."

When Lisa came back, Harry stood up and went back to the dance floor. He looked around for the girls. First, he saw Donna. She was almost dancing out of her dress. Harry, and everybody else for that matter, could see she was wearing sky blue panties.

34

He shook his head, looking for Sophia. His eyes narrowed when he saw her dancing with a man dressed in a gunmetal gray suit with a white shirt decorated with blue pinstripes. The shirt was open at the neck. Harry knew what happened on the dance floor. You would often find yourself dancing with someone you didn't even know with all these whirling bodies. It always happened with him and Sophia. He never thought anything about it. Nevertheless, this looked different. Sophia had the same expression she always had when dancing. She tended to get lost in the music. The man, however, was trying to talk to her. Harry watched. The man dropped his head close to Sophia's ear and said something into it. Sophia came out of her dancing trance. Harry could see her saying "no" to whatever the guy said. He said something else, and again Sophia shook her head. Now, the man reached down and grabbed Sophia's ass as he tried to talk to her again. She stepped back and went to push him off. She never got a chance.

Harry was there in five steps. He spent that time bringing his hand back. As he got to gray suit, he threw his fist forward with all of his strength and momentum. There was a sickening crack as he connected with the side of the man's face. Harry hit him so hard that the man's head snapped to the side and the blow propelled him into the dancers. There were screams and yells as he knocked people out of the way as he fell to the floor. Falling down with a splat, he lay there stunned. Slowly, he started to struggle to his feet.

Harry had his arms around Sophia. "What did he say to you?"

"He wanted to take me up to his office. He said he owned the place."

"That scumbag is the owner. He..." That's all Harry said as two large men wearing all black grabbed both of his arms and dragged him away from Sophia. They took him to a door off to the side of the main room. Harry looked toward Sophia and saw another black-clad bouncer pulling her toward the same door.

When they entered the room, Harry found himself inside an office that was done up to look like an executive suite in some

Harry Hid It

Manhattan high rise. It was all black and chrome and large glass windows. These windows looked out on the street side of the club and Harry could see a packed parking lot. He just stood looking out the window when the door finally opened again.

Gray Suit walked in. The glazed look was out of his eyes and replaced by burning anger. He walked up and planted himself in front of them. Harry had to look down at the scumbag since he was rather short.

The club owner punched Harry in the stomach. There wasn't much behind the punch. Harry thought he should double over in pain or something for show, but he wasn't that good of an actor. He took a step back but the two bouncers held him tight. Gray Suit said, "Do you know who the fuck I am?"

Several responses went through his mind. Instead of using any of them, Harry simply said, "I don't give a fuck who you are. Keep your hands off my girl!"

"I'm Anthony Russo. I own this establishment. Your slut girl-friend wanted me to grab her ass."

Sophia yelled through sobs, "You lying son of a bitch."

"Shut up, slut," said Anthony. He focused back on Harry. He raised his voice, "How dare you hit me."

"I'd hit you again if your goons weren't holding me," Harry said. "You owning this place gives you the right to make a move on any woman here, even after they tell you no?"

Anthony tried to puff himself up. "Who are you anyway? You're nothing. I run the best place on the South Shore. I have more money than you will ever have. Your girl should thank me for touching her." With that, Anthony punched Harry right in the jaw.

With fire burning in Harry's eyes, he said, "Pay back is a bitch."

Anthony screamed, "You can't touch me. My family will kill you and your skanky girlfriend." He turned and started to walk out but stopped. Looking at Harry with what he felt was a hard look, Anthony said, "I see you again, you're dead!" Facing the men holding Harry, Anthony continued, "Take him outside and teach him a little respect, and let the slut watch."

The man holding Harry's right arm said, "Sure, boss. We got this."

Anthony gave a little nod and left the office.

Harry focused on the two gripping him for the first time. With Sophia crying and begging the men to leave him alone, he knew that whatever he had to do, he had to act quickly. The man who just spoke was about six foot and built like a brick wall. His head was completely bald. The other was shorter with a crew cut and his face had a scar going from his left ear down to his chin. It looked like it came from a knife fight that went wrong.

Harry said, "You guys are okay with that clown touching other people's women?"

Neither said anything. They yanked Harry forward and pulled him towards a door that led to the outside. Harry tried to figure out how to get out of this. There was a good chance that these two were all muscle and no brains. After all, neither of them checked his pockets or patted him down. They were probably more used to throwing the drunks out than doing this rough stuff on a daily basis. As they went through the door and out into the night, Harry had an idea. With luck, it would only hurt a little.

He saw they were in a small area where there was some private parking. One small light bulb illuminated the area. The two goons threw him unceremoniously against the cinder block wall. Harry felt most of the wind in his lungs pushed out and he heard Sophia scream. Crew Cut grabbed her to keep her from running to Harry. Baldy pulled back his arm. Harry tensed all of the muscles in his stomach and took the blow full on. It hurt! Not as bad as if he didn't prepare for it, but the pain almost had him forgetting his plan. Harry let out a loud cry and lurched to the side. Thinking that the punch did Harry in, neither goon tried to hold him up. This is what he was hoping. Falling on to his side, Harry was able to reach behind him and grab the .380 he kept in a holster at his lower back. In the dark with the bad lighting, the two bouncers missed this move.

Baldy came over and reached down. He grabbed a handful of Harry's hair and started to pull him up. Harry got his feet under him, twisted around, and stuck the gun in Baldy's mouth, chipping some of the goon's teeth. Everyone stood stock-still for a few seconds. Crew Cut took a tentative step forward. Harry said, "Uh-uh. You take another step and I will blow his brains out. Now let go of her or you will be first."

The goon didn't say anything but did release Sophia. Harry told her to get behind him. When she did, he instructed the bouncers to lie face down on the ground. When they were lying side by side, Harry said, "If either of you get up and come for me, I will kill you."

Harry took Sophia's hand and headed for the big parking lot across the street. Trying to move as quickly as possible with Sophia in heels, he wanted to get lost in the sea of cars before Anthony got wise to what was going on and sent out more men looking for them. Harry realized that he left his phone in Sophia's purse back on the boat. He couldn't alert any of his friends to what was going on and he had to get out of here fast.

Harry looked around for a car he could steal. He spied a time-worn Oldsmobile Cutlass a row over and led Sophia over to it. Using a small knife he kept clipped to his belt, Harry shattered the driver's window. He reached in and opened the door. With the knife, he pried apart the steering column in front of the tilt control that moved the steering wheel up and down. He used his now bent blade to push the starting rod forward to start the car. When the engine roared to life, he yanked the steering wheel so hard to the left that the steering lock broke as if it were made of plastic. He reached over and opened the passenger door for Sophia to get in. Then he pulled out of the parking lot and away from the club.

Once on the main road, Sophia asked, "Are you okay, Harry?" She could tell that he was furious.

Harry Hid It

Looking over at Sophia, Harry calmed down. "Baby, I'm fine. But we need to find a phone so I can call Ozzie and let him know what's happening."

They went to four convenience stores before Harry found one that still had a pay phone. After five rings, Ozzie picked up. "Who's this?" he shouted over the background noise of the club.

"Ozzie, it's me," said Harry.

"Where the hell you at, Harry? Donna came back and told us something about you punching some guy and the bouncers taking you and Sophia away. Now people are running around here like a Chinese fire drill."

"I'll fill you in when I see you. The short version is that Sophia and I are fine, but we had to get out of there fast. Anyone there take an interest in you guys?"

"Not yet. John walked around trying to find out what was going on. Frank is three sheets to the wind and leaning on Lisa. What do you want us to do?"

"Don't make any fuss, but get everyone out of there. Go back to the boat and tell the captain to head up to Hewlett Harbor. There's a public dock there where he can pick up Sophia and me. I had to borrow a car and I'd rather leave it around here than drive it all the way back to where we started tonight. Got it?"

"We're already moving, Harry."

They hung up and Harry went back to the car. Sophia looked at him questioningly. He smiled. "Everything's cool, Soph. The boat's going to pick us up about ten minutes from here."

"What do we do with the car?"

"I'm going to drop you off at the dock and then go find a place to park away from the harbor area. I'll wipe it down and jog back to you."

Sophia nodded but Harry could tell she wasn't happy. He wasn't either. It had been such a good night until that asshole came on the scene. As he thought about it, his face tightened in anger. Sophia sensed this, turned to him, and said, "Harry, since

39

we're both fine, let's just forget about what happened tonight. We had a good time until that asshole started his shit."

"I know, baby." Harry set his face in stone as he approached the harbor. It was Sophia's way to forgive those that did her wrong, but it wasn't his. It never would be.

Chapter 5

HARRY PUSHED HIMSELF ALONG the park trail with Max thundering next to him. It was Sunday afternoon and anybody who came upon them jogging the trail would have to jump out of the way. For a big man and a big dog, they moved with a grace and fluidity. Max loved getting out of the house and running off excess energy. Harry needed to think.

Harry had hung out with Sophia and her family for most of the day. It had been pleasant enough, but he couldn't shake the dark feeling that had been with him since Saturday night. When the boat picked up him and Sophia from the public dock, Harry told his friends what happened. They were all outraged and wanted to go back and do something. Harry told them to cool it while he thought on it. He said, "Look, we go back now half-cocked, they'll destroy us. There are more of them than us. Don't worry, though, I'll get back at that asshole." With that, he grabbed a beer, went over to the rail, and looked out on the lights of the shore slipping by them. He refused to discuss the matter with anyone.

Sophia knew his moods and gave him a wide berth until they got back to his house. Finally, Harry relaxed and made the best out of the rest of the weekend. He sat through Sunday dinner at Sophia's. It was always a huge production and he enjoyed talking with her parents and sisters. After dinner, he begged off saying he had some things he had to do. When he got back home, he changed into shorts and a sleeveless T-shirt. When he said, "Run" to Max, the dog's ears perked up and he went over to the door. Together they walked to the park and started running once they hit the trail.

Harry's mind went back over the events of the week. He planned the car heist and it went off with barely a hiccup. Look-

41

ing back, the car chase was actually fun. "Yeah," he thought, "it was fun because I didn't get caught. I've been doing these penny-ante jobs for so long that I can pull them off without a hitch. And for what? A few thousand dollars!"

When he started to think about Saturday night, the rage made him run even faster. It was only when Max barked that he slowed down. Looking down, he saw the big dog moving with him panting heavily. Harry slowed back to a jog and brought it down to a walk as he went over to a water fountain. He took a long drink and pressed the pedal at the base. This squirted water into a basin from which Max greedily lapped it up. When they were both finished drinking, Harry led them over to a bench and sat down. Max plopped down at his feet and looked around with his tongue lolling out.

There were many people still in the park. Some were walking and others were jogging. Harry admired the ass of a blonde running by and going away from him and Max. Looking down at the dog, Harry said, "You're supposed to be a babe magnet. Why aren't you holding up your end of the deal?"

Max looked up at Harry, yawned, and turned on his side. Harry absently rubbed the dog's belly with the toe of his sneaker. He thought some more about the past few days. With a force of will, he put the nightclub incident out of his mind for now. He would definitely be revisiting it later and would figure out a way to wage war on Anthony Russo. That little shit had to stand up on a ladder to look Harry in the eye and he would pay. For now, something was bothering Harry even more than that.

This week made Harry feel like he was at some kind of cross-road in his life. He enjoyed the idea of owning a boat like the one he chartered Saturday night. He was a good mechanic at the airport, but that kind of work wasn't going to make him rich. He was damn good at planning and executing jobs like pinching the Mercedes, but there was no real money in that. Yeah, when he was twenty, a few thousand dollars seemed like a lot, but it was peanuts. What he did for Tommy Petrillo was a favor to an old friend. If he did enough of that work, it would add up, but Harry didn't like the risk versus reward ratio. He would rather do one big, dicey job for a hundred times the payoff.

Harry stood up and clipped the leash he was carrying onto Max's collar. He didn't like running with the leash but kept it with him for the walk back home. The dog got to his feet and stretched. Then they strolled back to the entrance to the park and headed to the house. The sun was dropping below the horizon and Harry noticed the shadows around them were getting longer and creeping around them. When he had a childish thought of the shadows swallowing him up, Harry made a decision. He wasn't going to be swallowed up by anyone or anything ever again. Harry was going to up his game. Not just a little, but in a way to make himself independently wealthy in five years.

Harry smiled. He knew tonight wasn't a big epiphany; it was the culmination of a great deal of thinking over the last several months. This week's events were the catalyst to crystalize his thinking. It was time to see just how good he was at pulling off a really big job. Not for someone else, either, but for himself. He had resources to find out where money was at, and he had friends he could rely on to help him. If he were smart, they could all be rich beyond their dreams.

By the time he got home, Harry felt like a weight fell off his shoulders. He hadn't even realized until now just how long he had been deliberating taking this step. "Max," he said as he took the leash off, "I feel like I finally decided to go into business for myself. We're going to keep the company small and lean. And you know what?" The dog looked up at him expectantly. "We're going to start tomorrow. What do you think of that?"

Max was a good sport and barked at his owner's enthusiasm. Harry rubbed the dog's head and got his stuff ready for work the next day. He felt his brain firing on all cylinders as he thought about all that he had to do. He already had an idea in mind and he was looking forward to putting it into action. Harry's friends sometimes kidded him with how methodically he thought things out, but they could never accuse him of being a procrastinator. Once he made up his mind on something, there was no stopping him. Harry went to bed feeling exhilarated with what was in front of him.

Monday morning dawned with rain in the air. The gloomy weather didn't dampen Harry's enthusiasm as he motored towards the airport in his Camaro. Pulling into his usual parking spot, he went into his workshop area and looked at what he had to work on today. It was all routine stuff and he knew he had ample time to do some extra research. When Harry started playing around with the concept of finding something big to rip off months earlier, it wasn't lost on him that he worked at one of the largest airports in the world. The amount of valuables that came through Kennedy Airport as luggage or cargo was practically infinite.

Harry drove a golf cart out to a plane parked at one of the gates. The plane was okay. He was heading there to fix the conveyor belt that fed luggage into the belly of the airliner. It only took him ten minutes of tinkering until everything was working perfectly again. After one of the baggage handlers high-fived him, Harry went back to his workshop and made his way over to the administrative office. Everybody in there knew Harry and there was a chorus of greetings. He chatted everyone up as he made his way through the office. It always reminded him of a maze built for rats with all of the cubicles in there. Harry could think of several preferable ways to die rather than chained to a desk in a cubicle. He finally got to his destination.

"Hey, Debbie," he said to a blonde in her forties.

She sat there peering intently through her glasses at the computer screen. Hearing her name, she looked up and focused her eyes on the intruder. Breaking into a smile, she said, "Harry! How the hell are you? What brings you into this part of the world?"

"I wanted to find my favorite girl in here," replied Harry.

"You say that to everyone," said Debbie, but her cheeks flushed at the attention. Debbie was an attractive woman, but Harry knew from the scuttlebutt around the place that her marriage was on the rocks. She was a little too old for him, but there was no reason not to be nice.

"I think I told you that one of my brothers in Florida works for United Airlines," said Harry.

"Don't all of your brothers work in the industry?"

"Yeah, in one fashion or another. What I wanted to ask you is that my brother was going to send me some family paintings. They're worth a little bit of money. If he ships them up to me here, is there some way that I can keep an eye out for them so I can snag them when they arrive?"

Debbie looked thoughtful for a minute. "It shouldn't be hard. Every airline logs in all cargo that it ships here, or any airport for that matter. Each item has instructions where it goes so that people on this end know what to do. Your brother could ship it up and list you as the contact person to pick it up. Since it isn't flying international, you shouldn't have a problem."

"Is there a way I can get into the system so I can keep track of it?" asked Harry.

"Not for your clearance as a mechanic. I can't even get into it. I deal with vendors and insurance so the powers that be figure I don't need that information."

Harry pointed to Debbie's computer screen. "So, only people with specific access can look on here?"

"That's right. You use the system, don't you?" asked Debbie.

"Sure," said Harry. "I log in with my ID number and password to see what jobs I have that day."

"Those with access get in the same way," said Debbie. "If you want someone to find out about your shipment, just get someone with that access."

"I didn't think it would be that complicated," sighed Harry. "Do you know anyone that can do that for me?"

Harry Hid It

"There's only one in this office, but he's the assistant director for the entire airport." Debbie screwed up her face in thought again. "Most people with access to that info are in another building, and then they filter it out to whoever needs it." Suddenly, she brightened up. "I have an idea." She quickly typed on her keyboard. Harry saw the screen change in front of him. Debbie smiled and hit one more key. Her desk printer started making noise and two pieces of paper spit out. She handed them to Harry. "This is the list of people in the department that takes care of that stuff. It's not like it's top secret information. Take that and see if you know anyone that can help you."

Harry beamed at Debbie, "You're a princess, girl. Thank you very much. Maybe we can go out for a drink after work someday."

"I would like that, Harry," said Debbie. "Don't be a stranger."

"I won't, darling." Waving the two pages Debbie gave him, Harry left the rat's maze and went back to his workshop.

Once he got there, Harry logged into his computer to check on his jobs for the rest of the day. It was a light load, which worked for him today. He looked at the list of names Debbie gave him. He did recognize one or two, but they were just acquaintances. There wasn't anyone he knew very well. As he absently tapped on his computer keys, Harry remembered how the captain on the party boat told him that a twelve-year-old who played computer games could operate his craft. Aloud, Harry said, "Where is a twelve-year-old when you need one?" As he said that, a light went off in his mind.

He didn't know a twelve-year-old, but he did know a twenty-year-old. When Harry was taking art courses at a local college, he ran into a kid who was pounding in despair on the windshield of a car. He was next to his Camaro and Harry ran into him as he was getting back to his car to drive home. When Harry asked what was wrong, the young man told him that he had locked his keys in the car and he didn't have the money to call a locksmith. Harry took pity on the kid and told him not to lose his cool. He opened his trunk and pulled out a few tools. Looking at the driver's door, Harry had it open in a matter of seconds. The boy was astonished, and then extremely grateful. He said his name was Zac and he would be glad to buy Harry a cup of coffee the next time they were on campus together.

True to his word, the following week Zac did just that and he and Harry got to know each other. Harry found out Zac was a computer expert, or more accurately, an ace hacker. He had almost gotten into trouble breaking into some bank accounts, but his father had hired a crackerjack lawyer and the charges were dropped. Zac had to promise his father that he would get his computer science degree and use his knowledge in a constructive way.

Harry started to walk outside and pulled his phone out. He scrolled through his contacts and found Zac's name. He pressed the number and after three rings, he heard Zac say, "Hey, Harry, haven't seen you around school in a while."

"No, I took about all the art courses I could. What are you doing?"

"Finished my degree and working on my master's. Not sure why, but I don't have anything better to do."

"What are you doing for money?" asked Harry.

"Oh, I do a little of this and that on the computer for some extra change."

"Does Daddy know?"

"Hell, no," said Zac. "I told him I advise at an Apple store. Even found a shirt on eBay so it looks like I work there."

"Want to make some money?" proposed Harry.

"What do you have in mind?" asked Zac.

"I need some information. Actually I need passwords for some people."

"How much?" asked Zac.

Harry smiled. The kid didn't seem too concerned about where he would be looking. Harry realized in this day and age, someone who knew his way around computers and software would be very helpful. Harry was comfortable with a computer, but he would much rather putter around in an old car engine than try to keep up with the information world. He did some quick calculation.

"Tell you what, Zac, for what I need today, I'll pay you one thousand dollars. If it goes well, I'll put you on retainer."

Zac didn't have to think. "You're on, Harry. I know you're good for the money. What do you need?"

Harry pulled out the paper from Debbie and looked at the six names he circled. "I'm going to give you six names, Zac. They work at Kennedy Airport. I need their ID numbers and their passwords. Can you do that?"

"Give me a couple hours, Harry. I want to go over to the school and use one of their computers. It's safer and harder to trace. I'll call you in the afternoon."

"Good man," said Harry. "Talk to you later." Harry clicked off and went back to his shop. Trying not to think about it too much, he lost himself in his work. He signed off on some inspections that he did. He was just finishing a late lunch when his phone rang.

"Harry," said Zac, "that was a piece of cake. Give me something harder next time."

"You found all that out already?" asked Harry.

"Something you have to realize, Harry, is that information like that is usually kept in a central place. Somebody in a company like Kennedy Airport has the keys to the kingdom. They keep track of who has access to specific information and keep a list of passwords and other data in case there's a problem. It's not like I needed to guess what someone's password is."

"It was that easy!" said Harry in astonishment.

"If I were trying to crack an airline's database, it probably would've been a lot more difficult. The airport had a bunch of security measures, but it wasn't hard to snoop through."

"Zac, I'll meet you tonight after work at the parking lot where we originally ran into each other at the college. I'll pay you and we'll talk about a long-term arrangement."

"Sounds good. I will send this information over to you in a text. You can do whatever you want with it. I'll see you later."

Harry hung up. Two minutes later, his text alert went off. Harry logged off his computer and entered the ID number and password of one of the names on his list. He held his breath and was about to hit the "enter" key when he stopped. He remembered how Zac said he went to the school to keep his hacking activities hidden. Harry thought this was a good idea and went to a back corner of the workshop area. Here was an empty workstation. It was good they were understaffed in his department. Harry booted up the computer and when it came on, he entered the appropriate information. Soon, he was treated to a menu of items to choose from.

Looking through the information, Harry moved the mouse around and clicked on different entries. Finally, he found the one that showed shipments coming into the airport on different airlines. They covered everything from the entire manifest of a cargo plane, to a couple choice items arriving on a passenger airliner. Scanning page after page, Harry's eyes started to glaze over until he saw a word that made him stop. Diamonds!

Chapter 6

"HARRY, THIS IS BIGGER than anything we've ever tried before," said John. He was sitting on the bumper of an old Corvette Harry was working on in his garage. He had his motorcycle boots up on a crate next to the car and looked comfortable in his biker garb.

He had driven over when Harry called him that evening. Max stretched out in the middle of the floor and Ozzie sat in a chair he had leaned against the garage wall.

Harry said, "It struck me that I'm tired of all the little bullshit jobs we've done the last few years. And for what? We make a little bit of extra cash to buy some toys or have a little fun. To quote a line from a movie, 'I'm getting too old for this shit.' If we're going to put ourselves out there on the line, let's do it for ourselves and for enough money to make it worthwhile."

"You have this all thought out?" asked Ozzie from his corner.

"I believe so. What I propose is that we zero in only on the big money."

"How much is that?" asked John.

"One hundred thousand dollars or more. We keep everything we do tight and small. It's basically just us. There are three main reasons that people get caught. One is that the planning of the job is shabby and the idiots doing the job are nabbed while carrying it out, or within a day of doing it, the cops track them down. The second reason is that too many people know what is going on. Somebody opens up his stupid mouth and starts bragging or blabbing. This is only for us and we don't work for anyone else."

"What's the third reason?" asked John.

"People get greedy," said Harry. "By that, I mean they hit a big score and are out there in a day or two blowing their money

50

on fancy cars, women, drugs, or whatever tickles their fancy. We will not do that."

Ozzie asked, "What are you saying?"

"Look, we all have okay jobs. They pay the bills. What I propose is that we take a very small percentage of what we take off each job and pocket that. It will be fun money. However, the great majority of it we put away for a year or two. More criminals get caught because the cops and feds follow the money."

The garage was quiet for a minute as John and Ozzie thought this over. The only interruption was Max letting out a loud snort and turning over. Finally, John spoke, "I know you're right on that. I've known my share of buddies that got nailed for any combination of those reasons you mentioned. What do we do with any loot we get? Start a bank account in the Cayman Islands?"

"I will look into that for any cash. Overall, I'm thinking of hiding all we find in a safe place. If we do this right, we can start filtering it out in large quantities after a couple of years go by. By waiting to do that, the heat will be off any jobs we did. If it's cash, nobody will really care that we're spending it, and if it's merchandise, we can convert it into money without someone watching over our shoulders."

"Harry, how much you looking at us accumulating in a couple years?" asked Ozzie. "A couple hundred thousand?"

Harry pushed himself off his workbench he was sitting on. He spread his hands up to the garage's ceiling. "No, Oz, that's the problem. We've been thinking too small. Last week John and I had to deal with dogs and cops at the car lot. You shot out a jewelry store window. And for what? A few thousand dollars. No, I propose that in two years we have about two million dollars apiece. It can even be more if we work it right, but that's the minimum. What do you think of that?"

John let out a low whistle. "That's big bucks. I'm down for that. Hey, I get a rush out of what we do. I don't want to do it all my life though."

Harry said, "I feel the same. I have been giving a lot of thought to this. Let me ask you something." He paused and looked pointedly at John, and then at Ozzie. "Do you guys trust me?"

John and Ozzie looked at each other. Ozzie spoke first. "Harry, we would trust you with our lives. You're the most honest crook I know. I remember a couple of years ago when you lifted a Lexus for someone. When you found out it was the wrong model, you returned it and then stole the correct one."

John laughed. "I never did understand why you didn't just unload that one too."

"I thought about it but figured if I went back to the same spot to steal the right car, it would've increased the chances of me getting pegged. To this day, they probably don't know I took that one first."

"So, yeah, we trust you, Harry. Why?" asked John.

"Because I want to be the only one to know where I stash our loot. I feel very strongly that a secret known by more than one person is not a secret. I want to protect you assholes if someone catches on to us. If we're careful, that won't happen, but it's better to be safe."

"Gee, Harry, thank you for the sentiment," said Ozzie sarcastically. "Look, I'm OK with that. I think John is too." John nodded his agreement. "But what if something happens to you, pal? It doesn't even have to be on a job. What if your parachute doesn't open on one of those crazy jumps you do? Why a person would want to leap out of a perfectly good airplane is still beyond me."

Harry grinned. "Ozzie, my man, I'll take you on a tandem jump with me anytime. You'll be attached to me and all you have to do is enjoy the ride." Harry laughed out loud at the horrified look on Ozzie's face. "Seriously, I thought about all of this. Tell you what, you two know me about as good as anyone does. There's no way I want to hide millions of dollars never to be found if I do croak. I will figure out a way to lead you to the cache. You'll be able to figure it out if you ever really need to."

Harry Hid It

"I have a feeling you already know where you're going to stash the stuff," said John.

"I do," said Harry. "Are you two in?"

"I am," said John.

"Me too," chimed in Ozzie.

Harry went over and shook both their hands. "Good. Because we're going to make our first deposit into our retirement fund tomorrow."

"Wow. You mean those diamonds you told us about?" asked John.

"That's right. They're coming in on an early evening flight from South Africa tomorrow. According to the manifest, it's about seventeen pounds of uncut diamonds. Conservatively speaking, that's worth almost three hundred grand. That's if we tried to move them right away. We stash them for a couple years, we can probably get more."

"So how do we do it?" asked Oz.

Harry went back to his workbench and spread out a street map for the area around the airport. "Gather around. Here's how I think we can pull this off."

The next evening around 7:30, the sun was starting to drop lower in the sky. It was one of those times where the wisps of clouds seem to be on fire with their orange glow. It had been a hot and humid summer day and people hoped the night would bring some cool relief. Harry leaned on a lamppost at a corner a couple of blocks down from the delivery gate of Kennedy Airport. His stomach was doing little flips inside as he tried to quiet his anxiety. He had to rush the planning for what they were about to do quicker than he would've liked. He knew he had to take advantage of the opportunity. So much money wrapped up in a small pile of rocks was too good to pass up.

When Harry saw that diamonds were coming into the country today, he quickly did some research. The manifest he unlocked on the computer showed who was picking up the diamonds. They were going to a store in Manhattan's Diamond District. The listing showed the carrier that would be picking up the diamonds after they cleared customs. This was a situation where an individual was bringing the gems over in a carry-on. Once he checked through the custom inspectors, the guards from the carrier would sign for the diamonds, get in their van, and hightail it to Manhattan.

As Harry approached the problem, he decided on two things. Even if he could think of a way to do it, he didn't want to make the heist at the airport. It seemed like a good idea not doing it on his home turf. He also knew that there were too many routes the truck could take going to Manhattan. It would be impossible to figure out how the truck would travel. Maybe if he had time to observe the carrier on several runs from the airport, Harry could figure it out. Without that luxury of time, he decided that a short and quick ruse was their best chance of snagging the diamonds and making a clean getaway.

Harry looked over at Ozzie who was half a block down. He was sitting in his truck with the engine running. A lot depended on Ozzie and the timing. Harry felt like making the sign of the cross when he thought about that, but he didn't want to draw any attention to himself. He just had to trust Ozzie. He knew John would do his part. It all came down to the first part of the plan working.

The way Harry figured it, this street was the only way out of the airport for delivery trucks and carriers like the one bringing the diamonds. They were lucky that the plane bringing in the diamonds was coming in so late. That cut down the amount of traffic leaving the airport this time of day. Harry had double-checked the manifests as well as he could and it looked like this particular company had only the one pickup tonight.

Harry pressed the app on his phone that tracked flights. He saw that the plane from South Africa had landed on time. He figured that by now, passengers should have cleared the plane and gone through customs. It shouldn't be much longer of a wait now. He texted John to let him know it should be soon. John texted back that he was ready. He was stationed next to one of the first buildings right outside the airport. With his motorcycle next to him, one of John's jobs was to alert Harry and Ozzie when the truck was coming.

As far as Harry could tell, everything was in place. He knew that if this crazy idea worked, they could never do it again. Everybody would be wise to it so this was a one shot deal. He would have to come up with another idea if he found anything else coming through the airport that he wanted to get his hands on. Harry hoped there would be more jobs. He wanted this first leap into the big time to go well.

The sound of a text broke his contemplative mood. It was John telling him and Ozzie, "They're coming." Harry looked up and saw a small white van leaving the gate of the airport and heading in their direction. He breathed a sigh of relief when he saw that nobody was in front of or behind the vehicle. This was a one-way street coming out of the airport so he didn't have to worry about traffic coming from the other direction. When it was still a block and a half away, Harry started to walk across the street. When he got part way across, Ozzie pulled his truck away from the curb and aimed it at Harry. At the last second, Ozzie swerved so that the front corner of the truck barely missed him. Harry actually thought the idiot was going to smack into him, but by swerving his hips, the truck missed by a fraction of an inch. Harry, however, made as if the truck hit him. He spun around twice and flopped face first onto the street. On the way down, he brought his left hand up and smeared a fistful of ketchup all over his face. When he landed, Harry made sure his right hand was under him. He lay out in the middle of the road like a sack of potatoes.

When he landed, he made sure he turned his head away from the truck. He heard the brakes squeaking to a stop. One of the doors opened and Harry heard a man shout, "Call 911. I think we need an ambulance here. That asshole in the truck just pulled right out and whacked him."

Harry felt the footsteps coming to him. He felt a hand on his shoulder and the person flipped him over. There was a gasp above him when he saw Harry's face covered in red. Through slits in his eyes, Harry saw the guy was wearing one of the carrier's uniforms. The man twisted his neck and shouted, "He looks bad. You better tell…"

That was all he got out when Harry swiftly rose and shoved the gun he had been holding in his right hand into the man's stomach. He growled, "Don't even utter a sound. Let's move, now!" With his ketchup-covered hand, Harry propelled him back to the van. Getting to the open driver's door, Harry pushed the driver's face into the seat. The driver's partner was still on his phone yelling into it. When he looked up, the gun was pointed at his nose. It looked like a creature from a horror movie was holding it with the blood dripping from his face. "Drop it now," Harry hissed.

When he did, Harry said, "Smart man. Now, with two fingers take out your gun and drop it on the floor." While he complied with this, Harry reached down and plucked the gun out the holster of the driver under him. He threw that down next to the other gun. "Now, we'll do this quickly. You hesitate for half a second and you're dead. Got it?"

The man in the passenger seat nodded and Harry heard an undistinguishable grunt from under him. Harry gestured with the gun. "Open that door." There was a metal door behind the driver and passenger seats leading to the back of the van. When he opened it, Harry said, "Get in there and lie on your stomach." He pulled the guy out from under him and pushed him all the way into the van. "You too, move!"

Harry followed the second one in and was happy to see the first man lying on his stomach. Giving a slight push to the driver, he said, "Get down with your friend." The driver hesitated and Harry felt him start to swing his arm. With a sharp thrust, Harry drove the butt of the gun into the driver's head. That took the fight out of the man as he pitched into the back of the van. "Damn it, I told you to do what I said," shouted Harry. "Put your hands behind your back." The man lying down did. Harry grabbed a pair of zip ties from his pocket and secured one around the guy's wrists. The other man was on his knees and rubbing his head. Harry grabbed his hands, pushed him all the way down on the floor, and bound him. The back of the van was empty except for a small suitcase. Harry grabbed it and tried to open it. It was locked.

He carried it up to the front of the van and closed the door to the back. Shutting the driver's door, Harry turned the keys that the driver left in the ignition. The van roared to life. Harry shoved it into gear and pressed on the gas. The van responded like a horse to spurs and leaped forward. There were sirens in the distance closing in on the area. Harry knew the streets here like the back of his hand and had figured out ahead of time where any ambulances or cops would come from. He set out on a prearranged route away from the noise. After ten minutes of zigging and zagging, Harry pulled into a narrow alley between two buildings. He pulled all the way up until the nose of the van hugged the wall at the end of the alley.

Harry reached down, grabbed the two pistols, and stuffed them into his jacket. He pulled out his pocketknife and forced open the lock on the little suitcase. When it popped, he pulled the top up, and saw a bunch of leather boxes. Opening one, Harry grunted in satisfaction when he saw small stones in there. Hearing a motorcycle pulling up behind him, Harry took out a cloth and wiped down everything he touched. He tucked the suitcase under his arm and got out of the van. It was difficult because the size of the alley barely let him open the door. Stumbling around to the back, Harry saw John pull up on his bike. Taking a helmet from John, he put it on his head while John pivoted the bike around. Getting on behind him, Harry hung on to John and the suitcase as he felt the motorcycle accelerate.

It wasn't long before they were miles away from Kennedy Airport. Nobody followed them. Even when they passed the occasional cop car, no one even glanced in their direction. The streetlights were on as the motorcycle glided onto Harry's driveway. Ozzie's truck already had parked out front. As they pulled off their helmets, John said, "That went sweet."

"I don't know, man," answered Harry. "Once we got started, I just went with it. It seemed like I was hanging around that truck forever."

"No, I watched you. You were there all of three minutes before I saw you drive off. They could never identify you with all that pretend blood on your face. The sirens weren't even close as you got away from there."

Harry nodded and they went in the side door to the garage. Harry grunted as Max placed his paws on his chest and licked his face. The dog licked off what ketchup was left. Gently pushing the dog down, Harry went over and placed the suitcase on the workbench. Ozzie came into the room from the hallway leading to the house. He had three beers in his hand. "You were great, Harry! It looked like I hit you."

Harry put his face up to Ozzie. "You fucking idiot, you almost did hit me. If I didn't twist away, I would've needed the ambulance those guards were calling."

"You told me to get close."

"Close, not on top of me." Harry took a beer and took a swig. He sighed. "Well, we did it. You guys did good." He glared at Ozzie. "Even you, but next time we do anything like this, we practice first."

"Works for me," said Ozzie. "Let's see the booty."

Harry went over and opened the suitcase. He took out one of the leather boxes and spilled its contents on the workbench. Ozzie looked at them and said, "They're just rocks. Where are all the glittering diamonds?"

"That's what uncut diamonds look like, Oz. I swear, what you don't know could fill up Yankee Stadium," said John.

"Really?"

Harry Hid It

"Yeah, the jewelers cut them up and polish them. You're looking at a hell of a lot of dingy bling right there."

Ozzie looked at Harry. "So, what are we going to do with them?"

Harry finished his beer and set it down. "I know a guy who will take a couple of these off my hands for a few bucks. We'll split that up. The rest goes into the stash that I will store away."

John raised his beer bottle. "May this be the first of many good hauls."

He and Ozzie went off to the side and started arguing about something. Harry looked at the small pile of rocks. This just may be the start of something big.

Chapter 7

THE ACTIVITY IN THE FBI field office in Manhattan was constant. There was always something going on in the nation's largest city. Crime was still one of the city's prime components of commerce and plenty happened throughout the five boroughs that crossed over into federal jurisdiction. Whether it was terrorism threats, kidnapping, or a Wall Street executive doing something funny, there was plenty to occupy the bureau.

Karyn Dudek entered the building located at Federal Plaza and slowly entered the elevator that whisked her up to her floor. She wished everyone around her would just shut up. They were talking too loud and it hurt her head. As the elevator doors opened, Karyn had to admit that it was her own fault that her head hurt. She had way too much to drink last night. She had to stop doing that. In the old days, which was only three months ago, Karyn would have a glass of wine with dinner now and then. Since moving to this madhouse of a city, she started to get in the habit of hitting the bar near her phone booth of an apartment for a drink after work. Last night it had turned into several drinks, or at least she thought it did. When she was honest with herself, Karyn knew she lost count. She vaguely remembered having to show her FBI credentials and her gun to the guy who kept hitting on her and wouldn't take "no" as an answer. The creds and the pistol finally got him to leave her alone.

Karyn plopped down at her desk and pulled out a bottle of water and extra-strength aspirin from her pocketbook. She had already taken three pills when the alarm went off. Now, she gulped down three more with a long pull of the water. As far as she knew, she didn't have anything pressing to do this morning. She was investigating some financial shenanigans that a small brokerage firm in Brooklyn seemed to be doing. "Good," she thought, "I can pretend to be researching on the computer until this hangover eases."

The loud drop of a file folder on her desk made Karyn grimace. She looked up at the source of the sound and saw Caitlyn Nemeth looking down at her. The woman was a senior administrative assistant here. When Karyn first met her, she thought Caitlyn was here because of her looks. She was medium height, a lot of blonde hair, and a body that would put most models to shame. Karyn soon found out the young woman was a very smart graduate from NYU, seemed oblivious of her looks, and was a nice person. She was going to law school in the evening and as they started to get to know each other, Caitlyn told Karyn she wanted to become a full-fledged FBI agent. Caitlyn looked down at Karyn with a sympathetic smile.

"I'm sorry. It looks like you had a bad night."

Karyn's smile was more rueful. "You can say that. I guess I haven't been adjusting to life in the big city too well."

"Big difference from Arizona, I imagine."

"That's an understatement. Whenever I was outside of the main cities in Arizona, it would take me a year to see as many people as I do coming into work in the morning. I guess I was feeling a little sorry for myself last night. I may have had one drink too many."

"Drink lots of water. That's what I do," said Caitlyn. "It flushes the alcohol from your system." She was silent for a minute and shuffled her feet. "Uh, I hate to break this too you, but Assistant Director Gonzales wants to see you in twenty minutes."

Karyn groaned. "Really? I thought I could keep to myself until lunch. I figured I would start feeling alive by then."

"I guess you better fake it until you make it," said Caitlyn. "You know how he can get."

"Yeah, anyone who feels like they're on the fast track to Washington, D.C. tends to be bastards," mumbled Karyn. A little louder she said, "Well, he seems better than most at least. I'll be there. I guess I better get some coffee in me."

She grabbed her mug from the desk and stood up. Anyone looking, and some of the men did, would see the physical contrast between Karyn and Caitlyn. The blonde with the long hair was almost five feet ten inches and had the look of an athlete with her tall, statuesque figure. Karyn was five inches shorter and had dark brown hair that barely hung to her shoulders. While Caitlyn was model pretty, Karyn was cute. She liked her nose, brown eyes, and knew she had a good smile whenever she flashed it. She wasn't plump, but she definitely had a curvy figure due to her hips and breasts. She was very fit, at least before she moved to the city. She used to run half marathons every other month when she was out west. Now she seemed to be getting out of breath heading to the coffee machine.

Sitting back down at her desk, Karyn tried to gulp down as much hot brew as she could without burning her mouth. She wasn't looking forward to meeting Assistant Director Gonzales this morning. The man didn't seem to like her, she thought. It wasn't just him. Karyn felt like all of the agents above her and many of her peers didn't care for her. She felt like a pariah in this huge office. That was one of the reasons why she spent too much time in the bar last night.

Karyn looked down at the one photo on her desk. Her ex-boy-friend took the picture last year when they were hiking around the Grand Canyon. Jerry did a great job shooting her standing out on a ledge with the sun setting in the background. She was wearing a tank top and shorts and Karyn liked the definition she had in her arms and legs. Even though she only gained a few pounds since then, she felt like a blob here in the city. She remembered fondly the frolicking they did in the tent and out under the stars that night. Jerry had been great in the sack, or wherever they did it at the time. Karyn actually thought she was falling in love with him. That time backpacking had been her last real vacation and her life turned to shit three weeks after that.

Harry Hid It

The FBI assigned her to the Phoenix field office after spending her first three years as a junior agent in Miami. That's where she went after graduating Quantico and her investigative record had her marked for bigger and better things. She turned out to be something of a dynamo in busting up drug rings and sniffing out the shipments of cocaine being smuggled into South Florida. Her promotion to Phoenix was both a promotion and a safety measure. The word on the street in Miami was that killers were looking to put Karyn out of their misery.

Her first two years in Phoenix were equally phenomenal. She was assigned to the drug squad and she quickly caught on to how the drug traffic filtered into the area from Mexico and points south. Her crowning achievement was finding a meth lab that took its inspiration from the TV show *Breaking Bad* and made its product in an old Winnebago out in the desert. That collar gave her a certain amount of local publicity because of the similarities to the show. She took it in stride and moved on with other cases. She met Jerry in the courthouse when she was waiting to testify on a case one afternoon. He was a federal prosecutor working on another case. Conversations turned into meeting for coffee, then going out to dinner, and then becoming an item for a year. Then came the "incident."

That's the word Karyn used for what happened. It was twenty days after returning from the Grand Canyon area. Karyn was working with a squad of FBI tactical operatives. Basically, they were the bureau's SWAT team. They were there under Karyn's leadership to bring down a large drug operation she had been trying to break up for the past three months. One of her confidential informants gave her a tip that a large shipment of drugs was coming to a location over in Scottsdale. It was going to be exchanged for a huge amount of cash. If Karyn timed it right, she could nab both the distributors and purchasers. It would be a huge feather in her cap. Like most agents, Karyn's aspirations were to end up in the J. Edgar Hoover Building in Washington, D.C.

Harry Hid It

From all the information Karyn could unearth, the buy was happening this night. The target location was an old, abandoned church of all places. It was located on a corner in one of the seedier sections of Scottsdale. Karyn figured there would be at least six to ten bad guys around between the buyers and sellers. Not knowing what kind of firepower they would have, she solicited the help of the tactical unit. Ten men outfitted in flak jackets, helmets, black combat fatigues, and high-powered weaponry were ready to do her bidding. Karyn had on a bulletproof vest and wore a jacket with FBI emblazoned on the back. She would stay in the background while the squad made the initial rush. For now, they were two blocks away with several black SUVs and a truck. With binoculars, Karyn had a clear view of the church. The information she received said the drop was going down at eleven. It was a clear night with almost a full moon that lit up the area.

It was 10:45 when Karyn saw the first car drive up. It looked like an old Lincoln Town Car and it pulled right up to the front of the church. Karyn saw three people go inside. In another five minutes, a white van parked next to the Town Car. Four more individuals went into the church carrying several packages. Karyn saw enough. She signaled to Robert Adams, the leader of the SWAT team. He got his men together and eight of them slowly jogged the two blocks to the church. Two others drove the truck and one of the SUVs. They crept along behind the men. Karyn watched the maneuvers through her binoculars. As soon as the warriors did their job, she would speed over with the other SUV. She had Scottsdale police stationed even further out and they were ready to come racing in on her signal. She could hear the tactical team over her ear jack.

As the men got closer, Karyn saw Adams split the force up. Four raced around to the back. When the leader of that team reached the rear, he signaled Adams. She saw his men burst through the front door. There were many screams of "Freeze, FBI" in her ear.

Then it was quiet. She heard Robert address her directly. "Agent Dudek. There's nobody here."

Karyn felt her stomach go hollow. "We saw them go in. The cars are still there."

"I know, but it's empty. Wait a minute, one of my guys found something. What is it, Gonzo?"

Karyn heard one of the agents say, "There's something glowing underneath this pew."

"Check it out," ordered Adams.

After a few seconds she heard, "Holy shit! It's a timer attached to a package. It's counting down. There are seven seconds left."

Adams screamed, "Get out. Everybody out. Run!"

Karyn looked up at the church and it erupted into a fireball. The orange flames illuminated the steeple and then it slowly toppled over onto the Town Car and van. Her mouth dropped in horror as she watched. Karyn tried to will her feet to move, but she was rooted to the spot. She heard the drivers of the SUV and the truck shouting in her ear as they pulled up and ran to the conflagration. When she saw them try to get inside, Karyn finally made her way to her SUV and drove the two blocks. Some men were stumbling out of the building and collapsing. She knew the rest were still inside. She made her way to the church entrance when the driver of the truck came out and grabbed her arm. "Don't go in there, Agent Dudek. We can't get through the fire."

Karyn looked in disbelief as sirens started to wail in the distance. She stood there watching as fire engines and ambulances showed up. The old wooden church slowly settled to the ground in fire and smoke. For the first time in her life, Karyn went into shock. Soon her supervisor found her leaning against the car. He gently helped her into his vehicle and they eventually drove back to the FBI office.

The next couple of months were hell. As it turned out, the entire drop was a setup. Whoever actually showed up that night had set the bomb and exited through a passageway that ran under the church and opened up in an old gardener's shack at the back of the property. They had all gotten clean away. Robert Adams and five of his men died in the explosion. The other three agents who were inside the church escaped with terrible burns and injuries. As more intelligence filtered in, the FBI determined that the drug lords of the area needed to get the federal agency to back off. Whether they meant it as a specific warning to Agent Dudek was a matter of debate. However, she was a great scapegoat for the FBI.

Their internal investigation decided that she had not thoroughly vetted out the information and her actions led other agents into an extremely dangerous situation. Karyn couldn't fault them on their findings because she felt the same way. During the course of the investigation, her superiors regulated her to desk duty and she felt like she was in prison. She went over everything in her mind and couldn't figure out what she would've done differently. Privately, her boss and other agents said they would've done the same exact thing. Officially though, she was demoted a level and sent to New York City for "reassignment and further training." What it meant was that she would no longer be leading any investigations and would have to take a backseat to every other agent for a while…or forever.

Karyn stopped her walk down memory lane and looked at the photo again. Jerry had dumped her two weeks after the explosion. He told her that she would be a detriment to his career now and he was sure she understood. Karyn mumbled "asshole" to herself and stood up. She smoothed down her black pantsuit and white blouse. She rubbed her eyes and hoped they weren't too bloodshot. Squaring her shoulders, she headed down the hallway to Assistant Director Gonzales' office. The door was open, but she stopped and knocked on the doorframe.

Enrico Gonzales looked up from his chair. He was a handsome thirty-five-year-old man wearing the obligatory FBI dark suit and tie. He gave a small smile and said, "Dudek, you're prompt. I do like that. Come in and close the door." When Karyn did, he continued, "Have a seat."

Karyn sat down in front of his desk. She normally wasn't a fan of closed-door meetings. They were usually bad. She saw a photo of Gonzales on the desk with a beautiful Latin woman and two small children. Obviously, it was his family. They probably had a nice house in Brooklyn or something while she barely fit into her apartment. She started to sigh, but physically put aside her feeling of self-pity. She had been carrying that around with her forever it seemed. She had to stop!

She focused on Gonzales when he cleared his throat. "Agent Dudek, I've watched you over the past few months. I like what I see when you're working on a case. You're good. But your file told me that anyway. I know what happened to you out west. At worse, I would call it a bad judgment call on your part."

Karyn tried to hide her surprise. This wasn't what she expected. He sounded almost supportive. She felt confused. The pounding headache didn't help. She looked blankly at Gonzales and all that she could manage to say was, "Sir?"

"I'm not an idiot, Dudek. I wouldn't have this position in New York if I were. I have been in the bureau for almost fifteen years now and am very familiar with the bullshit that goes around. I've had a few cases in my career that blew up." He looked surprised for a moment. "Uh, I didn't mean that literally. Not like what happened to you...oh, fuck, never mind."

Karyn was startled at the outburst and how uncomfortable he looked. She listened harder as he went on. "What I mean to say, there were a few times I was almost on the end of a reprimand. So these days, I try to look beyond the official report. I've had supervisors who took all the credit for my busts, but I don't work that way. I believe that if my people are successful, then I am too. We're a big enough agency that if something good happens, then there's enough room to spread around the glory. Unfortunately, as you know, blame works the other way."

At this point, Karyn didn't know what was going on. "I appreciate that, sir. I certainly have experienced all the ins and outs of the FBI the past year. I still believe in what we do here."

"I realize that, Agent Dudek. It's been brought to my attention, though, that you're rather mopey if you aren't out in the field working with your team. It's a bit of a downer. You're better than that."

Karyn decided to be honest. "I admit I'm having a hard time adjusting to the city."

"Is that because you're a western gal?"

"I did grow up on a ranch in Colorado," said Karyn. "I love the outdoors, but I enjoyed my time in Miami. I do like the city life."

"While I have no reports that you do not play well with others, my guess is that you excel when out doing your own thing," said Gonzales.

A blush spread over Karyn's cheeks. This man knew her. She thought he ignored her since being under his command. "You're probably right, sir. It was something that just sort of happened in Miami. I was getting more responsibility without looking for it."

"It didn't just happen, Agent Dudek. I'm friends with Agent-in-Charge Esposito from Miami. His version is that he didn't have a choice in giving you more responsibility. You earned it and he needed you. That got me to thinking. I believe you're a race horse who has been cooling your hoofs too long at the starting gate."

"I'm not quite sure I understand," said Karyn.

"New York has the most of everything in the country," said Gonzales. "That includes crime. What kind of manager would I be if I didn't have my best people do their thing? I'm pulling you off the team you've been working with and giving you a case. You're still responsible for the work you're doing with them, but more as a consulting agent. You are to head this up." He pushed a folder over to Karyn.

"What is it?" she asked.

"A bunch of diamonds were stolen a couple blocks from Kennedy Airport. Obviously, somebody knew how they were coming in. They may be connected with other crimes, but that's purely speculation. We have been dealing with a lot of smuggling and stealing around the docks and airports. I don't have a lot of resources to throw at this problem with everything else we deal with, but I have you. I would be stupid not to take advantage of your talent."

Special Agent Gonzales stood up and held out his hand. Karyn stood and grasped it. Looking directly into her eyes, he said, "Karyn, put Arizona behind you. I think you're better than that. Don't let me down."

Finding her voice, Karyn croaked out, "Thank you, sir. I won't."

She turned and left. Before going back to her desk, Karyn went into the restroom. She leaned over the sink and splashed water in her face. Looking up into the mirror, she was happy to see that her eyes weren't red and there was a spark in them again. She had no idea that the day was going to turn out this way. She lifted up the file from the counter and said aloud, "I'll get whatever dirtbag stole those diamonds, come hell or high water."

Chapter 8

WIND TORE THROUGH THE open door, buffeting Harry as a bump threw him off balance. He reached up and grabbed the edge of the doorframe to brace himself. He saw a glimpse of trees, meadows, and hillsides down below. The sun streamed down and bathed everything in a golden light. It was truly a glorious Saturday morning. Looking forward, Harry saw the signal and launched himself.

He loved that thrill of first stepping out of an airplane. It was a feeling of freedom, peace, and excitement that he could never quite describe to somebody who hadn't experienced it. He felt the air whistling past his ears as he set himself in a flat position to free fall for a while. Looking through his goggles, he could just make out the Delaware Water Gap area a bit to the west of him. He followed the course of the river north until he lost sight of it. He was getting to know that area. The mountainous area of northwestern New Jersey surrounded him as he plummeted to earth.

Harry had a couple of places he enjoyed parachute jumping from, and this one was quieter than where he went to on Long Island. When he really needed to get away from the Island and New York, he enjoyed coming here. As he pulled his ripcord and felt the reassuring tug of the parachute opening, he thought about a few places he saw early this morning that would be great scenery for a painting. As the ground came up below him, Harry nodded to himself that some mountain and river canvasses would be a nice addition to his landscapes.

He was such a veteran of parachute jumps that he didn't even consciously think what to do as he came in for a landing. It came as naturally to him as breathing. His right foot dragged across the exact middle of the landing zone as he brought his legs under him to softly land in a stand-up position. His knees buckled a little on impact, but he stayed upright. Quickly gathering his chute, he looked around to the couple who had jumped with him. He saw that they'd missed the landing zone by about fifty feet. Rookies! Still, they jumped solo and not attached to anyone in tandem, so they didn't do badly. They were a young married couple and Harry knew from his conversation with them on the plane that this was only their third jump on their own.

From the perimeter of the field, he heard a dog bark and looked over to see Sophia holding Max's leash. Harry waved and jogged over to them. When he got close, Sophia hugged him. "Harry, I get so damn nervous when I watch you jump."

"That's why I don't like bringing you, baby. But it was so beautiful today that I couldn't resist." Harry patted Max, who was sniffing at the parachute. "Was Max good for you?"

"Max is always good for me. It was funny though. He started barking when he saw you jump out of the plane. How he knew that was you ten thousand feet up there is beyond me."

"What can I tell you? Max is a special dog. Give me a few minutes. By the way, you look great."

Sophia smiled at the compliment. She was wearing white shorts and a salmon-colored sleeveless blouse. Her legs and arms were tan and her outfit wasn't hiding her figure at all. Harry liked when she dressed that way. "I'll meet you at the car."

Harry walked over to the hangar building that housed the jump school at Blairstown Airport. He'd discovered this area making a trip from Long Island out to the Poconos in Pennsylvania to deliver a car several years ago. It was a small town right before the Delaware Water Gap area and he made his way to the airport when he saw the sign advertising parachute jumping and glider rides. He made a jump that day and had been back here a few times since. After he discovered a nice little bed and breakfast on a small lake nearby, he and Sophia would occasionally escape out to this area. The big plus was that it allowed dogs and Max could come along.

Harry Hid It

He turned in his parachute and changed out of his jump suit and back into his jeans and black T-shirt. He stuffed his suit, boots, goggles, and helmet into his duffle bag and joined Sophia and Max at the Camaro. Sophia was leaning against the car with her legs perched out in front of her. She had on sunglasses and watched a little boy of about four walking with his dad past the car. The boy said, "Daddy, can I ride the pony?" He was pointing towards Max.

Coming up behind him, Harry said, "That's a dog, son. You can't ride him, but you can pet him. His name is Max." When the father looked at him questioningly, Harry added, "He's big, but he loves kids. It's fine."

The two tentatively approached Max. Max let the boy lightly touch his nose. When Max licked the hand, the boy giggled and went to hug him. The huge dog allowed the attention and wagged his tail. After a couple of minutes, the father thanked them and walked away. Sophia turned to Harry and said, "That was cute. You ever think of having a kid, Harry?"

"Yeah, but not quite yet." He opened the trunk and threw in his stuff. "Tell you what, Soph. I'm working on a few things. If it all pans out, we can seriously start talking about all that stuff in a year or so."

Sophia lifted her sunglasses. "Really, Harry?" she asked with genuine surprise.

"Really."

"What kind of stuff are you working on? A new job?"

"Uh, something like that. It's things you don't like to talk about."

She lowered the sunglasses and sighed. "Harry Strickland, why I put up with you, I'll never know."

Harry opened the passenger door and let Max climb into the backseat. Grinning, he exclaimed, "Because you love me!"

"That or I'm crazy," said Sophia as she got in and buckled up. "Where's this place we're going?"

Harry Hid It

"Town called Belvidere. It's only twenty minutes away. They have a big car show there this same weekend every July. That's why I wanted to come out here. That and getting away from everyone for a couple days." He went to the driver's side and got behind the wheel. He started the car and they began to move.

Once they started down the road, Sophia asked, "Why did you get up so early? I looked at the time and it was six o'clock. Didn't I wear you out last night?"

Harry reached over and caressed her thigh. "No, you'll have to try harder tonight." He moved his hand to the inside of Sophia's leg and felt her shudder slightly. "I needed to take Max out and I wanted to do a little hiking along the river. I'm trying to find a really nice spot to do some painting. I want to change up from all the seascapes I do out on the Island."

Sophia put both her hands around Harry's arm. "When are you going to paint me? I hear all artists like to do a nude sooner or later."

"And what artists have you been hanging out with?" asked Harry. Sophia just grinned at him. "When I feel ready to do a nude, believe me, you'll be the first one I'll call. Besides, what do I do with it when I finish it? Give it to your mom and dad as a Christmas present?"

"Mom would be appalled and my father will just think I'm that much closer to getting out of the house," said Sophia.

Harry laughed and they chitchatted during the rest of the ride to the car show. When they came around a hill, they saw a huge field with cars of all types. Harry followed the parking signs until a boy with an orange flag directed them to a spot in another field. With Max in tow, they made their way to the car show.

There was no admission, but a large sign said the Northwest New Jersey Veterans Association sponsored the show. A table was set up with brochures and information along with a huge tub for donations. Harry dug into his pocket and put some bills in the tub and they walked into the show area. The first part of the field had every type of car vendor imaginable. There were places to buy parts, transport your car, buy a classic car, accessorize whatever type of vehicle you had, and many more. Food vendors encircled the perimeter of the field.

When they finally reached the car area, Harry approved of what he saw. It seemed that whatever automobile had ever been built, it was here on display. Most were classic cars that ranged from a 1912 Stanley Steamer to every muscle car or sports car built. The automobiles' owners lovingly took care of them and enjoyed showing them off. Harry was in his element as he, Sophia, and Max weaved in and out of the rows of cars.

At one point, Sophia started talking to two women who were there with their husbands and their cars. They lived the next town over from Sophia on Long Island, and the three stood under a pop-up awning yakking away as if they'd known each other for years. Harry yanked on Max's leash and the two of them started to walk through the cars again.

As they passed a light green 1955 Thunderbird convertible, Harry looked up past the gleaming lines of the car and saw a security guard sauntering past the crowds. Harry felt a momentary pang of guilt. As well as the diamond heist had gone, he did feel bad that he had to pop the one guard in the head. If only the idiot did what Harry told him, it never would've happened. Even after a week and a half, Harry still wished it didn't come to that. At least the asshole didn't do something that would've forced Harry to pull the trigger. He never had to shoot anyone and while he'd never admit it to anyone, it wasn't something he particularly ever wanted to do.

Just as Harry shook those thoughts out of his head, he pulled up short and stared. Max stopped in his tracks and looked up at his owner. Then he followed Harry's gaze over to a beautiful 1962 royal blue Corvette. It wasn't the car Harry was looking at, though. It was the car's owner. When he first saw him, Harry thought it was that shithead Anthony from the club on the Island.

Harry Hid It

Harry felt himself get hot in the face and his fists started to clench. He calmed down after a minute when he realized this guy was taller than that jerk and had a much friendlier demeanor.

Taking a deep breath, Harry looked around for Sophia. She was still back there talking. He led Max over to a quiet spot off to the side and took out his phone. He pressed a name in his contact list and listened to the phone ring. "Hey, Harry, what's up?"

"Where you at, John?"

"Montauk Point. My group rode out here today. It's worth it just to see people's faces when we cruise through the Hamptons."

Harry laughed. "Yeah, I can see that. Listen, John, I want you to put some inquiries out in your motorcycle gang. Remember the fuckhead I had the trouble with at the club a few weeks back?"

"Yeah, how can I forget? What do you need?"

"I'd like to find out more about him. In fact, I want to know everything I can about him."

"You really have a bug up your ass about him, don't you, Harry?"

"Wouldn't you?"

John was silent for a moment. "I would. Okay, when we break for dinner, there are a couple boys here who are good at that. One is a detective in his day job. He's a private one, not a cop."

"Cool. I'd really appreciate it."

"How you and Sophia enjoying New Jersey?"

"It's been nice. We're at a big car show now. They have some vintage motorcycles here. You'd like them."

"I'm sure. You take care, Harry. I'll talk to you next week."

Harry clicked off and he and Max continued circulating around the cars. When he went back around to gather up Sophia, he said, "Jesus Christ, I thought you were going to ask them to adopt you!"

"It was fun. We had a bunch of mutual acquaintances." She put her arm through Harry's. "Want to buy a girl some lunch?"

They walked over to check out the food wagons. They decided

on meatball subs. Harry bought three and fed one to Max. After a couple more hours walking around, they started to head back to the car. When they were near the entrance gate, Sophia said, "They have a bunch of port-a-potties over there. I hate the things, but I'm not going to make it back to the B&B. Wait for me here, Harry."

She hurried over to a line of women. Harry sighed and looked at Max. "Well, what can you do? She lasted longer than I thought."

Harry found himself drifting over to the entranceway. A man in his late twenties stood up from the veterans' table and began walking towards Harry. He had the stiff gait of someone trying out a new pair of shoes. Looking down at the man's ankles, Harry could tell that his left leg was a prosthetic.

"Hey, man," said Harry, "how did you guys do today?"

"It's been a good weekend. Beautiful weather and big crowds are the best we can hope for. Everything else takes care of itself from there."

"I'm from out on Long Island," said Harry. "I have a couple friends out there who are veterans. I have a friend stationed in Afghanistan now. All I can ever think to say to you guys is thank you."

The man smiled and held out his hand. "Dan Groth. I appreciate that."

Harry shook his hand and said, "I'm Harry. What kind of things does your group do?"

"We do everything from helping vets figure out all of the damn paperwork to promoting activities for the families. All of the proceeds from this particular event provide scholarship money to veterans' kids going to college."

"How do you select who to give it to?" asked Harry.

Dan said, "We try to have a big enough pool so that we can give some to as many kids as deserve it. We have criteria we follow and try our hardest to make it fair."

"The government should send all your kids to school for what you guys deal with."

Harry Hid It

Dan laughed. "Harry, if you ever run for office, we'll all vote for you. Even if we had to move to Long Island to do it!"

It was Harry's turn to laugh. "I'm not cut out for politics. My bullshit meter is at a very low level and I wouldn't last two days." He reached into his pocket and pulled out some money. He counted off ten bills and gave them to Dan. "Here's a little extra for some worthy kid. Maybe he'll get through college and then enter politics and fix this mess."

Dan's eyes widened as he looked at the money. "Holy shit, Harry, this is a thousand bucks!"

"I had a nice payday this week," said Harry. He did. He had fenced a few of the uncut diamonds to give him, John, and Ozzie three thousand dollars each before hiding the rest. He sent them through someone in Florida so he knew they wouldn't point back to their heist.

At that point, Sophia came up and took Harry's hand. "I'm ready. We can go now."

Dan looked at her. "Hi there. Is this guy your man?"

"I guess he is."

"He's a saint."

Sophia smiled. "Not something I usually hear him called, but thanks. I guess I'll keep him."

Dan held out his hand to Harry again. "Thanks, Harry. Feel free to come back anytime."

"Best of luck to you guys," said Harry. With that, he led Sophia and Max back to the parking field.

"What was that all about?" asked Sophia. "You seemed to make his day."

"I just gave them a small donation," answered Harry. "All the money they make at this thing goes into a scholarship fund for veterans' kids for college."

"I don't care what others say, Harry," said Sophia. "You're a good man." She stopped and reached up to kiss him firmly on the lips.

"Oh, Sophia…here? Can't you wait until we get back to the room?"

"C'mon, you big goof. Take me there and I'll show you. Then you can take me out to dinner." Sophia started walking in front of him, giving him a good view of her ass as she exaggerated her walk to the car.

Driving back to the bed and breakfast, Harry thought about the coming week. In the schedule that he created in his mind, he wanted to do one or two big jobs a month for the next two years. He wanted them to be different so that it'd be difficult to detect any pattern. If he planned well and their luck held, then he could start thinking of some type of future with Sophia. For now, he wouldn't think about that much. He worked best when he was dealing with one thing at a time, and bringing in the big bucks was what was important now. Their next job depended on how well Ozzie was doing in the observation department. The success of their next caper depended on Oz. God help them all!

Chapter 9

JOHN LOOKED OUT ON the street from his truck. The rain lazily hit the windshield as he watched the armored truck pull away. As it lumbered away from the curb, John could see the storefront where the armored service delivered. It read Citywide Check Cashing. He could see with amusement that besides cashing checks for payroll, social security, and pensions, the place also sold lottery tickets. He said, "Friggin' incredible. They charge ridiculous fees for taking people's checks, and then they sell them lottery tickets. I'm surprised there isn't a beer cooler and wine rack in the back."

Harry snorted from the passenger seat. "Give it time, John. That's the funny thing about this world. It's full of thieves. However, a bunch of people have a license to steal. For people like us, we're just wildcat contractors."

John couldn't help smiling. "I'd like to hear you use that line in court."

"There won't be any court. We vary our jobs, do it methodically according to the plan, and slip into the night. By not flashing around wads of cash for a while, there won't be any heat on us."

"Harry, you know I have all the confidence in the world in you. But what are the odds of Ozzie fucking this one up?"

A frown crossed Harry's face for a second. Then he said, "Probably better than even. It's only a woman and a kid. How hard can it be?"

"I don't know, Harry. Remember that time you filled that truck up with the big screen televisions in Newark? You had Ozzie drive it while we covered his front and flank in our cars. It was a night like this with rain and we thought we lost him. We finally found him in the drive-thru of a McDonald's, with two cop cars parked in the lot because they were eating their dinner. I didn't think Ozzie would be able to sit for a week the way you tore into him when we finally delivered the stuff."

"First, I couldn't believe he just turned off without letting us know. Geez, you were a block ahead and I was a block behind. Between the traffic and the rain, he decided he needed a snack. I wanted to tell the cops to arrest the guy in the truck for being a dumb ass."

John laughed. "Yeah, sometimes he really comes through, and other times he can be bloody dense." He looked at his watch. "Shouldn't we hear from him soon?"

Harry clicked on his phone. "It's almost six. He better or we're going to have to wait another week to do this."

John looked across the street at the store. "He was right about the schedule. I'll give him that."

"Yeah. Tomorrow is Friday. People are going to be storming this place wanting to cash their paychecks. They need to lay in extra bucks today to pay everyone. Ozzie did good staking this place out. Now if he…" Harry's cell phone interrupted him talking to John. He looked at it and said, "It's Ozzie." He pressed the speaker and asked. "Did you do it?"

"Harry, the kid kicked me in the balls!" Ozzie's voice sounded pitched a little higher than usual.

"No names, idiot," snapped Harry. He looked over at John with a shake of his head. "Are they secure?"

"Yeah, I had to slap the kid around, but they're tied up in the kitchen. I'm in the living room. They can't hear me."

"Jesus Christ, you said he's ten!"

"He's a feisty ten-year-old. I'm hurting here."

"Shut up. You should be getting a call in ten minutes or so. Don't hurt them," emphasized Harry.

"Sure, boss," a resigned Ozzie said as Harry clicked off.

"Not a moment too soon," said John. "The place closes in five minutes. You ready."

"Into the breach," said Harry. He pulled the bill of his Yankees cap down low on his head and pulled the hood of his sweatshirt over the hat. "I hate these damn hoodies. Let's get to the alley."

John looked in his mirror and pulled into traffic. He made a left at the corner and stopped across from the alley that bisected the block where the check-cashing store sat. Harry lightly sprang from the cab of the truck. As soon as the door closed, John took off around the corner. Hunched over, Harry jogged through the rain down the alley. This job took a couple of weeks to plan and most of it relied on Ozzie observations. He'd watched the place and noted the comings and goings of the proprietor, Victor Elgort. Ozzie had actually gone in near closing time to cash a couple of checks and told Harry about the layout of the place and its routine.

According to Ozzie, the owner sent the lone employee out of the store about five minutes after the closed sign went up on the front door. Then Mr. Elgort exited about ten minutes later to his car parked at the rear. Going through the front door wasn't going to work since all the check transactions were done through two inches of bulletproof glass. The best chance Harry had was to catch Elgort as he left and herd him back into the store. His biggest worry was a camera somewhere catching him confronting the owner. Harry had walked around here last night and as far as he could tell, the store itself had a camera trained on the back entrance, but none of the other buildings had any pointed in that direction. The trick was to stay as unobtrusive as possible until he made his move. The dark skies and rain were a blessing.

Slowly sauntering down the alley, Harry tried to make himself as small as possible. The brim of the baseball hat was dripping water and Harry felt like he was trying to look through a waterfall. Harry saw the back door of his target open and a large Hispanic man came out. He ran through the drops and got behind the wheel of a battered Chevy pickup. With a roar that told Harry the vehicle needed a new muffler, the truck backed out and went right past Harry. Leaning against the wall of another building and trying to give the illusion that he wasn't feeling well, Harry cursed as the truck hit a big puddle that soaked his jeans. Shaking his left leg to throw off the extra water, Harry moved closer to Victor Elgort's shop.

Still bent over as he approached the corner of the property, he saw a three-year-old Lincoln parked there. Harry slipped on a mask and stayed there crouched against the corner of the adjoining building. He counted off the seconds in his head as he kept his eyes on the heavy steel door that served as the back entrance. If anyone came down the alley at this moment, Harry knew he'd have to abort. The adrenaline pumped through him and he knew he was ready to move. He kept wondering if he'd get his chance.

In thirty more seconds, he had his answer. The door started to swing open. Harry raced to it as a body started to emerge. Harry hit the door with his shoulder, squeezing the man between it and the frame. He heard an explosion of breath come out of the man as the impact hit him. Harry pulled the gun out of his pocket and jabbed it hard enough into the owner's neck so the man knew he meant business. Without wasting time, Harry said, "Back inside. Now!"

Grabbing the man's arm, Harry pushed him back through the heavy door, which Harry pulled shut behind him. The entire encounter took twelve seconds. With the gloom of the weather, Harry was confident that nobody saw what he did. If so, he'd hear sirens soon. John, who should now be sitting at the other end of the alley, would warn him if any troubles were coming his way.

With the door closed behind them, Harry couldn't see anything. The room was pitch-dark. He growled, "Put the light on." He kept his grip on the owner but allowed him to feel around on the wall. Harry heard a click. As the light came on, he found himself in a small room. Shelves lined three of the walls, and it looked like it was full of paper and supplies. In the wall opposite from the door they entered, in the middle of the shelves, was another door. This one was wooden and didn't seem to have a lock on it. Harry pushed Elgort to it and kicked it open with his foot. It opened wide and banged on the wall as it pivoted all the way around. This time Harry saw they were in a small office. He pushed Elgort down into the chair behind the desk and pulled it out so that it was in the middle of the floor.

Since he wasn't hanging onto the man now, Harry relaxed slightly. He quickly went over to the remaining door in the room and opened it. He saw this went into the area behind the thick glass walls where the employees served the customers. He could see where the customers stood. For all the money that went through the store, it wasn't a very big space.

Turning his attention back to Victor Elgort, Harry sharply said, "Alarm?"

"Huh?" said Elgort with a quaver in his voice.

"Did you set the alarm as you were leaving?"

Sweat streamed down the man's face. "Yeah, but it engages after the door is closed. It didn't set until you pushed me back in here."

Harry gave a grunt of satisfaction. He figured the system probably operated that way. Ozzie didn't see any motion detectors when he cased the front part of the shop, and a quick scan told Harry it was also clean in this rear section of the store. There shouldn't be any sudden rushing to the area by the police and Elgort couldn't hit any button sitting in the middle of the floor.

"Okay, Mr. Elgort. Let's do this fast and easy. I want the money in that safe there." Harry motioned with the gun to a large steel container sitting in the corner of the room. "Do it now. You don't get hurt and I'm out of here."

"B...b...but there's not that much money in there."

Harry took his arm and, in a sudden movement, cleared the top of the desk. Phone, laptop, papers, and a mug half filled with coffee that proclaimed, "Have a Great Day," crashed to the floor, making a lot of noise. Harry put his face in Elgort's and said as menacing as he could, "Don't bullshit me. I know what was delivered today. I know you have lots of people coming in tomorrow with their paychecks. I know what I want."

He could see the fear in the man's eyes. Harry actually admired the owner when he said, "It's not that simple. It's a special safe."

The guy was terrified, but he was putting up a brave front. Harry sighed and stepped back. Elgort eyed the gun still pointing at him. Harry said, "Take out your phone. Carefully. Use two fingers. If I see anything in your hand other than a phone, you'll lose the hand." The gun pointed unwaveringly at Elgort.

Victor Elgort looked at the dark eyes peering at him between the mask and the hat brim saturated from the rain. He reached into his right jacket pocket with a shaking hand. Pulling out a cell phone, he almost dropped it from the terror he felt.

Harry instructed, "Put it in your lap. Dial your wife. Put on the speaker."

The man looked at Harry with a puzzled expression. Then it dawned on him that this intruder had done something to his wife and son. He quickly put the phone down and did as he was told. Elgort couldn't quiet the new rush of fear he felt as the phone started to ring.

Harry hoped that Ozzie did what they planned. He was to instruct the wife to place her cell phone on the table in front of her. When Ozzie heard it ring, all he had to do was press the button to answer it. Harry began to silently curse as the fifth ring started. Finally, he heard it being answered. For a few seconds, nobody said anything and the room was silent.

Finally, Elgort sputtered out, "Violet, are you there? Can you hear me?"

Harry could hear sobbing on the other end. "Vic, is that you? Some man came in and has me and little Victor tied up here."

"Are you okay, Violet?

"Y...yeah. He pushed Victor Junior around though and slapped him."

Elgort looked up at the man with the gun. "What kind of people are you, hurting a little boy?"

For a second, Harry actually wanted to apologize. He was

thinking of a good retort when Violet spoke up again. "Victor tried to defend me, honey. He kicked the man in the nuts."

In any other situation, Harry would've cracked up. Part of it was thinking of Ozzie trying to handle a little kid and not faring well. Getting his head back into the game, he growled, "Hang up. Now."

"Victor, what's going on..." That was as far as Violet got before Victor broke the connection. He looked at Harry. "You took my wife and kid."

"Look, you see on TV how these things are long and drawn out. I prefer it go fast and we part friends. I don't think I need to spell it out. Open the safe and your family will be fine. If there is any alarm attached to it, deactivate it. If any cops start showing up here, two phone calls will be made. One to me to let me know they're coming so I can leave. And one to take care of your family."

They looked at each other for a moment. Then with satisfaction, Harry saw Elgort's shoulders sag in defeat. "Fine. Can I go to the safe?"

Harry took a step back and nodded. With the gun still trained on Elgort, the man tried to stand but sat down again. He took a deep breath and struggled to his feet. Looking sheepishly at Harry, he said, "My knees are shaking."

He took a few tentative steps and made his way to the safe. Harry stayed close and watched his every move. The safe stood on four steel legs so there was an opening on the bottom. As Victor started to reach under the safe, Harry stuck his gun hard against the man's neck. "What are you doing?"

"It's okay...nothing...I'm shutting off the alarm to the safe."

"Do it slowly," muttered Harry.

Elgort's hands were back to shaking. Harry saw him do a couple movements and then brought his hand out empty. He looked at Harry. "I can open it now."

"Good man. Go ahead."

Harry Hid It

The front of the safe was very old-fashioned, but effective. It had a round combination lock on it, and a handle to open it after the lock was disengaged. To cut through it would take heavy equipment. Harry wasn't a safecracker and had no desire to learn. While he wasn't crazy about involving the wife and kid, this was the simplest plan he could come up with. He knew if there were too many moving parts in any operation, there were more chances to fuck it up.

He heard a click and Victor pulled open the safe with a grunt. As the light hit the inside, Harry saw many neatly stacked bundles of currency on the safe's shelf. Under the mask, he smiled. Keeping his voice gruff, he told Elgort, "Back to the chair. Put your hands behind your back. When the man did, Harry took some zip ties out of his pocket, attached Elgort's hands to the chair, and bound his ankles together. Going over to a small bathroom, Harry saw a small towel on the sink. He grabbed it and formed it into a tight ball. Going back to the owner, Harry instructed him to open his mouth. He was about to stick the towel in the man's mouth when he stopped and asked, "What's the alarm code for the outer door, Victor?"

Victor gave him five digits. Harry nodded and said, "You know if that doesn't shut off the alarm, I'll be back."

The miserable-looking man quietly said, "It's the real thing. Just get out."

With that, Harry stuffed the towel in Elgort's mouth and tied a length of rag over it that he'd also brought. Satisfied that the trussed and gagged man wasn't going to be a bother, Harry put the gun into his belt at his back and went to the safe.

He looked at all the cash sitting there. Reaching to his side, he pulled two contractor strength garbage bags out of his pants. When trying to figure this part out, he wanted something strong enough to hold the money but not anything to draw attention to him. He hoped that if anyone saw him after he left here, they'd figure he was one of the countless denizens who wandered around New York carrying their possessions around with them in garbage bags.

Harry Hid It

He opened one bag and put half of the money in it. Then he did the same with the other. Harry tied their ends together and picked them up. Damn, money was heavy. He muscled them up to his shoulder and started to leave. He stopped at the door. "Victor, this was nothing personal. Somebody will call the cops and let them know about your wife and kid." With that, Harry went into the rear room and shut the door to the office.

He went to the big steel door and stopped at the keypad next to it. He punched in the number Elgort told him and was happy to see the green light turn red. The alarm was off. He reached over and shut off the light. In the dark, he opened the door and stuck his head out. Doing a quick and thorough scan of the area behind the check-cashing store, Harry saw nobody. He happily noted that if anything, it was now raining harder.

Walking out the door, Harry hunched himself over. He wasn't acting this time, as the two bags full of cash were quite heavy. Walking through a couple of puddles, Harry reached the alley. He turned left, reached up, and ripped the mask off. Reaching the end of the alley, he turned right and walked down until he reached John's truck. He opened the door and shoved the bags into the space behind the front seats. As he closed the door, John pulled into traffic and cautiously made his way out of the area and to the highway.

Harry pulled out his phone and called Ozzie. "It's done. Get out of there. Don't say anything to the mom and kid. Just leave. Meet you back at my place."

"Sure, Harry. It go okay?"

"Goddamnit, stop using names!"

"Sorry, Har...I mean, I'll see you later."

Harry sat back and took off the hoodie and hat. John glanced over to him. "That seemed to go well."

"For the most part, I think it did. However, I don't always know where Ozzie's brains are. Sometimes I think we need to trade him for a future draft pick or something."

"But, Harry, who would want him?" asked John.

Chapter 10

BOUNCING INTO WORK ON Tuesday morning, Harry went over to his workstation to see what planes and machinery he had to work on today. Even though it was getting to be the end of August, the day was one of those three "H" days that could plague the greater New York City metropolitan area – hot, hazy, and humid. Harry could feel the sweat slithering down his back already, but it didn't bother him. He was still riding high from the success he and the team had on Thursday.

Ozzie got back to Harry's house just as he and John pulled up. When they got into the garage, Harry dumped out the cash they took. He'd estimated that they could bring in a haul of one hundred fifty thousand dollars or so. To everyone's delight, it was closer to two hundred fifty thousand. John clapped him on the back after they counted the money. Max jumped around at the excitement and wanted to be included. Harry saw Ozzie give a weak smile and sit down.

"Hey, Oz, what's wrong? Your balls still hurt?"

"It isn't funny, Harry. That little bastard almost put me into the fetal position. He must be a soccer star or something."

Harry glared at Ozzie. "If this job got fucked up because of a ten-year-old kid, I'd put you in something worse than the fetal position."

"I knew what was at stake. I taught the kid a lesson."

"Yeah, I know. If you can't handle a kid, Oz, what happens if you run into something bigger…like a teenager?"

John let out a guffaw. "Harry, it went pretty smooth. We got a hell of a lot of loot in the past few weeks."

"Yeah," said Ozzie sullenly, "And we can't spend it."

"What the hell are you talking about, Ozzie," exploded Harry.

Harry Hid It

"I gave you a few grand from the diamond heist. Remember, we agreed to this. If we keep up this pace, but start flashing around big bucks, people are going to catch on. When that happens, the cops and feds won't be far behind. Wouldn't you rather be able to spend it in a couple of years without looking over your shoulder?"

"Harry, I could be dead before that."

"You keep talking like this, and you will be." Harry sorted through the bundles of cash in front of him. He checked one carefully and threw it at Ozzie. "Here, that's five thousand in older bills. The new ones might be recorded so I'll definitely stash them away. Are you happy?"

Ozzie flicked through the bundled cash. His smile became a little bigger. "I guess so."

"Remember why we do this," said Harry. "We'll try to do every job differently. Between that and being low-key with our spending, it's going to be difficult to trace anything back to us. Don't get greedy, Ozzie. Do you know how many cars we'd have to lift to equal what we did in the past two jobs?"

"A hell of a lot," mumbled Ozzie.

"You're damn right! Don't worry, Oz, I'll make sure you have enough money for a little fun. Please try to do what we need you to do, though. I wasn't happy to hear you were battling a child. We're trying to do this without people getting hurt, especially kids, for Christ's sake."

"It won't happen again," said Ozzie.

"I hope not!" retorted Harry. He sorted through the money again, stuffed a bundle of hundreds into his pocket, and tossed another one to John. "You good?" he asked John.

"Definitely," replied John. "You hiding the rest of it right away?"

"I try to get it out of here in a day or two. I do sleep easier when it's not under my bed. I think Max does too." He reached down and patted the dog's head. "I don't think he likes the responsibility of guard dog."

"I do want to make sure," said John, "that if something happens to you, God forbid, we can find the cache."

"For sure," said Harry. "I started devising a trail for you to follow. I hate being that mysterious about it, but everyone I know who got caught or killed was because too many people knew what was going on. A secret known by more than one person isn't a secret. To tell you the truth, I'll be glad when our two-year marathon is over. Personally, I hope I have enough money to buy an island off the Florida Keys; I'm going to enjoy my life in the warmth."

John started putting the piles of cash back into the bags. "Sounds like a plan. I need to head home. Harry, this was a profitable evening. It's a pleasure doing business with you."

Soon after that, Ozzie and John left. Harry wasn't kidding. He placed the money in waterproof containers and carefully sealed around the edges. Then he pushed the bags under his bed, put a leash on Max, and went for a long walk to unwind. He went to work on Friday. He was up bright and early on Saturday morning. He shoved the money and his painting supplies into his car and took off. By the late afternoon, he was with Sophia out at the little summer home her parents had near the Hamptons out toward Montauk Point on the southern fork of Long Island. It wasn't one of the rich McMansions that the celebrities owned, but a nice, comfortable bungalow. They spent Saturday night at a club, and on Sunday, they walked the beach and bummed around.

Now it was the second day of the workweek and Harry still felt the high of a successful job. He knew that he had to figure out their next score. While he didn't have a firm timeline in his mind, Harry knew he wanted to average about two big jobs a month. He wanted to get to the point that the three of them would have about five million dollars each when they retired from this work. To do that, he needed to figure out what they'd do next.

As his mind was half on what he needed to do today at work and where to look for their next job, Harry heard the clicking of heels on the concrete floor. He looked up from his computer and saw a woman walking through the maintenance area in the company of an airport security guard. She was of medium height for a girl and strolled with an air of authority. As she got closer, Harry could see that the look on her face was more unsure than her walk. He also noticed that the face was quite pretty and framed by curly brown hair. The body was curvy and moved well under the red blouse and navy blue jacket and skirt. Harry smiled slightly at the muscular calves he saw. He liked toned women.

Special Agent Karyn Dudek looked around the work bay she was walking through. Ever since Assistant Director Gonzales gave her the assignment of solving the diamond heist, she'd been running into dead end after dead end. So far, she had questioned people from the courier company that was robbed and the jewelry store that was supposed to receive the diamonds. She originally thought that it could be an inside job, but she didn't know which company to zero in on, so she checked out both. When that went nowhere fast, Karyn made some long distance inquiries to South Africa to the company that sent out the diamonds. Of course, they knew the courier who would pick up the jewels when they arrived in the United States, but that was all. It was another brick wall.

Karyn knew it wasn't a random robbery. Somebody identified and targeted the particular courier van that held the diamonds. She spent all Monday at the airport trying to figure out who had the knowledge that the diamonds were coming in on that particular flight. It was a long list and Karyn methodically tracked down every office and person that would know. She still had a way to go when she called it a night yesterday and resolved to spend all day Tuesday at the same task.

However, her phone rang at six in the morning. It woke her and she flopped on her bed like a beached fish looking for her phone. She'd stopped at a bar on the way home the previous evening to ease away some of the stress of the investigation. Karyn knew she couldn't keep doing that every night, and feeling disoriented this morning reminded her that she better start changing her habits. She found the phone and grunted, "Dudek here."

"Agent Dudek, this is Simon Wilde. I'm a cyber specialist here at the FBI."

"Yeah," said Karyn, desperately trying to rub the sleep out of her eyes. "Why did you call me?"

"I received the material you sent over from Kennedy Airport last night concerning the cargo manifests."

"Did you find out anything?" asked Karyn.

"We were able to connect with Kennedy's system. If anyone hacked into their computers, I found no trace of it," Wilde said.

"Oh," said Karyn, obvious disappointment in her voice. "Thanks for trying."

"No problem." Before Karyn hung up, she heard, "There was one tiny thing though."

"What's that?" she barked.

"Only certain personnel have access to the manifest lists."

"I know. I started talking to those people yesterday."

"As near as I could tell, this list only showed up on computers where they were supposed to…with one exception."

"Where was that?" asked Karyn.

Simon Wilde said, "On a computer in one of the maintenance areas of Kennedy."

"Don't they need passwords to get into the manifest?"

"That they do. The password that accessed the manifest was somebody not even employed there anymore. They took a job at Chicago's O'Hare Airport and went there four months ago."

"When was the manifest looked at?" Wilde gave her the date and she knew that was three days before the diamonds were stolen. She asked a few more questions and hung up. She avoided looking at her reflection in the mirror as she went in the bathroom and quickly showered and dressed. She drove out to Kennedy excited that she had something to look for, no matter how small it was.

Harry Hid It

Once at the airport, Karyn quickly found out that the keeper of the passwords didn't do a good job purging the list as people left their job. There were quite a few on there and Karyn had a feeling that the list would be cleaned up before she left the airport that day. She was starting to get a feeling that Simon Wilde's information would lead nowhere like everything else had to this point. When nobody could give her a good explanation why a computer terminal in the maintenance area would access the manifest files, she asked to go out there and see it for herself. One of the officers from the airport's police force took her there.

Walking through the area, Karyn looked around. The order and organization impressed her. There were different vehicles all around as well as tools and machinery she couldn't begin to identify. She looked off to her left and slowed down for a second. She saw an incredibly good-looking guy standing near some kind of workbench. He was tall, with dark wavy hair. He had a two-day growth of beard and he looked incredibly fit in the tight black T-shirt he wore. He looked at her and winked. Karyn blushed as she stumbled a little. Quickly regaining her composure, she looked away and continued following the airport cop.

He stopped in the back corner and said, "This is it, Agent Dudek."

She looked down at a keyboard and computer screen. It was old, since the monitor was the blocky-type that was common until the flat screens took over. Karyn knew that was quite a long time ago. The entire workbench area looked like nobody had worked here in months. Dust covered everything. On the other hand, this was a maintenance area so things might get dirty quickly. Karyn sighed. Any number of workers could've been back here for anything. For all she knew, a glitch in the software made it look like this computer accessed the manifests. She was learning that a computer whiz was a master of illusion when they wanted to cover their tracks.

Karyn reached up and rubbed her right temple. Her headache was almost gone and she swore that she wouldn't stop for a drink tonight. Thinking on what to do next, she figured she might as well not waste her time here. She said to the cop, "Excuse me for a moment; I'd like to go question that employee over there. I think I can find my way back."

"Sure, ma'am. Give the office a call if you need any assistance." He walked away towards the exit.

Karyn wanted to kick him in the ass. She wasn't old enough to be called "ma'am." Putting that thought out of her mind, she smoothed out the skirt of her outfit and walked over to where she saw the tall, handsome dude. She found him hunched over a clipboard making notes. He looked up as he heard her footsteps approaching. He straightened up and gave her a devastating smile. For a brief moment, Karyn forgot why she was here as she looked up at the man. She had a quick flashback to high school when the quarterback walked up to her to ask her out.

Trying to get her wits back, Karyn reached into the pocket of her jacket and pulled out her FBI credentials. She flipped it open to show the man and said, "I'm Special Agent Karyn Dudek." She wasn't totally sure if her voice cracked.

The man looked at her ID and then looked directly into Karyn's eyes. "Yes, I can see that you're special. Where do you hide your gun?"

"Uh, it isn't hidden. I have it in my purse." "Why am I sounding like an idiot?" she thought.

"How can I help you, Special Agent Dudek?"

"I'm here investigating a robbery. Your name?"

"Harry Strickland." He held out his hand. She briefly shook it and liked how warm and rough it felt. "What was stolen from the airport this time?"

"Oh, have there been many thefts from here?"

"Nothing in maintenance, but you hear about things over the years. Sometimes it sounds like more merchandise leaves this place than Wal-Mart."

"Actually, I'm here to investigate a robbery that happened right outside the airport. A courier van was robbed."

Harry's eyes twinkled. "Well, this place isn't in the greatest of neighborhoods. What was taken?"

"I'd rather not say. It's an ongoing investigation. I came here because I think someone used the computer in the back to access some sensitive information. Has anyone out of the ordinary been back here recently?"

Harry shrugged. "It's hard to say. There are people in and out all the time. Me and the other guys aren't always here. We're often out working on some plane or equipment. In fact, I have to go out and look at an aircraft now with a bum loading ramp." He picked up his ID off his workbench and placed the lanyard over his neck.

Karyn looked as the ID settled on a nicely muscled chest and she could see that this was definitely Harry Strickland. She mumbled, "You haven't seen anyone strange back here then?"

"Hey, sweetheart…I mean Agent Dudek, we're all a little strange back here. It must be all the airplane fumes we breathe in." He smiled. "I'm kidding. And sorry about the 'sweetheart' thing. I forgot who I was talking to. Seriously, there are many people going through here all the time. I never noticed anyone who seemed to be slinking around or anything like that."

Karyn couldn't explain it, but she didn't want to leave Harry yet. There was something captivating about him. She tried to convince herself that it was because she had to make sure that she conducted a thorough interview. She fished out a business card from her pocket and gave it to Harry. "Please give me a call if you think of anything that may be of help."

He took it and said, "I might be of more help if you can tell me what you're looking for. You learn about the airport in this job and I might have some insight."

She hesitated for a moment and then said, "It was diamonds. A courier was hit as soon as it left the grounds."

"Wow," said Harry. "That's big stuff. Was anyone hurt?"

"Thank God, no," replied Karyn. "It was obvious, though, that they knew these diamonds were coming into the airport and when. They also had information on how they were transported out of here. I guess my question for you is if there's any easy way for someone to find all of that information out?"

Harry took a moment to think. Karyn watched his expression as he looked off into the distance. She thought that this guy should be in movies or something. Why was he here as a mechanic? He seemed to have an innate intelligence about him. She glanced over his work area. She saw various technical manuals, a book on famous artists, and another on Dutch settlers in colonial America. Karyn tried to stop her brain from going off on a tangent as he started talking again.

"Well, Agent Dudek, it's not like much here is a secret, I guess. I see people every day that work here, and most of them I never recognize. It's like a small city. All I can tell you is that with all of the stuff that goes in and out of here, I reckon people can figure out patterns. With all of the security that we have here since the terrorists in the world went nuts and looked at airplanes as weapons, it's hard to sneak a fart in or out of this place. If I go anywhere without this thing," Harry fingered his ID badge, "I'd be on my belly with five cops around me. Sorry, but I don't think I'm being much help."

Karyn took a breath. "I want to thank you for your time, Har… uh, Mr. Strickland. You have my card. Please feel free to contact me if you can think of anything that will be a help."

"Sure." Harry stuck the card in a rear pocket of his jeans. "It was nice meeting you." He picked up a toolbox and walked toward the door leading out to the tarmac. Karyn admired the almost catlike way he moved. She slowly started following in the same direction to go back to the main administration building.

Karyn had mixed feelings. Part of her was depressed because she didn't feel any closer to solving this case. She knew this diamond heist could make or break her career. At this moment, with her job hanging in the balance and her future uncertain, Special Agent Karyn Dudek had one overwhelming thought: "Why can't I meet a guy like Harry Strickland?"

Chapter 11

SITTING IN A BACK corner of Art's, Harry slowly ate a small steak, occasionally throwing a bite to Max who was lying at his feet. He walked directly over to the tavern as soon as he arrived home. The heat was still stifling outside. By the time they made the walk, Harry could feel his shirt sticking to him and Max was panting as if he'd just traversed the Sahara. When Harry eschewed the bar for the corner table, Jeannie brought a bowl of water out for Max that the huge dog drained.

While Harry waited for his food, Art walked over. "How they hanging, Harry?"

"Too damn hot to do much of anything," said Harry. "I may have to call a cab here for my friend." Max opened one eye at Art, gave a half-hearted wag of his tail, and then closed it.

"It's supposed to be like this for three more days at least," said Art. "You'll be missing this when we're up to our ass in snow in a few months."

"Don't even start in on that shit," said Harry. "I hate that stuff. I try to take as much vacation time then visiting family in Florida."

Art looked at the table. "You usually sit at the bar. Expecting company?"

"Yeah, John and a friend of his are stopping in. He texted me on the way home from work. I figured that I'd come over early and get a bite to eat and exercise Max." The big dog grunted when he heard his name, but didn't move.

"Ok," said Art, "let me know if you need anything." The ex-football player went back to his position behind the bar. Harry idly registered a woman with two young children coming inside and going up to the bar. They were quiet and didn't interfere with his thinking.

Harry Hid It

Harry certainly had a great many thoughts on his mind. While he gave no indication of it at the time, Special Agent Dudek showing up this morning shook him. He knew that the police and feds would cover the airport about the diamond heist, but he never thought they'd show up in his work area. In hindsight, he was thrilled he trusted his instincts not to use the computer at his own workstation when he was looking through the cargo manifests, but he was also kicking himself for not trying to find another computer to use. Kennedy Airport was a great place to target something worth taking, but now he had to figure out another way to look at future shipments. Harry sighed. It was one more thing to do as CEO of his own enterprise. He'd figure something out. He always did. One thing he knew was that he wasn't going to go back to that well until the agent finished snooping around the airport.

In spite of himself and thoughts of Sophia, Special Agent Dudek intrigued Harry. She was an attractive woman, that was for sure. Harry couldn't help wondering what the body under the federal agent costume looked like. She was definitely in shape and had a certain sexiness about her. It was more than that, though. When Harry looked in her eyes, he saw intelligence, but also pain. Her eyes were definitely bloodshot as if she'd been out drinking all night, but she didn't seem like someone who was a habitual drinker. He interpreted that as someone who was hurting. In other circumstances, Karyn Dudek would've been someone he'd have chatted up.

Harry looked up when he heard whimpering next to him. He saw a girl about six years old sitting at a table with her head in her hands. Her shoulders were shaking and she was crying as silently as possible. The mother came up, put her arms around the girl, and pulled her up to her feet. Looking past the mom, Harry saw Art indicate a small table for them to sit at on the other side of the room. It looked to Harry that the little girl's brother was about eight years old. He was trying to look older than he was and was careful to keep his face emotionless. Art stopped Jeannie, who was walking by, and sent the petite blonde over to the family.

Harry Hid It

Art was shaking his head when he saw Harry looking at him. The big man came over. "Sad story. The woman came in here looking for a job. I have more people than I need now. Apparently, her husband moved to Wyoming last year to work at the new oil rigs out there. Good money in those jobs. A crane crushed the poor bastard. She has a lawyer suing the company, but those things take years to settle."

"I wish I could think of something out there for her, but I have no clue," said Harry.

"Yeah, I know. They got thrown out of their apartment and have been making the round of shelters for a few days. She wants to find something before school starts for the kids."

Harry sighed. "We can't save the world, Art."

"Don't I know it. I told her to order anything off the menu. I have a friend who works for Catholic Charities. I'm going to give her a call and see if she can help her." Art pulled his phone from his pocket and started looking through his numbers as he meandered back to the bar.

Harry looked over at the table. The kids were quietly sitting there and the mother looked exhausted. She was pretty, but her face looked worn by crying and worry. He wondered if the marriage had been a happy one. It certainly couldn't have been easy to have her husband go across the country to work in some oil fracking wilderness. Harry sighed again. He hoped John was bringing him some good news to get him out of this mood. The text he sent Harry was vague, just that he wanted to meet tonight and he had a friend with him.

The door to the tavern opened and John came strolling in with a very tall man behind him. John was dressed in jeans, motorcycle boots, T-shirt, and leather vest. The guy bringing up the rear must've been almost six and a half feet tall. A cowboy hat and boots exaggerated his size. When the door shut, John looked around and made a beeline for Harry. As Harry stood up, John said, "Harry, this is Ralph Lennon. Ralph, this is Harry."

Harry Hid It

They shook hands and Harry felt a firm grip and looked the man over closely. He appeared to be about forty years old or so. He had green eyes and red hair that hung out from under the cowboy hat. The jeans, boots, and hat all looked worn and well lived in. The shirt was black with white trim and had a very western look to it. As they all sat down, Harry signaled for Jeannie to come over.

Max perked up and stood on all fours. The tall man looked at him and said, "Does he come with a saddle?" Harry watched as the man made a fist and held it out for Max to sniff. After Max sized up the fist, he rubbed his head against it. The man smiled, relaxed his hand, and began petting the huge dog.

After the two newcomers ordered beer from Jeannie, John said, "This is the detective I told you about. He's been part of our motorcycle gang for three years now. He's the one I asked to look into the club where that little shit gave you and Sophia such a hard time."

Harry looked at Ralph. "I appreciate that. What do I owe you for the service, Ralph?"

"First of all," said Ralph with a decidedly Texan twang to his speech, "call me Cowboy. That's what I'm known as around these parts. The motorcycle guys laid that name on me when I first got here and it stuck. My clients even know me by that now. I should put it on my business card."

"Okay, Cowboy, I'll do that," said Harry.

"And you don't owe me anything. John here took care of it."

Harry raised an eyebrow at John. John took a gulp of the beer Jeannie placed in front of him and said, "You've been taking care of me fine. I wasn't happy with what went down that night either."

Harry nodded and said to Cowboy, "Have you been doing this type of work for long?"

"It seems like all my life. I worked intelligence for the United States Army and from there was a Texas Ranger. When I came to New York City to apprehend a drug runner from Fort Worth, I kind of fell for the area. My wife had just divorced me and it was time for a change. I got licensed here and been making a living ever since. I fell into the clutches of John's group and been riding with them for a while now."

"You like motorcycles better than horses?" asked Harry.

"Hate horses. Love bikes!" exclaimed Cowboy.

Harry roared with laughter at that. He needed a laugh and that relaxed him. He liked Cowboy. When he got a hold of himself, he asked, "So what can you tell me about our boy Anthony at the Ocean Club?"

Cowboy reached into the left breast pocket of his western shirt and brought out some folded sheets of paper. He smoothed them out on the table and plucked a pair of glasses from the other side of the shirt. Her perched them on his nose and started to look over the information. After taking a swig of beer, he started reviewing the pages. "Anthony Russo is actually Anthony Russo Jr. He's twenty-seven years old, had a few complaints against him by women when he was in college, but never arrested or anything. The club underwent an ownership change a year and a half ago and he was installed as manager."

"Manager!" said Harry. "That little asshole bragged to Sophia that he was the owner."

"Not exactly. Anthony Russo is the owner, but it's Anthony Russo Sr., his father."

John joined in. "Harry, you know of the father. Around town, he's known as Fat Tony."

Harry's eyes widened at that. "Fat Tony is that little shit's daddy! I'd never have put the two together. Fat Tony isn't exactly a class act, but he runs a tight ship from what I understand. Is he trying to teach his son the family business?"

Cowboy shook his head. "I called a friend I made in the city. He works organized crime for the state police."

Harry held up his hand. "Ugh, I can appreciate you were a Texas Ranger and all, but just how closely are you connected with the police?"

Cowboy drawled, "They're just a resource, Harry."

John said, "I vouch for him, Harry. He's helped the boys in the gang out on a few things."

"It's funny what being a private detective is like," said Cowboy. "The line between right and wrong gets very blurry. It's not like being a cop. I like not having a bushel of rules to worry about. As long as nobody is getting hurt, I'm very mercenary about where I make my money."

Harry felt better after hearing this from him along with John's endorsement. "What did your friend in the staties have to say?"

"His sources told him that if Fat Tony could unload his son without making his wife mad, he'd drop him in a minute. The boy is obviously a source of embarrassment." Cowboy traced one of the pages with his finger until he stopped halfway down. "The boy actually went to Harvard. The campus cops there hated him. He was constantly in trouble. I talked to the chief there and he said they get many rich assholes there, but Anthony Junior was one of the biggest. He threw parties, thought he could jump on anything with a skirt, and arrogantly believed his money and daddy could get him out of anything. They threw his ass out before he graduated."

"That description certainly matches what I ran into that night," said Harry. "What happened after college?"

"Fat Tony got him into C.W. Post to graduate. He was supposed to go to law school, but he could never pass the test to get in. Even his father's money wasn't going to help him with that. Daddy finally put him in as an assistant manager at a small club in Hartford, Connecticut. He was supposed to learn that side of the business - the legit side - from the bottom up. From what I learned, the manager of that club threatened to shoot young Anthony if Fat Tony didn't get him out of there. He bounced around in other areas of his father's business until he became manager at the Ocean Club. It sounds like Fat Tony put him there so that he could keep an eye on his son. Apparently, Tony has three other kids who are quite successful on their own and not in his employ. Anthony is the fucking idiot of the bunch."

Harry sat back and digested this. His desire for revenge on Anthony Russo had been simmering for weeks now, but it was still there. Being he was the son of Fat Tony meant Harry should tread carefully. However, that wasn't something he always did. He looked up at Cowboy, who was watching him closely. "I know Fat Tony by reputation. What's he into?"

The former Texas Ranger referred to the third sheet of paper. "For a crook, you have to admire the guy. He's been operating up and down the eastern seaboard for thirty-five years and has spent all of three weeks in jail. I think he was hoping to send Junior to law school to help with the family business because Fat Tony must've paid a fortune for attorneys all these years. However, with what I've discovered about Junior, he probably would have daddy on Death Row for jaywalking!" They all laughed at this, and then Cowboy continued.

"Fat Tony has several legitimate businesses including clubs in five states, restaurants, storage buildings, and some office properties. My friend with the state is sure that he uses these places for laundering money, storing stuff, and arranging meets. But he's slick. Nobody has been able to nail him on anything substantial. When the cops or feds get close to someone, there's too much space between the people they bust and Fat Tony to make a solid connection."

"What's his non-legitimate enterprises?" asked John.

"Pretty much all the biggies," stated Cowboy. "It's suspected that he's into drugs, prosecution, gun running, illegal gambling… you know, all the big cash cows. Apparently, he has plenty of personnel and protection all around him and good lieutenants that run the nuts and bolts of his operation."

"Now about Junior…" Harry's voice trailed off as something caught his attention across the room. John turned and saw a woman and two young kids getting up from a table. They headed to the door. Harry said, "Would you two excuse me for a minute?" He got up and walked over to their blonde waitress.

Harry took Jeannie by the elbow and walked her over to the bar. "Jeannie, do me a huge favor." He stuffed a wad of bills into her hands. "Go give this to that woman who's leaving. Please don't tell her where it came from. Just tell her," Harry stopped to think, "tell her a guardian angel is looking out for her tonight."

Jeannie looked down at the money in her hand. "Jesus Christ, Harry, this looks like two grand."

"Yeah, whatever. Just go before she gets too far." They both saw the door close behind the family. Jeannie took off out the door. Harry looked over and saw Art looking at him from the far end of the bar. The owner had a bemused smile on his face. Harry shouted at him, "What the hell does a guy need to do to get another beer here?"

The smile turned into a grin and Art plopped a beer out of a cooler and popped the cap. With a deft flick of the wrist, he propelled the bottle down the bar at Harry. In one motion, he scooped it up as it was going by and took a long pull. Harry waited a minute. He saw John and Cowboy talking. Max's head was on Cowboy's knee and his new friend was scratching the beast behind his ears. As Harry took another drink, the door opened and Jeannie came back in. She had tears in her eyes. She went up to Harry and said, "Damn you, Harry, I'm never going to be able to call you a bad name again. The mother was overwhelmed. She wanted to come back in and find out who gave her the money, but I asked her not to; I said our Good Samaritan was shy."

She fished a tissue out of her apron and dried her eyes. "It's no big deal," said Harry. "I had some extra money on me. Besides," he swatted Jeannie on the ass, "I'm sure I'll do something soon enough for you to call me something evil or perverse."

"Well, you get a break from it tonight," growled Jeannie as she went back to the kitchen.

Harry returned to the table. He looked at Max who was still content with Cowboy scratching him. Collecting his thoughts,

Harry said, "As I was about to ask, is Junior involved in any of his father's shit?"

"So far, there's been no indication of that. The official book on Anthony Junior is that he's a fuck up and his father doesn't want him involved in anything where he can really mess up things."

Harry looked at Cowboy with a quizzical look. "I noticed how you said 'official.' Is there more to the story that you know, but others don't?"

Cowboy smiled. "John told me you were sharp, Harry. There's this informant I use when I'm trying to find certain items stolen from my clients. He's one of these old boys that know everything that's going on in the city or the Island. I was having a beer with him last night picking his brain on a completely different matter. When I was done with that, I asked him on a whim if he knew anything about Anthony Junior. He said what I just told you about his father keeping him out of the business. However, he also told me that his father was stuck on a location for moving some product and was going to use the Ocean Club Thursday night."

"What kind of product?" asked John.

"My guess is guns or drugs," said Cowboy. "If I were a betting man, I'd put my money on drugs. It's smaller to move and you make a hell of a lot more money."

"I wonder if Junior will be there when it goes down?" muttered Harry.

John gave him a sharp look. "What are you thinking?"

Harry's gears were turning at top speed. This was an opportunity for revenge in spades, but he wasn't quite sure in which direction he wanted to go yet. "Cowboy," he asked, "how good is the intel?"

"Pretty solid. I went to a few other sources and I'd give it an eighty-five percent rating of accuracy."

"Why wouldn't you tell your friends in the cops about this?"

"Hey, Harry, I didn't say they were good friends. I promised I'd find out all I could on Anthony Russo for John and I don't go back on my word. That means something to me. Must be those years in the Army and the Rangers."

Harry liked people he could respect. He had that feeling about Cowboy. Besides, Max liked him. He said, "Look, I want to keep you at arm's length with all of this. I think it's called 'plausible deniability.' But if you'd like to make a few extra dollars, could you find out more information about what's going down Thursday night?"

"Intelligence is all," said Cowboy. "I can do that."

Harry gave Cowboy his phone number. "Give me a call or text when you have more and we'll meet. Hate to put a time crunch on it, but as you know, this is happening two nights from now. I'd also love to know if the cops have any inkling about this happening."

"And if they do?" asked John.

"Then I'll do everything in my power to make sure they apprehend all the bad guys and put Anthony Junior's ass in jail. If not, then I may just crash their party."

Chapter 12

THURSDAY AFTERNOON AT LUNCH, Harry was munching a sandwich and sketching out what he remembered about the Ocean Club from his one ill-fated night there. Cowboy sent him a series of texts during the morning detailing what he found out. He cautioned Harry that the information that he was able to discover was about seventy-five percent reliable. Still, Harry was pleased with what the man unearthed in a day's time.

Whoever Cowboy talked to said it was drugs being exchanged for money. Fat Tony was providing the drugs and taking home the cash. The club closed down at two o'clock on Thursday nights and the purchase would take place about a half hour after that. Cowboy couldn't provide any information on how many people were involved or exactly where it'd take place on the property. One thing that Cowboy was fairly sure of after checking out different contacts was that the police didn't know what was going down and wouldn't be a factor.

Harry sat back and looked at the floor plan he drew of the nightclub. He had to make a few educated assumptions with what he now knew. Cowboy didn't know how many drugs or how much money were involved, but drugs took up less room than if this was a gun deal. That meant less people involved...at least he hoped so. Because of the volume, it was probably something that would be done inside the club, rather than out in the parking lot or on the loading bay, though that was still a possibility. If Cowboy were correct that this was the first time Fat Tony Russo was using the Ocean Club for such a transaction, it would probably not be a huge shipment that he was delivering.

There would be people with guns; Harry knew that. Fat Tony and his goons wouldn't easily give up the cash he wanted. Harry wanted nothing to do with the drugs. As far as he was concerned, the buyers could take all of that shit and leave. Harry wanted Fat Tony to know that the only reason he was here was because his son had a big mouth. Harry wanted young Anthony's father to know his son was a stupid asshole and couldn't be trusted. That was the worse seed of doubt Harry could sew into a family like the Russos.

On the practical side, Harry was going to do his best to leave with the cash. The problem was that he was going to go up against a bunch of people with guns and he had three men. The only possible way this was going to work was with the element of surprise. As he gazed at the club sketch, he began to get an idea of how to make this work. In fact, it'd be rather easy. Harry actually started chuckling. It would depend on a little luck and how many people showed up, but he'd have to make those judgments on the fly. The fact that he knew what was going down and that it was happening in a nightclub made everything a little easier.

Harry placed his drawing under a piece of copper ore he picked up in his travels and used as a paperweight. He pulled out his phone and called John. "Hey, you ready for tonight?"

"I don't know, Harry. This is a little ambitious, even for you. It's you, Ozzie, and me. We aren't exactly a fucking army going up against Fat Tony and the others."

"I know, but I have a plan. Did Cowboy fill you in?"

"Yeah, on the basics. But then again, he only seems to know the basics. Unless he told you something different, he has no clue how many people are going to be there or how much is going down in the deal."

"I know," said Harry. "Don't worry. You know if it gets too sketchy, I'll abort the job. However, I think I know a way we can do this. Call Ozzie and tell him to get a car or truck for tonight. We don't want to use his. You two drive up to the edge of the club at about one in the morning. Stay out of sight and observe. I'm trusting you on this, John. Make sure you can see the vehicles coming in and out of the club. You'll be able to tell if something looks different than the usual partiers coming and going. Text me your updates and I'll do the same."

"Where are you going to be, Harry?" asked John.

"I'm going to be in the club already. If they're stupid enough to want to do this at a place that has lots of people in it before they close up the joint, I'm going to use that to my advantage."

John sounded doubtful. "If you say so, but how's this going to go down?"

"I'll have you and Ozzie come down when I can either let you in, or to pick me up. I have to figure this out as we go."

There was silence on the phone. Finally, John said, "Harry, I'm in, but can't we just leave this asshole alone? I know you want to screw over Anthony Junior, but there will be another way."

"We have to act now," said Harry. "This is like a peach on a tree just ripe for the taking. It's too good of an opportunity to pass up. Besides, Fat Tony and his posse probably aren't really worried about someone being there tonight. What idiots would ever interfere with a drug deal like this?"

"Just idiots like us, Harry. Okay, let me call Ozzie. We'll be on station at one."

"Good, John, and make sure you have masks, guns, and your cell phones are charged. See you tonight."

As he hung up, Harry felt a shot of adrenaline go through him. This was different from the other jobs they'd recently pulled. This one certainly had the potential for more fallout, considering the parties involved. Harry only knew Fat Tony by reputation and it was a ruthless reputation. On the other hand, they wouldn't have to worry about cops looking into this if they pulled it off. Harry's same philosophy pertained to this situation. If they succeeded tonight and made off with the cash, by keeping quiet about it and maintaining a low profile there was nothing to lead Fat Tony back to them.

Putting aside the rest of his lunch and the sketch, Harry picked up his tools and headed out to the tarmac. He had a plane to work on and it'd keep his mind off everything until he went home. He wasn't totally at ease with what he planned tonight, but Harry knew he was moving ahead the best way he could with the information that he had. While he was dead set on extracting revenge on Junior, Harry knew he'd back off if the situation were beyond him and his men.

The rest of the afternoon sped by. Soon, Harry was back home after the end of the working day. He took care of Max and began getting ready for the night. Looking in his bathroom mirror, Harry looked at himself carefully. He hadn't shaved in three days and he had put off getting a haircut. The day they partied on the boat and visited the Ocean Club, Harry remembered he'd cleaned up for the evening. The scruffiness and the longer hair should throw off any of the men he encountered before from immediately recognizing him. He planned to be as unobtrusive as possible, but even a few seconds of doubt on someone's part could make a difference.

Harry dressed all in black. Black shirt, pants, and sport coat. He looked perfectly fine for clubbing. He needed the jacket to hide his gun, mask, and a few other things. He put on comfortable black shoes that not only looked good, but also sported rubber soles that had good traction and were quiet. Harry would feel a little better if he could carry an Uzi, but since he didn't own one, he'd make do with what he had.

Harry called a taxi at ten to take him to the club. He had the cab meet him near Art's. Fortunately, the driver didn't speak much English and Harry could run everything through his mind again without having to deal with idle conversation. His immediate goal was to get into the club. He knew he could do that in a couple ways. The one thing he worried about on this job, and every job for that matter, was cameras. Between security cameras and everyone in the world with one on their phone, you could never be sure when you were in someone's lens. The hardest thing with committing crimes these days was the abundance of technology. Harry didn't want Fat Tony to look over any surveillance footage or the random YouTube video taken by someone at the club and find him in the picture.

This thought occupied Harry all the way to the Ocean Club. He paid off the driver and looked at the entrance from the curb. People were coming and going. It was getting near the end of summer and the vacation crowds were still around. The heat from the last several days tainted the night with humidity that had Harry feeling his shirt sticking to his body. This wasn't a night to be wearing a sport coat, but he didn't have much of a choice.

Taking a deep breath, Harry started for the entrance and then changed his mind. Keeping his face bent forward as much as possible, he forced himself to stroll casually around the corner of the building. This was the direction of the kitchen and he saw a parking area for unloading trucks. As he kept to the shadows of the wall, he saw two glowing eyes up ahead. The eyes were moving all over. As he got closer, Harry saw what he expected, two employees outside a door having a smoke. The red eyes were the cigarette tips going up and down toward their mouths.

Harry stood silently watching. They were dressed in white pants and shirts, which meant they were probably part of the kitchen staff. Harry could barely make out that the door behind them was propped open with a mop handle. The soft voices he heard coming from the men were Spanish. Harry realized he had an opportunity here, but he had to time it right. This was either his way in, or this mission would be over before it began.

When he saw the two men throw their butts to the ground, Harry tensed his muscles and got ready. As they turned their backs to him and started to go back inside, Harry started silently jogging in their direction. He sped up as he saw the door closing behind them. The door was a quarter inch from banging shut when Harry grasped the handle with a finger. He kept the door exactly in that position so that it didn't close. Harry figured that it was one of those self-locking doors that could only be opened from the inside. That's why the employees kept it propped open.

Harry slowly counted to ten, and then pulled back on the handle. The door effortlessly opened. Continuing to keep his head down from any cameras mounted above him, Harry peeked inside. It was an empty corridor. He could hear kitchen noises up ahead. Harry swiftly entered and quietly closed the door behind him. Not wasting time, he walked forward. As he passed the kitchen on his left, he kept going. Where the corridor intersected with another, Harry thought he knew where he was. Going left was the same way those two goons dragged him and Sophia outside that one night. Anthony Junior's office was to the right. Stuck in the hallway going to the left were two other doors. Harry tried one and saw that it was a small closet. That wasn't quite what he needed right now. As pushed open the other one, he saw that this suited his purpose much better.

The second door led him into some type of large utility room. It contained several hot water heaters and various control panels. Harry reached into his pocket and took out his mask. He quickly put it on to hide from any cameras in here and so that he could look around easier. Scanning the panels, he saw that heat, air conditioning, fire suppression, and almost everything else were controlled from here. He didn't see any cameras in this room, but he kept his mask on just to be safe. Going to the back corner of the room, he saw a closet. Inside were cans of paint and drop cloths. Harry sat down on an old chair near the closet. This was perfect! He would hang here until the club closed. Unless something went wrong with the air conditioning or something else in the club, nobody would come here. If he started to hear the outer door open, he would dart into the closet. If somebody needed a can of paint for something at this late hour, well, then things would get nasty.

Harry felt fairly confident he got this far undetected. Anybody who saw him after this would only see a man in a mask. His original idea was to mingle with the party people in the club and find some place just like this to lay low. Lucking out and coming in the back way was fortunate. He forced himself to relax and stay alert. He had a long wait.

When it got to be one he sent a text to John. "Are you there?" The reply came back almost instantaneously, "On site." Harry texted, "Keep me posted of anything out of the ordinary."

Harry kept waiting in the dark. It wasn't an absolute darkness as the different control panels shone with varying degrees of light. He wished he'd stuck a bottle of water in one of his pockets. After an hour had gone by, he glided over to the door and opened it a tad. He could tell that the noise in the club had greatly tapered off. He texted John asking what he was seeing. The reply was that cars were leaving. Harry started pacing in the dark. If the information Cowboy dug up was wrong or there had been a change in the exchange location, he was going to be incredibly pissed off. Looking at the paint closet, Harry began to hatch a backup plan of burning the place down if this night crapped out.

It was almost 2:30 when Harry got another text. "White SUV arriving. No other car. Driving up to the entrance. Still plenty of cars in the parking lot. Partiers still hanging around as well as staff. Advise?"

Harry thought for a moment. He thought they were doing this drop with too many people around. They were probably going to make it as quick and low key as possible. He went into the back corner of the room and dialed John. Speaking as quickly and quietly as possible, he said, "Drive down to the left of the building. There's a place there for unloading trucks. Fifty feet down from the double doors into the kitchen is a regular size door. I'll open it and keep it open. Come in there with your masks on and guns drawn. I'll be waiting for you. Move. Now."

Harry heard John say, "Got it. Move down to the building, Oz."

Harry Hid It

Pocketing the phone, Harry took out his gun and went back to the door. He put on gloves and took a deep breath. Steeling himself for whatever was coming, Harry slowly opened the door and looked out. The corridor was clear. He hurried back the way he came in several hours ago and pushed open that door. He found the mop that the kitchen employees used and stuck it into the opening around the hinges so it wouldn't close shut. As he got the mop in place, he heard the soft squeal of brakes outside. Praying it was John and Ozzie, Harry scurried back to the junction of the hallway. Carefully looking around the corner, he saw a large man disappear into Anthony Junior's office.

Hearing footsteps behind him, Harry abruptly turned and saw John and Ozzie. Like him, they were dressed in black and had ski masks on. They were holding their guns and Harry could tell they were nervous. He whispered, "I think they're in the office. Here's the deal. Ozzie and I will go in. John, keep your eye on the hallway. Oz, you cover everyone. I'll do the talking. There isn't going to be a lot of chitchat. We make the grab and go. Everyone good?"

Two apprehensive faces nodded yes. Harry signaled to move forward. Hopefully, all of the staff were doing their closing up things and this hallway would stay empty for another couple of minutes. John stayed crouched near the intersection of the corridors and Harry quietly moved forward. He could tell by Ozzie's heavy breathing that he was right behind him. Stopping at the door, Harry leaned his ear against it. He heard someone saying inside, "I'm glad we could do business. If this worked out for you, we can continue to use my son's club as a place to meet."

It was now or never. Harry turned the knob and pushed it open. Making his voice sound huskier than normal, he barked out, "Freeze! Nobody moves, nobody dies." He saw someone's hand jerk to his waist. Harry pointed his gun at the man's head. "Nope. You'll be the first."

The man stopped and Harry looked around. It felt like he stepped into a photograph. Everybody was still with shocked looks on their faces. Seven people were in the office. It was a big room, but it seemed filled with all these bodies. To Harry's left were three neatly dressed Asians. The one in the center had that look of being the leader. The man on his left had three large boxes in his hand.

On Harry's right were Anthony Russo Junior, his father, Fat Tony, and two large goon types. Harry had pointed his gun at one of these. At their feet was a large nylon bag. The zipper was half-open and Harry could see a few stacks of cash in there. Bingo! He didn't want to play games. He just wanted to get the hell out of here.

Fat Tony said, "Do you know who I am?"

Harry said, "I don't care."

The lead Asian asked, "Mr. Russo, is this some kind of double-cross? I just paid you for this merchandise."

Harry glanced at him. "You can take your merchandise. I don't care about that. I want this." He smoothly bent down and pulled up the nylon bag. He almost grunted with the effort. The fucking thing was heavy. How much money was in here anyway?

Fat Tony looked at him. "You'll be dead before you can spend it."

"I got men in the hall with guns," said Harry. "Don't even try to come after us." He could feel Ozzie start to open the door. Then he remembered. Looking directly at Anthony Junior, Harry said, "You've got a big mouth. Thanks for tipping us off on this deal. It was a pleasure knowing you."

It was then that all hell broke loose. Harry saw the other goon draw his gun. Before Harry brought his all the way around, Anthony Junior ran at him. Harry's comment triggered his temper off the charts and he lunged at Harry shouting, "You son-of-a..."

A shot rang out. Anthony's head exploded as he toppled over. Harry pointed his gun at Fat Tony and his goons and fired. It went wide, but it made everyone duck. The Asians dove to the floor and one of them was pulling out a gun. Before anyone else fired, Harry pushed Ozzie out of the door in front of him. His hand came down on the light switches and plunged the room into darkness. Harry fired two more shots above everyone's head and closed the door.

Turning, he could see John pivoting around trying to see if anyone was coming. Ozzie was already heading to the door to the outside. Harry said, "Move!" He and John sprinted right behind Ozzie. Breaking out into the fresh air, Ozzie pushed one of the kitchen staff who was leaning on the truck out of the way. He jumped in the driver's door and fired up the engine. Harry heaved the nylon bag into the truck's rear and followed John into the passenger seat. Ozzie got the truck into gear and whipped it around past the club's entrance. In a matter of seconds, he was on the main road, heading east.

Finding his voice, Harry shouted, "For Christ's sake, Ozzie, slow down. The last thing we need is a cop pulling us over. Head back to my place, but take it slow. I think we were too fast for them. Nobody is following us."

Back in the club's office, Fat Tony was looking down at his son. His face was stoic as he looked at the blood soaking into the carpet. Looking over at the Asian trio, he said, "Go. Take your stuff and get the hell out of here." Without a word, they did what he told them.

He looked at the taller of the two men that were with him. "You killed my son, Billy."

"It wasn't my fault, Fat Tony. I had a clear shot on that asshole who barged in here. Anthony jumped in my way."

"I know, Billy, accidents happen. Let me see the gun that killed him."

Billy reluctantly handed over his Glock. Looking it over carefully, a look of sadness crossed Fat Tony's face. With a sudden movement, he brought the gun up and shot Billy between the eyes. When Billy crashed to the floor, Fat Tony threw his gun on top of the body.

Turning to the other man, Fat Tony said, "I don't know how, but find the people that came in here tonight. If I don't clean up this mess I'm going to lose respect and business. I want whoever was here dead. I want it long and painful. And I want my money back. Do you understand me?"

With a quiver in his voice, the remaining goon said, "Y…yes, boss."

Chapter 13

FRIDAY FOUND HARRY SLUMPED over his workstation at the airport. He had no energy. It was so long since he felt drained like this that he couldn't even remember when that was. Part of it was coming off the adrenaline high he had early in the morning with his adventures at the Ocean Club. He always laughed when he saw in the movies or television how nonchalantly people aimed and fired guns at each other. They never seemed to show the fear that swept through a human being when something like that was going down.

Harry knew that surprise and luck were the only things that got them through last night. The entire exchange in the office took less than three minutes and they'd ran out with a bag full of money and no holes in their bodies. While Harry would've shot anyone who was about to shoot him, he was glad it didn't come to that. What he didn't plan on was Anthony Junior getting shot. When he, Ozzie, and John got back to the garage, Harry was a little nauseated to find blood and brain matter on his clothes. He promptly stripped down and threw jacket, pants, and shirt in a metal fire pit he kept in his backyard. Splashing it all with some lighter fluid, he immediately burned it all.

Ozzie had missed any of the blowback from the shot that killed Anthony. Harry had him thoroughly vacuum out the truck, just in case something fell off him. As he watched Ozzie in the cab of the truck, Harry took his first good look at it in the light. It looked vaguely familiar to him. When the vacuum shut off, Harry asked, "Oz, where did you get the truck?"

"It's Spanky's, Harry. I borrowed it from him."

"What! You used Frank's partner's truck for a job?!"

"Yeah, John told me we needed a truck, but not to use mine."

Harry Hid It

Harry slumped in a chair and held his head in his hands. With everything tonight, he was starting to get a headache. He muttered, "Why didn't you pinch a truck? You knew what we were going to do tonight."

"I didn't think of that." Ozzie started to look nervous. "I'm sorry, Harry, I wasn't thinking."

"Oz, if I had a dollar every time you said that, I wouldn't need to do this shit. I'll write you out a fucking list next time detailing what we need." He was too tired to chew Ozzie out. With a sigh, he got up and walked over to a small workbench in the corner where John was carefully counting the money. "Did you add it up, yet?"

John used the calculator on his phone and finished punching in numbers. He looked up at Harry with a gleam in his eyes. "Goddamn, Harry. I don't know what kind of drugs Fat Tony was selling, but there is a million dollars here."

The vacuum fell to the floor as Ozzie ran over to look. "A million bucks! I've never seen that much money."

Harry hadn't either. He looked at the pile of money John had neatly stacked on the bench. No wonder the bag had weighed so much. John explained, "They're all hundred dollar bills wrapped in ten thousand dollar bundles. There are a hundred bundles. I randomly checked a bunch of them and they're all consistent so I'm assuming they're all the same. It comes out to a million however you do the math."

Once again, Harry had the urge to sit down, but he settled for leaning against the wall. "I had no idea. I figured we'd pick up maybe a couple hundred thousand. This was a major buy. Jesus Christ, Fat Tony is going to be pissed."

"And you said his son is dead?" asked John.

"Yeah, his head exploded like a piñata. Except what little brains he had poured out instead of candy. The poor bastard was dead before he hit the floor." Harry gave a snort. "The little shit saved my life. I'm not one hundred percent sure if I'd have seen the guy pull his gun on me."

"How did Daddy react?"

"We didn't stick around to find out, John. You saw us coming out about five seconds after the shot." Turning to Ozzie, Harry asked, "What did you tell Spanky when you borrowed his truck?"

"I told him mine is in the shop and I needed to pick some things up. I told him I'd have it back at the construction office by the morning."

Harry looked at the truck. "Thank God nobody shot at us. I wouldn't want to explain bullet holes to Spanky or to Frank. If Frank knew we were using it for a job, we'd never hear the end of it. He'd want to know why he wasn't included. Plus Lisa would have my balls for breakfast." Harry gave another audible sigh. "Nobody can ever hear about this job. We'll be dead, or at least constantly looking over our shoulder for the rest of our lives."

He turned back to the money and grabbed two bundles. He threw one to Ozzie and handed the other to John. "That's the cut from tonight's haul." He looked at Ozzie. "Do not flash that around. Make it last."

"I get it, Harry. I don't want to be dead."

"Good. Go get Spanky's truck back to him. It's been a hell of a night."

Ozzie pushed the button to raise the garage door. He waved to John and Harry and backed the truck out. As Harry walked over to lower the door, John said, "You think we got in a little too deep with this one?"

Slowly shaking his head, Harry said, "I'm not sure. I'd feel a lot better if we ripped off an armored truck for a million, rather than Fat Tony. Then all we'd have to worry about are the cops. However, I don't believe they can identify us and we got away clean."

John started to shove the money back into the nylon equipment bag. "I certainly hope so. You thinking about laying low on other jobs for a while?"

Harry thought for a couple of minutes on that one. "No. This haul tonight helps us get to our goal a little bit quicker. So far, nobody is wise to us for anything we've done. I'd rather take a break if the heat picks up for some reason. Otherwise, I want to do as many as possible. That way we're done with it all a lot sooner."

"You're the boss. I'm just the math major." He zipped the bag shut with a certain finality. "There you go. Sleep well with that under your bed."

"Sure, with luck I'll get a nap in before heading to work." They bumped fists. John went out the side door of the garage and Harry went into the house carrying the money. He dropped it onto the living room floor with a thud and plopped into his easy chair. Max picked himself off his favorite rug and put his big head on Harry's lap. Harry rubbed his head and said, "Looks like you never have to worry about running out of biscuits, boy!"

Harry thought about making himself a drink but decided against it. The sun would be rising soon. As he considered going up to his bed, he dozed off in the chair. He woke up in time to let Max out, stuffed the money under his bed, showered, and left for work. Now he sat here feeling like half a zombie trying to get his energy back.

Deciding that working would make the day go faster rather than sitting here, he checked his emails and saw that he had to pick up some special work order from the main administration building. As he trudged over to it, his cell rang. He looked at it and answered, "Hey, Cowboy, what's up?"

"I don't know," said Cowboy, making his Texas twang more pronounced than usual. "I reckon I'd give you some info that fell in my lap. Seems like there was some trouble at the Ocean Club last night. Actually, it was this morning if you want to get specific. I regret to inform you that Anthony Junior is where scumbags go after they die. Unless, of course, you already knew that."

"Why should I?" asked Harry. "I can't say I'll lose any sleep over Anthony going to the great beyond."

"Whoever caused it may lose some sleep because Fat Tony is

on the warpath. Just wanted to drop that tidbit to you. If you know anyone involved, tell them to watch their back."

"Appreciate it, Cowboy. Let's have another drink sometime.

"Sure thing, Harry. You take care." Cowboy clicked off.

Harry didn't expect anything less. Nothing he could do about it now. He wanted to do the hit on the club to exact a little revenge on Fat Tony's son. Harry wasn't sorry that he was dead, but he knew the theft and death would make Fat Tony as friendly as a wounded tiger. Harry uttered a prayer as he walked into the administration building.

Going in, he gave a friendly wave to Debbie. "I was told to come over to pick up some kind of emergency work order."

"Damn, Harry, you look exhausted."

"I love you too," said Harry.

"Really, you look like shit. Anyway, the work order is back in Tom's office. He's the assistant director. It's about checking equipment for a stairway that will be wheeled out to some VIP's plane coming in. Apparently, he's too important to come into the terminal. Whoever it is will come down the stairs right into a limo. Tom wants to make sure it all goes smoothly. C'mon back, I'll take you there."

Harry followed the blonde through the maze of cubicles to an actual corner office rather than a cubicle. Debbie poked her head in. "He's not there." Turning to a girl at a desk outside of the office, she asked, "Dawn, is Tom in?"

"Yeah," a petite redhead answered. "He'll be back in ten minutes are so."

"This is Harry," said Debbie. Dawn gave him an appraising glance. "Tom had some special job for him to do. Is the order on his desk or something?"

"I'm not sure. He can go inside and have a seat. He'll be right back."

"OK, Harry, you're on your on." With that, Debbie went back to her station and Harry went into the office. It was a mess. Paper covered every inch of flat surface. He sat down in an empty chair next to the desk.

He was idly looking around when Dawn popped her head in. "I just called Tom…uh, Mr. Fleming. It's going to be more like twenty minutes before he gets here. He asked that you just sit tight. Can I get you anything?"

Harry gave her his biggest smile. "I'm fine. I can use the rest."

"Good. I have to run over to a meeting. He might be back before I am." With that, the redhead made her exit and Harry was alone.

He could see that there was a large flat screen monitor on the desk. Harry began to get a wild idea. He didn't dare to use any of the computers in his area again to get a look at upcoming cargo schedules. While he had abstractly begun to think of ways to access other computers, here was a golden opportunity right in front of him. He leaped up and put himself in front of the screen. Moving the mouse, the monitor sprang to life and Harry could see that Tom Fleming never logged off the airport's computer system before leaving his office. He scanned the icons on the desktop of the screen. Happy that he'd done this once already, Harry quickly found what he wanted and clicked on it.

Pulling the desk chair out, Harry sat in it and studied the screen. There were plenty of manifests showing what was coming in over the next two weeks. He glanced at the clock and frowned. There wasn't enough time to study all of this information. Impulsively, Harry hit the "print" button. The printer on the side of the desk started chattering. Fortunately, it was a fast printer and paper started spitting out. After a few minutes, it stopped. Harry picked up a stack of printouts an inch thick. Cursing himself for not bringing a bag or something with him, Harry lifted up the back of his shirt and stuck the papers down into the waistband of his pants. The shirt hung down enough so that nobody should notice them.

Harry clicked out of the program and made sure everything else was in order on the desk. Just as he sat down, Tom Fleming walked into the office. He was a lean man in his forties and he held out his hand to Harry. "Sorry to keep you waiting. I hope you weren't too bored."

Standing up to shake hands, Harry said, "Not at all. I seem to always find ways to occupy myself."

"Sorry to call you in like this, but we have to kiss the ass of certain bigwigs when they fly in. I just want to make sure the ramp for the plane is in good shape. This particular VIP thinks he owns the airport. The sooner he's out of here, the better for everyone." Tom Fleming rooted around on his desk and pulled up a folder. "Here you go. I appreciate this."

"No problem. Feel free to give me a shout anytime," said Harry and he left.

Hurrying back to his work area, he stuck the manifests in the backpack that he always brought into work with him. He immediately went to check out the piece of equipment and found everything in good working order. When that was done, Harry picked up his backpack and went into a secluded corner of the maintenance building. He took out his pilfered paperwork and started going through it. He took photos with his phone of pages that interested him. When he was done, he went back to his area and ran everything he'd printed out in Fleming's office through the shredder.

When the workday was over, Harry went home and took care of Max. Then he shaved, showered, and went over to pick up Sophia. Tomorrow they were heading over to New Jersey for an overnight camping trip. Frank and Lisa had a cabin in the woods out there and the same group from the night on the party boat was all going. They called it camping, but it was a nice cabin with four small bedrooms and plenty of room for everyone. Sophia was going to stay with him tonight so they could get an early start in the morning. Now, he was picking her up and heading out to dinner first.

When he arrived at her house, it was strangely quiet. When Sophia came to the door, she explained, "There's some fundraising dinner going on at the church and everyone is over there." She threw herself in his arms and kissed him. Standing back, she said, "Harry, you look like you haven't slept in three days."

Calculating in his head, Harry replied, "You're close. Guess I've had some things on my mind. I'm actually looking forward to the weekend out in the woods. I can use the rest."

Harry picked up Sophia's bag and they went out to his car. They drove to a small Italian restaurant they liked for dinner. After drinking some wine and finishing their salads, Sophia said, "I'm worried about you, Harry. You've been very busy lately and I miss you. You don't come over quite as much as before. I don't think you'd cheat on me, so I can only assume you're doing some of that other stuff I don't like to talk about."

Harry took a long drink of Chianti. Where the hell was this coming from? "I'm sorry, Soph; I've been doing some other things. With summer almost over, I've been doing some painting and skydiving. I'd also like to get in some scuba diving before it gets too cold. I guess I've been trying to get a bunch of stuff in before the days start getting shorter. Plus, work has had me doing some overtime lately."

Sophia looked closely at him. "OK, Harry, I just worry about you. I guess I'm fine with everything as long as you stay out of trouble."

Harry lifted his wine glass up to Sophia. "Hey, you know me. I'm always in some kind of trouble."

"Seriously, Harry, if you're really thinking about getting married in the future, I want you to start thinking about getting away from that other part of your life."

"Sweetheart, didn't you say you fell for me because I'm 'dangerous'?" Harry actually made the air quotes.

Sophia laughed. "It had a certain appeal. But you're getting older now. Shouldn't that all stop?"

Harry took a quiet breath and tried to think of the best way to answer this. "All I can tell you, Soph, is that stuff I used to do is pretty much a thing of the past." He wasn't lying. Harry had certainly upped his game in the past few weeks from the car thefts and little stuff he used to do.

Sophia looked a little doubtful but said, "I'm glad, Harry. I love you, but I don't know how long I could stay with someone who could end up in jail…or worse."

"Nobody's going to jail. Look at it this way. How much trouble can I get in on a nice weekend in the Jersey countryside?"

"Harry Strickland, sometimes I think you say things just to tempt fate. All I want this weekend is you and some fun. Is that too much to ask for?"

"Not at all. Tell you what; I'll make sure I put more time into us. Maybe we can get out to your folk's place in the Hamptons next week and a few times in September when it's still nice out. I like it then when the summer crowds are gone."

"Oh, Harry, you always know what to say to me." She reached out and took his hand. The rest of the dinner was a lot more relaxed. Harry felt like he dodged a bullet just as lethal as the ones he avoided last night. God, he was tired.

When they went back to Harry's home, they took Max for a walk together. Harry puttered around in the kitchen pulling things together that he was bringing with them on the trip. This included some food and treats for Max who'd be joining them. He knew what Sophia expected when they went upstairs. He figured that even in his exhausted state he could find his second wind for sex. At this point, it would actually be his third or fourth wind of the day.

Sophia went upstairs ahead of him. When he got there, he found her lying on the bed wearing nothing but lavender bra and panties. She stood up and kissed him. She helped him take off his clothes and pressed herself against him. With a little tug, she pulled him on top of her as she fell backwards on the bed. Whispering in his ear, Sophia said, "Harry, you make me feel like a million dollars."

Thinking about what was under the bed they were on, Harry said, "Sweetheart, you have no idea."

Chapter 14

"WHAT'S WITH YOU GUYS this weekend? You all seem really out of it." Frank came out of his cabin with a handful of beer bottles. He passed them around to the three other men around the fire. Looking at Harry, he said, "You guys probably did some kind of job. Damn, Harry, I'd be glad to lend a hand sometime."

Harry smiled a little. Frank had no idea that he inadvertently did help with the Ocean Club fiasco with his partner's truck. "Frank, if we're doing anything, we can't worry about holding your hand. I've been telling you this for years…you aren't cut out for it."

Frank pouted for a minute, but he'd heard all of this for a long time. "Maybe someday, I'll be able to show you what I can do. I don't have to tell Lisa nothing. I mean, you don't tell your girls anything, do you?"

John took a drag from his beer and said, "You never mix business and pleasure, Frank. Never. You see how much we'd have to teach you."

It was dusk and they'd all just finished supper. The women were inside the cabin finishing the cleaning. Frank had a nice cabin out here in Sussex County, New Jersey. It was off by itself in the woods, but only a ten-minute drive to the nearest town. He'd built a small fire pit off to the side of the house and surrounded it with logs to use for benches. Ozzie got up and walked over to the edge to the trees.

"I really don't like it out here. There's no lights, no noise. How do you sleep? The silence drives me crazy."

"Shut up, Ozzie. Take advantage of the quiet and chill. You'll be back in the hustle and bustle of everything tomorrow. It's nice to have a chance to relax." Harry said this with great conviction.

He certainly needed the break. Then in a quieter voice, he said, "After the other night, we're lucky to be here."

From the doorway, Lisa stuck her head out and said, "Frank, can you come in here? The sink is backed up."

Frank stood and said, "My work is never done around here. I'll be right back."

As he disappeared into the cabin, Ozzie hissed, "Harry, why did we decide to come here? It's boring!"

"Ozzie, I'm not the fucking program director. I meant it. Take the time to relax. Fat Tony almost killed us. And I have some news for you. The man is out for blood."

"Why?" asked Ozzie. "We didn't kill his asshole son?"

"No," said John sarcastically. "His kid wouldn't be dead if it weren't for us. Fat Tony wouldn't have lost a million dollars and been embarrassed in front of his Asian buyers. By now, he must feel humiliated in front of the greater criminal element on Long Island and in the city. Nothing is going to satisfy him until he eliminates the people who stole from him. By the way, Oz, that's us."

"No shit, Sherlock. I was there, remember?"

Harry said, "Calm down. I think we're all a bit rattled."

"You think Fat Tony will find us?" asked Ozzie with real concern in his voice.

Harry looked at him for a moment before he answered. He never knew Ozzie to be really afraid. "I don't think so, Oz. We had masks. We wore gloves. Even if we showed up on some surveillance camera, it was dark and I don't see how they could recognize us. We just keep our ear to the ground and our eyes open."

"How about all that cash?" asked John.

"Taken care of already," replied Harry. "I took a stack of bills for myself like I gave you two. It's safe, along with everything else."

"Are we going to close up shop and lay low for a while?"

"You know, Ozzie, John asked me that the other night when all this shit went down. I don't see any reason to quit. We do not target criminals to rip off. Fat Tony was a one-time thing and a bit of a fluke. If it weren't for his son, I never would've been there that night, even if I knew a million dollars was on the table."

John chimed in, "So, what's next?"

"Funny you should ask. I perused the cargo manifests for the next few weeks and found a couple possibilities."

"Was that safe, Harry?" asked John. "You had that FBI agent there checking you out."

"She may have been checking me out," said Harry with a smile, "but it wasn't for stealing the diamonds. I think I convinced her that there were too many people coming in and out of our area to figure out who used that one computer terminal. Nah, this time, I was in an assistant manager's office. I borrowed his computer to do my research."

"I may have said this before, Harry, but you got balls." John drained his beer. "What did you see that you liked?"

"Another shipment of jewels is coming in on Wednesday. The flight arrives at seven in the evening. The gentleman bringing them lives on the Island. I'm thinking we follow him and encourage him to give us the rocks."

Ozzie asked, "Is it diamonds again?"

"The shipment appears to be a mix of diamonds, rubies, and emeralds. He's coming in from one of the Bahama Islands. They have jewelry stores there on every corner. It looks to be about two hundred fifty thousand dollars in gems."

"Not bad," said Ozzie. "Can I take one of the rocks to give to my girl?"

"Jesus Christ, Ozzie, Donna is a nice kid and all, but your track record with women is about three months."

"I really like her, and she likes me," said Ozzie with a smile.

John said, "Oz, she has nice tits and legs that she likes to show off, but I wonder how much she'd like you if you didn't have any cash to flash."

"That's not fair, John. You don't know that. What do you say, Harry?"

130

"Oz, I don't care if you were in a fifty-year relationship. You're not going to take a rock we snatch to give to anyone. It doesn't work like that. You can be such a fucking idiot." Harry put the cold bottle of beer on his forehead. He felt like another headache was coming on. It had a very busy day. He really needed to catch up on his sleep.

"Sorry, Harry," Ozzie said sullenly.

Noise was coming out of the cabin. The three men around the fire looked up and saw Frank and the four women coming toward them with Max trotting behind. All the women had wine glasses and they were laughing with each other. They all seemed to be wearing shorts and sleeveless blouses of one kind or another. Donna's shorts were cut shorter and her blouse was tighter than the other three.

Sophia sat down next to Harry and put her arm around him. "How you holding up?"

"I'm fine, Sophia. I guess you girls are done."

"Yup, the kitchen is all cleaned up and Frank unclogged the kitchen sink."

"I knew Frank was good for something," said Harry, raising his voice.

Julia sat on John's lap and said, "Harry, I don't know if I ever saw you so tired."

Before he could answer, Sophia broke in, "He's been on the go since six this morning. I was still in bed and he was off with Max running around to some garage where he gets parts for cars. Then we drive out here and he's off with his painting supplies while I hang out here with Frank and Lisa."

"When are we going to see some of your paintings?" asked Lisa.

"He was gone for five hours doing landscapes. He should have enough to do a gallery showing by now," said Sophia.

"Hey, who knows?" said Harry. "Maybe I'll do a display someday in my garage."

"Do you paint any people?" asked Julia.

"I've been a nude model for an art class," said Donna. "I'll model for you."

"That's not happening," said Sophia, and everyone laughed.

The rest of the night was a lot of the same back and forth between everyone. Harry, John, and Ozzie didn't discuss any more business. They managed to forget about everything and had some fun. When it was time to go to bed, Harry finally crashed and got a good night's sleep. He awoke feeling refreshed on Sunday for the first time in several days. They all went to a diner for brunch and then made their way back to Long Island. Harry and Sophia stopped at Harry's home to leave Max there and then continued on to Sophia's house.

As Harry walked Sophia to her door, she said, "I had a lot of fun this weekend, Harry. I'm glad we talked on Friday night. It makes me very happy that you're getting away from your old tricks."

"Maybe I'll figure out some new tricks," said Harry with a devilish grin.

"As long as they aren't illegal, Harry Strickland. Now kiss me before we go inside."

They did and Harry took Sophia and her bag into the house. He stayed for a half hour visiting with her family and then begged off because of having to get to work the next morning. On the ride home, he felt a little relieved without having to dodge Sophia's questions about what he was up to. The constant fencing over his "dark side," as Sophia called it, was making him weary. He thought they had a "don't ask, don't tell" policy on that stuff. Obviously, he missed the memo revoking that rule.

Pulling up to the house, Harry heard a text come in over his phone. After parking, he pulled it out and saw it was from Cowboy. It said, "Got time to meet for breakfast tomorrow?"

Harry texted back a time and location. When Cowboy replied that he'd be there, Harry got out of the car and unloaded his gear.

Harry Hid It

He took Max for a quick walk and then settled down. Before bed, he pulled out his laptop and did some searching on the person flying in with the gems from the Bahamas on Wednesday. He marveled at what he could find on the Internet. When he matched up the name with an address, he began to visualize how to pull off this job. The only question was whether Hans Bamberger would take the gems to his home or to his store when he left the airport. As he drifted off to sleep, Harry went through various scenarios in his mind on how to make this work.

The next morning he was at a table at his favorite donut shop that was five minutes away from his job. Sipping coffee and eating a plain donut, he saw a tall figure with a cowboy hat heading toward the entrance. When Cowboy came in, he found Harry and walked over. Harry indicated another cup of coffee at the empty seat across from him. "It's black. I didn't know how you took it. There are a couple more donuts in the bag there."

"Thank you, Harry. Black is how my mama taught me to drink it. I had you pegged as a stand-up guy. Thank you." Cowboy lifted a long booted leg over the back of the chair and sat down. He took a sip of the coffee and looked at Harry over the cup.

"I do believe that you're a good guy, Harry. That's why I'm here. I wanted to share with you some of the scuttlebutt I heard on the street this weekend."

"What about?" asked Harry.

"Fat Tony."

"Why would that interest me?"

Cowboy looked at him. "As far as I'm concerned, Harry, there's no reason that you need to know any of this. I look at it as simple gossip. Nothing wrong with that, right?"

Harry saluted him with his coffee cup. "You got that right. And I thrive on gossip. What did you hear?"

"A few more details came out about Fat Tony's son being killed last Thursday. Fat Tony killed the bodyguard that accidently shot his son. Right then and there. The people that robbed him prob-

133

ably weren't out of the area yet when Fat Tony dropped him."

"Sounds like he was mad," said Harry.

"You got that right. His people are trying to find out anything they can on who hit them. So far, they've turned up nothing. The word is that there is five thousand dollars out there for anyone who can provide any information."

"Only five thousand!" said Harry. "Kind of a lowball figure, if you ask me."

"John said you were a cool customer," said Cowboy. "I'm sure that whoever robbed Fat Tony that night knows they can never utter a word to anyone."

"Do you think that anyone who might suspect something would be tempted by the five grand?"

Cowboy grinned. "Never. For instance, if somebody like me had an inkling of what was going on, he wouldn't take any amount of money from the likes of Fat Tony. When I was in Iraq with the Army, I saw firsthand the definition of evil. As a Texas Ranger, I learned the difference between a criminal and a really bad man. Fat Tony is totally evil and bad. I think the bodyguard shot the wrong Anthony Russo. The son was an asshole, but the father should be exterminated."

Harry took a bite of his donut and slowly chewed it. "I like how you make distinctions in the people you meet."

"That's the world, Harry. In the detective business, I do some things that the law may frown on, but it doesn't mean I'm a bad person. I think that's true of a lot of people I know."

"You got that right," said Harry. "You know, I'm more than happy to keep you on a retainer to keep your ear to the ground about all of this."

"I'd probably do it anyway, but I won't say no to a few bucks. John has been great to me, and I'm glad we met. I'll do what I can."

Harry reached into his pocket and pulled out a wad of bills. He counted them under the table and slipped a portion of them over to Cowboy. "I appreciate this. I have enough on my mind lately without having to concentrate on what Fat Tony may or may not do."

"I wouldn't make this offer to just anybody, Harry, but I'm damn good with a gun. If you need any defensive help, give a yell."

Standing up, Harry said, "I'll definitely keep that in mind. I have to get to work. Take the rest of the donuts with you. Keep in touch." With that, he left the shop and went over to his car. Driving over to the airport, Harry was glad Cowboy was on his side. He had a good sense of people and believed he could trust the Texan. Too many people would sell him or anyone else out for five thousand dollars. Harry felt as if Cowboy would stick with him even if the price went up to a hundred grand. As it was, he was feeling a little insulted that the current reward was so low.

When he got to his workstation, Harry fired up his computer. The first thing he saw was an email addressed to all airport personnel with instructions on how to change their passwords. Everybody who had any access to the airport computer system would have to be able to log into the system with a new password by the end of the week.

Harry didn't know whether to punch his desk in frustration or laugh. Somebody finally got off their ass about the security of the computers. All the information that Zac accumulated for him was now worthless. He was sure that any passwords to access the cargo information were already changed. Harry also had a good idea that Special Agent Dudek was the one who encouraged the airport to make those changes. Oh well, he had some information for the next three weeks or so that he could make use of if he chose to. He and the guys were definitely going to steal some gems on Wednesday. He'd decide after that job if he'd exploit the rest of the info he obtained from the airport's computers or if he'd find marks in another way.

Harry had confidence that with time, he could still tap into what was coming in and out of the airport somehow. What he had to worry about now was how to smoothly execute Wednesday's job. Before he started doing his mechanic's thing, Harry pulled out a road map of the area and started formulating a plan.

Chapter 15

JOHN PERCHED ON A chair outside the exit for a series of gates at Kennedy Airport. This area was fifty feet down from the TSA checkpoint that all passengers had to filter through to get to their flights. Where John sat, he could see the one TSA agent stationed where the people came out from their planes. Her job was to prevent anyone from taking the back door into the gate area and bypassing security. That suited John fine. He wanted people to come down this way from their flights with no fuss or confusion. He was here to put the eye on Hans Bamberger when he got off his plane.

Opening the newspaper he held, John looked at the photo he held between the pages. It was actually a printout from a jewelry company's website that displayed its management staff. This particular business acted more as a wholesaler to smaller jewelry stores. Mr. Bamberger was the chief purchaser for the company. He was the one coming in from the Bahamas carrying an assortment of gems. John didn't think he'd have trouble eyeballing the man. Hans looked to be in his forties, with a big round face and a very thinning band of blond hair covering his pate.

It was easy for Harry to find out about Bamberger from the information he gleamed from the manifests. Even though Hans was personally carrying the shipment, he had to notify the airline of the gems. Mr. Bamberger was carrying a sizable amount of them and he'd be going through customs. Doubtless, he'd done this many times and had all the proper paperwork to make his life go as smoothly as possible. Once Harry had the name and the company, it was a simple matter of doing some research on the Internet. Life got easier for Harry and the crew when he found Hans' smiling face on the company website.

Harry Hid It

With that insight, Harry told John that he'd hang out at the airport and ID Hans Bamberger when he arrived. John's job would be to follow Hans and identify the car he got into when he left the airport. Harry and Ozzie would station themselves in the area to follow the car. What Harry didn't know was if the jewelry company's chief purchaser would be heading to the office or to his home with the gems. Harry planned to snatch the gems at whatever location as soon as Hans stopped.

John usually had great confidence in Harry's plans. He wasn't so sure about this one. There were too many loose variables for his peace of mind, but they'd pulled in a huge amount of money in a relatively short amount of time. John was also spooked a little by what happened on the hit at Fat Tony's. While they got away safely with a hell of a lot of money, that job was a split second from being a total fuck up. Cowboy shared with John just how furious Fat Tony was acting. Hopefully, he'd just go away after a little bit of time passed.

Even though he was downplaying it, John also knew that Harry was feeling the heat from that one too. He had to be feeling the pressure of hiding cash and jewels. It was a lot of money. None of them figured they'd come into this much so quickly. John occasionally speculated on where the cache was, but he trusted Harry for keeping it secure. On the other hand, if anyone found it, it would be as if they won the fucking lottery!

John understood Harry's motivation. Get as much as they could as fast as possible, and then lie low for a year or two. After that, they could slowly get rid of the jewels and spend the money in a way that would keep everything under the radar. For every day that went by between a theft and spending the proceeds, the safer it was for him, Harry, and Ozzie. John had no desire to be in jail or get killed. The faster they finished their crime spree and quit, the better their quality of life would improve. Still, John wasn't feeling very positive about being here at the airport on this assignment. Too much of this job felt like it was being done on a wing and a prayer. They already experienced that with infiltrating the club.

Looking over at the screen showing the arriving flights, John saw that the plane from Freeport in the Bahamas had landed on time. It would still be a little while before people from that flight started to file out through here. John became aware of other people gathering around the area where he was sitting. He noticed most of the people were in suits and holding placards with names on them. These were drivers from car and limo companies waiting for their clients. A few of the more high-tech chauffeurs were holding computer tablets with a name on them.

With a sudden inspiration, John leisurely stood up and stretched. He slowly walked over next to a wall so that he could take in all of the drivers. It took him a few minutes, but he did see a huge Hispanic driver in a black suit holding up a sign with "Bamberger" clearly printed on it. Next to him, another individual stood in an almost identical suit. This guy was black, with his head shaved clean, and looked like a heavyweight fighter in his prime. "This isn't good," thought John.

Keeping his eyes on the two, he slid further down the wall and called Harry with his cell. Harry greeted him with, "Is he there already?"

"Not quite, Harry, but his driver is." John explained about the gathering of drivers. "Harry, this isn't some old retired guy. He's got the look of a bodyguard and so does his friend."

"There are two of them?"

"Yeah, Harry, the dude is bringing in a shitload of jewels."

There was silence on the other end. Finally, Harry said, "Oh, fuck, I don't know why I thought he'd just go to his own car and ride out of here. Dammit, dammit, dammit!"

John could hear Ozzie in the distance say, "What's wrong, Harry? Are we doing this?"

Harry must've lowered the phone, but John could hear him say, "Shut up while I think. Geez, Oz, do you always have to be talking." Then to John, "You think they're packing?"

"That would be my guess. They have the look of armed security. What are you going to do? Abort?"

More silence, then, "Maybe. Tell you what. Follow them and give me the info on the car they use. Ozzie and I will follow them and play it by ear. If I see an opening, we'll take it. Otherwise, this will be a lesson in jerking off."

"Hey, Harry, we can't win them all."

"I know." John could hear the frustration and anger in Harry's voice. "Good job, John, in seeing those two. I should've known that this wouldn't be so easy."

"Don't be so hard on yourself, Harry. The last couple weeks have been crazy. I'm getting off this call. I'll let you know what car they get into." John clicked off and continued watching. He slid off to the rear of the crowd. He didn't see much problem in following the two big guys. Hans Bamberger would find them and John wouldn't have to worry about identifying him.

It took another twenty minutes, but people finally started to stream out into the terminal after clearing customs. John watched a roly-poly man walking towards the driver and bodyguard. He matched the photo John held, but he was a little shorter and rounder than expected. He had a large leather satchel draped over his shoulder and was wheeling a small suitcase behind him. The large black man took the suitcase, but Hans hung onto the leather bag. As they started towards the exit, John slowly strolled after them. He was careful not to watch them too closely, but he had no trouble keeping tabs. They weren't in a hurry and other than the occasional glance around, didn't seem too concerned about anyone around them.

When they walked out into the parking area, John walked parallel to them, but kept two rows of cars in between. It wasn't long before they stopped at a pearl white Lexus. The black man opened the rear door for Hans, who maneuvered his bulk inside. The other man got in the driver's seat while his partner placed the suitcase in the trunk, and then got into the passenger seat. Then the Lexus pulled out and headed to the exit. John was on the phone before they even backed out of their parking space. He gave Harry the particulars on the car, including the license number. As he shut off his phone, John knew it was now all up to Ozzie and Harry.

At that moment, both of them had their eyes glued on the airport exit. They had been slowly circling the area for the last thirty minutes in a stolen Ford Taurus that Ozzie had lifted a couple of hours earlier. Harry was glad they were looking for a light-colored Lexus. It should stand out with all of the dark-colored limos and luxury cars passing by. It was actually Ozzie who saw it first. "Is that it, Harry?" he asked, pointing.

Harry looked through the binoculars hanging around his neck. Focusing on the rear of the car, he saw that the license number checked out with what John told him. "That's it, Oz. Follow him, but stay back a bit. We'll know soon enough where they're going."

Ozzie fell in behind the Lexus. He kept three to four cars in between the Taurus and the Lexus. It was easy to follow since the driver of the Lexus was smoothly going with the traffic flow and not doing anything crazy. Harry knew that the company's headquarters was in Brooklyn, while Hans Bamberger lived on the North Shore of Long Island in one of those golf course communities. With the traffic, it was another fifteen minutes before the Lexus took the road leading up towards Glen Cove, which was the location of Hans' home.

Harry weighed the situation in his mind. It was getting to be early evening, so heading up to the house made sense. He had a feeling that transporting around this much in jewels was common for Hans Bamberger. Harry did only a quick search when he was checking out Bamberger and his company, but it didn't look like they'd ever been robbed. That was one of the reasons he targeted Hans. People who have been robbed tend to be a great deal more cautious than somebody who never experienced it.

"Ozzie, pass them. I know where they're going. I want to get there first. Don't go too fast, though. We don't want to attract any cops."

Glancing over with a quizzical look, Ozzie knew to do what Harry told him. He accelerated and pulled the car out into the far left lane. As they passed the Lexus, Harry glanced over, but he couldn't see anything through the tinted windows. He started to give Ozzie directions on where to go. Oz blurted out, "How do you know all of this?"

"I took a long drive last night. I checked out the company's offices in Brooklyn and then drove up to the guy's house up near Glen Cove. It was easy to get his address. I thought it would be a good idea to case out both places since we didn't know where they'd go. I originally had a few places picked out to force the car off the road and snatch the gems." Harry was quiet for a moment. Then he grunted, "But I didn't think about him being escorted by a couple of bodyguards."

"You can't get it right all the time, Harry," said Ozzie.

"Yeah, but I'm supposed to. I want to get up near his house before they get there. If the car just lets him off at the house, we still have a chance of doing this."

"Is it a nice house?" asked Oz.

"Looks it from the outside," replied Harry. "We lucked out. It's in a good neighborhood surrounding a golf course. It's older, though, so it isn't a gated community. You'll see when we get there."

Ozzie drove according to Harry's instructions. Soon, they were off the highways and winding their way through neighborhood streets. Finally, Harry said, "There it is. It's that big brick house with the pillars on either side of the driveway." Ozzie slowed down as they passed it. Harry instructed, "Go past the neighbor's house and pull into the side street across from it."

Ozzie did this and parked the Taurus next to a big colonial that was set back from the road. It was about as isolated as they could hope. Harry said, "Put your hat on low and bring your mask. Follow me, and no talking!"

They left the car and walked across the street. Harry knew there was a path between Hans' two neighbors to the right of his property. This took him and Ozzie to the fringes of the golf course. Harry was thankful for the twilight that was rapidly descending to darkness. Looking around, Harry could see that the remaining golfers still playing were far away. Once again, Harry counted his blessings that Hans' home wasn't on the eighteenth fairway or every golfer left on the course would be going by them right now.

A row of trees bordered the golf course and the homes lining it. He and Ozzie stayed close to the tree line as they quickly walked past the neighbor's house. As Harry cut through the trees, he got down on his hands and knees and crawled to the short stone fence surrounding the Bamberger property. As they got to it, Harry heard an automobile pulling into the driveway. Cautiously raising one eye above the stone wall, he saw the Lexus come to a stop. Hans got out of the car, as did the bald, black man. The suited man opened the trunk, fetched Bamberger's suitcase, and gave it to him. Harry could hear Hans say, "Thank you," and start walking to the side door of the house. When he was safely inside, the other man returned to the car. This was the moment of truth. Harry didn't even realize he was holding his breath until the car backed out of the drive and took off. They were only delivering Hans to his home. They wouldn't be hanging around.

Harry turned to Ozzie. "Put your mask on. We're going down hard and fast. We get the gems and get the hell out of here."

"OK, Harry. I'm right behind you." Ozzie put on his mask and took out his gun when he saw Harry pull his.

With a nod, Harry vaulted over the fence and lightly landed on the lawn. Oz tried to emulate Harry, but his foot caught the top of the fence and he tumbled over onto his back. Harry looked at the house, but nobody seemed to see them or hear the whoosh of air when Ozzie landed. He waited until Ozzie picked himself up.

Then he quickly trotted over to the back of the house.

Harry looked in a window and saw that he was staring into a dining room. The table was set for dinner and a plump woman with very blonde hair was at one end. The chair on the opposite side was empty, but the two seats on either side of the table had children in them. Harry's head almost bounced against the window as he let out an inaudible sigh. "Fuck," he whispered.

"What's wrong now?" asked Ozzie.

"Kids! Four kids are in there. I didn't know he had so many brats."

"I'm not going to take any shit from kids this time," sputtered Ozzie.

"Shut up, Ozzie. You don't hurt the kids. Just follow me." Harry went around the corner of the house to the back patio. He slowly pushed on the sliding door there, and it started to move. He opened it wide enough to slip through. Ozzie was right on his heels as he crossed some type of family room and went into the dining room. He heard a chorus of "Daddy!" as Hans Bamberger entered the dining room from the other direction the same time Harry did.

Bamberger's eyes went as wide as saucers as he said, "What's the meaning of…"

"Shut the fuck up and sit down." Harry covered everyone with his gun as he went over to Bamberger. Ozzie went in the other direction, watching everyone at the table. Harry clamped a strong hand on Hans' shoulder and forced him down into the vacant chair. There were screams and cries from the man's wife and kids. With as much vehemence as he could muster, Harry snarled, "Everybody just shut up and maybe you'll live through the next five minutes."

It took a few minutes, but eventually everyone quieted down. The family took turns looking at Harry and then over at Ozzie. Harry saw that there were two boys and two girls around the table. The oldest was a boy who looked to be fifteen or so. He looked terrified and defiant at the same time. The youngest was a four-year-old girl who started to cry. Harry signaled Ozzie to stay and he went into the kitchen. Looking around, he saw a door next to the kitchen and opened it. It was a laundry room with a big washer and dryer, but no other door or windows.

Going back into the dining room, Harry said, "Everybody up and into the laundry room. Now." Nobody moved. Harry placed the gun to Hans' forehead. "You don't want Dad to die, do you?"

Hans' wife let out a cry. She got the kids to their feet and marched them into the kitchen. Harry grunted to Ozzie, "Stay with them. Put them in the room and keep near the door."

When they were gone, Hans could see the man's eyes burning into him through the mask. The masked man pointed the gun at him and said, "I want the gems you brought home. Now."

Hans looked at the gun. Trembling, he said, "You must be mistaken. There are no gems here. Everything is at the office."

"Listen, asshole, you just came back from shopping in the Bahamas. I know you came right here from the airport. I want them and I want them now."

"I have some money in the house, but that's all," said Hans. "I can give you that and then you and your man can go."

"Do you think I'm stupid or something?" shouted Harry. He slammed the gun into the bridge of Bamberger's nose. With a loud yelp, the man's head flew back and his momentum made him and his chair fly backwards. Hans slammed onto the floor with a loud crash as blood spurted from his nose.

From the other room, Harry heard a boy cry, "Dad!" Then there was the sound of scuffling and Harry could hear several punches landing in someone's face. Looking down at the motionless Hans who had his hands up to his face, Harry leaped over him and looked in the kitchen. The older boy must've flown out of the laundry room when he heard his father yelled. Ozzie had hit him or tripped him, but the kid was on his back. Ozzie knelt on one knee with the gun pointed in the direction of the laundry room and wailed away at the boy's face with his free hand. Harry could already see blood coming from the kid's nose and bruises starting to well up around the eyes.

"Goddamnit!" Harry took one step, pivoted, and kicked Ozzie off the kid. For a split second, he thought about shooting Ozzie and just leaving. Spitting mad, Harry said, "Cover them and that's all." Heading back toward the dining room, Harry saw a block of wood with kitchen knives sticking out. Grabbing the longest one, he marched back in. He found Hans Bamberger trying to stand up. Reaching down, he pulled the man up by his collar and propped him against the table. "Where are the fucking jewels?"

"I told you, I don't have any here."

Harry took the knife and carefully put it down the waistband of the man's trousers. With a sharp motion, he gave the knife a yank and sliced through the material. Most of the material fell away. Bamberger now had a look of terror in his eyes as Harry did the same to the man's boxers. Now Hans was pretty much naked from the waist down.

Very deliberately, Harry brought the knife down. Hans shuddered when the cold metal touched his scrotum. Through clenched teeth behind his mask, Harry snarled, "Since you have four kids already, you don't need your balls anymore. One more time before I cut them off, where are the gems?"

The defiance evaporated out of Hans Bamberger. He stuttered, "Th…they're in my office."

Harry withdrew the knife and stepped back. "Show me."

Hans tried to gather up his pants. Harry said, "Leave them." Hans stopped fumbling for his ripped clothes and led Harry to his office bare-assed. Any other time, Harry would find this hilarious, but he wanted to get out of here as fast as possible. They went through the kitchen. Harry saw Ozzie's eyes widen as the half-naked man walked by. Harry saw that the kid must be back in the laundry room. The door was closed and there was a lot of crying going on behind it. Blood covered the floor where the boy fell.

Harry Hid It

Hans led Harry down a hall and into a small office. In the corner was a steel safe. Without being asked, Bamberger crouched down and twirled the combination. When the door opened, he backed up. Harry looked around. "Sit in the desk chair." When he did, Harry took out zip ties and fastened the man's arms together behind the back of the chair. Satisfied that he wouldn't be a problem, Harry went back to the safe and looked inside. He saw the leather courier bag that Hans had with him when he got out of the Lexus. Opening it, he saw many envelopes like the kind a bank puts money into when you make a withdrawal. Harry opened one and blood red rubies shone inside. Another contained green emeralds. Several looked like they held diamonds. Harry quickly counted twenty-five or so envelopes

As Harry was about to stand up, he looked deeper into the safe. Two shelves were stacked with several boxes. He grabbed one of the boxes and opened it. He let out a loud gasp when he looked inside. The light reflected off many gems of all colors. The other three boxes were the same. This guy kept precious stones around here like he kept doggie treats for Max. Why he had all of these here and not at their company office was beyond him, but Harry didn't need the details. He put the boxes in the satchel. The last item in there was a velvet bag. Harry reached in his hand and pulled out gold coins. "Holy shit," he thought, "this is the mother lode."

Harry placed that in the leather bag and hoisted it to his shoulders. Standing up, he went over and put a gloved hand on Hans' mouth. "You just keep quiet and your family will stay alive. It was nice doing business with you."

He quickly trotted back to the kitchen. He waved at Ozzie to follow him. They left by the patio door and retraced their steps back across the lawn. As they landed on the other side of the fence, Ozzie asked, "Shouldn't we have tied them up or something?"

"We're on borrowed time now," hissed Harry. "I'm hoping they think you're still there and that will keep them quiet for a few more minutes. We need to get out of here."

They ran along the trees and back up the path to the street. They took their masks off and tried to calmly walk across the road to their car. They got in and Ozzie drove away. Harry whipped out his phone and called John.

"Yeah, we got it…and a shitload more. Pick us up at the shopping plaza we agreed on before. We'll leave the car there."

As he hung up, Harry rested his head against the back of the seat. He felt incredibly tired. "Oz, if you ever hit a kid again like that, you're done. Got it?"

Ozzie gulped and said, "Sure, Harry, but I couldn't help…"

Harry held up his hand to shut him up. "Just drive or I swear to God I'll shoot you and leave you on the side of the road."

Chapter 16

Caitlyn Nemeth stood at the corner of Karyn Dudek's desk. Glancing out of the corner of her eye, all Karyn could see were long legs sticking out of a red skirt. She sat back and looked at the rest of the assistant looking down at her. The woman looked stressed, which matched Karyn's mood exactly. The last week had been extremely hectic in the FBI office. Crime seemed to skyrocket as the summer was coming to an end.

"He wants you now," said Caitlyn.

"Of course he does. It's not like I have anything more to tell him than this morning. I've hit more dead ends than a rat high on drugs in a maze." Karyn stood up and looked at her watch. "What the hell are we doing here so late anyway? It's eight o'clock. Shouldn't you have left hours ago?"

"You'd think," said Caitlyn. "I've been doing some extra work for the organized crime unit. They've been working on that guy who was shot out on the Island. It was some crime boss' son and nobody is doing much talking so far."

"There's a surprise," said Karyn. "A crime lord who doesn't want to say anything." She started across the room to the door at the end. "I guess I'm off to get my ass chewed…again."

She looked around. The room was still more than half filled with agents. Everyone was either hunched over laptops or talking on the phone. Over the past several weeks, numerous killings, robberies, kidnappings, and other crimes fell into the bailiwick of the FBI. For her part, she had nothing more to go on with the diamonds stolen from the courier leaving JFK. It was if the diamonds and the perpetrators had vanished into thin air.

Finding herself at Assistant Director Gonzales' door, she glanced in. He was busy talking on the phone and writing something down. Gonzales sensed her presence and looked up. He waved her in and indicated the chair in front of the desk. Karyn sat down and realized she needed to get out of her clothes. The light tan pantsuit she wore still looked fine, but she'd been wearing it for the past fourteen hours. It had been a long day and she knew a shower would feel good. She sighed. Maybe a drink in the shower would heighten the experience.

She focused back on Enrico as he hung up the phone and continued writing for a few more seconds. Then he looked up and said, "You need to go out to Glen Cove."

"Why would I want to do that?"

He thrust the paper he'd been writing on at her. "We just got a call from the Glen Cove PD. There was a home invasion only a half hour or so ago. Thieves came in and took a bunch of gems."

Karyn looked at the notes and address on the paper. "You think this is connected to the robbery outside the airport?"

"I don't have a lot of information so far, but this Hans Bamberger just returned home with the precious stones. The police called us because he'd only arrived from the airport about an hour earlier from the Bahamas with the rocks." He looked at Karyn with a tired smile. "He came in through JFK."

The tiredness Karyn had been feeling instantly left her. Like most cops at any level, she didn't believe in coincidences. They did happen, but where crime was concerned, they were rare. "It's about fucking time," she blurted out. "I haven't been able to find shit on the first heist."

"I know. I've read your reports. I don't know what else you could've done." Gonzales hesitated for a moment. "Unfortunately, my supervisors aren't as discerning as I am. They're putting pressure on me to solve that one and about twenty other cases that have turned the greater New York area into a cluster fuck." He smiled again. "I'd apologize for my language, but you don't seem to mind."

"God, don't start treating me like the delicate woman," exclaimed Karyn.

Harry Hid It

"I'm not. I'm also not going to sugar coat it," said Gonzales. "You know that shit rolls downhill. I can protect you and my other agents, but only to a certain extent. You need to solve the jewel heist. To add double jeopardy to the equation, you now have this one too. Go see if they're connected."

Karyn got up and left without a word. Going back to her desk, she picked up her pocketbook and headed out. Caitlyn gave her a questioning look as Karyn passed her desk. Without slowing down, Karyn called over her shoulder, "Well, I didn't get my ass chewed. I may actually have a lead on the missing diamonds."

Caitlyn said, "Good for you. Lots of luck."

Karyn went down to the garage below the building and signed out a Chevy Malibu for the ride. She keyed the address into the onboard navigation system and maneuvered out into the streets. The roads and highways of New York City and Long Island were still a labyrinth to her. When she lived out west, she could be on one road for miles before there was a turnoff. In this part of the world, there were eight possible directions to go along a quarter mile stretch of road. She carefully guided the car, matching the GPS instructions. She breathed a sigh of relief when the speeding highways turned into quieter, suburban streets. She knew she was at the right place when she saw squad cars with flashing lights up ahead of her. As far as Karyn understood it, the actual crime took place about two hours ago at this point. Why did the police insist on lighting up an area like a circus, even when the criminals were long gone? Nothing like inspiring fear throughout the neighborhood!

Karyn parked across the street from the Bamberger home and got out of her car. Flashing her ID at the patrolman stationed outside, she asked, "Who's in charge?"

The cop lit up and smiled at the pretty FBI agent. "Detective Warner is inside. You can't miss him. He's the grumpy one."

Though she tried to always remain professional, Karyn grinned at that. "Thank you." She walked past and up the front steps. The patrolman couldn't help but follow her sexy curves up the stairs.

Karyn entered the foyer to the house and saw that the living room to the left was full of people. She quickly took in the occupants. She first noticed two boys and a girl on the couch. Their ages varied, but the one teenage boy had his nose bandaged and was sporting two awful-looking black eyes. On one chair was a blonde, slightly chubby woman with a young girl on her lap. Sitting across from her in a matching chair was a short, fat man with very thinning hair. He had on a dress shirt but was wearing sweatpants. He also had a bandage on his nose. Standing in the middle of them was a tall man with dark blond, bushy hair wearing a worn blue sports jacket and gray trousers. He was taking down information in a notebook.

As Karyn walked in, the man with the notebook barked at her, "What can I do for you, Miss?"

"I'm Special Agent Dudek with the FBI," said Karyn.

The man looked like he was going to say something, but decided against it. In fact, he seemed to shrink into himself a little as he grudgingly said, "Glad you're here. Detective David Warner is my name. I'm sure you'll want to interview the victims yourself, but the short version is that Mr. Bamberger here landed several hours ago with a good amount of rubies, emeralds, and diamonds. He's the purchaser for a wholesale jewelry concern that sells stones to smaller shops. Almost as soon as he got home, two men came in and robbed him. They roughed up their son, Richard, here. Since the goods came in from the islands, it seemed a good idea to alert your office." He looked over at a clock on the wall. "You didn't waste any time getting here," finished Detective Warner.

"It may be connected to something else I'm working on, Detective," said Karyn.

The detective closed his notebook. "I'll leave the family to you. I want to take another look around the crime scenes."

"There's more than one?" asked Karyn.

"Apparently a lot happened in a short time," said Warner. "We can compare notes if you want when you're done." With that, he left the room and Karyn could hear his footsteps clomping down the hallway.

Karyn withdrew her own notebook from her purse. She also pressed the recording app on her phone and set it down on the coffee table. "As I told the detective, I'm Special Agent Karyn Dudek with the FBI and will be trying to find out who did this." She looked at the man. "Could you please state your name and tell me what happened?"

"I'm Hans Bamberger and this is my wife, Heidi," said the fat man. He indicated his oldest son, "This is Richard. He can stay, but can my other children go up to their rooms? They do not need to hear this again."

Nodding, Karyn said, "That's fine. I may have to ask them some questions later." Heidi told the second oldest child, whose name was Leyla, to take the two youngest children up to their rooms. When they left, Karyn turned back to Hans and said, "I know you had to go through this with the police, but could you relate to me everything you remember?"

Hans took a deep breath and did so. Karyn winched when he got to the point about Richard getting beaten. She asked the boy, "Why did that happen?"

"We heard a loud crash coming from the dining room and Dad yelled out. I didn't think about it. I threw open the door and went running out. The big jerk in the kitchen whacked me with his gun and I fell into the cabinet. Then he said something about no kid was going to get the best of him again and starting hitting me hard."

Examining the boy's face, Karyn said, "That was very brave of you. You're lucky the man stopped hitting you."

The boy beamed at the compliment from the beautiful woman, but it was Heidi who replied. "The man didn't stop on his own. The other masked man came into the kitchen and kicked him away from Richard. He was really mad at his partner and cursed at him. When that man went back into the dining room, Leyla and her other brother came out and helped Richard back into the laundry room. There's a sink in there and I tried to clean the poor boy up the best I could." Heidi was starting to tear up as she told all of this to Karyn.

Karyn shifted her attention back to Hans. "So then you took him to your office."

Hans looked sheepish. "I tried to bluff my way out of it, but then he threatened to…to…"

"Cut his testicles off," said Heidi.

Hans' face turned crimson. "They weren't the exact words he used, but he cut off my pants and had the knife touching me there. I didn't have much choice."

"I should say not," said Karyn matter-of-factly. "Then what happened?"

"He tied me to the chair in the office and took the gems I just brought back from the islands plus a bunch of others I had in the safe. When I didn't hear anything for five minutes, I started yelling. Heidi and the kids came out, cut me free, and we called the police."

"I'm really sorry you had to go though that ordeal," said Karyn sincerely. "I'm happy you all got through it. Can you tell me about the men? Any kind of description that might be helpful."

Heidi answered, "They both had masks on. You know, those winter wool hats with the eyeholes in them. They also wore gloves. One was tall and thin, while the other was short and stocky. They had on black pants and sweatshirts. The tall one did all the talking."

"What did he sound like?" asked Karyn.

"Kind of a husky voice," said Hans.

"But he sounded different when he yelled at his partner for beating Richard," said Heidi. "It was a deep voice, but not like when he was talking to us in the dining room."

"Maybe he was trying to make his voice sound different," said Karyn, almost to herself. She looked around the living room. "I don't suppose you have any security cameras around here?"

"No," said Hans. "We have an alarm system we set at bedtime and when we're out of the house, but that's it."

"Can you take me to your office?" asked Karyn.

"Sure," said Hans. He stood and Karyn followed him down a hall. A techie from the police department was just finishing up taking photos. He nodded to Karyn as he exited the room. She could see the open safe and the chair where the intruder had bound Hans. She walked around the small space looking for anything that might resemble a clue, but she found nothing.

"What was the value of the gems taken from you?"

Hans looked crestfallen. "What I brought back with me today were valued at almost four hundred thousand dollars."

It took all of Karyn's self-control not to exclaim, "Holy shit!" Instead, she said, "Who knew you were coming in with them today?"

Hans replied, "I've been going over that ever since this happened. The only person who knew I was coming back with that much in gems was the owner of the company. He doesn't even tell his wife how much money he makes, so I can't see him leaking information. I had to tell the airline I was flying on and the customs office how much I planned to bring back about a week ago. You may find this hard to believe, but this is fairly routine for me. One reason that I never had any trouble before is that I don't advertise what I'm doing."

"Why bring them here instead of the office?"

"Whenever I arrive in the early evening, I bring any jewels here and lock them right up. If I come back during the day, I go to the office." Hans hesitated. "Not that I'd have been able to do that on this trip anyway."

"Why?" asked Karyn sharply.

"We're having a new state-of-the art safe installed at the office. The place has been a mess for the past two weeks. We've kept our inventory to a minimum, but both the head of the company and

I have had some of the merchandise in our home safes until the construction is complete."

"So you had more stuff in the safe?" asked Karyn. "How much?"

Hans looked like he was going to faint. In a squeaky voice he said, "About a million and a half dollars' worth of gems and gold coins."

Karyn felt a little faint. She closed her eyes and said through tight lips, "You're telling me that two masked men came in here and took off with almost two million dollars tonight!"

"Yeah." Hans looked like he was about to cry.

"Did they say anything at all that would help?"

Hans thought hard for a minute. "The tall one did all the talking. Most of that was threatening me. When I was trying to tell him he was wrong about there being precious gems here in the house, he said that he knew I just brought them home from the airport."

Karyn pondered this nugget of information. It was a stretch, but the airport was the connection between this robbery and the diamond heist. It was flimsy, but still, it was more than she had to go on for the past couple of weeks. She closed her eyes. She'd have to do a ton of investigative work, but she knew hard work helped make your luck. She was determined to solve these thefts. It would be her ticket back into the good graces of the bureau and out of New York.

"Mr. Bamberger, I need copies of everything you filed with the airline and U.S. Customs as well as your flight information. I also need the contact information for your boss and the service that drove you home from the airport. I also want to question your other children. Nothing in depth, but you'd be surprised what kids sometimes see that adults miss. My only chance of getting your merchandise back is if I have as much information as possible."

Hans nodded. "I understand. I already informed my boss. He isn't happy, but I told him I didn't think keeping our inventory in our homes while the safe at the office is being replaced was a good idea. I guess it's one catastrophe at a time. I'll have Heidi bring the kids back downstairs."

They want back to the living room and Heidi reassembled the children. Karyn asked questions in every way possible to try to nurse some pertinent memory out of the family, but she didn't really find out anything new. When she finished questioning everyone, she walked through the office again as well as the kitchen and dining room. She walked through the patio door and out to the lawn, but didn't see anything that would be much help. She finally wandered back out to the front of the house. She found Detective David Warner leaning against a cop car, sipping out of a coffee cup.

He toasted her with the cup as she approached. "I'd have had my men bring you one, but I didn't even know they were bringing me any."

Karyn leaned against the car with him. "That's fine. I'll either drink some later or go home and catch a few hours of sleep before hitting this tomorrow. Mr. Bamberger tell you how much was taken?"

"Almost two million, you mean? Yeah. I almost shit when he told me. I'll tell you, Agent Dudek, I'm not much for inter-agency bullshit. As far as I'm concerned, we all want to catch the bad guys. But when he told me how much was swiped, I was kinda glad you'd have the lead on this one. I don't need my boss on my ass with that much loot at stake."

"Funny how the pressure goes up in direct proportion to the amount taken," said Karyn.

"You said this may be related to another case?" asked David Warner.

"Yup. A bunch of diamonds were stolen right outside of Kennedy Airport a couple of weeks ago."

"Heard about that. After talking to the family, you still think they're connected?"

"Both sets of jewels came through Kennedy and they were taken shortly after they arrived there."

"Kennedy is a big place," said the detective. "It's bigger than a lot of towns."

"Still, you take what you can," said Karyn. "Did your men find anything inside or around the grounds?"

"Nope. We can tell they came in over the wall into the yard and through the patio door. It looked like they left that way too. I have men combing the area behind the house and all around. For all we know, they drove over here across the golf course on a golf cart with clubs on the back, pretending they were golfers. To make things worse, we're supposed to get thunderstorms tonight. If that happens, it'll wash away anything we might see in the daylight." He took a gulp of coffee. "As my first partner used to say, this is a real shit sandwich."

Karyn gave a grunt of appreciation. "Sounds about right. The neighbors see anything?"

"Of course not," answered Warner. "We've already knocked on doors within two blocks of this place. They came, they stole, and they vanished. Was there anything odd in what you heard from the Bambergers?"

After a few seconds of thought, Karyn answered, "The part where the one guy kicked his partner off the kid? That was a little strange for a home invasion team."

"I thought so too," said Warner. "I don't know what it means, but in this business you never know." He stood up straight. "I'm heading home. I think we're about done here." He handed Karyn a business card. "Give me a call if I can be of help."

She fished out one of hers and held it out. "You do the same."

"Sure. As I said, we're in the same business. I don't want the creeps of the world to think they can hit the homes in my town like this. I'll never get any rest." With that, he waved a casual salute at Karyn and walked down the sidewalk into the gloom.

She slowly headed over to her car. Getting in, Karyn felt the fatigue of a very long day hit her. She was exhausted. A few hours of sleep and then back into the office was the way to go. As she started up the car, she thought of the detective's words, "Kennedy is a big place." It looked like she was going to make more of a nuisance of herself tomorrow at the airport. For no good reason, she wondered if she'd run into the handsome mechanic again. There was just something about him. She violently shook her head. She had a lot more important things to deal with than a good-looking man. What was his name anyway? Henry…Barry…no, Harry – that was it.

Chapter 17

THE COFFEE PASSED TASTING terrible a long time ago. Karyn took another swig anyway and tried to put some order to the papers in front of her. The main printout showed who had logged into the airport's computer system to access the manifests of what was coming in and out of the airport. Since the thieves had knocked off the diamond courier a couple of weeks ago, the administration had greatly cleaned up who had access to that particular information. As far as she could tell, the people who pulled up the manifests had permission to do so. That could mean that if someone in JFK had used that data to pull off the two gem thefts, then it was a very inside job. Or someone paid for the information and nobody here was actively involved in the thefts. Or it was a coincidence that both sets of jewels just happened to come through the airport and the perpetrators stealing them had some access to New York City's jewelry industry.

Karyn stood up from the desk where she sat in the security office of John F. Kennedy International Airport and went to the ladies' room. After getting rid of the coffee she had been drinking for hours, she washed her hands and splashed water in her face. She had been hoping that something would stick out in the reports that would make this a little easier. Now she faced having to do background checks on everyone that could access the manifests. It was a big list. It ran from the executive staff of the airport to the people who unloaded the planes to custom officials. Her heart sank at the prospect. She was really upset at what the thieves had put the Bamberger family through, but she didn't feel any closer to figuring this out than she did yesterday.

Going back to her desk, Karyn looked at the printout again. She noticed certain notations by some of the entries. Looking at the top of the pages, she didn't see any key telling her what they meant. Taking the printout, she took it down a hallway and into a room that was the IT center for Kennedy. Everything except the radar and communications ran through this office. The electronics that had to do with landing and flying the planes were the responsibility of the FAA and headquartered in another building. Karyn's head went right and left as she tried to find the head geek, as she called him. He was a nice guy, but he wasn't much taller than she was and he must have weighed almost three hundred pounds. Worse yet, Bob Fletcher kept trying to flirt with her.

She spied him hunched over a young woman at a computer terminal. When she came up behind him, he turned and beamed. "Agent Dudek, is there anything I can do for you? I told you that I'm at your service."

Karyn heard the woman Fletcher had been talking to trying to stifle laughter that she turned into a cough. Karyn smiled and held up her printout. "I saw something on here I didn't understand." Bob came closer. She used a pen she was holding to indicate a series of numbers. "What does that mean?"

Bob took the paper and took his glasses off. He looked up and said, "That's the machine that printed out that particular manifest." He looked at the printout again. "I take it that this shows the information on the gems you told me about." Karyn nodded. "All our systems show when official documents get printed. Some of our offices have one central machine that does all the printing, and others have individual printers at each workstation."

"Thank you, Bob. I'm not sure how that helps me, but you never know." She spun to go back to the security office.

"Anytime, Agent Dudek. Hey, if you need to grab lunch, I can show you a couple places around here."

"You're a dear, Bob, but the FBI likes us to keep our noses to the grindstone." Karyn said this over her shoulder as she kept strolling away. She wasn't sure, but she thought she heard the woman near Bob say, "Loser."

Harry Hid It

That made her grin. She didn't have a lot to smile about today, but she was glad that she wasn't imagining Bob's flirting. As she got closer to her desk, she had an inspiration. It probably wouldn't matter worth a damn, but she had another printout that gave a general idea of where every employee was at any given time. It was very general because to get from certain sections of the airport to another, employees swiped their ID cards. This was one of the security measures of the airport because some areas were restricted. What it did do was time stamp an employee when he left one area and swiped into another. She didn't know if it would show anything, but she could see if there were any correlation between the gem manifest being printed and the employee going somewhere away from his building or station.

Karyn was going on the flimsy premise that the person printed the manifest and then he or she took it somewhere…maybe to give to some contact who then gave it to the thieves. As she sat back at her desk, she quietly said aloud, "Oh, hell, that's way too complicated. A person could just take a picture of the paper or even the computer screen and text the information out." She knew she was only killing some time before she called Gonzales to suggest they needed to do a deep background check on everyone who had direct access to knowing the gems were coming in yesterday. He'd flip. That sounded easy and routine on the TV shows, but it was a ton of work and she knew resources were thin.

She started playing around on the computer in front of her. Bob had shown her how the system worked when she got there in the morning and the security officers in the vicinity answered her questions when she got stuck. It was only a week and a half ago that Hans Bamberger alerted customs and the airline that he would be bringing in a sizable amount of jewels. According to the security chief, this was routine if someone was personally bringing in merchandise of any value for business. The people who did this regularly had it down pat. They'd give preliminary information and then finalize it right before they actually boarded their flight.

Hans had indicated that he would be bringing approximately two hundred fifty thousand dollars in assorted gems back with him from his trip. Karyn started with this entry and checked who had printed any manifests from that point up to yesterday.

On television, it would've taken five minutes to cross-check all of this information. For Karyn, it was almost two hours and a bottle of coke before she was finished. After all that work, she found nothing obvious, but there was an anomaly. At the time Assistant Director Tom Fleming's printer was pumping out the manifest in question, he was two buildings over from his office. He clocked back into his building about ten minutes after his printer started. Karyn knew this was thin. It could've been someone else like his assistant doing the work. Still, it delayed her having to call the FBI office to report another dead end.

She asked a security officer what building Tom Fleming worked in. The woman started to tell her and then said, "Look, I'll just drive you over there. It will be easier." They went outside and hopped into a golf cart. When they arrived at their destination, the security officer said, "I'll wait here to take you back."

"Thanks," said Karyn. "I appreciate that. I can't imagine I'll be too long." She went into the building, showed her ID, and asked for Tom Fleming.

In a couple of minutes, a small, pretty redhead in her twenties came out with her hand extended. "Hi, I'm Dawn Kramer. Mr. Fleming is in Washington today. I'm his assistant. Can I help you?"

Karyn said, "I'm Special Agent Dudek with the FBI. I had a couple of questions for him, but you can probably answer them. Can we go back to his office?"

Dawn looked puzzled but smiled and said, "Sure, come with me." She led Karyn through the array of cubicles. When she got to an office, she stopped and said, "Here it is. What do you need?"

Karyn said, "I'm investigating the theft of some items. They happened outside the airport, but they were stolen soon after arriving here. Anyway, going through the airport's computer information all morning, I saw that Mr. Fleming printed out the manifest from the aircraft that one of these items came in on."

"That's not unusual," said Dawn. "He often is the one who makes sure certain people or certain shipments get through here effortlessly. He's sort of in charge of anything reeking of VIP status."

"Well, as near as I can tell, this particular printing operation happened when he was in another building. Do you or anyone else ever use his computer or office?"

"Not that I ever saw, at least not when I'm sitting out here." She indicated her desk. "I have my own computer and printer setup. When did this happen?"

"Last Friday morning. Do you keep a log of Mr. Fleming's meetings?"

"No, except for things like his trip down to DC today. He's always called into meetings or calling one of his own at the last minute. It's the nature of the business here."

"Was there anyone around here last Friday out of the ordinary?"

Karyn watched Dawn's forehead crease as she thought about that. "I'm sorry, Agent, I can barely remember yesterday. The days around here are absolutely crazy."

Taking out one of her cards, Karyn handed it to her, saying, "If you think of anything, please let me know. It's important."

"I will. Is there anything else?"

"No, just point me the way out of this maze." Dawn did so and soon Karyn was back outside and climbing back into the golf cart. She said to the security officer, "Well, that wasn't much help. Let's go back." As they were halfway back to the security headquarters, Karyn asked the woman driving, "That building we were at…does it have security cameras?"

"Most of our buildings do, ma'am."

This "ma'am" crap was getting to Karyn. She bent over to

look at the woman's nametag. "Listen, Officer Bertel, can you get me some footage from last Friday? And call me Karyn."

"I'm Alice," said Bertel. "Everything is digital, so we keep video for a long time. Last Friday is no problem."

"Let's go watch some TV, Alice," said Karyn.

Bertel took Karyn into a room with multiple flat screens standing on a long table. She asked the FBI agent, "I take it you want the video from the building we just came from?"

"You got that right…from last Friday."

The security officer went to work on a keyboard. Soon, three of the screens came to life. Each one was divided into four quadrants with different images in each section. Karyn could see the view from several outside cameras focused on the building. The other scenes were from the inside. Alice said, "I'm starting this from six a.m. Is that good?"

"Fine. I think the time I need is more near ten. Why don't you just fast forward these until that time?"

Alice Bertel hit a few keys and everything speeded up. Karyn got the feel for everything she was seeing. As the digital readout neared ten Alice slowed down the action to normal speed. Karyn kept her eyes between the scene of the main entrance and the one that showed the area around Tom Fleming's office. She could see Dawn at her desk off to the side. Suddenly, Karyn sucked in her breath. The good-looking guy from the maintenance area was coming in the front door. Harry! She watched as he called over to a blonde woman. They disappeared from that camera. Karyn scanned all the screens and then saw them walking over to Dawn's desk. As they were talking, Karyn wished these things had audio. Dawn escorted Harry into Fleming's office and went back to her desk. After a short wait, Dawn leaned into the door and then completely left the area. Looking at the clock, Karyn saw fifteen minutes go by without anything going on at all on the screen. Too bad Fleming's office didn't have a camera.

Finally a man dressed in a suit strolled into the picture and entered the office. Karyn assumed this was Tom Fleming. After five minutes or so, both the man and Harry came out shaking hands. Karyn finished watching Harry walk out of the building. She sat back in her chair.

Alice asked her, "Did you find something?"

Karyn looked at the times she jotted down in her notebook. The time Harry was in the office by himself coincided with the printer spewing out the manifest. It was something. It was purely circumstantial and wouldn't hold up in court or even be enough to obtain a warrant, but it was an avenue to pursue. It was actually more like an alley, but it delayed admitting defeat to her boss. "Yes, I did. Nothing big, but something I have to follow up on. Oh, there was a maintenance building I was in a couple of weeks ago. Are there cameras in them?"

"Right now, only on the outside. A security upgrade is hitting in a few months where some cameras will finally be placed inside them."

"Okay. Alice, thank you for your help."

"Anytime. See you later."

Karyn left the room and went back to her desk. Checking her notebook, she brought up the employee directory on the computer and called Dawn Kramer's extension. When she answered, Karyn said, "Dawn, this is Agent Dudek. I have one quick question. I did some checking around and saw that a Harry from the maintenance area was in your office on Friday morning."

Without any hesitation, Dawn said, "I'm so sorry. I forgot all about that. Mr. Fleming had a special assignment for him and asked him to come over. He was still at a meeting so I left him in Mr. Fleming's office. I end up doing that a lot with Mr. Fleming running all over the place constantly."

"Were you there the entire time?"

There was silence as Karyn pictured the girl thinking. "No, I had to go over to another administration building for a committee meeting that I'm part of." Dawn was quiet. "Am I in trouble?" she asked, almost in a whisper.

"No, I just needed to verify a few things," said Karyn. "Thank you." She hung up, looked blankly at her computer screen, and thought it through. Her mind started imagining different scenarios of what could've happened. When she started imagining a conspiracy at the highest levels of JFK, she shook her head and decided it was time to do some straight police work before she blew everything out of proportion.

Leaving the security building, she made her way over to where she found Harry the first time she was here. Walking inside, she saw him at his workstation intently looking at the monitor on his desk and tapping on his keyboard. Looking at him in profile, she realized what a handsome man he was. His hair was slightly tousled and today he was clean-shaven. If he wanted to, he probably could make some good money doing ad work in Manhattan. He had the looks to be up on a billboard in Times Square. "Maybe in an underwear ad," thought Karyn. Her next thought was, "For the love of God, Dudek, get your head in the game. You're not a stupid teenager."

She put on her game face and started walking towards Harry. She purposely planted her feet hard so that her heels would warn him of her coming. He looked up from what he was doing. He looked surprised to see Karyn walking his way. Recovering, a big smile lit up Harry's face. "Agent Dudek, I believe. What are you doing back in my part of the world?"

"Mr. Strickland, I hope I'm not interrupting something important?"

"Not at all. I was just finishing some reports. I work with tools all day, but I think I spend more time doing paperwork than I do fixing anything."

"I hear you on that. Paperwork is the bane of an FBI agent's existence."

"Unless you're here to ask me out on a date, why are you back here, Agent Dudek? Something else get stolen?"

167

Karyn felt herself blushing a little. Ignoring the question, she said, "Mr. Strickland, I'm investigating an information breech here at JFK."

"Harry."

"Huh?" asked Karyn.

"Call me Harry. People call me Mr. Strickland and I start looking around for my father."

"Sure, Harry. According to the records and a lot of double-checking with security cameras and people, I discovered that you were in Tom Fleming's office last Friday morning."

Harry looked blank for a moment, and then light returned to his eyes. "Oh, yeah, he wanted me to check out one of our ramps for some high muckety-muck landing here."

"You waited in his office for him?"

"Yeah."

"When you were there, did you touch anything?"

"Like what?"

"His computer."

"Why would I do that? I have one right here." Harry pointed to the laptop he had just been working on.

"How about his printer?"

"I have one of them too. What's all of this about, Agent Dudek? Is something missing from Mr. Fleming's office? Are you accusing me?" Harry's tone got very serious.

Karyn thought, "I'm totally fucking up this interview." Karyn was pretty good at reading people. Harry hadn't looked concerned or guilty when she started asking questions. She tried again. "Going by the records, some confidential information was printed out in Mr. Fleming's office while you were in there."

Karyn wasn't sure how to react when Harry started laughing. "Going by the records? Sometimes we think all they do in the IT department is have a circle jerk because these machines spew out so much garbage. We constantly have to verify information about the jobs we have to do." Harry started moving around papers on his desk. With an exclamation of discovery, he plucked out a sheet and handed it to Karyn. "You see that work order. What does it say?"

She scanned the page quickly. "I'm no engineer, but something about going out and fixing the landing gear on a United 737."

"I traveled out to the runway. The only thing that work order had correct was the landing gear. However, it was for a JetBlue plane and it was an Airbus, not a 737. When I called up the jackass who sent me out there, he insisted that he entered the correct information. I couldn't yell at him, because I've seen stuff like this before."

"But the computer showed that the printer was working while you were in there."

"The computer also showed that this entire maintenance area was shut down one week. It was a big surprise to all of us who were working here."

"So there was no printing going on when you were in Fleming's office?"

"Listen, lady, I was exhausted that day and I think I dozed off and rested my eyes waiting for Mr. Fleming to return." He snatched the work order back from Karyn and put it on his desk. "Do you have anything else to ask me?"

Karyn's mind was blank. What was it with this guy? She wasn't getting anywhere. It was better to retreat and regroup. Besides, everything he said was plausible. "No, Harry, I'm sorry for taking your time. Thank you for your help."

Harry calmed down and gave her another big grin. "Sorry if I got a little worked up. I hate being accused of something where I have no idea what you're talking about." He held out his hand. "No hard feelings?"

Karyn took it and said, "Of course not. Just doing my job."

Harry held her hand a little longer than necessary. Looking her in the eyes, he said, "I know you are. I am too."

Chapter 18

HARRY WATCHED HIS BUBBLES lazily ascend to the surface. He loved the freedom of soaring through the sky or swimming under the ocean. It was Friday and the afternoon light still allowed him to see clearly, even though he was thirty feet down. This was one of the unique pieces of geography on Long Island. He was in the Long Island Sound off the north fork of the Island. Unlike the south shore, the landscape next to the water was rocky and rough. In some locations, huge hills descended right down to the water's edge. The areas that passed for beaches were very pebbly as opposed to the soft sand of the shoreline along the ocean.

He needed this time to decompress after a long day. It was Friday and Agent Dudek's visit the previous day had shook Harry up a little. He knew that in terms of real evidence, she had absolutely nothing on him. All they knew is that he was in the office when manifests were supposedly being printed. The truth was that the computer system at JFK wasn't the best and that it often had unexplainable hiccups. To make sure there was no sign of the pages he took from Fleming's office, Harry took care of them last night. While grilling hamburgers for him and Max, Harry made sure that he deleted all the photos off his phone of the manifests he took from Fleming's office. At this point, most of those cargos had already arrived anyway. Harry made the prudent decision not to snatch any other shipments coming through the airport, no matter how tempting. That was off-limits for a long time.

Harry swam upwards until he was only ten feet from the surface. He moved along the rocky wall that the waves crashed against along this section of the shore. When Harry was working on his SCUBA certification a few years ago, one of the group dives was along here. What fascinated him at the time and what he was looking for here were caves that dotted the rocks. The entrances were right below the waterline at low tide. You could swim into them and crawl up to huge hollowed-out caverns. The rumors were that pirates used to hide their loot in them. None was ever found, but that didn't dissuade treasure hunters.

Slowly entering a cleft in the rocks, Harry turned on his flashlight and followed the passage until he surfaced in a quiet pool of water. He knew he shouldn't be diving alone, but he needed to think. This was about as quiet as it got and the physical exertion also helped relax him. It was hard for someone to interrupt him under the ocean or in a cave.

Keeping his air tank strapped on, Harry scooted up until he was sitting on land with his back against a large rock and his flippers still in the water. He swept his powerful light around the open area. The beam barely reached the far back wall. Shining it up, Harry could see that high tide and storms flooded this cave right up to the roof at times. Unless pirates were very good at waterproofing their booty, this wouldn't be the best place around to hide it. Harry idly wondered if any tunnels honeycombed this section of the Island. That would offer more potential for securing away treasure. As much as he was an adrenaline junky, exploring caves alone was foolhardy and not on Harry's list. Maybe he would look up on the computer if people found any kind of cave or tunnel system around here. Right now, he had more pressing problems.

Harry called in sick and took today off. While he got rid of any evidence of possessing the airline manifests last night, he still had a shitload of diamonds, gems, and gold coins to get out of his house. While he didn't believe Karyn Dudek had enough evidence to get a warrant to search his place, you could never tell who knew who in the judicial system. He was going to hide everything on Saturday, but it seemed prudent to move that operation up a day.

Bright and early, Harry was up with Max and they hit the

road. Dressed in jeans, his hiking boots, and a sweatshirt, Harry could feel the early morning coolness in the air. August's heat had broken and it felt like autumn this morning, even though Labor Day was next weekend. He stopped for donuts and coffee before heading out to fight the morning traffic. Max sat beside him looking outside the window at the ever-changing landscape. Today meant making several stops. Harry first pulled off into a section of Brooklyn where a friend had lent him the use of his garage. It wasn't until he left there and maneuvered through two traffic jams that Harry finally got out of the city.

It was midafternoon when Harry crossed back over the George Washington Bridge. He stopped at home to give Max a bathroom break in the yard and so he could get his diving stuff. Back in the car, he headed for the Long Island Expressway and went east. After driving long enough for even Max to get antsy, Harry pulled into a small marina near the village of Baiting Hollow. He had become friends with the owner and his wife when he started diving in these waters. The wife adored Max and watched him while Harry rented one of their boats and set his two duffle bags of gear into the craft. Casting off, he made his way to the area he liked exploring. He raised the red diving flag so people wouldn't think the boat was abandoned and jumped into the sound. Resting in the cave, Harry wondered what to do next.

He felt like he was being squeezed from two directions. On one side, there was the pretty, and rather sexy, Agent Dudek. Harry had to admit there was something that appealed to him about that woman. Too bad she was a damn Fed! Harry also knew he had Fat Tony to think about. So far, he had no reason to believe he was on Tony's radar, but like an unseen shark in the ocean, he knew that situation could change. While he couldn't put his finger on it, Harry never felt like he and the boys got out of that mess completely free.

With summer almost over, Harry wanted to figure out at least one more job before the weather turned cold. He had a couple of ideas, but now he needed to flesh them out. Harry mentally kicked himself for becoming a person of interest in the eyes of the FBI. He had no record for them to nail on him, so he hoped they'd find someone else where they could focus their attention. Maybe Harry should've done something to steer the authorities in another direction after they pulled off the thefts. Aloud, he said to the cave, "Fuck that. Simple is better. That would've made everything more complicated. It's just bad luck that Agent Dudek figured out I was in the office when the printer was going."

Sighing, Harry cleared his face mask and put it back on. Putting the regulator in his mouth, he made sure he was still getting smooth airflow from his tank. Satisfied, he plunged underwater and made his way out of the cave. Reaching the opening, he started heading in the direction of his anchored boat. He suddenly stopped as he saw a large shape drifting about twenty feet away. You couldn't mistake the outline and movement of a shark. This one was about Harry's size. He watched it, but the big fish showed no interest in him and glided away in the other direction.

Harry methodically made his way to the boat, checking every now and then for any other predators. When he grasped the short ladder on the side of the boat, he hauled himself aboard with all his equipment, which was no easy task. He quickly took off the tanks, vest, and weight belt. He stripped out of his wetsuit and allowed the sun and air to dry his body as he sat in one of the seats for about ten minutes in his bathing suit.

Sitting back enjoying the warmth, Harry looked at the coastline. He knew that a glacier had carved out Long Island eons ago. Well, this was where the glacier dumped all of its garbage. It was rocky and hilly all along the northern fork of the Island. The shore went from small flat beaches and suddenly turned into very high hills. Harry saw the reflection of the sun catch something high up in the hill off to the right of where he anchored. He suddenly wondered if anyone was watching him. God, he was getting paranoid. He knew that area was a park and it was still summer. Plenty of people were out today enjoying the beautiful weather.

Harry grabbed his T-shirt and pulled it on. "I got to get out of this funk," he said as he revved up the boat's engine. He piloted the craft back to the marina and tied up. As he unloaded his equipment onto the pier, a big wet tongue slobbered up the side of his face. Max was leaning down toward him with his tail wagging quickly.

"He saw you coming from a half mile away," said Kara, the owner of the marina. Actually, she and her husband Randy owned it together. She was a tall, lean woman in her fifties whose tanned arms and legs indicated the time she spent in the sun. Harry liked the couple and was glad he could connect with nice people like this out here. "Sophia isn't with you today?"

"No, I'm meeting her down at her folks' summer home in the Hamptons after this," answered Harry. "She likes getting out on the boat, but she gets nervous whenever I go diving."

"I won't lecture you about the dangers of diving alone," said Kara, "but I'm going to be pissed if I find my boat abandoned someday with no signs of life out there."

Harry gave her his biggest smile. "I hear you, Kara. Don't worry; when I do this by myself, I stay near the coast."

"Not exploring any of the wrecks out there?" asked the woman.

"I'm not that stupid," answered Harry. "I only do those dives with groups, or your husband, if I can pry him out of the office."

"You know how it is when you have your own business," said Kara. "There's always something to do. When it quiets down in the winter we take a month in Florida and finally relax for a bit."

"That's my goal in life. With each passing winter, I hate the cold more and more." Harry shouldered his duffle bags. "Thanks for watching Max for me."

"Always a pleasure. You be careful heading down to the Hamptons. I'm sure the exodus from the city out to there started hours ago."

Harry whistled for Max to follow. "At least I'm already out

east," he said. "I only have to drive with those idiots a little."

He dumped his gear in the car and drove away. He drove south through the town of Riverhead and slowly joined the line of cars heading out to the south fork of Long Island and the Hamptons. He knew it didn't pay to get mad at the traffic, so he listened to music and talked to Max until arriving at the summerhouse. Sophia's parents had owned this small bungalow in East Hampton before this area became the place in the summer for the rich and famous. Harry new that Sophia's dad had turned down outlandish offers for the house and the property. He did this partly out of enjoying having a place here that the family could go, and partly because he was a stubborn bastard who enjoyed making the real estate weenies sweat.

As he got out of the car, Harry saw Sophia's sister, Janine, walking towards him. "Hey, Harry, how was the water?" She was about the same size as Sophia, but her body was more on the petite side. She wore blue shorts and a red bikini top. As near as Harry could remember, she was in her fifth year of engagement to Fred, a man who rarely left his office on Wall Street.

"It was great," said Harry. "You should come with me some time."

"I love the water, but I don't know about wearing all of that stuff." She stood on her toes and gave Harry a peck on the cheek.

"Once you're in the ocean, you don't even notice it. The astronauts used to practice in the water because you have a weightless feeling when diving."

"Then I wouldn't have to worry about losing these last five pounds," said Janine.

Harry looked her up and down. "Sweetie, you have no five pounds to lose. Why do women always say that?"

Janine laughed. "Because we are woman! Sophia will be right out. We got here about twenty minutes ago. Traffic sucked. I like coming out here after Labor Day when it isn't such a struggle."

Harry was about to respond when Sophia came out of the door

of the bungalow. She had on a black two-piece bathing suit. It wasn't quite a bikini, but it didn't leave much to the imagination. She ran over and kissed Harry hard. "Whew, you smell like fish," she said. "I figure that since you've been swimming already, you wouldn't mind hanging with us on the beach for an hour. Then we can get cleaned up and go out to dinner."

"Sounds like a plan," said Harry. He looked over to where Janine had Max's big head in her hands as she hugged the large dog. "Is Fred joining us this weekend?"

Janine glanced up with a grimace on her face. "No, he said he had too much work to do. I don't even know why I put up with him."

Sophia grinned at her sister. "I think it's because of that large portfolio that you keep talking about." She looked up at Harry. "And I'm not talking about his money, though that probably helps too."

Janine said, "Well, fuck you too. I'll go get towels and we can head to the beach." As she walked towards the house, she called back to them, "And don't worry, I'm meeting up with a couple friends later so I won't be a third wheel for you two lovebirds."

When she came back outside with a beach bag, the three people and one dog walked the five-minute path to the beach. It was getting to be six o'clock and the place was deserted. They laid out blankets and Harry took off his shirt to absorb the last of the day's sun. Janine shrugged out of her shorts and Harry could see that she had the briefest of bottoms on to match her top. "Can I take Max into the ocean with me?" she asked.

"Sure," said Harry, "as long as you hose him off when we get back to the house."

"No problem. C'mon, Max," Janine shouted, and the two ran down to the water.

Sophia looked at Harry watching the two. "Stop ogling my sister's ass, Harry," she said.

He put his arm around her and pulled her tight. "Sophia, you know you have the best ass in your family. I keep telling you that." To emphasize, he placed his hand on one of her cheeks and squeezed hard.

Sophia leaned in and kissed him. "I like that. I plan to give you as much of it as you can handle this weekend. I want you to relax and enjoy yourself. So why did you take off from work today?"

"I needed a break and had a lot of running around to do," explained Harry. "I'd been feeling a little stressed lately and figured a little underwater exploration would be good for the soul. You told me Janine was coming out this weekend, so I figure it would work out meeting you here."

Sophia broke off the embrace and lay on her back. She reached up and pulled her bathing suit straps off her shoulders to negate any tan lines. Harry said, "Why don't you just take off the whole top?"

"You'd like that, wouldn't you?" Sophia quickly lowered one side of her suit to give Harry a quick peek at her boob. "For later," she said with an evil grin.

"I may not be able to wait until dinner," said Harry.

"You certainly will, Harry Strickland. You know Janine. She'll be out until all hours. You can have your way with me after dinner."

It was Harry's turn to lie on his back. Maybe this weekend was just the thing he needed. Anything that could connect him to the jobs from the past few weeks was now out of the house. A few days of fun and sex would put him back on an even keel. John, Ozzie, Frank, and their women were coming out for the day tomorrow. He would put everything out of his mind until Monday.

Then Sophia spoke, "I forgot to tell you, Harry. You remember that douchebag that gave us all that trouble at his club? I heard from some girlfriends who went up to the place last week that he's gone. The scuttlebutt going around is that he was killed. His father is some kind of gangster."

Harry tried to keep his voice casual. "Couldn't happen to a

nicer guy. Anybody hear exactly what happened?"

"You know how it is," said Sophia, "one person tells another who tells somebody else and so on. Whether he's dead or not, the one fact is that apparently he won't ever be at the club again. Not that I want to ever go back there. I was never so scared in my life!"

"Nice things don't happen there," said Harry, "that's for sure. I'm good with never seeing the place again in my life," he finished truthfully.

"I'm glad you didn't do anything stupid about revenge," said Sophia. "That little asshole wasn't worth it. I could've taken him down if he didn't have his bodyguards with him. Because he owned the club, he thought he was God's gift to women. You probably needed a magnifying glass to find his dick."

That made Harry laugh. He didn't want to dwell on this subject, but Sophia was probably right. "Just be glad he's gone, sweetheart. Nothing for us to ever have to worry about again."

Chapter 19

Special Agent Karyn Dudek felt silly. Here it was a beautiful summer day and she finally made it out to the Hamptons. She was dressed in shorts and a sleeveless blue shirt. She wore a stupid floppy hat and big sunglasses that hid most of her face. She was sitting on the sand, peering over a dune at three people and a really big dog on the beach. They looked like they were having fun. She was miserable.

When she returned to headquarters yesterday, her interview with Harry Strickland kept going through her mind. Karyn accessed the FBI's databases, but found no criminal file concerning Harry. She found his address and driver's license, but that was about it.

When her boss, Enrico Gonzales, stopped by her desk on his way out, he asked, "How did things go at the airport?"

"It was a very tedious investigation, to say the least," said Karyn. "I spent most of the day looking at spreadsheets and reviewing security tape." She hesitated, "It isn't much to go on, but I have a hunch about someone." She then proceeded to tell Gonzales about tracing manifest printouts and how the only odd one was from Tom Fleming's office.

"I don't know, Karyn. Sounds kinda flimsy to me."

"Yeah, I know. It was even flimsier when the geek squad at the airport told me exactly what this Harry Strickland said. Their computer network does do many weird things without any reason. Apparently, the notation indicating the manifest was printed out at the time Strickland was in the office could've been a mistake."

"You're still pursuing it, then?"

"Dammit," Karyn said in frustration, "I don't have anything else to go on. My luck is so good I seem to be interested in someone with no criminal record at all. He hasn't even had a parking ticket in the last five years!"

"Why are you still barking up that tree?"

"I don't know. Call it a feeling or woman's intuition. There was just something about my conversation with him that I can't quite put my finger on."

"Does he seem like someone that could do these thefts and terrorize the Bamberger family?"

"No, he doesn't. Maybe he's selling the information to someone who's pulling off these jobs. I have some phone calls into some of my contacts in a few police departments in his area." She smiled at Gonzales. "You know how there are always cops who want to join the Bureau? Some of them become very good sources. When I was out west, I even recommended a couple to the agency."

"We're all looking for the bad guys," said Gonzales.

"Yeah, if we didn't have all the interagency and departmental bullshit. Anyway, I hope to hear back from them in the morning."

"Far be it from me to tell someone not to follow their hunch," said Gonzales. "See what you can find out, but don't spend a lot of time on this guy if it's a dead end. I'll see you tomorrow."

Karyn stayed at the office for another hour, but it got to the point that she couldn't keep her eyes open anymore. She went home to her small apartment. She shed her clothes along the floor as she stumbled to her bed. When she got there, she flopped onto the sheets naked and promptly fell asleep. She slept restlessly and when she woke up, she knew some of her dreams had Harry in them. She couldn't quite remember the context, but he was there.

Back in the office sucking down coffee, she started fielding some calls from her police sources. As the time was approaching eleven, Karyn sat back and looked at the notes she took. There wasn't much to review. Harry Strickland's name had come up in connection to some car thefts and other minor crimes, but almost as an afterthought. There was never enough to warrant a full investigation into the guy.

Karyn reached into her pocketbook and found a bottle of aspirin. She took a couple and washed them down with the coffee. As she massaged her temples, she couldn't shake the feeling in her gut that she should look further into Harry. Maybe it was because he was so good-looking and she was completely losing perspective.

She leaped to her feet and went into Gonzales' office. He looked up and said, "You look determined. What's up?"

"I can't shake this feeling I have about Harry Strickland. For my own piece of mind, I want to follow him around for a few days. Maybe see what he does until Monday at the latest. It's like I have this itch that I can't reach."

Gonzales put the file down that he had been looking at and studied Karyn. "I take it you didn't have any plans for the weekend."

Karyn sniffed. "I haven't had any plans since I got to this city. I want to solve this case. If I get a feeling that I'm off base with Strickland, then I can move on without any doubts holding me back."

"You have no other leads?"

"Nothing. I have people doing thorough background checks on anyone who had official access to those cargo lists, but I'll be surprised if anything comes of that."

Enrico Gonzales sighed. "I hate shit like this. There is never the perfect crime, but sometimes you wonder. And between the two jobs, we're talking about a hell of a lot of gems and diamonds." He looked out his window for a minute. Turning back to Karyn, he said, "Okay, do what you want. I guess if you can come to a better evaluation on this Strickland, one way or the other, it will help."

"Thank you. I'll let you know what I find out." Karyn left his office and gathered up her file, such as it was. She signed out a car and went back to her apartment. She shuddered at the mess she had left it in this morning. Karyn was usually very neat, but she had let herself go the past year. She felt as if solving these jewel thefts would set her back on the right path again.

Going into a closet, she pulled out a nylon bag she used for overnight trips. Experience taught her to prepare for various situations when following someone. She threw in some clothes, bathroom articles, shoes, and even her little black dress. She took off the skirt and blouse she wore into work and put on shorts, a shirt, and sneakers. She might as well be comfortable.

Getting into her car, Karyn headed for JFK. She figured that she would pick up Harry whenever he left there. She switched on her cell phone and called the human resource assistant director that she came to know on her visits there. She wanted to find out how long Harry worked there. When she heard a man saying, "Hello," Karyn said, "Bill, this is Agent Dudek from the FBI. I was wondering if you could give me a little information on one of your employees."

"I'll give you what I can, Agent Dudek. As I told you yesterday, there's only so much I can tell you without a warrant."

"I understand. I just wanted to know how long someone has been working there. His name is Harry Strickland. I don't know what his title is, but he's one of the mechanics or engineers there."

"Let me see," Bill said. Karyn could hear the clicking of a keyboard. "Mr. Strickland has been here for a little over six years. Well, except for today. He called in sick."

Karyn almost swerved into oncoming traffic when she heard that. Instead, she pulled into a McDonald's and parked. "He isn't there today?"

"Apparently not. Doesn't look like he misses work much, but there you go. Hope that was a help."

"I appreciate it, Bill. You have a good weekend." Karyn clicked off the phone and thought. It seemed like too much of a coincidence that she visited Harry Strickland yesterday, and he takes off from work today. Was he feeling guilty about something?

She looked up Harry's address in the file and punched in the address on her phone. She pulled back into traffic and followed the GPS app until she found Harry's house. From the road, she looked it over. It was a nice little house, with a big two-car garage and a good size yard. Everything looked very neat and maintained. It also looked like nobody was home.

Karyn quickly concluded that she really didn't have a lot of choice but to wait for Harry to return. All she had for him was his work and home address. For all she knew, he was actually sick and at the doctor's right now. She drove away from the house and drove a few blocks until she found a deli. Hurrying inside, she ordered a turkey sandwich and grabbed some bottles of soda and water. Driving back to Harry's house, she parked a half block down from his home. There were other cars on the street so she figured she would blend in. She settled in to wait.

As stakeouts went, this one wasn't bad. It was a warm summer day, she had food and drink, and Harry pulled into his driveway two hours later. She had a pretty good view of his driveway as he stepped out of his car with a very large dog bounding out after him. Harry was dressed in jeans and dirty hiking boots, and wearing some kind of green baseball hat with a green jacket thrown over his shoulder. She watched Harry open the gate of the yard so that the dog could enter. Then he disappeared into his house. It was only twenty minutes later when Harry came out with two large duffle bags that seemed heavy. He placed them in his trunk and then herded the dog back in the car. After that, he drove off with Karyn keeping a respectable distance behind.

After an hour of driving, Karyn said aloud, "Where the hell are you going, Harry? Sooner or later this island ends." They had been driving east for the entire time. Following was easy. There were plenty of cars to weave in and out of in order to stay out of sight. Harry was driving fast, but not enough to catch the attention of any cops out on the road with radar. Finally, they left the highway. Karyn knew that Long Island split into two forks at its eastern end and that they were traveling the north fork. Soon, she saw Harry pull into a marina. She kept on going another one hundred feet before she pulled over. Getting out of the car, she stretched her cramped body as she jogged back to the marina entrance. She perched behind a tree and looked down.

Harry and the dog were out of the car and walking to a dock. He was carrying the duffel bags. When a woman came out to greet them, the dog stood up on his hind legs and rested his head on the woman's shoulder. She was laughing and patting the dog's head. Pushing the dog away, she led Harry over to a small boat. He put his gear into it and got in. As he started up the engine, the woman untied the line and threw it into the boat. Harry waved and slowly piloted the boat away from the dock.

What the hell was she going to do now? Karyn watched the boat head into open water and turn to the right. She ran back to her car and got in. The road seemed to follow the coast. Gunning the engine, Karyn took off. In between the houses and trees, she caught glimpses of the water. Whenever she could, she pulled over. Pulling out binoculars, she found Harry's boat. For whatever reason, he seemed to be contently following the coast.

This cat and mouse game went on for a half hour. The road went past a park that loomed high on a big hill between the road and the water. Karyn went past this. When she could see the water again, she stopped to look for Harry. At first, she couldn't see him. Then she looked back and saw that he had anchored his boat. Even with the binoculars, she couldn't make out what he was doing. Fishing?

She drove into the park and found a parking lot that looked out over the water. It wasn't a great angle for spying, so she took her binoculars and a bottle of water and found a path that wound around the hill. She followed it for five minutes and then veered off on her own. Soon she found a spot near a few trees that looked right out over the boat. Focusing her glasses on him, Karyn was surprised. Harry was in a wetsuit and putting on an air tank. She watched in fascination as he geared up, grabbed some kind of container, sat on the side of the boat, and tumbled backwards over the side.

Karyn sat there sipping her water, wondering how long someone could stay underwater like that. She liked swimming and had snorkeled on a cruise once, but never tried diving with all the equipment and air tanks. After forty-five minutes, she saw Harry emerge from the depths. He hauled himself into the boat. He methodically stripped off all his gear. Then to Karyn's delight, he stripped off his wetsuit. Soon, he was sitting back in just a bathing suit or shorts, drying off in the sun. Karyn felt like she had switched from an agent to a voyeur watching an almost naked Harry in the boat. "If Harry was somehow tied up in this jewel business," Karyn thought, "it would be a shame to send a man like that to jail." She sighed. "Maybe I should start dating again," she decided.

Soon, Harry put on a shirt, pulled up the anchor, and started up the boat. Karyn watched as he made a lazy circle and headed back the way he had come. She ran back to her car and exited the park. She figured Harry was heading back to the marina, but she periodically stopped to watch his progress. When she was positive he was heading there, she stopped at a little diner to use the bathroom, and was waiting for his car when he pulled back out on the road. She let two more cars go by and was back to following him.

She thought that he was heading home, but he headed south and then east again onto the southern fork of Long Island. She passed small bungalows and huge homes overlooking beach. "So this is where the rich and the famous play in the summertime," Karyn said. "Guess snooping on someone is the only way I get to come out here."

Harry finally slowed down and pulled into a driveway. As she passed by, Karen glanced at a modest house where he stopped.

As soon as she could, she made a U-turn and went back along the road. She passed the driveway again and pulled into the parking area of a small store about a quarter of a mile down from the house. Out of her bag, she pulled out a cloth hat with a big, floppy brim. She placed that on her head and the biggest pair of sunglasses she owned. Suitably disguised and feeling a bit like an ass, she walked down the road to the house. There were no fences and she cut across the neighbor's property before reaching the house. The home on her right was eight times the size of the one Harry pulled into. It was quiet and she kept to the few trees on the property. She knelt down on one knee and looked for Harry.

Karyn had no trouble finding Harry since a pretty woman was wrapped around him like a blanket on a baby. She was kissing him hard. From somewhere deep inside, Karyn felt a pang of jealousy. She violently shook her head and watched the two of them, another woman, and the dog head down a path. Karyn paralleled their course until she came to a beach. She scrambled behind a high dune and watched all the happenings in front of her.

She liked seeing Harry in his bathing suit again but wasn't so happy about him being next to that other woman. Karyn reflected on this when it hit her that she wasn't learning a damn thing. Who the hell cared if he had a girlfriend? Was this what she bought into for a weekend? Watching a marginal suspect frolic and get laid while she was slinking around in the bushes, or in this case, the sand! Karyn knew the drudgery of her work well, but she also knew she had to figure out a course of action.

Keeping low, she backed away from the dune until she knew that she was out of sight. She shook sand out of her sneakers when she got to the road and made her way back to the car. She figured she had some time while they were on the beach. If they were heading out to eat, she had time to get back here before they left. She got into her car and took off, heading further east.

After driving a couple of miles, Karyn saw a small motel. Much to her delight, the owner was just hanging up on a cancellation as she waited. It was the last room available and she took it. She almost gagged when she saw how much it was and already started to figure out how to justify it on her expense report.

The room was small and clean. She leaped into the shower for five minutes. Karyn dressed in black capris, black tank top, and black flat shoes. Color coordination was easy on a stakeout. She took her car and once again parked at the store. Soon she was back behind the tree on the neighboring property. She figured if she saw people leaving the house that she could get back into her car in time to follow.

The first person who came out was the petite woman with the big dog on the leash. She was walking him around and letting him do his business. Karyn became nervous when the dog went still and sniffed the air. He looked right at her and whined a little. The woman gave him a gentle tug and headed back into the house. In about ten minutes, all three people went towards Harry's car. The woman who brought the dog outside said, "You can drop me off at the pub. My friends will bring me home sometime tonight…or tomorrow morning." As soon as they all started laughing, Karyn made her way to the road and back to her car.

Just as she was approaching the driveway, Harry pulled out before the car in front of her and headed down the road. They drove past Karyn's motel and after ten minutes of slow driving in the terrible traffic, they came to the town of Bridgehampton. Harry pulled into a parking lot. Karyn drove into the next one and walked back to see Harry and his girl go into a restaurant.

She cautiously walked inside and glanced around. She saw Harry and his date sitting at a table way in the back. Karyn was famished and took a chance. She walked over to the bar and found a seat. She ordered a hamburger with fries and a beer and tried to unobtrusively blend in. Unfortunately, this was the night every guy in the place seemed to come over and hit on her. She was flattered but declined every drink offer. She didn't need to get shitfaced. However, she did make a mental note that maybe she would return here for a fun weekend sometime. She did like the attention. It seemed like all she was meeting in the city were derelicts!

The rest of the night was uneventful. By the time Harry and the woman left, Karyn was outside and a respectful distance away. She followed them back to the house, decided that she didn't really want to know what they were doing in there, and went back to the motel and crashed.

In the morning, she was back at her lookout spot bright and early. She again had on the shorts and the floppy hat. Today, she brought along her Canon ESL and the telephoto lens. Being at the beach taking photos was a good cover, and she wanted to get some good shots of Harry and the people with him. Much to her surprise, she saw Harry coming out of the house with an easel and a bag. He headed to the beach and she watched him set up and start painting the shoreline and ocean. Looking through the telephoto lens, Karyn was impressed with his skill.

As it turned out, the rest of the day was uneventful. Around noon, people started arriving at the house. Three more couples showed up. Two of the couples arrived by car and the other one drove up on motorcycles. Karyn spent the day going back and forth between her two hiding places taking plenty of photos of everyone. She muttered a prayer of thanks that nobody seemed to be living at the big house behind her this weekend.

As the alcohol and food intake among the party increased, Karyn made periodic trips out to use the bathroom and get food. By the time midnight arrived, she was beat. Nothing was happening today that would lead her anywhere, but maybe she could find some information on Harry's friends. She had pictures of everyone, even the dog, as well as all the license plate numbers.

The next day also wasn't much help. All of the Saturday visitors were gone. Harry and the two girls headed back into Bridgehampton. There was some kind of street festival going on. Brightly colored canopies held different craft or food items.

Harry Hid It

Some of them were sponsored by different charities. Karyn tried to blend in under her floppy hat and big glasses. As she observed Harry, she noticed a commotion break out when he left one of the tents. Sliding over, she caught a woman overcome with excitement.

"I don't believe it. The generosity of some people."

"What happened?" another woman asked.

"See that tall, good-looking guy? He asked what kind of work we did. When I finished telling him, he reached into his pocket and gave me some bills. I thought it was a few dollars. When he walked away, I counted it. He gave me sixteen hundred dollar bills!"

Karyn went closer and saw a sign hanging from the top of the pavilion. It said, "Disabled Vets of Suffolk County."

Sixteen hundred dollars was quite a bit to be giving away like that. It would take her weeks of saving to give that kind of money away. Karyn looked after Harry with a very thoughtful expression behind her sunglasses. "Okay, Mr. Strickland," she whispered to herself, "that was incredibly generous. Where do you get that kind of pocket change?"

Out of the entire weekend, that was the most eye-opening event. Sure, scuba diving and being a painter were a bit different from what Karyn initially thought about Harry, but the money he gave away was very interesting. The rest of the day consisted of following them around town. In the evening, Harry drove away in his car and the two women in another. All Harry did was take himself and the dog home. Karyn called it quits and drove to her apartment where she showered the weekend off and fell into bed.

Her last thought as she fell into a deep, exhausted sleep was, "Sixteen hundred dollars? What mechanic has that to give away?"

Chapter 20

THE TUESDAY AFTER LABOR Day was an especially gray and wet day. The remnants of a hurricane were far to the east in the Atlantic Ocean, but water was still dumping buckets of water over New York City and Long Island. Tony Russo was sitting in his son's old office at the Ocean Club. Fat Tony didn't exactly miss his son. As kids go, he had been a total disappointment. Tony had to prop him up and get him out of trouble since he was twelve. "Setting him up as the manager here should've kept the little shit out of trouble," Fat Tony murmured to the empty room. He was brooding over his son's death. Not that the idiot jumped in front of the gun, but the fact that none of Tony's men found out who did it. For a second, Tony thought about shooting one of them to create a little more incentive but decided that would actually be bad for morale.

There was a tiny knock on the door. Tony grunted out, "Come."

A skinny young man entered the office. He had shaggy dark hair, big horn-rimmed glasses, and his skin was so white that it looked like it had never experienced sunlight. He came over, stood in front of Tony's desk, and said in a voice that cracked, "Uh, Mr. Russo, I may have found something."

"What, Kevin? The fucking IRS trying to get up my ass again?" Kevin Hook was Tony's bookkeeper. He was a numbers freak and great with computers. Despite his appearance, he enjoyed hiding Fat Tony's wealth in various ways to keep the government snoops away. To him, it was a game.

Kevin said, "No, it's nothing like that. I might have found something from the night your son got shot and the money stolen."

This certainly made Fat Tony sit up straighter. "What is it?"

"I know you got men out there shaking the bushes trying to

190

figure out what happened. In my spare time, I've been trying to see if I could find anything out there on the Internet. I was getting close to giving up when I found this today."

He slid a paper across the desk to Fat Tony. It was a photo that Kevin printed out. Fat Tony squinted at it. "Yeah, it's a truck. What about it?"

"I found it on Facebook. I was doing a search for anything that had to do with the Ocean Club. Somebody posted this on his page. The entire picture had a bunch of people laughing and drinking in the parking lot. The caption said, 'Still partying after a night at the Ocean Club.' It was posted the night of the, uh…incident. The time on the actual photo was right before you said everything happened. I cut the truck out of it and blew it up. You can see two people in it, but the glare of the parking lot lights obscures them. However, I was able to get the license number off it." Kevin slid another piece of paper across to Fat Tony.

Tony was impressed. He didn't even know how to turn on a computer. He was old school and that's why he only thought to have his people go out into the criminal community and see what people heard. People always talked. However, there wasn't a peep from anyone. It was as if the men who robbed him came out of nowhere and then disappeared. To think this little geeky kid may have found something!

Tony asked, "Did you run the number?"

"I can hack the Motor Vehicle Department from here," answered Kevin, "but I didn't want to take a chance that it could be traced back. I can go somewhere else to do it."

"You're a smart kid," said Fat Tony with a small degree of admiration. Praise didn't come easy for him. "Nice work. I have some people who can find out for me."

"It might just be other customers driving around," said Kevin. "I thought the time frame fit."

"I know, but it's more than I've had to go on for almost a month now. Believe me, I'll get it checked out."

As Kevin exited the office, Tony picked up the phone. He dialed and when it was answered, he simply said. "It's Tony."

"Jesus Christ, Tony! What are you calling me here for?"

"Now, now, Sergeant, I'm just a simple taxpayer looking to the police for a little help."

Tony only heard silence for a few moments, and then a very loud sigh. "Yeah, Tony, but I wish you wouldn't call me at the precinct."

"I think my contributions more than allow me that luxury now and then," said Tony with steel in his voice.

The cop on the other end of the phone was immediately contrite. "You're right, I'm sorry. What can I do for you?"

"Simple. I need to know who owns this vehicle." Fat Tony read off the number. "I'll hold."

"You don't even have to hold. I'm right here on the computer." After thirty seconds, the sergeant said, "A company called Sunshine Construction owns the truck. The address is somewhere in Queens. Got a pen? I'll give this to you."

Tony jotted down the number and said, "Thank you. You've been a big help." He hung up before the sergeant said anything else.

Raising his bulk off the chair, he went out into the hallway. Two big men were sitting in chairs near his door. "Riley, I have a job for you."

Sean Riley stood up and followed his boss back into the office. As Fat Tony sat back in his chair with a huff, he said, "This might be nothing, but I really don't care. It's a possible lead to the assholes who invaded the club that night. Take the photo and that address. Find the one who drives it and find out if he came here when my son was killed. I trust you not to disappoint me. I don't care if you have to hurt someone. I want the street to know I will tear anyone apart to find out who hit me that night. I don't care who it is."

"Don't worry, boss, I'll look into this. I still regret I wasn't there that night. I keep thinking I could've stopped it."

Harry Hid It

"Maybe you could have," said Tony. "That's why you got a promotion when I fired Billy." Neither of them smiled at the joke. Tony looked into the eyes of the big redhead. "I need to clean this up, Sean. I lost a lot of face out there and business has slowed down. We need to let people know not to screw with me."

Riley made a motion as if to salute. "I'm on it." He started to the door and turned. "Uh, just so I'm clear, boss, I do whatever I need to do to find out information?"

"You got it." Tony bent over his desk and started to shuffle some papers.

The bodyguard went out to a new Cadillac and looked at the address. He pulled away from the club and made his way over to the borough of Queens. He found the construction company. It was set behind a tall fence and contained a small building that appeared to be the office and three larger buildings that must store equipment and supplies. Riley pulled over to the curb across the street. The rain was still pouring and he checked out the trucks scattered around the construction yard. None of them looked like the one in the picture.

With nothing else to do, Sean leaned back in his seat and waited. The road he was on was a slight hill and he idly watched a stream of water rushing down the street. Whenever a truck came to the construction company, Riley checked it out. One finally matched the photo, but the license number was wrong. It was getting to be near five o'clock when his patience paid off. The truck he had been waiting for finally pulled into the yard. Riley watched closely as a small man with blond hair jumped out of the truck and ran into the office building. Without any real plan in mind, Sean continued observing.

About an hour later, the yard started emptying. The man he saw before got into his truck and came out on the street. Riley put his car in gear and got into line behind him. Soon he realized the truck was heading back the way he originally came from. Riley thought, "At least when this is over, I won't have far to go home."

Harry Hid It

With the rain and the traffic, the guy ahead of him was oblivious to being followed. When the truck pulled into the parking lot of a food store and stopped, Riley did the same and parked two spaces away. Riley watched the guy run into the store, trying to minimalize the soaking he was getting. Sean looked around. If anything, the weather was the worst it had been all day. The rain was almost blinding and the clouds made it seem like night already. There weren't many cars in the parking lot.

Riley sighed. He didn't feel like getting wet, but this was an opportunity that he couldn't pass up. If nobody came out at the same time as the man, Riley would take a chance.

He only had to wait ten more minutes. The man came jogging out of the store carrying a plastic bag. As he got close to his truck, Riley leaped out of his car, intercepted the man, and body checked him into the door of the truck. The bag fell out of his hands and broke when it hit the ground. Apples and cans started to roll around. Just as the man started to say, "What the fuck," Riley brought his hand down on the man's head. The steel knuckles he had wrapped around his fist stunned the guy. Riley reached down and dragged him up by the color. Hitting the button on his key fob, the Cadillac's trunk popped open and in two steps, Riley flung the man into it. He slammed it shut, got in the car, and drove away. The entire event took less than twelve seconds.

He thumbed Fat Tony's number on his phone. "I got the guy. I need a place to question him." He listened for a few seconds. "I know it. Thanks." He listened again and said, "Don't worry; there won't be any loose ends."

***

In Manhattan, Karyn Dudek was looking at the darkness and rain settling in over the skyline. She was in Enrico Gonzales' office again. He was looking at the file she brought in and she was looking over his head out the window. As usual, she felt like she had been here too long today. It had been a week since her stint in the Hamptons and she had found out a couple of things from that trip. It was weak, but she hoped that Gonzales would go for an escalation into the investigation. If he didn't, she might as well start looking for work as a bartender. She had nothing else.

Gonzales closed the file and looked up. "You know what the most amazing thing is in here?" Karyn shook her head. "The amount of money that you had to pay for a room out in the Hamptons. I'll sign it, but we're both going to get grief on that."

Karyn smiled. She couldn't remember the last time she did that. "I know. I'm glad I had enough room on my credit card. What do you think about what I found out?"

"Sketchy doesn't begin to cover it. You were out there a week ago. All you have is the fact Strickland dropped a hunk of change to a charity group and he has some questionable friends. I don't see a whole lot worth pursuing. His finances are clean. He's been with the same job for a while. He has no record. What are you going to tell me? He's too clean and, therefore, we should suspect him?"

"You know, when you say it like that, it does sound silly," Karyn said lamely. "I also followed some other empty leads on both of those thefts. I've found nothing. The only person I've run into with any criminal record is that friend of Harry's. That Ozzie guy."

Gonzales opened the folder and looked. "Ozzie Marcos it says here. Small-time stuff that the cops busted him on. Hardly someone to pull off two huge jewel robberies."

"I know, but he could've been part of it. He and Harry seemed very tight. Also, the other guy that showed up that weekend. His name is John and he rides around with a motorcycle gang."

"So does the pastor of my church," snorted Gonzales. "It's a Christian group called the Sons of God. He rides around wearing one of those leather dusters and an old Army helmet. You wouldn't know he leads a church." He paused and collected his thoughts. "Look, Karyn, my ass is up against a wall here. Because those diamonds and gems came through JFK, they landed in our lap. There was a home invasion during the second theft. I won't even bore you with everything else going on in this city that finds its way to my desk. Against my better judgment, I'll give you another week on this thing. If something doesn't break, whether it's with this Strickland character or something else, I'll have to assign you to something else next Monday. Got it?"

Karyn stood up. "Uh, I have one more request."

Slightly exasperated, Gonzales asked, "What is it, Agent Dudek?"

"May I have a few junior agents for surveillance? I want to put them on the three guys that showed up at the Hamptons. Besides the two we talked about, there was one more man. He owns the construction company. His name was Frank somebody."

"Are you sure you don't want agents to follow their women too?"

"Can I do that?"

"No!" roared Gonzales. "What the hell do you think we have here? I don't have enough people for what we do now." He calmed down. Gonzales knew solving the jewel thefts was a priority. "Fine," he said, "but only till the end of the week." He wrote down some names and gave it to Karyn. "Go. Or do you need something else?"

"No, I'm good, sir. I will keep you apprised of what I'm doing."

"Not necessary, Agent Dudek; just let me know if you find out anything. If you don't make any progress, I'm going to have to reassign the jewel heists to someone else and give you some smaller cases." He looked Karyn in the eyes. "I really do not want to do that."

"Understood. I don't want that either." On that note, Karyn went back to her desk. She sat down and put her hands in her head. She really didn't have much. But like all good cops, she didn't believe in coincidences. It was too much of one that Harry was in an office by himself when cargo lists were being printed out. Maybe it wasn't enough for a warrant to do a search of Harry's place, but that didn't mean she couldn't snoop from a distance. She clicked on her computer screen and brought up the calendar. She would spend the next three days following Harry the best she could. If that didn't work, then she would make herself a little more visible to him. Maybe she could force him into a mistake.

As she got up to head home, she slowly shook her head. Harry Strickland seemed much too cool a customer to rile easily. Still, you never know. Something might turn up. She gathered up her things and headed out the building. She planned on being up bright and early to follow Harry and she desperately needed some sleep. Karyn knew she wasn't in a position to make any mistakes at this point. Otherwise, her entire FBI career would look like one big mistake.

***

Harry was driving back home through the rain. He had a feeling their window of opportunity to pull off these big jobs was closing. He was feeling nervous. One thing Harry never felt was his nerves. He had to admit that ripping off Fat Tony wasn't the smartest thing he'd done recently. The haul in cash was incredible, but you don't want to wake a sleeping bear. His little jerkoff of a son deserved what he got, but Harry knew being in the room when it happened was a bad omen. There was still no noise on the streets that Fat Tony's men had found anything. Harry hoped that held true for about another hundred years.

He and Sophia had been back out in the Hamptons again for the Labor Day weekend. It was even more crowded and crazy than the week before. While relaxing on the beach, Harry decided they'd do one more big job and then call it quits. He'd actually underestimated what they'd take in on every caper so far. He'd stashed a lot of gems and cash away at this point. He reviewed his hiding place. Stashing loot away as he did worked for pirates and thieves for years. It should hold up for him. He figured it only had to stay hidden for a few years and then he could put all of this behind him forever.

As he soaked up the sun on Saturday, not listening to Sophia yammer away, Harry knew he had to find something that met his criteria: short, quick, and result in a big payday. He knew he wasn't going to snatch anything going through the airport again. That cute Agent Dudek had also added to the anxiety that started with Fat Tony. Damn, he even thought he saw her last week when they were walking around town on the east end of the Island. He saw a chick with a nice body that reminded him of Dudek, but the woman had on some big hat and glasses. When Harry tried to find her again, he couldn't. Maybe he was seeing ghosts or something.

"Oh well, paranoia is a good thing," he said to his windshield. "It keeps me alive and out of jail." His wipers were barely keeping up with the deluge falling from the skies. Harry was driving home through this storm because he had a brainstorm on Sunday morning while going out to breakfast with Sophia and a couple of her sisters. There was a copy of Newsday, Long Island's newspaper, on the seat of the booth at a diner. While the women were talking, Harry flipped through it. An article caught his eye.

It talked about a real estate tycoon who had plans to rival Donald Trump in New York City. The story talked about how he wasn't afraid of taking bags of cash to entice sellers so that they parted ways with their buildings in the city. The paper quoted Bill Dean as saying, "Nothing talks like cash." As Harry was agreeing with that, he continued reading and saw that Mr. Dean talked about how his wife led a quiet existence as a writer in their big home in Huntington, Long Island. "I'm out making deals everywhere, so my sweetheart can follow her passion," Dean said.

Harry Hid It

Harry gave a slight grunt as he kept reading. He put the paper down and looked into the distance. This article gave him his idea. It was a plan so simple and audacious that it had to work. Just to make sure nothing went wrong, he would take John with him instead of Ozzie. John wouldn't let a teenager get the best of him!

Chapter 21

WEDNESDAY WAS A BEAUTIFUL day. Harry marveled how big storms like yesterday's seemed to wipe everything clean. The sky was a bright blue, the air was fresh, and there was just a hint in the temperature that summer was drawing to a close. He was out in his yard watching Max run around. He drank from his coffee mug and walked over to the gate. He opened it and went around to his garage. Harry heard Max's big paws padding behind him. When he pulled in last night, it looked like a piece of siding came loose and he wanted to check it out.

He found what he was looking for and saw he could fix it easily enough. It would be fine until the weekend. He casually looked up and down his street. He had a big day ahead of him and he thought he should get to work. For a half second he stopped and then continued back to the gate and into the yard. Harry knew the cars of all his neighbors. Part way down the block was a dark blue Taurus he had never seen before. He wondered if someone bought a new car or had visitors.

With that, Harry made sure Max had water, picked up the things he took to work, and headed out. On the way, he called John. "Hey, what are you doing tonight? I want to do one last big one."

"Sorry, Harry, Julia's godmother passed away over the weekend. We're heading upstate this afternoon for the service. Can it wait?"

"I would like to, John, but there's a small window of opportunity this evening. Besides, I have this nagging feeling that this should be done tonight and then we can stop."

"I can't say I'm unhappy to hear that," said John. "Ever since that night at the club, I've been feeling uneasy."

"Hear you on that, bro. Shit, I guess I'm going to have to call Oz."

"You don't sound happy about that," said John.

"I'm thrilled to death. Maybe I can find a toddler for him to pistol whip this time."

"The man doesn't always think," said John. "It will be OK."

"I certainly hope so. Don't worry; you'll get a cut from this one. I would've done the same for Ozzie if you came with me."

"You the man, Harry. Best of luck."

"Thanks. Please give my condolences to Julia."

Harry called Ozzie and woke him up. He got him to agree to help this evening and Harry told him when and where to meet. As he finished that call, Harry began thinking that he should just pull the plug on this one. On the other hand, by midnight tonight, he would be out of the crime game for good.

As he drew closer to the airport, Harry pulled into a coffee shop to pick up breakfast. When he got out of his car, he saw a Ford Taurus glide by the entranceway and keep going. He always thought it was a shitty car and so many people seemed to have one. He picked up coffee and a muffin and went into the airport.

When Harry got to his station, he checked what was on the work orders as he ate breakfast. He wanted to get everything done as quickly as possible so he could have a little thinking and planning time. His trip last night was to case out William Dean's house in Huntington. Much to his surprise, the house was big but didn't fall into the mansion category. He didn't plan to break into the house this time, but he did want to get the lay of the land. After that, Harry drove around the town of Huntington scoping out the police station and a few other landmarks. It was only then that he headed home through the monsoon.

Harry spent most of the day working on planes and equipment. He spent an hour after lunch putting some thoughts on paper. When he needed to check out some information, he used his phone rather than the Internet on his terminal. He'd be damned if he'd use his computer for researching anything ever again of a questionable nature. As for his phone, even the NSA couldn't nail him for the data he was looking up now.

As the workday wound to an end, Harry felt the old adrenaline rush start to kick in. He liked getting keyed up before a job. He always believed it heightened all his senses and kept him sharp. He knew that everything could hinge on a split second. He and his boys had already found that out in the past couple months. He was happy when quitting time finally came. Now, it was time to really go to work...hopefully, for the last time.

Harry headed home first to take care of Max. When he stopped at a light near the airport, he glanced into his rear view mirror and saw a dark Ford Taurus two cars behind him. Harry's inner alarm started to go off. This was now getting to be too much of a coincidence. He kept his eye on the car in his mirrors. At one point, he turned into a small shopping center and stopped at a PetSmart. He went inside and came out carrying a fifty-pound bag of Max's dog food. As he continued the journey home, he found the car still following at a discreet distance. He had memorized the plate number so he knew it was the same car.

This caused a dilemma. It was either Fat Tony or the cops. Neither was desirable. Harry tried to think this through. He thought that if it were Fat Tony, somebody would've shot him going into the store. He didn't think Tony would be very subtle at anything. Conversely, it could be the pretty Fed that had interviewed him almost two weeks ago. If she had more to go on, they'd show up with a warrant and search his house. He wasn't worried about that. There was nothing there. He even had a permit for the gun in his bedroom. The one he had taken on jobs was stashed away, but not on his property. Ozzie was bringing one with him tonight, even though Harry didn't think they'd need it.

"Oh, fuck it," said Harry. "Let whoever it is follow me. I'll pull a disappearing act for the evening and they'll be at a complete loss." He thought about how to do this and got an idea. He called Ozzie. "Been a slight change in plans."

"What is it, Harry?"

"Where are you lifting a car from?"

"I'm going to the mall. I'll park my car on one side, walk through the place, and come out on the other. I'll find something and meet you like we said at 6:30."

"Really watch your back, Oz. I think I have someone on my tail."

"Do you want to cancel?"

"Nah, I don't know when we'll get this type of play again. Listen, do you know where the community college is?"

"Yeah, not that I ever took any classes there."

Harry almost said something but bit his tongue. Instead, he said, "There are three buildings there. Park behind the big one and keep the engine running."

"Sure, Harry, that's easy enough."

"Two things; when you do your mall dodge, watch your back. If you think you have someone keeping an eye on you, lose him. And steal an SUV or something like that. Ideally, if you find a van, take that."

"Gotcha, Harry."

He hung up on Oz and continued home. Once he arrived, he took his work stuff and the dog food inside and came out with Max on a leash. He saw the phantom Taurus parked where it was in the morning. He started walking that way, whistling a tune as he went. As the driver saw Harry headed that way, the Taurus pulled out and drove down the street and past Harry. The windows were sufficiently tinted so that he couldn't see the driver. As it was, he only tried to look out of the corner of his eye. He didn't want the driver to know that he knew that he was being followed. If it were someone in law enforcement playing cat and mouse, then Harry was perfectly fine with becoming the cat. He would eventually confront whoever it was, but not now.

Harry Hid It

After doing a circuit of the neighborhood with Max, Harry didn't see the car, but he had a hunch it would appear again when he started driving. With the big dog flopped out on his rug in his bedroom, Harry changed into black jeans, white T-shirt, and dark sneakers. He stuck a black sweatshirt and his ski mask in his little backpack. He put in a couple more items. On the way out to his car, he picked up an easel and his painting supplies. He started out and made a call while he was driving.

"Vicki Light," said the voice answering his call.

"Vicki, honey, it's Harry."

Instantly the voice changed from professional to a more sultry tone. "Harry! How's my favorite student?"

"You must have others that were better artists."

"You being my favorite has nothing to do with your painting ability. You taking me up on modeling for your first nude?"

Harry smiled. Vicki was a plump brunette. She was very pretty, and if he did do a nude of her, it would look like a Rubens' painting. She had that zaftig quality Rubens' models had in the seventeenth century. "Very tempting. Tell you what; we will make a date for that. I do need a favor though."

"I think whatever you need can be arranged."

"You still give that four-hour class on Wednesday evenings?"

"Yes, it's tonight. You coming by?"

"Sort of." Harry thought about how he was going to spin this. "There have been thefts at the airport. For no good reason, the FBI has set their sights on me. I think I have one following me. I'd like to come into your studio there at about 6:30. If anyone comes looking for me, can you vouch I'm in the room painting away?"

Vicki was quiet for a minute. Then she said, sounding a little breathless, "I always thought you had that dangerous vibe about you. Did you steal anything from the airport?"

"No," said Harry truthfully. "I didn't steal anything from the airport. I value my job too much."

"And if I do this, you'll lay me out naked and paint me?"

"At the least," said Harry.

"Sounds like fun. See you soon, darling."

Harry laughed to himself. Spending time with a naked Vicki Light wasn't a bad thing. He actually wanted some practice sketching and painting people. Of course, he would never tell Sophia that she wasn't his first nude model if it came to that.

While he was on the phone, he saw that the Ford was following him again. The timing on this thing tonight was tight. He hoped he could pull it off. He would really be happier using his spare time painting rather than planning this shit!

As he pulled into the college, he saw that there were some parking spaces near the largest building. The small campus had the huge brick building as its centerpiece, and two smaller, modern structures framed it. Vicki's studio/classroom was on the top floor of the four-story building. There were only the big center doors going into the building and no side entrances. Harry hoped his ruse would work. Vicki would be the icing on the cake. She ran her classes with an iron hand. If anyone came into class to look for him, she would keep them at bay.

Harry made a show of taking out his easel and bag with his art supplies in it. As if it were an afterthought, he looped the small backpack on his shoulder and casually strolled to the entranceway. As soon as he was inside and out of sight from the big glass doors, he turned and sprinted up four flights of stairs. He walked into the familiar classroom and was happy to see Vicki here by herself. "You look good," he said. "New haircut?"

She ran her hands through her hair. "You noticed! Yes, it was time for a change." She watched Harry go over to a corner and lean his stuff against it, except for the backpack. "You're obviously in a hurry. Do you have to leave right away?"

"Unfortunately, I do." He came over and gave her a quick kiss on the cheek. She turned so that their lips met. "Thanks for covering for me. I have an idea who these agents are really looking for and I need to slip away unnoticed for a bit. I want to find out if this guy may be the one they're looking for. Then I can get them off my butt."

"Harry, I think a lot of people would like to get your butt," teased Vicki.

"Thanks, I guess. Anyway, if you can wait for me, I appreciate it. I'll try to get here by eleven when class lets out." As he turned to go, he spun back to her and said, "I have to admit, I don't miss the four-hour class."

"When you only meet once a week and spend so much time setting up and cleaning up, it was the best I could do for all the would-be artists with day jobs. Besides, I'm a night owl. If you want, we could do the painting of me up here one night after class. We'll have privacy."

"Sounds like a plan, Vicki. We can set a date for the portrait session when I return."

"I like that," said Vicki, almost purring. "How are you going to get out of here? Through the basement and the back door?"

"You're half right. I'm going out the back." Harry went to the far rear corner of the studio. Vicki had strung curtains up strategically throughout the room so that students could work without everybody watching. As he pushed the last curtain aside, it didn't look like anyone used this space. It was where he always worked when he was in the class. He pushed up on the old window in the corner. For an old building, it had old windows, and more importantly, an old-fashioned fire escape. He nimbly climbed out of the window and stood on the escape. "See you soon."

Before setting out, he pulled out his sweatshirt from his bag and pulled it over the white T-shirt. Then he quietly descended the fire escape. He passed some students sitting in the classrooms on the other floors, but nobody noticed him. When he got to the ladder that you lower to the ground, he saw a dark enclosed van idling right below him. "Wow," he thought, "Ozzie did good this time."

Harry Hid It

He pushed down on the ladder and cringed at the grating noise it made. The thing probably hadn't been greased since men first landed on the moon. When he had it lowered, he slid down it to the ground. The van's driver door opened and he heard, "Harry?"

"Yeah, it's me." He pushed the ladder back up, giving a slight push so it was just out of reach. He could easily jump up and grab it. He ran to the other side of the van. "Let's get out of here. Go slow and take your time. Don't draw any attention to yourself."

Harry looked around the van. It looked like it had been a work vehicle at some point, but now it was empty. Harry saw the pavement split at the corner of the building. One way wound around into the parking lot and the other went to the back of the adjacent building. Harry directed Oz to go to the back of the next building. As they slowly rolled behind that, Harry saw that they could access the main drag out of the college from here without going into the parking lot at all. "I don't suppose you came in this way, did you, Oz?"

"As a matter of fact, I did," said Ozzie proudly. "After what happened to me, I thought it was best to stay to the background."

Harry turned sharply to Oz. "What did happen to you?"

"You were right. I was being followed. After you gave me the head's up, I paid attention. It did look like a car kept behind me. When I got to the mall, some jerk in a suit stayed on my ass. He tried to act like he was just wandering around, but I could tell."

"Did you shake him?"

Once again, Ozzie beamed proudly, "I sure did. I went to the movie theater there and bought a ticket. As soon as I got into the theater, I went to the little back door they have there. As soon as I went through it, I went up a couple of floors of the parking deck and found this beauty." Oz patted the steering wheel. "These old ones are so easy to get into and start up. I was gone in about two minutes of hitting the theater."

Harry was impressed with Ozzie's ingenuity. "Great job, Oz. By the way, we're heading up to Huntington."

207

"Yeah, that's what you said on the phone this morning. I was half asleep, but I remember that." They drove in silence for a couple minutes. "Harry, why are people following us?"

Harry had been wondering the same thing. "I'm not sure, Ozzie. I told you out in the Hamptons I had an FBI agent talk to me. All I can think of is she got a bug up her ass about me."

"Then why was someone checking me out?"

Harry didn't have an answer, but it got him to thinking. Out of the three of them, Oz was the only one with a rap sheet. The police caught him several years ago trying to steal a car on his own. He had spent nine months in jail. If Agent Dudek was behind this, how did she latch on to Ozzie? The only time he and Ozzie had been together since the Bamberger mess was when everybody went out to the Hamptons a week and a half ago.

"Jesus Christ!" said Harry aloud.

"What?" asked Ozzie in alarm. Harry tried to get his thoughts together. "She must've been out in the Hamptons last weekend. I'm so fucking careless." Harry cursed a few more times as he hit the door with his fist.

"Who was in the Hamptons? We were all there."

"That damn FBI agent. I don't know how, but she must have seen us all together. That's all I can think of." He had a sudden thought and pulled out his phone. He called John. When he answered, Harry asked, "Can you talk?"

"Give me a sec. I'm in the funeral home." Harry heard people, as John must have been walking outside. "What's up? Ozzie not show up?"

"No, he's here. Look, we're being followed." He told John about his theory on the FBI agent seeing them together at the Hamptons. "If she did, it's all my fault. Have you noticed anyone interested in you?"

"Funny you should say that. Julia drove and there did seem to be this one car I kept noticing. Hang on a minute; I'm in the parking lot and it's a pretty big one." There was silence and then

John said, "Holy shit. It's parked across the street. You think they made us?"

"I'm thinking I'm…and now by extension us… all they have to go on. They're fishing. We did such good work on the jobs that they have nothing solid. Except, of course, for your esteemed leader playing with the computer at work."

"Stop beating yourself up, Harry. You and Ozzie going to cancel tonight's shindig?"

"Nope. Still going through with it, and then we'll be done."

"Is that wise?"

"No guts, no glory, pal."

Chapter 22

OZZIE AND HARRY WERE going over the plan when Harry's phone rang. He looked in surprise at the name on the screen. When he answered he asked, "What's up, Frank?"

"I wasn't sure who to call, Harry. You haven't seen Spanky around, have you?" Charlie "Spanky" MacGregor was Frank's partner in the construction business. Harry was friendly with Spanky but never really hung out with him.

"No, Frank, I haven't run into Spanky since the middle of the summer. What's wrong?"

"He never came home last night. Madeline, his wife, is worried sick. Spanky isn't one to go running off without telling anyone. I just thought I'd see if you happened to see him. I don't know what to do."

"Did you call the cops?"

"Yeah, but they have to wait another day until you can file a missing person's report."

"When did you last see him?" asked Harry.

"Yesterday, at the end of work. He got in his truck and took off right before me."

Harry could tell his friend was distressed. "I'm sure he'll turn up, Frank. Hang in there. Keep me posted. I'm up on the north shore, but I'll keep my eyes peeled for him when I get back down there."

"Thanks, Harry." Frank clicked off.

"What did Frank want?" asked Ozzie.

"Spanky's missing."

"Really! That's surprising. You can always find him. That's why I went over to him when I needed to borrow a vehicle that night we went to the club."

Harry Hid It

Somewhere in the back of Harry's mind, a distant warning bell started to go off. He ignored it and said, "Oz, when I told you to borrow a vehicle that night, it was a euphemism for stealing one. You know, like you did tonight."

"Harry, when you want me to steal, just tell me to steal. Borrow is borrowing; stealing is stealing. Why do you make everything so complicated?"

"Oh…just shut the fuck up and drive," Harry commanded.

They were silent until they reached the town of Huntington. Harry gave instructions to the Deans' home. As they got closer, Harry said, "Don't stop, but slow down as you go by."

Ozzie did just that. He saw that it was a nice size house, and not set too far back from the street. He could see a BMW sports car sitting in front of the garage. The garage was being renovated and Ozzie saw that the doors were off and a big blue tarp covered the roof. "What did you want to see here? You said we weren't going into the house."

"That's right. When I drove past here last night in that big storm, two cars were in front of the garage, the BMW and a Lexus. I figured the BMW belonged to Bill Dean and the other was his wife's. I was hoping this is what we'd find. Now, keep going down the road and we'll go to the library."

"How do you know she's going to be there?"

"She's a writer. She wrote some kind of romance novel. She's giving a reading tonight between six o'clock and 7:30. I'm hoping her husband didn't go with her. If he did, we'll get them both and negotiate from there."

"Wow, she wrote a book. I have a hard enough time trying to read one."

"Oz, you never cease to amaze me," said Harry. "Don't worry; we won't be going into the library so you won't have to hurt your brain."

"That wasn't very nice, Harry."

"I didn't mean anything by it, Ozzie. Did you bring me a gun?"

Harry Hid It

Oz reached down into a small leather bag between them and brought out a small .22 revolver. "Best I could do on short notice."

"That's fine; it's just for show," said Harry. "I hope," he thought.

Following Harry's instructions, Oz soon reached the library. Driving into its parking lot, he drove around until they saw a red Lexus parked off to the side. It was facing the trees that lined the back of the building. There must not have been many people at the reading because the lot was only half full. To Harry's delight, to the right of the Lexus was an empty space. Pointing, he said, "Pull in there."

When Ozzie braked to a halt, the side door of the van was even with the driver's door of the Lexus. Ozzie asked, "What do we do now?"

"We wait. If there are people with her when she comes to the car, we'll force her to the side of the road on her way home and take her. If she's by herself, I'll pull her into the van and you take off."

"Harry, if the FBI is already sniffing around you, is kidnapping a good idea?"

"Not particularly, but this is hardly a kidnapping. It's more like a detainment. I expect this to be over within an hour. I need to get back to the college by eleven. If for some reason it gets fucked up, we dump Mrs. Dean somewhere in town and get out."

"You mean we kill her?"

"No, you dickhead moron. No killing. No hitting. If you fuck this up, Oz, I will never work a job with you again. Jesus Christ, it's a good thing we aren't kidnapping a teenager or you'd be afraid."

Oz gritted his teeth. "I told you he kicked me in the balls. It hurt."

"OK," Harry said, trying to calm things down. God, he was on edge tonight. He also realized that he hadn't told Oz that this was their last job. He'd bring that up when this was over. He knew that would upset Ozzie. He also knew he would then be putting up with a couple years of, "Harry, when do I get my money?" Since getting to their stash wasn't quite the same as going to the bank, Harry made a mental note to keep some cash out to keep Ozzie happy until it was safe to bring all of it out of hiding. If tonight went well, he'd do that with some of the cash he planned to take from Mr. Dean.

The van had no rear window, so Harry angled the mirror on his side of the truck so that he could see behind them. At about 7:40, he saw several people exiting the library. They were walking together and then stopped. It looked like they appeared to be saying good-bye to each other as they reached the parking lot. Harry saw a woman peel off from the group and head their way. She had a large cloth bag in one hand and her pocketbook hanging from her other shoulder. It was twilight and there was enough light for Harry to see that it was Sarah Dean. She was a good-looking woman in her mid-forties, with long blonde hair that billowed behind her. She was thin and wore dark pants and jacket with a light pink blouse under it. "Put your mask on. I'm going to grab her."

Harry pulled his on and saw that Ozzie did the same. They had been wearing gloves the entire time so as not to accidently leave any fingerprints in the van. He wiggled his tall frame between the two seats and crouched at the sliding door on the side. He could hear the sound of her heels on the pavement. When he sensed that the woman was directly outside the door, Harry threw it open, reached out, put a big hand over the woman's mouth, wrapped his other arm around her torso, and yanked her back into the van. Sarah Dean didn't even have a chance to react. Harry twisted his body so that he brought the woman under him. He pressed his weight down as softly as he could, whipped the door shut, and hissed to Ozzie, "Go! Slowly."

Ozzie complied and smoothly drove the van out of the parking lot. Harry kept his hand over Mrs. Dean's mouth and continued to press down on her. From the light coming through the front windows, he saw her eyes wide in fear, but she didn't seem hysterical. She appeared to have control of herself. He pulled out the gun he had in his pocket and pressed it into her cheek. He kept his voice low and guttural. "I will take my hand away and get off you, but you can't move or scream. Do you understand me?"

Sarah Dean nodded her head the best she could with Harry's wrestling hold on her. First, he took his hand away. When she did nothing more than suck in air, he eased himself up to his knees. The woman didn't move. Harry said, "You can sit up and lean against the side there."

Mrs. Dean slowly picked herself up and untangled herself from her bags. A few buttons on her blouse came undone and Harry could see the top of very nice breasts pushed up by a red bra. She looked down at her exposed breasts and back up at Harry with a questioning look. He said, "Don't worry, we're not here for that. You can button up."

She said, "Thank you." She closed her shirt and sat straight up. She smoothed back her hair, stuck her legs straight out, and appraised the masked man before her. She said in a deep throaty voice, "If you don't want sex, then obviously you want money."

He couldn't help it. Harry liked this broad. He just kidnapped her and she was as calm and classy as she could be. He admired people who kept it together under pressure. Not many folks could.

"Not yours; I want your husband's money. I want to do this as quick and clean as possible. My intention is not to hurt you."

"As long as you get your way, I'm sure, young man."

"Well, yeah, that's how this works."

"Are you doing this because of that fucking article in the newspaper? My asshole husband bragging how he has bags of money to take in to close the deal?"

"Ugh," was all Harry could think of saying. This wasn't the reaction he expected. He thought he'd have to hog-tie and gag the woman by now. He stayed on his guard. Anyone this calm might actually be a problem.

"I told him not to talk like that to the reporter. But he knows *everything*. He has this plan to make big bucks in real estate and then run for political office. He couldn't even purchase our house without mucking up the deal."

"Mrs. Dean, please be…"

"Call me Sarah," the woman said.

"Okay, Sarah. Now I need…"

"And what's your name, young man?" she interrupted again.

In spite of the situation, Harry smiled under the mask. This gal was a pistol. "Nice try. Now will you please shut the fuck up?" He didn't say it with very much malice, but Sarah just nodded. "Thank you. Now is your husband home?"

"Yes. He came home right before I left."

"Does he keep cash in the house?" asked Harry. Mrs. Dean nodded. "Good. This is what we're going to do. We're going to call him from your phone. I'm going to give him all of five minutes to gather up the cash, bring it to us, and we go our separate ways. Sound good?"

"Works for me, but lots of luck with Billy. He makes himself out to be this big tycoon, but he doesn't handle stress well."

"Do you have any security at the house?"

"Like people? No. We have a security system, but I'm the only one that ever remembers to set it. Bill always forgets the code."

"Where's your phone?"

"In my purse there." Sarah gave a slight point to the bag between the two of them.

Harry kept his eye and the gun on her as he cautiously reached forward. He rooted around and pulled out an iPhone. He handed it over to her and said, "Call him and put it on speaker. And let me see the screen as you're doing it."

Sarah lit up the screen and pushed the code to open it. She tilted the screen towards Harry; he could see the name "Bill" on the screen as the phone started ringing. It was answered on the third ring and Harry heard, "What do you want now? I'm watching the ball game."

Harry Hid It

Sarah said, "Oh, my book reading went very well. Thanks for asking."

"What are you busting my balls for? Why aren't you home yet? You're not home are you? I'm up in my study."

"You're study is a spare bedroom with a lounge chair, a bottle of scotch, and a big TV. Don't be pretentious with me, Bill."

Harry waved his gun in a "get on with it" movement.

Sarah nodded. "Bill, I'm in a bit of a situation here. This very nice man in a mask kidnapped me from the library parking lot and I'm in some type of van. They want money."

On the other end of the phone, there was a roar of laughter. "That's rich, Sarah. Don't you have anything better to do tonight? Are you out with your girlfriends? Is this because I didn't want to go with you to your stupid book thingy?"

Harry broke in. He kept his voice low and made it more menacing. "Listen, douchebag, we have your wife. If you don't do exactly what I say, she's dead. If you put me on hold or hang up, she's dead. You do one thing out of line, she's dead."

Bill Dean said, "You're good. Are you boinking her? She used to be a good piece of ass."

Before Harry could respond, Sarah roared, "You stupid shit, he isn't kidding."

As Bill started talking again, Sarah leaned forward and pressed the mute button. "Look, things haven't been good between us lately. I write romances because I have none in real life. He does think I'm trying to pull something."

Harry's mind raced. This part certainly wasn't going as planned. "Scream. Pretend I'm beating the shit out of you."

Sarah looked thoughtful, and then she nodded. Bill was still babbling away when she killed the mute button and started screaming. Then she said, "That hurt, you son of a bitch. Get off my tits." She screamed again.

Harry hoped nobody was outside the van. He had told Oz to slowly head back to the Deans' house and to cruise around the neighborhood. Harry was impressed with Sarah's performance as he heard Bill stop talking. Finally, her husband stuttered, "Th... this is real?"

In response, Harry said, "For a supposed real estate mogul, you're not too bright." Harry saw Sarah role her eyes in agreement. "Your wife's got a nice rack. I'm sure you want her to come home with both of them."

Very subdued, Bill Dean asked, "What do you want?"

"All the cash in your house. From what I read, I think you can spare half a mil."

"Are you fucking out of your mind? I don't have that here. You said you're real?"

"Yup."

"Kill the bitch."

Harry wasn't sure he heard right. "What?"

"Kill the bitch. You'll save me a fortune in divorce fees. Besides, I don't have that kind of scratch around here. I keep it in the office."

"You fucking son of a bitch rat bastard!" Sarah screamed into the phone. "You have two bags with seven hundred fifty thousand dollars in it you brought home tonight. You showed it to me before I left, as if I'm impressed by the money. You said you were taking it to bribe that condo group in the morning."

"Kill her and maybe I'll give you money for that," Bill Dean shouted into the phone.

Harry was about to say he needed counseling, when Sarah broke in. "Listen to me, Bill." She managed to sound like she was pleading and threatening at the same time. "This man made me record this conversation on the phone. Both sides of it," she emphasized. "If you don't do exactly what he says, he'll send it to the TV stations."

"What a great idea," Harry thought. "I wish it were mine." Aloud, he growled, "You got it, Bill. Now can we stop dicking around?"

On the other end, Bill Dean was seeing his political career and visions of grandeur dashed. Sullenly, he said, "What do you want?"

"First, you stay on the phone. After I tell you what to do, I want you to keep talking and give me a play-by-play of your actions. You take more than a breath, Sarah is dead and this recording goes to everyone I can think of. You won't be able to sell a dog-house, let alone run for office. Got it?"

"Yeah."

"Go get those two bags Sarah just told us about. Take them outside and stand on the curb. Have the bags open so that I can see in them. The clock is starting. Your ass better be out there in five minutes. Go!"

"Fine. I'm taking a drink of my scotch. Now I'm going into the bedroom where we have a big floor safe..."

Harry leaned forward and this time he pressed the mute button. He could still hear Bill explaining what he was doing. He could be trying to text someone while he talked, but that was a chance he had to take. In another four minutes, they should be out of here. Harry felt the van change direction. Ozzie was doing really well on this job. He hadn't opened his mouth and obviously paid attention to the conversation. He should be cruising back to the Dean homestead now. He said to Sarah, "You're unbelievable. What made you think to tell him you were recording this?"

"Because I am. I figured if nothing else, that I would have your voice. Obviously, you're disguising it though."

"I'm going to have to take it from you, you know."

"Yeah. That's okay. Asshole doesn't know it yet, but he's being served with divorce papers and a restraining order tomorrow. You taking the money means he has that much less to spend on lawyers. Other than the cash he drags around to meetings, he has no liquidity. You see, what he didn't tell the reporter is that he carries this money in, but he never actually gives it to anyone. It's a very expensive prop. When they see it and they do want to deal, he tells them he'll just write the money in the contract so that it's legal and all. The bottom line is he screws the sellers over. I'm sick of it. You would have a million tonight, but he spent two hundred fifty thousand dollars yesterday to get out of a potential lawsuit."

"So you want him to go down?"

"Oh yeah! You just took care of the one thing I was worried about. No cash, no power. I'll be divorced in three months, with the house." She stopped and looked at Harry. "Guess it would be inappropriate to thank you for kidnapping me."

"Yup. This has been fucking weird anyway. That would just be the cherry on top."

She looked at him coyly. "You think I have a good rack?"

"Definitely, and don't listen to that shithead of a husband. You're still a great piece of ass!"

From the front seat, Ozzie growled. "We're here and so is he."

Harry told her, "I'll keep the phone. You can take the rest of your stuff."

"That's fine. I'll tell him I still have it and will bring it to court if he contests the divorce. He's a wimp."

"Well, nice meeting you," said Harry. "In any other circumstance…" His voice trailed off.

"I hear you," said Sarah Dean.

When the van stopped, Harry slid the door open. He took the flashlight he had clipped to his belt and shone it into Bill Dean's face, blinding him. He saw a red face under a red crew cut. The man screwed up his eyes in protest to the light. Harry used the light and ran it over both bags. They were the zippered nylon bags like Fat Tony carried money in. He could see plenty of hundred dollar bills in each. He took one and threw it in the back of the van followed by the other. He then took Sarah's arm and helped her down out of the van. He yelled, "Go," and Ozzie did. As he started sliding the door closed, he saw Sarah wind up and knock Bill Dean on his ass.

Harry Hid It

From up front, Ozzie yelled out, "That was the most fucking bizarre kidnapping I ever saw. What the fuck do you call that?"

As Harry went to retrieve the bags that he threw to the back, he replied, "Marriage!"

Chapter 23

THEY DROVE IN SILENCE thinking about the evening. Harry figured that after the last two jobs, they were due an easy one. He was happy that nobody got hurt, he didn't really have to threaten anyone, and Ozzie did a good job. All in all, it felt like a great victory to go out with. If the money in the two bags did add up to three quarters of a million dollars, then he was retiring on top. It didn't get any better than that.

Now he had to figure out what to do with the money. He didn't want to leave it at the house. If his hunch was right about the FBI, he didn't want anything around just in case they figured out a way to search his home. However, it took time to cart the money out to the vault, as he called it. "What the hell," he concluded, "I've gone without sleep for an entire day before. Better safe than sorry."

Ozzie said, "Did you say something, Harry?"

"Sorry, talking to myself."

"I do that all the time."

"The problem, Oz, is that you start arguing with yourself."

"Not usually. Am I taking you back to the school now?"

"No, we need to stop at my house first. I want to drop the money off. They are two big bags. Neither of us is going to be able to sneak them into our cars."

"How much do you think we got?"

"Sarah said her husband had seven hundred fifty thousand dollars. We have twenty minutes until we get back to my place. Let me see." Harry squeezed between the two seats again and knelt in the back. He clicked his flashlight on and held it between his teeth. He checked a few rolls of money and saw that they all were hundred dollar bills banded up into bundles of five thousand

221

dollars. After carefully counting, he found there were one hundred forty-nine packs of hundreds. "Well, Oz, if these bundles of money are consistent, we have seven hundred forty-five thousand dollars. Not bad for a few hours' work, huh?"

"I like it. Can we spend this money?"

"We'll each get a little, Oz. It's like I keep telling you. We can't afford flashing around big bucks. If anyone on the street gets a whiff of big spenders, there's no telling what people might start thinking. You don't want Fat Tony to start looking into us, do you? It's bad enough that I got the FBI's panties up in a bunch."

"I guess so. We've taken in more money than I've ever seen."

Harry thought about telling Oz this was the last job and then decided against it. This job went even better than he could've dreamed. It was a good night. Why ruin it now? "Yeah, we've done good, Ozzie." Harry maneuvered into the front seat again. "Let's get back to my house. I'll only be a minute. Then you can get me back to the college and you to the mall."

When they got near Harry's place, he told Ozzie, "Drive slowly down my street and then around the block."

"Why?"

"I want to check out the cars on the street. I need to make sure nobody is watching my home."

Ozzie did this. Harry scanned the street, but he recognized all the cars. The same was true with those parked around the corner. After the circuit, Harry told Oz to pull into his driveway. Hopping out, he grabbed the two nylon bags from the back of the van, unlocked his side door, and went inside. He braced himself for one hundred sixty pounds of dog leaping onto him. After a quick pat and pushing him aside, Harry went into the garage through the connecting door. Finding a couple heavy-duty plastic containers, he threw the money inside. He opened up the trunk of his Cruze and placed the bins in there along with waterproof duct tape. After promising Max that he would be back soon, Harry pushed him back into the house and closed that door. He started the Cruze and pressed the button to the garage door. He backed out, closed the garage, and turned into his street. He went around the corner and drove three blocks with Oz following behind him. He parked between an old Lincoln Town Car and a pickup truck. Harry made sure he locked the Chevy and he jumped back into the van. He gave a nod and Ozzie took off.

When the van stopped behind the large college building, Harry looked at his watch. It was 10:50. Man, he couldn't have timed this better than if he had been planning the job for months. "What are you going to do with the van?" he asked Ozzie.

"There's another shopping center next to the mall. I'll drop it there and hoof it back to my car. Do you think the FBI guy is still hanging out?"

Harry smiled. "Tell you what. Can you get back into the theater through the rear door?"

Oz looked embarrassed. "Yup. Sometimes I sneak into the movies that way. I did it last week."

Harry shook his head. This guy was part of a crew stealing millions of dollars and he still snuck in for a free movie. He blew out some air. "Go back that way then. If he's waiting for you, then you won't disappoint him."

"Great idea! Thanks, Harry."

"You did good tonight, Oz." They fist bumped. "See you later."

Harry got out, making sure he had his backpack with him. He wanted to leave the building with the same stuff he had when he entered. He didn't know if Agent Dudek was following him or someone else, but Harry didn't want to underestimate the FBI. They'd pick up on something like that. Besides, they were on his ass. That said something about them. Not for the first time, Harry wondered if he should've planted some red herrings on the jobs so the cops and feds would go on wild goose chases. By not having anywhere to look, they were now grasping at straws. Unfortunately, Harry was one of the straws.

Determined not to tarnish such a good night, he shook his head to dispel the self-doubts. Looking up, he saw the bottom of the ladder to the fire escape. Crouching, he sprang up and grabbed the bottom rung. His weight pulled it down with the same sickening noise from before. He scrambled to the first landing of the fire escape and pulled the ladder up. Lightly, he went up the stairs until he was outside the window of his old classroom. He raised it a few inches and put his ear to it. Harry could hear Vicki saying good night to her students. Since it didn't sound like anybody was in the back corner, he raised the window more and climbed into the room. Shuffling through the maze of curtains, he saw the last student going out the door.

As Vicki closed the door, he said, "Maybe I'll do your portrait from the back. You look really good from this angle."

Vicki gave a little yelp of surprise, turned, and flung a paintbrush at Harry. He deftly caught it in his left hand. "Damn, Vicki, you better bring more than a brush if you're ever attacked."

"Fuck you, Harry. I thought everyone was gone."

"They were. I just got here. Told you I'd try to be back on time."

She looked at the clock on the wall. "You're good, but I always suspected that about you," she said with a smile. "Did you have any luck with what you needed to do?"

"I think so. Time will tell. Anyone come looking for me?"

"Not exactly. There was a woman who looked in here though. I noticed she was doing that to all the rooms on this floor. I asked what she wanted and she just said that she was lost."

"What did she look like?" asked Harry.

"About my height, dark hair that barely reached her shoulders, and a lot of boob and hip."

Sounded like Agent Dudek to Harry. "Vicki, I can't thank you enough. I need to go. I want to come out with the rest of the students." He peeled off his black sweatshirt and stuffed it in the backpack. Then he went over and picked up his easel and artist material bag. "Text me your dates for the next couple weeks when you're free, and we'll do that portrait." He went over and kissed her cheek.

As he was at the door, Vicki asked, "Do you really want to do me from behind?"

Harry grinned. He didn't know quite how she meant the question, so he simply said, "Yes. You have a cute ass." With that, he quickly descended the stairs. As he went out the entranceway, Harry saw that not many cars remained. College security was patrolling the lot to make sure everybody got their cars without a problem. Walking to the Camaro, Harry scanned the area as subtly as he could. There she was. Parked way off to the side so that she had a clear view of the entrance. Fortunately, she was sitting on the direct opposite side of where Oz entered and exited with the van. She probably didn't even notice the vehicle going behind the buildings.

Harry put his art stuff and backpack in the trunk. He slowly exited the college and headed for home. He stopped at a 24-hour grocery store to pick up a few things he needed for the house. This wasn't something he would normally do at this time of night. It still wasn't time to let Karyn Dudek know that he knew she was following him, but that didn't mean he couldn't fuck with her head. If she wanted to keep observing him, then far be it for him to cut her night short.

He left with a couple bags from the store and then stopped for gas. His last stop was a 7-Eleven where he bought a very large coffee. If he didn't have some place else to be tonight, he would stop at Art's for a nightcap and anyplace else he could think of. She had to be getting tired. Harry just wanted to show her that his life was very mundane so that she would look somewhere else or just quit.

Back at the house, he pulled into his driveway and parked in front of the garage. He made two trips to get everything into the house. He did notice that the Taurus parked up the street where she had stopped earlier. He sat down and drank more of his coffee. Max placed his head on Harry's lap.

"Hey, pal, sorry I haven't been around much today. I'll make it up to you tomorrow. I'd love to take you for a ride tonight, but I need to slip out of here. You haven't managed the trick of turning into beagle, so you watch the house."

Max gave his tail a wag and seemed to whine in acknowledgement. Harry made more coffee, which he poured in the cup. He set it on the counter and started shutting off all the lights in the house. He had a small guestroom that looked out on the street in the direction that the Taurus sat. Harry got his binoculars from his room and went there to look out.

"Goddamn, you're one persistent broad," he said aloud. "Hope you enjoy watching an empty house. Well, except for a big fucking dog."

Harry used the bathroom and put the black sweatshirt back on. He substituted hiking boots for sneakers. Down by the back door, he looked at the rack on the wall where he hung coats and jackets. He found the one he was looking for and the matching ball cap. He plucked a key from a bowl near the door. He carefully stuck the key into his pocket and placed the folded coat and hat in his backpack. Going to a cupboard in the kitchen, he found a high-powered flashlight and that also went in the pack. Finally, he gave Max a good-bye pat and picked up his travel cup of coffee.

Heading to the back corner of the house that was out of view of the FBI agent, Harry entered a room he planned to turn into an office one day. Right now, it held everything that had no real place in his home. Dodging a couple of cartons on the floor, he went over to the window. It looked out on the backyard and was ten feet from the fence that separated him from his neighbor. Thankful that there was no moon tonight, all Harry could see was darkness. He slipped the latch, raised the window, and dropped the backpack outside. Being careful with his coffee, Harry clambered through the window and jumped like a cat onto the lawn. Picking up the pack, he looked left and right, and then went directly to the fence and vaulted it.

Without looking back, he went across his neighbor's lawn and out their gate. Keeping to the shadows, he made his way to where he parked the Chevy Cruze. He got in and turned it over. As he slid it out of its parking spot, he thought about seeing if the FBI agent was still in the same place. Deciding not to tempt fate, Harry made a beeline for the highway. He had barely enough time to do what he had to do and make it back in time to get ready for work. As it was, he had never done this in the dark. "Oh hell," Harry thought, "it's the adventures that make life interesting."

As he started out, Harry switched on the radio. He turned off his usual music station and put on the 24-hour news channel for the area. After hearing that the Mets won and the Yankees lost, the announcer went back to the news reports for the city and vicinity. Harry heard about a huge fire in Newark, New Jersey, two murders in the Bronx, and a mutilated body found in a warehouse in Valley Stream. Identities of all the victims were being withheld until next of kin were notified. "Poor bastards," Harry said. There were more stories on crime, traffic reports, and then the sport scores again. There was nothing at all about a kidnapping on the north shore.

Harry wondered how Bill Dean was going to handle the situation. If he were able to think after Sarah belted him in the kisser. Remembering that made Harry laugh out loud. How the hell was Dean going to explain his face when talking to the cops? Say that the kidnapper hit him after Dean handed over the money?

It occurred to Harry that Bill Dean probably had some connections and might try to keep the incident low key. On the other hand, maybe he had acquired his money with less than legal means and didn't want anyone to know what happened. Sarah had plenty of reasons from tonight alone to divorce the dirtbag. Harry felt bad about throwing her phone away. He had a gut feeling that she wasn't going to do much to help the police track down her kidnappers. He wondered when she found the packet of hundreds he took out of one of the bags and stuck in her pocketbook when he helped her down out of the van.

Harry put the music back on. After an hour, he found a place to get some more coffee. Now that the adrenaline rush was over, he needed to substitute caffeine for it so that he could keep going. As it was, everything went as smoothly as possible. Usually when he did this run, he had Max with him to keep him company. When he arrived at his destination, it was a little difficult making his way to his cache lugging the two containers in the dark, but he managed. His only mishap was banging his head once in the low enclosure. This was also the first time he couldn't just take his time and paint some landscapes when he was done.

It seemed like no time at all before he was back at the same stop off the highway getting more coffee on his return trip. Dawn was beginning and he could see the sun rising in front of him. It was going to be a beautiful day. As he was thinking about where at the airport he could hide and take a nap, he found himself back in his neighborhood. Hoping that Karyn Dudek had finally gone home at some point, he carefully reconnoitered the area. She wasn't where he left her last night and the area all around his block was clear. Taking a chance, he raised the garage door when he was three houses down and rolled right into the garage. When it closed behind him, Harry gratefully eased himself out of the car and stretched. He was beat. Even with all the coffee he drank, he knew that if he rested his eyes he'd be out for the count.

He went into the house and Max bounded over to him. Harry opened the back door and Max bolted into the yard. Just as he did this, he saw a Ford Taurus slide past his house and go up the road. It kept going. Harry closed the door and ran up the stairs. Going into the guestroom, he looked out the window. This time the car parked on the opposite side of the street.

Going into the bathroom, Harry shook his head thinking that he had to give her props for persistence. When he looked in the mirror, he said to his reflection, "I hope she looks as shitty as I do." Harry stripped off all his clothes and threw them in the hamper. He brushed his teeth and decided to shave today. He figured anything to improve his appearance had to be a help. After that, he stood under the hot water of his shower for a solid twenty minutes. Then he turned it all the way down to cold and endured that for as long as he could. It was an old trick that refreshed him and he felt better as he toweled dry.

Harry dressed for work and went downstairs. He let Max in and fed him. Deciding a big breakfast was needed, he made himself sausage and eggs with toast. Feeling as if his stomach would revolt with one more cup of coffee, he made tea. He threw a sandwich together for lunch and was soon traveling to work with his rearguard in view. As Harry neared JFK, he saw the Taurus suddenly peel away, do an illegal U-turn, and head in the opposite direction.

"Hmmm," Harry thought, "either she doesn't want to sit here all day waiting for me to come out of work, or she got called to something."

Soon, he was checking his work orders. "Thank God, it's a light day," Harry said, lifting his head up to where he thought the Almighty would hear him. Just as he was sitting down to plan out his work, his cell phone rang. He looked at who was calling, clicked it on, and said, "Hey, Frank, they find Spanky?"

Harry was surprised to hear a sob. Frank was many things, but he wasn't a crier. "They found him, Harry. He was hanging by his arms in a warehouse. He was all cut up and bleeding. I had to identify the body. They fucking killed him, Harry. He was a good man. He didn't deserve that." Harry looked at the phone as Frank's voice trailed off into a wail.

Chapter 24

KARYN ALMOST HIT A truck as she spun her wheel around and headed off in the opposite direction. She dropped her phone on the seat next to her and rubbed her eyes. Yesterday was an incredibly long day of sitting on her ass in the car. After four hours of sleep, she was feeling extremely cranky. Since she was already out on Long Island, Assistant Director Gonzales just called her and told her to head up to Huntington to interview the victims of a kidnap case.

When she asked who was kidnapped, he said, "The wife of some Donald Trump clone. She was kidnapped for all of an hour and her husband handed over almost a million dollars to the kidnappers."

"He had that much money on hand?"

"This entire thing is a little off. Since kidnapping was involved, the local police called us. I talked to the chief and he said he would be happy to wash his hands of it. Mentioned that he retires in four months and did not want to deal with rich people issues."

"I'll go see. I'm sure my friend Harry is going to continue heading to work. We're almost at the airport now."

"Find out anything yesterday?"

"No," said Karyn disgustedly. "He went to work, walked the dog at home, and then spent the evening at some class in the local college."

"Waste of time?" Gonzales asked.

"Feels it. Nobody else did any better. The guy John went to a funeral home in a town above the city and Ozzie went to the movies. The only bad thing is that the police came to get Frank to identify a body. From what little I heard, it apparently was his business partner."

230

"I saw that come across the desk this morning. Police are sitting on the details to the public, but it looked like a torture and murder thing. Hell of a way to go. Blood all over."

"I'm not crazy about this city of yours."

Gonzales said, "Not my city. I'm from St. Louis. Technically, it didn't happen in the city. It happened somewhere out near where you are now. Report back to me after you talk to the kidnap folks." With that, he hung up and Karyn found herself heading north.

Yesterday was such a waste of time. The only activity she had was when she cautiously poked around the college trying to find out where Harry went last night. Most of the doors to the classrooms had small windows in them, and it was hard to see much in the rooms. She didn't want to start knocking on doors because she didn't want Harry to know he was being followed. Sometimes, you wanted to unnerve a suspect by doing surveillance in plain sight. She wasn't ready to do that yet. She wanted to get a feel for what was going on with him. While her gut told her that she was on the right track, her head was telling her that she was operating on a skimpy circumstantial theory.

When she couldn't find Harry, she checked out the college on her phone and saw the administration office was in one of the smaller buildings. Going there, she introduced herself and said she was checking to see if Harry Strickland was enrolled at the school. She explained that she was conducting a background check on him for a job he applied for with the FBI. The young woman behind the desk was very helpful and told her that he had been enrolled here last spring, but not this year.

"I thought I saw him walking into the big old building here when I pulled up."

The woman looked at the computer screen. "He was taking an art class in the spring. Those artsy people are always coming back here and sitting in a class with their old teachers now and then. Painters, writers, and anyone like that do it all the time. I know the president here tells the teachers not to let them because they aren't paying." The girl dropped her voice in a conspiratorial whisper. "Everybody thinks he's a prick, so they ignore him."

"Is there an art class going on in the center building now?" asked Karyn.

The administrator clicked through several screens. "Yes, there are three in there. They are all on the top floor. It looks like Mr. Strickland took Vicki's class last spring. She does a once-a-week, four hour class."

Karyn remembered seeing classrooms with people drawing and painting. She sighed. That meant she had to wait here until eleven. "Thank you. You've been a big help. I really just needed to know if he actually went here last semester. Have a good night."

As she was exiting, she saw a couple of vending machines. She bought a soda and peanut butter crackers and went back in her car. She maneuvered it over to the fringes of the parking lot so she could see the entrance to the center building and Harry's car. When he finally came out a little after eleven, she continued following from a distance. Cursing at him for all the stops he made, she was thrilled when he finally went home. She parked up the street and waited. An hour after all the lights went out, she decided to call it a day and went home to grab a few hours of sleep and a shower. She actually welcomed the chance to do something different today as she zoomed up to Huntington.

A police cruiser without its lights blinking was in front of the Deans' house when she pulled up. There were two nice cars in front of the garage under renovation. It seemed like a very peaceful neighborhood. She went up to the front door, which a cop opened when she rang the bell. She showed her credentials and he escorted her into a large living room that looked out onto the water. Karyn figured her entire apartment could fit in here. Seated on a couch was a redheaded man with an older police officer. Across from them was a pretty blonde woman who was quietly drinking out of a teacup. "I'm Karyn Dudek with the FBI," she announced.

Harry Hid It

The cop got up and extended his hand. "Chief Harold Staats. Thanks for getting here so quickly."

"I was in the area and my boss directed me up here. What happened?"

The chief looked at the other two who seemed content to let him explain. "Mrs. Dean was abducted outside the town library at about 7:45 last night. Mr. Dean received a call from the kidnappers at eight. After some back and forth conversation with Mr. Dean ascertaining they meant what they said, they then told him to bring two bags of cash out on the curb in five minutes. They told Mr. Dean that they'd take the money and drop off Mrs. Dean. They told him that if he stopped talking on the phone while he got the money and came outside, they'd kill his wife. He complied with their wishes, and at approximately 8:20, a blue van pulled up. The kidnapper took the money, helped Mrs. Dean out of the van, and took off. For whatever reason, Mr. Dean waited until this morning to tell me the news."

Karyn wondered if this was the shortest kidnapping on record. She turned to Mrs. Dean. "Are you OK, ma'am? Did they hurt you?"

"I'm perfectly fine. After he pulled me into the van, the kidnapper was a perfect gentleman."

"That's good, at least. And you, Mr. Dean, why did you wait until this morning to call the police?"

Bill Dean looked like he was sucking on a lemon. "My insurance man told me I had to if there were a chance of getting my money back."

"That's the only reason you called the cops?" Karyn asked incredulously.

"Yeah. I doubt you're ever going to catch them. Why bother?"

"Why bother...are you serious?" Karyn calmed herself and got back on track with the questions. "How much money did they get?" Dean mumbled something. "I didn't hear you," said Karyn.

Almost in a roar, Bill Dean said, "Three quarters of a fucking million dollars!"

"How did they know you had that much money?"

"They didn't. That bitch told them." Dean pointed with a quivering finger at his wife.

Karyn shifted her attention to the woman. "You told them that, Mrs. Dean?"

"Call me Sarah. They knew he kept lots of cash around. My intelligent husband bragged to a reporter a few weeks ago how he likes to show up to meetings with big bucks to grease his deals. I wasn't going to tell them any amount until my darling husband here told them to kill me because he didn't have any money. Since I was afraid for my life, I blurted out how he bragged when he came home last night how much money he had for a meeting he was going to this morning."

"Which I had to cancel because of this shit," mumbled Bill Dean.

"Did you really tell the kidnappers to kill your wife?" asked Karyn.

"I was stalling for time," said Dean lamely.

Out of the corner of his eye, Karyn saw the police chief shake his head in disgust. As she was about to ask another question, the doorbell rang. The police officer who opened the door for Karyn stuck his head into the room. "Chief, there's a sheriff's deputy here."

"I didn't call the sheriff."

"She has something for Mr. Dean."

Bill Dean's eyes widened a bit as the chief said, "What the hell. Show her in."

A tall, statuesque black woman in the uniform of the Suffolk County Sheriff's Office walked in with a manila envelope. She looked at everyone and asked, "William Dean?"

All three pointed to the red-haired man. She walked over to him and said, "You've been served."

Harry Hid It

Dean dumbly took the envelope. The woman nodded to Karyn, gave a salute/wave to Chief Staats, and left the room. Bill Dean tore open the envelope and read the first page. The color of his face started to match that of his hair as he looked at his wife. Screaming, he lunged at her. "You fucking slut! You want a divorce?"

Karyn swept her leg and caught Bill Dean across the knees. He flopped on his face. As he started to get up, she jabbed the heel of her shoe into the back of his head and pressed hard. He gasped as she said, "Stay. Chief, could you please have your man take him to another room."

Chief Staats reached down and grabbed William Dean by the collar of his shirt. "I'll do it myself." Effortlessly, the older man yanked Dean to his feet and dragged him out of the room.

When they were alone, Karyn asked Mrs. Dean, "I take it he didn't know that was coming?"

"Nah. Can you blame me? As it worked out, I'm glad you and the chief were here. He doesn't handle stress well. Believe me, he's more upset about losing his money than me divorcing him, the self-absorbed jerkoff."

Karyn went across from Sarah Dean and sat on the couch. "You know, if I had a suspicious mind, I'd begin to think that you concocted this entire kidnapping thing to get the money. Set yourself up for your divorce."

Sarah raised her eyebrows and then laughed. "You know, I thought the same thing. The timing looks bad. The truth is, Miss FBI Agent, that I don't want his money or anything of his. I bought this house and it has always been in my name. I just want his ass out of here and to get away from his shady business dealings. Bill doesn't know it, but I have a pending contract for a three-book deal to write romance novels. I just want him to go."

Karyn said, "Let me get some of these questions out of the way. Are you seeing anyone on the side?"

"My literary agent, and for what it's worth, it's a she. I found out I enjoy it both ways. For now, I've had my fill of men."

"O…K. Tell me what happened last night." Karyn wrote down the events as Sarah Dean related them. "Did you get a good look at the kidnappers?"

"Nope. They wore those ski masks where they have the openings for the eyes and mouth. The one kidnapper stayed in the driver's seat the entire time. I think he grunted once. The guy I talked with was tall, seemed strong, and had nice eyes."

Karyn stopped writing. "Nice eyes?"

"Yes, they were soft and brown. I think he was disguising his voice when he talked. He tried to sound low and mean, but if asshole in there," Sarah indicated the door to the next room, "didn't pay up, I really don't think he would've hurt me."

"Any idea about the driver? Height, weight, anything?"

"No idea."

"What about the van?"

Sarah thought for a moment. "I think it was dark blue. I didn't give it a thought as I walked back to my car. My mind was on the reading I just finished in the library. When he pulled me in, I was more startled than scared at first. As I started to talk to my husband, the scared turned into fury. As for the inside of the van, it was empty. No seats or anything except for the driver and passenger seats. Numbnuts didn't get the plate number when he handed over the money."

"I noticed his face was bruised. I was going to ask him about that before the divorce papers got here. Did the kidnapper hit him to stun him when they took the money?"

"Oh no," said Sarah Dean breezily. "I did that. He had just told people it was perfectly fine to kill me. I was mad."

The woman had spunk, Karyn thought. She would've done the same thing. "Why did you only call the police this morning?"

"I wanted to call last night, but we fought for an hour about it. I finally got disgusted, took an Ambien, and washed it down with bourbon. When Bill found out that the only way the insurance company might reimburse him for the cash was to get the police involved, he called."

"Why did your husband go from telling them to kill you to handing over the money?" asked Karyn.

"Because I threatened him. I told him I had recorded our entire conversation and that I would broadcast to the world what he told the kidnappers. I think he saw his business career and political aspirations go up in smoke when I said that."

"You really think he would've done nothing?"

For the first time, Sarah Dean looked sad. "I really believe he meant it. You know how it goes. I thought I loved him in the beginning, but then I found out how self-centered he is. Men!" She gave a small laugh. "The kidnapper was at a loss when he said that. I don't think it would occur to him to be that way with a woman."

"How do you figure?" Karyn asked.

"He sympathized that my husband was an ass. Plus, he could've just thrown me out of the van onto our front lawn. It was quick, but he helped me out of the van in a very nice way. Go figure. My husband is fine with somebody offing me, and the bad guy shows kindness. We live in a fucked up world."

Karyn closed her notebook. "This is the oddest kidnapping I ever heard, Sarah. I'm sure there will be some more questions. I need to go talk to your husband again." She handed the victim her card. "Please call me at any time if you remember something."

"Thank you, Agent. It was a surreal experience. I certainly didn't plan it or anything like that, but the kidnappers made my divorce so much easier. People shouldn't do that to others, but if you never catch them, I'm not going to lose any sleep over it. I will continue to cooperate fully, but I wanted you to know how I feel."

Karyn stood and shook the other woman's hand. "I appreciate your honesty. I rarely run into that from the good guys or the bad guys."

The FBI agent left the room and found the chief and Mr. Dean in the kitchen. William Dean answered her questions in short bursts of answers. When Karyn asked about the bruise under his eye, he started telling her how the kidnapper had hit him when he took the money.

"Your wife told me she hit you when she got out of the van. Something about being pissed you told them to kill her."

With that, he shut up and just sat there looking down at his feet. Karyn nodded her head at the chief and together they went back to the foyer near the front door. They stepped out into the bright September sunshine. "What do you think, Chief Staats?" asked Karyn.

"Please, call me Corky."

"Corky?"

"Yeah, been a nickname since I was a rookie. I'm not one to stand on ceremony around here."

"So, Corky, what do you think of this mess?"

"I was tempted to shoot him myself when Mrs. Dean related how he told the kidnappers to kill her. I thought you were too nice to him when he went after her. It was only with great self-control that I didn't handcuff him and accidently push his face into the wall."

"Cops really don't do things like that, do they?" Karyn asked with a smile.

"Noooo, of course not," replied Corky Staats. "We're here to serve and protect. However, my tolerance for bullshit artists and assholes is getting less and less as I get older. From what I know, that pretty much describes Mr. Dean."

Karyn liked the chief. He reminded her of her father. "Any problems with him in town?"

"Not really, but I seem to get an inquiry every month for the last two years from government officials about him. People in the city, the state police fraud division, and the SEC even contacted me once. He seems to skate the fine line between legal and not legal with his business."

"What do you think of the kidnapping?"

"As in do I think it's real? I had thoughts on that, but I believe Mrs. Dean is telling the truth. She's not like her husband. I'm not even sure how she ended up with him, but I guess that's a moot point now." He chuckled. "This is one of those stories you tell over a few beers and people won't believe you."

"That's the truth. Were there any surveillance cameras at the library?"

"Yes, but not covering the parking lot. I have one of my officers going through what they have from the last few days to see if anyone out of the ordinary had been there looking over the place. I also have someone looking at footage from what few street cameras we have in this town to see if they can pick up the van."

"Thank you for calling us in," said Karyn.

"I've been doing this job for thirty years. I know kidnapping is your bailiwick. Besides, I needed someone else to corroborate the whole bizarre business. Think you can find these guys?"

"I don't know. It may be looking for a needle in a haystack. That seems to be all my cases right now."

"Sometimes, Agent Dudek, all we seem to do is keep the dam from overflowing. All this technology makes some of what we do easier, but there seem to be a lot more criminals out there. I wonder if the Deans even would've reported this if it weren't for the insurance company."

Karyn gave the chief her card and he did the same. "Let's keep in touch. Maybe something will break. I'm going to say good-bye to Mrs. Dean and then report to my boss. I don't know what else to do right now until I can find out if anything similar has gone down in recent months."

The chief went back to William Dean as Sarah entered the living room. Sarah was looking over the back of the chair at the blue water shining outside the huge window. "I'm leaving now, Sarah. Please call me if you think of anything."

Sarah stood up and started escorting Karyn to the door. She

looked at the card she still held. "I certainly will, Agent Dudek. As I said, I'll cooperate fully. Which is a lot more than you'll get from my soon-to-be ex-husband."

Karyn went out the door and Sarah watched her head to a car parked out front. She reached into her pocket and fondled the five thousand dollars she found in her pocketbook from the night before. She smiled a little and said to herself, "I'll cooperate, but I'm not bending over backwards to help you find them."

Chapter 25

THE TABLE IN THE back corner of Art's was quiet. Harry was buying drinks for Frank and Lisa trying to get them to calm down. It was Friday and he came here after work. He was still waiting for Sophia to join them. Max sat with his head in Lisa's lap so she could pat his head as she was trying to stop the tears running down her face. Not for the first time, Harry marveled at the ability of dogs, especially Max, to sense when a person needed comforting.

Frank downed a shot of whiskey and said, "God, Harry, I never saw anything so terrible. Spanky's body was so cut up. They at least cleaned up his face a little so that I could identify him. It was sickening, but it was better than his wife Madeline having to do it. After I did the ID, I had to go in the bathroom to be sick."

For once, Harry didn't know what to say. He knew Frank and Lisa were very close to Spanky and his wife. They'd been in business together for ten years. Harry had been surprised that their construction company had not only survived, but also thrived. In that time, Frank and Spanky not only stayed partners, but they also continued as great friends. The wives were close. Harry liked Spanky. He and Madeline had come to a couple of Harry's get-togethers. Harry was afraid to put into words why something so horrible had happened to Spanky. He couldn't shake the fear that this had something to do with Ozzie borrowing his truck when they hit Fat Tony. Harry prayed that he was being totally paranoid and his imagination was going wild.

Art brought over another round of drinks. Usually after two or three drinks, Frank would check out of reality. Tonight, he was on number five and showed no signs of slowing down. Harry often thought of Frank as a fuck-up. This was why he never brought

241

him onto any type of job no matter how hard Frank begged. One time, Frank only wanted to ride in the passenger seat when Harry lifted a car. Harry even turned him down for that, mainly because he feared the wrath of Lisa.

Harry saw Max's head lift up off Lisa's lap and look toward the door. He followed the dog's gaze and saw Sophia coming into the tavern. She saw them and came over. She gave Harry a quick hug and then went over and embraced Lisa and Frank. The three of them started to cry. Max settled on the floor and Harry downed the rest of his vodka and cranberry. Maybe he should've had all of them over to his house. People at the bar and other tables were wondering what was going on. Harry never liked being the center of attention and this was making him uncomfortable.

Finally, Sophia disentangled herself from both of them and sat next to Harry. She asked, "How is Madeline doing?"

"Terrible," sniffed Lisa. "Their kids are ten and eleven, and the entire household is a mess. We stopped over there before coming here. Her mother and a brother are there with her now."

"Nobody knows what happened?" asked Sophia.

"Nope," said Frank. "They did finally find his truck. Police found it parked at a store five minutes from his house. The cops think somebody grabbed him there."

Harry asked, "Frank, were you and Spanky doing any work for anyone odd or on the sketchy side?"

Frank downed his next shot. He wiped his mouth with the back of his hand and said, "Not at all. Except for a house we're working on over on Staten Island, all our current contracts are with schools or city government. As far as I know, none of our past customers are mad at us."

"Spanky into anything that would piss somebody off?"

"Jesus, Harry," exclaimed Lisa, "what the hell could he be involved in that would make somebody do that? There's being upset with someone and then there's psychotic. I could see maybe some people you come in contact with being sick bastards like that, but not Spanky."

Harry felt like cringing, but struggled to keep his face neutral. "There's nothing then?"

"When he wasn't at work, Spanky spent the time with his family," said Frank. "He coached the kids in sports, helped out in their church, and did all of that husband and father stuff. He often told me that he wished that we got a few more big jobs so we could hire more managers and not have to be so hands-on."

"Business been good?"

"Terrific. The last time I saw him was that rainy day we had – Tuesday. Right before we left, we both said how happy we were that things were going so well. That was the last time...the last time..." Frank couldn't finish. He wiped at his face with a napkin and picked up his glass. Realizing it was empty, he put it down. Harry waved over to Art to bring some more.

Sophia asked, "Any word on the services?"

"The viewing will be Sunday afternoon and evening. The funeral will be on Monday," answered Lisa.

Looking at Harry and taking his hand, Sophia asked, "We're going to go, aren't we, Harry?"

"Definitely. I have plenty of time coming. I'll take Monday off." Looking at Frank, he asked, "Are Madeline and the kids taken care of?"

"Yeah, a few years ago as we became bigger, we had a financial guy come in and we reworked our partnership agreements, insurance, and all of that stuff. Technically, Madeline is now my partner, but I think I'll get enough money to buy her out if she wants. We'll do all of that stuff next week sometime. I just know that's not a worry."

Art came over with another refill on the drinks and a glass of red wine for Sophia. "Hey, Frank, I just wanted to say how sorry I am about Spanky. He seemed like really good people whenever he was in here with you guys."

"He was. Thanks, Art."

As the ex-football player walked away, Harry raised his drink and said, "To Spanky."

The other three said, "To Spanky," clinked glasses and drank. As they put them down, Lisa said, "Honey, let's head home. You look beat."

"Yeah. It was hard being at work yesterday and today. Everyone was in shock. The crew all liked him." Frank sniffled and stood. He wavered a little and said, "Thanks for asking us over, Harry. I needed to get out of the office."

Harry and Sophia stood and took turns embracing Frank and Lisa. When Harry hugged Lisa, he asked, "Are you driving home?"

"Of course, you know who holds the liquor in this family." She was right; Harry could never recall seeing Lisa anything more than slightly buzzed, and she could keep up with the best of them. She straightened up and said, "Harry, I know what kind of crowd you hang out with sometimes. I don't know if you can, but if you can find out anything about what happened, please do. Those sons-of-bitches that did this need to die."

Harry nodded and watched the two of them leave Art's. He flopped back in his chair and felt drained. When Sophia sat back down, she said, "Harry, that is absolutely the worst. What could've happened?"

"Who knows, Soph. Unless we find out Spanky was into something nobody had any clue about, it could be something as simple as mistaken identity. Some asshole thought he was somebody else. If they did torture him and they found out they had the wrong person, they'd have to kill him anyway."

"We live in an ugly world, Harry," said Sophia.

"You got that right." He waved over to Jeannie, who was waiting on the tables in the vicinity. When she came to the table, she greeted Sophia. Harry asked, "What are the specials today, darling?"

Harry Hid It

"Fish and chips, lobster ravioli, and stuffed pork chops. You guys hungry?"

"I am," said Harry. "I didn't eat much today. I'll have the pork chops. Sophia?"

"The ravioli sounds good," she said.

"Bring that, another glass of wine for Sophia, and a plain hamburger for his lordship," said Harry pointing to Max.

"It will be a few minutes," said Jeannie as she headed to the kitchen.

"Harry, I know we don't talk about it, but I think if you need extra money, you should just find a better paying job than the airport or fix more cars on the side. I don't want you to do anything else that might be a little outside the law."

His face showed surprise. This topic rarely came up. "What brought that on?"

"I don't want you to end up like Spanky. Even if he were grabbed by accident, there are crooks out there who hurt people like this all the time. All you have to do is read the newspaper and you see people being killed around here every day. Two people were shot 'executioner style,' as the papers say, in the Bronx the same day they found Spanky. I don't want you dead."

"I'm not crazy about it either," smiled Harry. He thought about the kidnapping escapade on Wednesday night. He realized he could say this to Sophia for the first time without lying. "I'm not doing anything wrong now and won't be. As for extra money, I'd like to get into restoring some classic cars. Last time I talked to my brothers, they said they'd invest in something like that."

"We haven't seen them since last winter," said Sophia.

"Tell you what," said Harry, "I'll call Johnny and see if he can get us a couple round-trip tickets for next week. We'll go down to Florida on Thursday night and come back Monday. We can make it a long weekend. After hearing what happened to Spanky and going to his funeral, I think we could both use a break."

Harry's brother Johnny lived in Florida around the Miami

area. His other brother lived out in Lake Ronkonkoma and they both worked in the airline industry. Harry could often get free travel to wherever he needed it. It seemed like a very good idea to get out of town for a while.

"Oh, that's a great idea," Sophia squealed. "Let's do it."

They talked about what they could do for a few days down there. Harry was fine hanging out at South Beach and spending some time bumming around. Maybe he could check out some fishing boats and get an idea of what they cost. He still had to break it to Ozzie that they were done with any more jobs. Harry could see doing one or two in a year or so if he still needed some cash for getting out of New York for good. Until then, he would just jump out of airplanes or go scuba diving for his thrills. Maybe he would learn how to pilot a plane. He always wanted to do that.

He and Sophia continued chatting when their food came. Harry realized that if he could move to Florida permanently, Sophia would want to come with him. He wondered what that would be like. Would they get married? The thought didn't scare him, but he tried to think if he could stay with her for that long. One thing Harry liked about Sophia was her family. He liked that feeling of normalcy when they were all together. If they moved, they'd be getting away from that. Then Sophia would be spending more time with him without her sisters, parents, and about a thousand cousins around. It would be something he would have to give considerable thought to over the next couple of years.

Harry did give a small smile. If he decided to ask her to get married, he could design a hell of a nice ring with all the diamonds and gems he had stashed. He was imagining what kind of a bauble he could come up with when he felt someone stop at their table.

"Harry Strickland! Fancy meeting you here!"

Looking up, Harry saw Agent Karyn Dudek looking down at him with her hands on her rather shapely hips. She was dressed in a short leather skirt that stopped at mid-thigh, heels that called attention to her muscular legs, and a violet sleeveless blouse that advertised her toned arms and ample cleavage. Her dark hair hung loosely to the top of her shoulders and she had a big smile. Harry could see that the smile didn't touch her eyes.

What the fuck was this about? He saw Sophia looking at him, wondering who the attractive woman was that interrupted their dinner. Harry cleared his throat. "Uh, Sophia, this is Agent Dudek of the FBI. Agent Dudek, my girlfriend, Sophia."

Sophia reluctantly took the offered hand. "Where do you know Harry from?" she asked.

"There were some thefts at the airport I was investigating," said Karyn. "I met Harry when I was looking through his area. An old friend wanted to meet me here tonight. Just as I pulled up, he texted to say he couldn't make it. Since I made the trip, I thought I might as well come in for a drink."

"She's a good bullshitter," Harry thought. Aloud he said, "That's a shame, Agent Dudek. Have you been in this area before?"

"Quite a bit lately," she answered. "Please call me Karyn. I'm off duty."

"I'm sure you are," said Harry dryly.

"I don't want to bother you anymore. I was just surprised to see someone I knew here. You both have a good night," said Karyn as she walked over to the bar. She perched up on a corner seat so that she could still see their table. Sophia went back to her meal. When Harry glanced over at Karyn, she smiled widely at him and gave him a little wave.

As he tried to eat the rest of his pork chop, Sophia hissed at him, "Do they make all the FBI agents that pretty?"

"No, most of them have a bad case of five o'clock shadow," said Harry. "You can't be jealous of her, can you?" One fault of Sophia's is that she didn't take kindly to Harry flirting with another woman, or a woman coming on to him. Even though

Karyn did nothing but say hello, Harry knew how Sophia's mind could take off on that.

"Please, Harry, you should know me better than that. I'm more interested in why the FBI is interested in you. What have you been up to?"

Harry put his fork down and sighed. He didn't feel like eating the rest of his dinner. It was funny how life worked. He felt sky high on Wednesday after finishing the quickie kidnapping and bringing in a bunch of money. Then Frank told him about Spanky yesterday and now this tonight. He finally slept for a couple of hours last night, but he was still so bloody tired. He wasn't so sure he if he was up to any verbal sparring tonight with Sophia or anyone else.

"It's like she said, Soph. Stuff was going missing at the airport. You know how they are with security there if anything happens. Her and a bunch of other feds spent several days questioning everybody. I still don't know what they were investigating or if they ever found whatever they were looking for. All I know is that I'm exhausted and I don't want to play twenty questions."

Sophia looked at Harry and then her expression softened. She put her hand on his. "I'm sorry, Harry. I guess this whole thing with Spanky threw me for a loop. Then seeing how upset Frank and Lisa were didn't help. Having a sexy thing come up to you wasn't a help."

"Did you think she's sexy? I hadn't noticed," said Harry with a sly grin.

She slapped his hand. "You never shut it off, do you, Harry?"

"You wouldn't know what to do with me if I did." Harry sat back and finished his drink. "So you still want to go to Florida with me for a few days?"

"Sure, Harry, of course I'll go. It would feel good after doing the viewing and funeral. So you think Spanky just ran into the wrong person at the wrong time, or something like that?"

Harry looked off in the distance. In his peripheral vision, he saw Karyn Dudek drinking a beer. "I really don't know. It's a travesty what happened and I hope they catch whoever did it."

"Me too. I need to go to the ladies' room." She stood up. "I'll be right back. Then we can go back to your place for a while."

Sophia walked away. Max wrestled himself up into a sitting position next to Harry. He looked at the dog and said, "I'm not sure what's going on, Max, but I don't like it. I can't help feeling that Spanky bit the dust because of me." He wondered if Fat Tony had somehow gotten a line on the truck they used when they hit the club that night. There were still people in the parking lot when John and Ozzie showed up. If only that stupid fuck had just stolen a truck instead of borrowing Spanky's. Here he was about to give up a life of crime and he had to watch over his shoulder constantly. Florida was sounding like a better idea all the time.

As he continued patting the dog's head, he caught Jeannie's attention. He asked for the bill and then he called her back over. He gave her some instructions and borrowed her pen and a piece of paper. When she came back, he gave them back to her along with a handful of money. As Sophia came back into the room, Harry stood up and snapped the leash onto Max's collar. He said good-bye to Art and Jeannie, and even gave a friendly wave to Agent Dudek.

Out on the sidewalk, Harry put his arm around Sophia and walked her to her car. She would drive to his house while he walked home with Max. Her car was too small for both him and the dog. Besides, it was a nice late summer evening and he found that he had an awful lot to think about.

Inside Art's, Karyn finished what was left of her hamburger and signaled for her check. The big black man behind the bar walked over to her and laid down a piece of paper. She scrambled to get up and get herself together to see where Harry was going. Instead of a check, she saw that she was holding a handwritten note. It said:

Harry Hid It

Dinner's on me. You must be tired after following me most of the week. I am too. I'm going home, having sex, and then going to sleep. You should do the same.

Harry

PS – Leave a nice tip. These are good people.

Chapter 26

"DAMN, DID I PUSH it?" Karyn asked her boss.

Assistant Director Enrico Gonzales perched on the edge of his desk and looked down at Agent Dudek. He held the note she received at the bar. He knew she was upset, but he couldn't help himself from chuckling. "The man has got chutzpah; you have to give him that."

"When did you turn Jewish?" Karyn asked.

"Been in the city too long. It rubs off on you," said Gonzales. "Any idea how long he knew you were following him? Or do you think he just assumed that by you showing up at his local watering hole?"

"I think he knew. It's how he mentioned 'most of the week.' I have no idea when he caught on to me, but now I'm wondering how much I saw when following him was real."

"Did you ever think that he has nothing to hide?"

"Constantly."

"Did you keep following him all weekend?"

"Off and on. I actually took him at his word and went home Friday night. Saturday he went into Queens and worked on someone's car in their driveway. Sunday, he and his girlfriend went to the viewing of their friend that was killed this week. Today, I watched the funeral from a distance. I even took photos of everyone at the cemetery as if I were in an episode of *The Sopranos*. Didn't they do that whenever someone died or was rubbed out in the mob?"

"You'll have to ask the organized crime division about that. Find out anything?"

"Absolutely nothing. The same people I saw out in the Hamptons showed up. There were many other people, of course. Harry seemed to know many of them, but it was those same people that he hanged with. It was a very sad funeral. I guess the murdered man had a family and little kids. Are we working on that?"

"Right now, only in a cooperative manner with the town police and the state police. They're lead on this. As far as I know, they don't know anything yet."

"Does anything happen around here that we can solve?"

"Not lately," said Gonzales. "Have you seen any reason to continue with Strickland on the jewel thefts?"

"No," admitted Karyn dejectedly.

"I've been through your reports. If there were anything I could've suggested, I would have," said the assistant director. "I'm not going to pull you off it, though."

Karyn looked up at him in surprise. "Really?"

"Yeah, I don't know what else you could've done. I want you to delegate the background checks you're doing on your suspects at the airport. I'll give you the new agents you used in your surveillance work this week. They can learn doing that grunt work."

"I can do that. What do you want me to be doing then?"

"The kidnapping in Huntington needs to be closed one way or the other. The bad guys did get a hell of a lot of money."

"Why do you keep giving me these weird ass cases? The victims give up almost a million dollars and nobody seems to give a shit. I'm sitting there and she delivers him divorce papers. I believe that he did tell the kidnappers to go ahead and kill her. He struck me as that kind of scumbag."

"I get that, but this office is getting a ton of pressure right now from D.C. Between the city and Long Island, there's been more crime this summer than the past five years. We need to close some of these cases. We need to do something big pretty soon, or I'm out of here." Karyn's eyebrows shot up. "Oh yeah," said Enrico, "that's how they're tightening the screws right now. Get to the bottom of something, Agent Dudek."

He dismissed Karyn, who went back to her desk. She saw

that it was getting to be close to five o'clock already. Part of her didn't mind giving up on Harry Strickland. It was getting weary. Besides, she didn't think much of his girlfriend. He could do so much better. "I must be getting catty with lack of sleep," she thought. Karyn decided that she would spend one more hour at work and then go home and get a good night's sleep. Maybe she would even stop tonight for a drink or two. She was also starting to weary of acting like a nun lately.

For some reason, it got under her skin when Harry told her on Friday that he was going to go home and have sex. Karyn had been in a grumpy mood all weekend. If she were honest with herself, she had to admit that she didn't want to see Harry with Sophia or whatever her name was. Besides, if he knew she was following him, why bother? She was mad at herself for barging into the bar like that. She thought that maybe she could unnerve Harry by surprising him. She knew she was running out of time and wanted to try to force him into doing something stupid. Apparently, the only one who became unnerved from that encounter was her.

Her gut feeling didn't go away about Harry, but it was starting to fade. Maybe it was time to think about a different career. Maybe go to law school and finally make some big bucks. Whenever she divided how many hours she worked a week by her salary, the amount she made per hour depressed her. It sucked being a civil servant sometimes.

Karyn checked her emails. She saw that Gonzales had assigned her permanently the three agents who followed John, Ozzie, and Frank last week. She sent them all notes detailing the airport investigation and divided the list of people on whom she wanted in-depth background checks. She also threw in the entire IT department. Their computer system had more holes in it than Swiss cheese. If there were anyone who could figure out when valuables were coming into JFK and be able to cover their tracks, it would be that geek squad. For all she knew, they threw up all the notations of who accessed the cargo manifests as red herrings.

They might've even faked the one that made her zero in on Harry Strickland.

When she finished, she went from that unsolvable matter to the kidnapping. It was like going from the frying pan into the fire. Out of all the interviews connected to a crime she conducted since joining the FBI, the one with Mr. and Mrs. Dean took the cake. She tried to figure out how best to proceed. For a brief moment, she thought about figuring out exactly where William Dean obtained all that cash he handed over, but she figured that might lead her down rabbit holes she didn't want to travel right now. Karyn had a feeling there was a lot to William Dean that might lead to other investigations. For now, she needed to concentrate on the kidnappers.

The only thing she had to go on was that there were two of them. The one Mrs. Dean interacted with was on the tall side and was nice to her. The other was a total mystery. It could've even been a woman for all she knew. Sarah Dean said that the driver grunted and that was about it. The other thing she had was the van.

It was blue. As she went through the miniscule file she started, that's all she had on the van. It was a blue van with no windows in the back and no seats. Chief Staats had checked all the city cameras and any businesses that may have surveillance pointing out to the streets. In the time period they were looking at during that night, he could find nothing helpful to send her. In most kidnappings, the FBI did everything to slow down the ransom process in order to get some kind of fix on the kidnappers. This kidnapping was shorter than a Kardashian marriage.

Karyn tried to put herself into the heads of the kidnappers. "If I were going to kidnap somebody and use a vehicle, I wouldn't want it traced back to me," she said aloud. "I'd steal one."

Going back to her computer, she did a search for vehicles stolen in the area for the week before the kidnapping in the city or on Long Island. Her eyes widened at the size of the list. "Christ, more cars are stolen than are bought in a week's time," she thought. She changed the search parameters and started with the date of the kidnapping itself. She methodically went through the list to see if any stolen vehicles were vans. For all she knew, the kidnappers gave it a quick paint job before heading out that night.

She was almost through the list of Mercedes, BMW, Lexus, and the three eighteen-wheelers stolen that day when she saw a listing for a blue van. It was reported missing from a mall that evening and found the next day at the shopping center directly next to the mall. Maybe kids stole it and dumped it. She expanded the report and saw that no damage was done. The owner wasn't sure what mileage was on the vehicle or how much gas was used, to get an idea how far the thief had driven it. No security footage from the mall showed anything.

Karyn was about to dismiss the entry when the name of the mall rang a bell in her head. Then it dawned on her. She quickly pulled out the file on the jewel thefts. Paging through it, she found the report from Agent Wills. Looking up the number, she called him. When he answered she said, "Charlie, this is Agent Dudek."

"Yes, ma'am, what's up? Is this about the people you want me to check on at the airport? I just got your email."

"I'm not old enough to be a ma'am," she wanted to say. Instead, "When you were following Ozzie Marcos, you said he went to the movies. Did you go in after him?"

"No, I didn't think that would be a good idea. You told me not to be seen. Besides, it's one of those places with twenty-two screens. I waited outside the theater forever for him to come out. He must've left one movie after it finished and went into another."

"Is there a back door to the place?"

"I did go look," said Wills. "There was no other entrance except the one in the mall, but there were several emergency doors along the back."

"He could've left and come back that way without you knowing then?"

There was silence for a minute. "Uh, yeah, but why would he do that? He'd have to know that he was being followed."

Karyn thought, "Or someone told him that he was being followed." To the agent she said, "Just following up on an odd hunch. Go do the JFK stuff tomorrow. I may put you back on following Marcos. I have to check out a few things."

She hung up and sat back. An awful lot that was happening didn't make sense. Maybe she was so desperate that she was looking for connections where they didn't exist. Most criminals have a pattern. Thieves stole, kidnappers kidnapped, and home invaders broke into homes. The fact that crooks had a certain affinity for carrying out their jobs in a consistent way is what usually led to their downfall. That or they bragged about their crime and got busted for sheer stupidity. Could the same person have done the jewel heists and the kidnapping? Maybe the lack of a pattern was the pattern. Her peers would laugh at her for that one, but she kept coming back to the same basic problem – she had nothing else to go on except one man, his friend, and the timing of the kidnapping.

Karyn got up, ran outside, and got a large cup of coffee from Starbucks. For the hell of it, she was going to look at crimes over the last six months in the area. She would concentrate on ones that were still unsolved. If she were connecting threads, maybe she could find a few more and begin making a web out of them.

***

Fat Tony glared at Sean Riley. "That's all you found out? One fucking name? I read the reports – you really tore that guy up."

"I know, boss. I thought he was just holding out. As it got near the end, I began to realize that he really didn't know anything. Anybody would spill his guts out with what I was putting him through. He was crying like a baby. I almost shot him to put him out of his misery."

Harry Hid It

"When did he decide to talk?"

"It wasn't like he decided," said Riley. "He was about to die, when all of a sudden he got this look of serenity on his face. With all the screaming and yelling he had been doing, he quietly said, 'Ozzie, that son of a bitch, he borrowed my truck that one time.' Then he died. I left him there and made sure I got out without leaving any trace."

"According to my police contacts, you did that well. They have no idea who did it. Apparently, the guy led such a clean life they're baffled as to why this happened to him. Now, did you just sit around with your head up your ass while I was in Atlanta?"

"No, Mr. Russo, not at all. I started to make some inquiries if anybody knew an Ozzie. I've been running down any leads I can find, but it's been slow. Can I maybe have a couple more men to help?"

The chair moaned as Fat Tony leaned back and put his hands behind his head. He looked sightlessly at the ceiling as he thought. He had been to a meeting in Atlanta that would kick-start his business again, but it would help if he put this matter to bed first. If he successfully negotiated all the details of the deal, he'd be back in the black three weeks from today. As much as he was starting to get desperate for some positive cash flow, getting his reputation back meant a great deal in the city. He wanted to be the biggest drug broker on Long Island, but that meant he needed the respect of the Russians and the Mexicans. Right now, they were all laughing at him about the way a few men came in and stole his money. It didn't help that his former employee shot his kid in the process. If he didn't fix this mess, he was done.

"Listen, Riley, I'm going to lay it out for you. When I was down in Georgia, I arranged for a huge shipment of meth to be transported here in a few weeks. I put the rest of my money into it. What I'm going to be busy doing until it gets here is arranging buyers. That's not going to be easy after that fiasco that went down here in the club, but I'll appeal to their greed. I'll have a great deal of product at a discounted cost, and they'll show up. However, it will greatly enhance my reputation if people know that I do not suffer fools easily. You need to find out who this Ozzie is, if he was there that night, and who was with him. Then I want everyone to know how each one suffered greatly before dying. That should take care of anyone else who might think about crossing me."

"Does that mean I get some men to help?"

"Yes, but I still don't know how those people knew to crash here that night. I don't know if someone here was mouthing off or if it was those fucking Orientals I sold the stuff to. Do you know people outside my organization that you can use?"

Thinking for a few moments before replying, Riley said, "I do know a few. One is actually a woman."

"A woman," roared Fat Tony. "I don't need no broad getting involved with this. Got it!"

"Yes, sir, whatever you want," quickly replied Sean Riley.

"Pay them the usual rate. Anybody who gets a solid lead that pans out will get a ten thousand dollar bonus. Point out that time is at a premium and I don't care about tactics. My wife is already mad at me for the death of our son, and I really don't want to go into retirement and have to listen to her every day. Understand?"

Riley nodded. "Sure do, boss."

Fat Tony continued, "And Riley, you know how I deal with people who do not perform well."

Sean gulped. "Yes, I do. I'm very clear on that, Mr. Russo."

"I also reward." Tony reached into his pocket and pulled out a wad of hundreds. He peeled off fifteen and gave them to Riley. "You did good. I'm sorry the poor bastard didn't actually know anything about that night, but you can't make an omelet without breaking a few eggs."

"Thank you, Mr. Russo. We'll find these guys."

"You better. The clock is ticking."

Riley turned and went out of the office. He pulled out his

phone and called the men he thought he could trust. He told all of them to meet him at a small bar he knew not far from the club. It was nearing nine at night when all four of them were seated at a table with a pitcher of beer between them. Sean mapped out what had happened, and why they were looking for an Ozzie.

He concluded, "I was beginning to think the ones who attacked the club were from out of town. Obviously, the owner of the truck they used knew one of them. I have to imagine that at least he's local."

"We could really use Christine to help on this," said a tall, thin man with half of one ear gone. He spoke with an Irish accent. "My sister learned a lot when she worked intelligence for the boys in Ireland."

"The boss don't want no women," Riley said. "He said they're only good for fucking and having babies."

"Old school, huh?" said another at the table.

"Totally, and he's the one paying the bills. We don't have a lot of time. There's something going down in three weeks and he wants this cleaned up by then." He picked up his beer glass and said, "Success!" They all clinked glasses and drank down.

Chapter 27

CLIMBING FOUR FLIGHTS OF steps seemed very difficult this time of night. It was Tuesday evening and Karyn found out that Vicki Light had another class tonight, but it wasn't as long as her Wednesday offering. She managed to get here at 8:30, which was the time the class ended. She sat in her car waiting. She had retrieved a photo of Vicki from the school's website and was patiently waiting for her to come out. She needed to find out it Harry had been in her class last Wednesday.

When the clock was reaching nine, she got out of her car and went into the building. She trudged up the stairs wondering how many more wild goose chases she would go on before something paid off. It seemed as if it were a lot easier to crack cases in the west than in New York.

She found the classroom she wanted and turned the knob. The door was locked. Looking through the small window, she could tell there were lights on in the back. Her frustration got the best of her. She pounded on the door, shouting, "FBI. Come to the door now or I'll shoot it." As faces poked out from some of the other classrooms, Karyn flashed her credentials around. She realized she didn't really care if she caused a panic.

The door opened and a woman stood in front of her. She was Karyn's height, with hair that went past her shoulders, and was a little on the stout side, but very curvy. The white robe she was wearing highlighted her figure. Karyn thought, "Why a robe at school?"

"What the fuck is this FBI stuff?" growled the woman. "I'm in session with one of my students."

"Dressed like that?"

"I'm modeling for him. Who are you?"

Harry Hid It

Karyn put her ID in front of her face. "Special Agent Dudek of the FBI. I have a few questions for you."

"Concerning what?" the woman asked.

"Are you Vicki Light?" The woman nodded. "Can I come in?"

Vicki looked hesitant and then stepped aside. Karyn entered the room and realized it wasn't what she thought it would be. It was very large and it seemed that a series of drapes crisscrossed all over the room. "This is a classroom?" she asked Vicki.

"More like a studio. Sometimes I assemble the class in this outer room when I'm having group instruction. Usually, everyone gets their own little space and I talk to them individually as I try to help them. Planning on taking a class, Agent?" Vicki asked in a saucy voice.

"No, I'm inquiring about a student of yours, Harry Strickland."

"Lots of talent in that boy's fingers," said Vicki. "What do you want to know?"

"Is he a current student?"

"No, but Harry stops in from time to time to work here. I encourage my students to do that when they can. Especially the ones with talent."

"When was Mr. Strickland last here?" asked Karyn.

"Last Wednesday. He had a few canvases here that he was working on. Wednesday night classes this semester are small, so I let him set up in the back where he used to be when he took the class here. I didn't hear a peep out of him until the class was over. He didn't bother me or the students at all. He asked me to critique some of the work he was doing and then he left."

"He was here the entire time then?"

"Agent, he didn't leave my door until I was done with my students. I can't help you there."

"Sorry I barged in. I didn't mean to interrupt your work."

"Not mine; one of my students. He's starting to do some sketching with live models. The girl I usually pay to be here for that sort of thing was sick so I'm filling in. We got a late start.

Now if you would excuse me…" She escorted Karyn back to the door.

As Karyn was halfway into the hallway, she turned and asked, "Is Harry a good artist?"

Vicki looked thoughtful. "He really is. When he was in my class, he mainly did landscapes. Now he's branching into doing some stills of objects. I'm encouraging him to start doing people."

"Thank you," said Karyn. "You have a good night."

"You too. Hope you didn't terrify half the building screaming out 'FBI.' I'll hear about it tomorrow." She pushed the door shut behind Karyn with a resounding thud and engaged the lock. Then she went around a couple of curtains before entering the lit area. She shed her robe and stood under the lights naked and proud. Adopting a posture that made her breasts rise and stick out, she said, "You have all kinds of women after you, don't you?"

Harry was sitting on the stool behind the easel. He looked at her with an appraising grin and said, "You have no idea, darling. I had a feeling she would be back here to see if I was in your class last Wednesday. Clever way that you answered her question."

"I'll cover for you, Harry, but a girl has to watch out for herself. If I say that you were in the back corner and I didn't see you leave by the door at all, then they can come to whatever conclusions they want."

"I almost yelled out for her to come on back," said Harry, "but I didn't think this was the time to be cocky. As it is, I'm glad I didn't come over tonight in the Camaro. She might have spotted that in the lot and guessed I was here again."

"What would you have done if she came back here?" asked Vicki.

"Invited her to strip down and be in the painting with you. I could try for something a little more erotic than just one beautiful woman."

"You're making me blush, Harry." He could see no evidence of that and he was seeing the entire woman right now. "What would you want, a little girl-on-girl action? I'm an artist, you know, and not a stranger to that."

"Never had any doubt of that, Vicki. Maybe we'll talk about that for the next portrait. As for now, can you turn back around and go back to that pose you were in. Remember, this is from behind tonight."

Vicki grinned and turned. She put her back to Harry, but turned slightly so that she was in a slight profile. She put her arm up to hang her hand on a pole that ascended from the floor while angling her head so that her hair went down her bare back and almost touched her ass. Harry gave her a few directions to slightly adjust her pose and went back to work on the canvas.

***

The next afternoon, Agent Dudek dragged a corkboard over by her desk and started to pin up pictures and incidents related… or at least she thought they were related…to everything she was working on. She had pictures of Harry, John, Ozzie, Frank, and Spanky. She had notecards detailing the two gem heists that originated at JFK, the kidnapping, and an incident that she found yesterday right before she went to check on Vicki Light. She had added this additional one.

She discovered that a man owning a cash-checking operation had forked over a shitload of cash to a man whose accomplice had his wife and child hostage. Not exactly a kidnapping, but it was close. Karyn had contacted the detective in charge and found out they didn't have much to go on. The perpetrators wore ski masks. The one at the store was tall and fit, and the one who tied up and held the wife and kid hostage was short and stout. That could fit the description of the thugs at the Bamberger home. Unfortunately, that description and the ski masks were all that tied them together, but the similarity was worth noting. The other similarity was that all four of those jobs resulted in a great deal of money for the people that conducted them.

Harry Hid It

The detective running that case did tell Karyn one thing. Apparently, when the criminal at the house was trying to get the mother and son under control, the ten-year-old boy had given the man a hard kick in the testicles. He told Karyn, "It's a shame because he slapped the kid around after that, but the boy almost foiled the entire thing by kicking the guy in the balls. A little harder and he and the mother might have escaped. They weren't tied up yet when he did that."

Karyn went back through her notes of when she interviewed the Bamberger family on the gem heist. She found the quote from the son that one of the home invaders had roughed up. The boy said that the guy who started beating him said something like, "No kid is going to get the best of me again." Was the asshole who beat up on the teenager the one who the young kid kicked in the balls a couple weeks earlier? Again, it was far-fetched, but it was a connection.

The other thing these events all had in common was how the tall one was obviously in charge and seemed to go out of his way to make sure nobody got hurt. He yelled and threatened, but the closest he came to hurting anyone was when he held a knife to Bamberger's dick. Would he have really sliced it off if Bamberger didn't cooperate? From Karyn's point of view, it was a moot point. In her experience with men, they'd give up their own mother before they let anything happen to their penis.

The kidnapping still puzzled Karyn a great deal. She had gone over and looked at the van stolen from the mall. The owner used it to haul items he sold on eBay over to the post office. Since nobody connected it to a crime, the owner used it several times since it went missing. Of course, Karyn wasn't sure if it was used in the kidnapping and she didn't find anything to confirm or refute that suspicion. If only one of the Deans saw the license number. Too bad Sarah Dean was so intent on punching the shit out of her husband.

Karyn was sitting back and looking at the board when Gonzales came up to her desk. "You're thinking these are connected?"

"I can certainly imagine how they were," she answered, "but I've seen things that weren't really there in the past. I don't want to make that mistake again. I feel like a scientist with a good theory, but I need something to push it into the 'proved' category."

"Did your minions find out anything at JFK?"

"Yeah, nobody knows anything. They chased a couple of tiny leads concerning people's background checks. All they turned up was one affair and one employee sneaking off to the doctors to get ready for a sex change operation."

"Life is complicated," said Gonzales. "So where are you?"

"Look at that photo pinned up in the corner," directed Karyn. "I took that picture out in the Hamptons. I circled Harry and the Ozzie guy. They are the tallest and shortest of their little group. The description of the two people involved in the cash-checking crime and the Bamberger theft was that one man was tall and the other short. In the diamond theft and the kidnapping, the one person anyone saw was tall. I know it's not much to go on, but it could be those two."

"Karyn, you're missing something. It's called proof!" Gonzales' voice rose in volume on the final word.

"I know, I know," she said. "Look, sir, Harry is a cool customer. I don't think he would crack if we waterboarded him and stuck hot wires under his fingernails. However, if Ozzie were the one who went off on the kids in two of these incidents, then he might talk. I've told two of my men to finish up out at the airport tomorrow at noon and then follow Ozzie. They have instructions to make sure he can see them. I'm thinking we can make him nervous and see what he does. If he tries to rabbit, we'll pick him up and ask him why he's running."

"Why you waiting until noon?"

"They're finishing up interviews. After that, I'm just keeping Agent Burroughs on the airport people for now. She can handle what's left. I don't think there's anything there, but we'll go through all the steps before we write it off completely. Any suggestions for me?"

"No."

Karyn looked at her supervisor. "What's wrong, sir?"

"I'm going to tell you what I told a few of my key people, Agent Dudek. If this office doesn't have some kind of success soon, the bureau will be making wholesale changes up here. We need a big score to satisfy the brass and the politicians. I don't care what it is at this point. Keep working your cases. Push where you need to. Keep me informed."

"I will, sir," she said to the retreating man's back.

Turning back to her board, she said, "There has to be something here. There has to!"

***

Riley walked into Fat Tony's office with a feeling of trepidation. It wasn't fun to go in and talk to your boss and worry about getting killed if he wasn't happy with what you said. As usual, Tony was in a bad mood. A half-eaten sandwich was on the desk in front of him and he was yelling into the phone. "You and your boys would be doing yourself a disservice not to get in on this deal. The price is sweet and if you don't buy in, then your competition is going to undercut you. You'll be out of business."

Tony listened and motioned Riley to come forward. As he moved closer to the desk, Sean heard Tony say, "What the fuck are you talking about? We took care of that problem we had in the summer. There was a leak. I killed the leak." More listening. "We're getting closer to finding the fucks who broke in here. Don't worry, everyone will hear about it when they get theirs." Finally, after another minute of hearing the person on the other end, Tony shouted, "Fine! If you don't want to do business with me, your ass will be hanging out there in the marketplace, not me!" Winding up, he threw the cell phone against the far wall. It bounced off the wall but shattered when it hit the floor.

"You better have something for me, Riley. I'm having a hard

time drumming up business here. I need to show these shitheads out there that I'm back in control. What do you got?"

Riley looked at the shattered cell phone and cleared his throat. "Mr. Russo, one of my men may have gotten a line on this Ozzie. He's a two-bit hood who's done some small jobs for others. He's no brain, but he's usually the muscle or wheel man."

"He work for anyone in particular?"

"Doesn't seem to. He doesn't do any direct work for any of the big players around. He's the guy that others hire to help them when *they* do jobs for one of the bigwigs."

"Why do you think this Ozzie is the one we want?"

"One of the guys I hired went over to the construction company of the guy we killed. He was a co-owner. He's done construction work and went pretending that he was looking for a job. He started chatting up some of the people there. He told them Ozzie sent him over. Apparently, the guy who died and his partner were both friends with this Ozzie dude. They gave him a couple jobs driving different trucks to jobs."

"Is he still there?" asked Fat Tony.

"Nah. He kept fucking up. He'd go to the wrong site or show up late. Apparently, they let him go for good when he used one of their trucks to pick up a bunch of stolen computers and they found out he was selling them out of the back of the truck at a Wal-Mart parking lot. The one guy said he thought he was still friends with the owners...oops, owner now...but they never gave him anymore work. I guess he'd even been there begging for work when he was low on funds. They didn't give in. Sounds like he still pops in, though, to visit now and then."

"You got a full name on this dirt bag?"

"Ozzie Marcos."

"You know where he lives?"

"I have everyone working on it now," said Riley. "In fact..." His voice trailed off as his phone received a text. "Excuse me, Mr. Russo, this is one of my guys now."

Fat Tony fumed impatiently as Riley read his message. "We got his phone number. One of my other men reached out to a few people he worked for in the past and dug it up. Want me to go bring him in?"

"No, not here. I'd love to cut off his balls where my kid died, but I have to keep this place clean. It's been doing a good business and has built up again after the problem in the summer." Tony picked up the phone on the desk. "Can you come in here for a minute?"

Riley speculated on who Tony called, but he didn't have long to wait. Kevin Hook walked in and said to Tony, "What can I do for you?"

"My man Riley there needs a quiet place to ask somebody a few questions. I can't send him back to that old warehouse we have. The police are still hanging out there looking for answers about that other poor sap he questioned."

Hook brushed hair away from his face and shuddered. He heard about that on the news and received details through some other sources. "Mr. Russo, I urge you to do that kind of work somewhere that you're not connected to. There are layers of paperwork and ownership with these different properties, but that doesn't mean somebody can't find a link back to you. You shouldn't have sent them to that warehouse."

The flat of Tony's hand came down and rocked the desk. "If I want your fucking opinion, I'll ask for it. I need to clean this mess up and I don't have time to find some private place where Riley can do his work. Besides, I want to be there for this one. This could very well be one of the scumbags who robbed me that night." He raised his voice even higher. "Where can Riley take him?"

Hook turned even paler, if that were possible. He stumbled over his words for a few seconds and then found his voice. "W…w…we have that salvage yard near the Brooklyn–Queens border. There's also that cold storage facility in Rockville Centre.

We're going to renovate that for a legit business, but we're still getting bids from contractors."

Tony looked to Riley. "Take him to that one. Do it tomorrow. Soften him up and call me. If I can make it, I will."

Sean Riley looked at Kevin Hook. "I need the address for that place. I've never been there."

Kevin looked dejected, "Sure. Come by my office and I'll get it for you and a key." He turned and left.

As Riley started following, Fat Tony called out, "Hey, Sean, you know how you're going to find and grab him?"

Riley smiled, "I'm going to have him come to us."

Chapter 28

OZZIE'S PHONE RANG AS he was going into his favorite coffee shop. He looked at the display but didn't recognize the number. Stepping back outside, he answered it. "Hello."

"Is this Ozzie?" asked a man on the other end.

"Yeah. Who's this?"

"My name is Simon. I got your name from Billy Malone."

Malone was a man who lived in Nassau County that Ozzie had done some driving for in the past. The last time was about five months ago when Ozzie drove a car with questionable ownership down to Philadelphia to be delivered. "I know Billy. What did he say about me?"

"That you were a reliable man behind the wheel. And I need a wheelman."

"I'm listening," said Ozzie.

"There's this poker game that takes place over in Rockville Centre during the day. Bastards there cheated me. I'm going to take them down today. I had a driver, but he had an accident this morning."

"Who runs the game?" asked Ozzie.

"Some dickhead from New Jersey who's trying to move into the area. I want to send him back to Jersey. You want in?"

"How much?"

"Game gets big. Depending how many people are there, it can be anywhere between ten and twenty thousand dollars. I'll cut you in for thirty percent. All you have to do is drive me there and go like hell afterwards."

Ozzie gave it some thought. It was small potatoes compared to what he had been involved in lately, but it wasn't like he had seen a lot of that money. His girlfriend was always hounding him to go out and he needed cash for that. A few thousand bucks for an hour's work seemed like easy pickings. "Sure, what time?"

"Pick me up at noon from this Starbucks." He gave Ozzie an address on the outskirts of Rockville Centre. "You can get a car?"

"Sure. No problem. How will I know you?"

"I'm wearing a Yankees shirt and a Knicks hat. See you at noon." He hung up.

It wasn't unusual for Ozzie to pick up some odd jobs like this. It's how he lived most of his adult life. Harry was the only one that used him on a consistent basis, and that had to do more with friendship than anything else. If Billy Malone told this guy about him, then it must be okay.

Ozzie went back in to get his coffee and a corn muffin. Sitting at a small table eating, he kind of wished Harry would be a little freer with the proceeds from the jobs they had been doing. He had given Oz a packet of bills from the kidnapping job and said that he was sitting on another one for later, but everything else was going to wherever the hell Harry was hiding all the loot. For a few minutes, Ozzie fantasized about what he would do with a few hundred grand right now. Maybe he would take his girlfriend Donna to an island for a few weeks. They'd do nothing but eat, drink, and fuck. Then he could come home and buy a new car. Maybe get a small place further out on the Island or along the Jersey shore. He even thought about what kind of business he could invest in so he didn't have to steal cars or transport stolen merchandise anymore.

Ozzie trusted Harry since the guy had always looked out for him. He understood why he wanted to sit on the money and gems for a couple of years. Ozzie certainly didn't want to go back to jail. He spent almost a year inside and hated it. On the other hand, some of these little jobs he did were from contacts he had made on the inside.

When he finished eating, he got in his pickup and thought about where to go to find a car. He would steal one, of course.

Harry Hid It

You always did that on this type of job where people might see you. He was still kicking himself for not stealing one when they hit the Ocean Club. When he told Harry he had actually borrowed Spanky's truck, Harry had given him that "how can you be so fucking stupid" look. Ozzie hated when Harry looked at him that way. He knew he could screw up and he detested doing it in front of Harry. He knew that between that incident and beating up on a couple kids, Harry wasn't thrilled with him. That's why he tried so hard when they snatched the sexy broad from up in Huntington. He was getting worried that Harry wasn't going to have him help anymore.

Ozzie put it out of his mind and concentrated on finding a car. He wanted one that looked in good shape but wouldn't attract attention. He also needed to lift it from an area that didn't have cameras all over the place. That was the hardest thing about being a thief these days – dealing with the technology. One of the reasons Ozzie looked for older cars to steal is that there weren't as many bells and whistles to get through.

He drove to a Park and Ride that he knew about on Sunrise Highway. It was a parking lot where commuters would meet. A few people would park their cars there and then get in one car to continue their journey into the city. Ozzie had scoped it out the other week and saw there were no cameras around it at all. Since this was an afternoon gig, he could take a car and be back in plenty of time before the owner returned. He smiled at the brilliance of this and found a spot on the end to park his truck.

From his seat, Ozzie looked around the lot. His eyes lit on the vehicle he wanted. It was a 2007 Ford Edge. It looked in great condition and the small SUV made getting in and out easier when you were in a rush. It was also an easy car to get lost with in traffic. Everybody seemed to have an SUV these days. Ozzie grabbed the satchel he kept in the door of his truck and went over to the black Ford. Taking the appropriate tools out of the leather case, he quickly opened the door and disabled the alarm before it beeped more than once. Reaching beneath the dash he found the wires he was looking for and with a deft twist, he gunned the motor.

Sitting in the driver's seat, Ozzie pulled out of the commuter lot and headed for the Starbucks. He could feel his excitement building up along the way. It wasn't only the thrill of the job, but also the prospect of some extra pocket money that made him smile. This was going to be a good day.

Pulling up to the coffee emporium, Ozzie saw Simon standing in the front of the store looking around at the traffic going by. He was dressed exactly as he told Ozzie. Honking the horn, Ozzie lowered the passenger window and signaled to the man. Simon came over to the car and bent down. He looked through the open window and inquired, "Ozzie?"

"That's me. Get in."

Simon did so and Ozzie held out his hand. They shook and Ozzie pulled the car away from Starbucks. He said, "Where are we going and how is this going down?"

Simon told him where to drive to and said, "Very simple. You're going to stop by the main door where the card players enter. I'm going to go in, threaten the one goon they have for security, scoop up the money, and get out of there. I'll jump in the car, you drive us back to where you picked me up, I'll give you your cut, and we're done. Easy peasy."

"Sounds simple enough to me," said Ozzie. "They only have one guy there for muscle?"

"Yup. Like I told you, some lowlife who thinks he can make a name for himself here in the New York area runs it. The thing is that he cheats. He's not going to go far around here with that attitude."

"You got that right." Ozzie looked up at the large building looming up the block. "Is that it?"

"Sure is. See, you didn't even have to drive far. Pull up to that red door on the side."

Ozzie did so and said, "I'll be here."

Simon reached under his Yankee shirt and pulled out a 9mm Glock. He shoved it into Ozzie's ear and snarled, "Shut the car off, now!"

"What the fuck is going on?" yelled Ozzie. Simon whacked him in the temple with his gun. Ozzie saw stars and noticed two men running out of the red door and around to his side of the car. They pulled Ozzie's door open and yanked him out of the car. Holding both of his arms in grips of iron, they hustled him into the building. Just as his head was starting to clear a little, they smashed him face-first into a cement wall. Ozzie yelped as his nose broke and he felt hands patting him down. He felt himself relieved of the gun he had at his back in his belt and the switch-blade he always kept in his pocket. He felt the men turning him around. Then another blow to his head made everything go black.

When Ozzie woke up, he found himself naked and firmly strapped to a metal chair. He tried to clear his vision, but blood seemed to have covered his left eye. As his one eye cleared, he focused on his surroundings. The first things he saw were some kind of cables running across the floor and attached to where he was sitting. The other ends attached to a box plugged into the wall.

Looking around, he saw Simon, the two guys who grabbed him out of the car, and a third individual. This man was tall and wide. By the way the others stayed behind him a little, he must be the one in charge.

Ozzie spit out, "What the hell are you doing? What did I ever do to you?"

"Not us," said Riley, "but my boss thinks you're one of the assholes he's been looking for."

"Who's your fucking boss?"

"First of all, I ask questions, not you. Remember that."

Ozzie watched the man press a switch he was holding. Immediately, his entire body felt on fire as electricity surged through him. He strained against the straps holding him to the chair. He tried to cry out, but his mouth wouldn't move. After ten seconds, the man shut the juice off. If he weren't attached to the chair, Ozzie would've fallen to the floor. He hung there trying to get his breath back. One of the men made a face at the smell of burnt flesh that now hung in the air.

"You're here, Ozzie Marcos, because your name came up in a similar situation with a friend of yours. I think you called him Spanky. He was a brave man. He lasted for a long time. I feel bad about it, because I realized that he actually had no idea what I was talking about for most of the time." Riley grabbed Ozzie by the hair and pulled him up into a sitting position. "Do you know you were the last person he mentioned before he died?"

Ozzie heard the words but his brain couldn't put anything together. What did Spanky dying have to do with him in this hell? His head rocked back and forth with two hard slaps by the big man talking to him. The whacks actually cleared his head a little as he tried to see through his one good eye. The man walked away from Ozzie again and started speaking.

"I have good news for you. I'm not going to kill you. I'm just here to make sure you're in the right mindset for some questioning." He hit the switch again and Ozzie felt the tremendous pain flash through him. It felt like his hair was on fire. Oz tried to throw the chair over and realized through his pain that it was bolted to the floor. This time when the head goon shut off the current, Ozzie had passed out.

He felt like he was coming up through a dark and murky fog. He heard voices, but they sounded a mile away. The first thing he noticed was the stench. He must have relieved himself on this chair. He wanted to throw up, but he couldn't even do that. Ozzie stayed slumped over and tried to get his ears and eyes to work again. The voices became clearer.

"Jesus Christ, Riley, he shit all over himself."

"Sorry, boss, that happens when you run ten thousand volts through someone."

"Is he dead?"

"No, he should be coming around soon."

"Did you ask him any questions yet?"

"As soon as you said you'd be here, I only wore him down a bit. I thought you'd want that pleasure."

"Is this what you found on him?"

Ozzie could now distinguish voices. The one who had talked to him and turned on the electricity said, "Just that gun and knife."

He heard a clicking sound. It slowly dawned on Oz that he was hearing his switchblade opening and closing. The voice he didn't recognize said, "Nice blade. I think we can put it to some good use."

Ozzie willed his one eye to open. He seemed to be looking through a mist, but then things came into focus. He saw the fat man who was playing with his knife. His one eye widened. "Oh my God, it's Fat Tony. I'm going to die today."

***

Agent Charlie "Chuck" Wills didn't feel like calling Agent Dudek. He hated the fact that she seemed to think Ozzie Marcos had slipped away from him that night he followed Oz to the mall and the movie theatre. He sure as hell didn't want to tell her that he couldn't even find Ozzie today. She had him calling in every hour since two o'clock this afternoon to report in. Since it was almost ten at night, that equaled nine straight admissions of failure. He had been all over the places he knew Ozzie hung out at and had no luck. He called his contacts in the local police department and none of them had any record of picking up an Ozzie Marcos or even giving him a speeding ticket.

Chuck felt very tired. He spent the first half of the day chasing more ghosts at JFK Airport. Since he left there, he had beat the streets trying to get a line on Ozzie. He was just about to suck it up and call Dudek when his cell rang. It was a friend he had on the detective squad at Rockville Centre. "Hey, Chuck, you still looking for Ozzie Marcos?"

"Yeah, I am. Did he turn up?"

"In a matter of speaking. You out and about?"

"I'm in my car."

"Then come to this address." The detective gave it to Chuck.

"Can't you tell me what this is about?" asked Agent Wills.

"Not over the phone. You never know who has ears." The line went dead.

Chuck shrugged, put the address in his GPS, and followed the directions. As he approached a commercial street with many buildings lining it, he saw the telltale flashing of cop cars several blocks down. As he pulled to a stop, he saw at least eight patrol cars, several SUVs, an ambulance, and the coroner's van blocking the street. As he approached the yellow crime scene tape, a cop held up his hand to stop him. Chuck showed his ID and the cop waved him through. Making his way through the crowd of official personnel as he went through the building's door, Chuck saw his detective friend who beckoned him over.

"Did you bring a barf bag with you?" asked his friend.

"No, why?"

The detective gestured over to where CSI people were around a body and taking photos and examining the area for evidence. "Is that your Ozzie? The wallet near the body says it is."

Chuck Wills took in a deep breath and went in the direction of the body. What he saw made his insides turn to water. He wished there was something he could hold himself up with. The body was that of a naked man. He looked like he was face down, but then the upper torso was twisted on its side so the face could clearly be seen. Except for a cut over one eye, there wasn't much blood on the face. It was as if whoever did this wanted to make sure the body could be identified. It was Ozzie.

The face was the only part of the body that was relatively free of blood. The rest of Ozzie looked like he received a thousand cuts with a knife. His buttocks and back looked like it had been scorched away. As the coroner flipped the body on its back, Chuck lost it. He ran through the crowd and went outside. He went back to his car and threw up in the gutter. He heaved until there was nothing left. He leaned against the vehicle and tried to suck as much air into his lungs as he could. He opened the passenger door, reached in, and pulled out the bottle of water he had in the cup holder. He splashed a little on his face and drank a bit.

When his heart rate felt almost normal, he took one more big breath of air and dialed his phone.

A tired voice answered, "Dudek here."

"It's Agent Wills."

"Dammit, Chuck. Did you find him yet?"

"Yeah, I did."

Karyn heard something in the other agent's voice. Something that she didn't like. "Where are you, Agent Wills?"

"I'm in Rockville Centre. I'm in some industrial park. Ozzie Marcos is dead. He was killed. But it was more than that. He looked like he was burned and beaten and somebody tried to cut him up in little pieces. And…and…"

Karyn gripped her phone harder, "And what, Agent Wills?"

"And they cut his penis and testicles off."

Chapter 29

FRIDAY WAS BRIGHT AND clear. Karyn Dudek made her way through Kennedy Airport. She wasn't here investigating any crime this time, but to catch a plane. She was the last person on board the aircraft before the flight attendants closed the door behind her. She found room in the bin above her for her bag and she crept past two people to take her seat by the window. As usual, Karyn wondered how larger people manipulated their bodies into these tiny spaces. The Bureau, being cheap bastards, had their agents fly coach. At least the flight was only a little over two hours to Miami.

After sitting on the runway for a half hour, the plane finally took off. When allowed, Karyn took out her iPad and reviewed everything that she learned since last night. When Chuck Wills told her what happened, she told him to stay there. She jumped in a car and flew to Rockville Centre. The coroner had carted away the body, but the blood smeared everywhere gave her an idea of what occurred. Seeing the photos of Ozzie almost made Karyn lose her dinner, but she clamped her mouth shut and willed herself not to be sick.

When she got herself under control, she talked with the detective Agent Wills knew from the local police department. He told Dudek that all he knew is that they received a phone call at nine o'clock that something terrible had happened at this old cold storage facility. The patrol car that investigated found the body. After the cops in the car got their wits about them, they called the cavalry and everyone showed up. Chuck had called the detective earlier in the afternoon asking about Ozzie, so the detective returned the favor when they found Ozzie's wallet near the body. At this point, that's all he knew.

Harry Hid It

It was two in the morning when Karyn returned to headquarters. This was one coincidence too many. Why would two of Harry's friends die in such horrible ways within a week of each other? While she couldn't figure out how it connected with her investigations, something was definitely up. She told Agent Wills, who had returned with her, to stick with the police tomorrow and give her any updates on their investigation and what the autopsy showed. Karyn instructed him to offer the resources of the FBI to the police if it would help.

She then woke up the two other members of her team. Karyn told Agent Burroughs to stop with her work at the airport and told her to see what connections she could find between the two murders. Agent Smith was to keep an eye on Spanky's former partner in case somebody was coming for him. Karyn had no idea why that would happen, but it seemed like a logical chain of events. She wished she had someone to also track down John, but he seemed like a bit player in this drama.

Steeling herself, she called Assistant Director Gonzales at home. He seemed to have that veteran agent's ability to wake up instantly because he didn't even sound groggy when he answered with, "Agent Dudek, I really hope this is necessary."

"It is, sir." She filled him in on Ozzie's murder and the steps she was implementing.

When she finished, Gonzales said quietly, "Give me a minute." She heard moving on the other end of the call and figured he was heading out of his bedroom. Then he said, "Okay, it's easier for me to talk now. I agree there's some connection to these two murders, but I don't see how it relates to what you're working on."

"I don't either, but this might shake some birds out of the tree."

"How so?"

Karyn hesitated for a brief second, but then took the plunge. "I know Harry Strickland flew to Florida earlier this evening. When I heard about Ozzie, I did a quick search in the databases to see if Harry was doing anything unusual. His name showed up flying to Miami with his bimbo girlfriend and staying at a hotel in South Beach. I want to go down there and break the news about Ozzie to him. The cops are going to keep a lid on the identity of Ozzie for twenty-four hours at least. You know, that next of kin thing."

"Bimbo girlfriend?" said Gonzales.

"Did I say that? I have no idea why I said that," said Karyn. "Anyway, this might be my best chance to rock him enough for him to spill something. Or offer him protection if his friends are in trouble. Anything that will get us closer to what the hell is going on."

There was silence as Enrico Gonzales thought about what his agent said. It did make sense. When he was in the field, sometimes shaking up the suspect was the only thing that worked. "Okay, Agent Dudek, you can go approach him."

"Good, because I sort of already booked my flight."

Gonzales let out a noise of agitation. "Thanks for telling me your plans then," he said sarcastically.

"Sorry, sir."

"Fine. Don't forget, Karyn, that murder trumps thefts no matter how big they are. The same goes for kidnappings, especially when people are reluctant to report that it happened. I'll talk to the local and state police tomorrow morning and tell them of our interest in the murders. I'll see if we can get the lead on these. Nobody may mind if we head this up."

"Yes, sir, anything else?"

"Be careful. Somewhere in this mess are some not very nice people."

***

Karyn checked into the Marlin Hotel. Her room was very nice and looked out over the hustle and bustle of the street below. She stripped off all her clothes and took out something more appropriate to wear in South Florida than her navy blue pantsuit. She went into the bathroom and took a twenty-minute shower. She never had a chance to clean up before coming to the airport this morning. She barely had time to go home and throw some things together before catching her flight. Karyn also hoped the water made her look and feel more awake. She knew she was operating on fumes. A big part of her wanted to throw herself on the big bed in her room, but she knew she would sleep for hours if she did that.

After drying off, she spent more time in front of the mirror applying makeup than she usually did. She tried to convince herself that it was to hide the bags under her eyes. The honest part of her knew it was because she was going to talk to Harry. At least she would if she found him. It was important that she tell him about Ozzie. She hoped the word hadn't gotten to him yet in some way. She wanted to see his reaction on hearing the news.

Karyn learned from Harry's credit card that he and Sophia were staying at the Beach Paradise Hotel. She also saw on the computer that they flew down here on comp tickets. A little more research showed that Harry had a brother who worked for the airline they flew on, and that he secured the tickets for them. It looked like Harry had a brother who lived in Florida and another up in New York and they both worked with the airline industry in some way. Could they have a connection to the thefts from Kennedy? She wasn't going to worry about that now, but it was something to look into later.

When she was done with the makeup, Karyn stood back and looked at herself in the full-length mirror behind the bathroom door. She managed to hide some of her tiredness. She thought her body was starting to look better. She hadn't exercised worth a damn lately, but the hours she was putting in with work and the lack of drinking like a fish took about eight pounds off her frame in the past month. She liked how her breasts stood out a little and her curves no longer looked as if they were padded with fat.

She went back into the room, looked longingly at the bed, and dressed in a short denim skirt, striped tank top, and sandals. It was eighty-five degrees out and she might as well be comfortable. She made sure she had her gun, ID, and wallet in her small travel purse. Slinging it over her shoulder, she put on sunglasses and went looking for Harry.

It felt good getting out of the city and seeing palm trees. Many tanned and healthy looking people were walking the streets of South Beach as Karyn made her way to the beach. Harry's hotel was across the street from the Atlantic and she could smell the ocean as she walked toward it. Karyn was thinking that if she could scrape a few dollars together after this was over, maybe she would go escape to some island for a week.

The Beach Paradise Hotel was an art deco building like so many places in this area of Miami. It gleamed in the sunshine and Karyn could see a swimming pool in the back along with a large outdoor bar under a roof of palm fronds. She made her way into the lobby and walked through to the bar area. Stopping as she stepped back outside, she surveyed the pool and bar area. She didn't see Harry or his girlfriend. She went out a side gate and walked across the street to the beach. She propped her elbows up on the stone wall that separated the sidewalk from the beach and looked around. There was a good amount of sand between her and the ocean, with bodies lying out here and there. She didn't much relish walking around the beach looking for Harry.

She was wondering whether she should see if there was an unobtrusive place in the lobby where she could watch for Harry when she heard people passing behind her. A woman said, "Stop looking at her ass, Harry. I swear that's the only reason you come to the beach."

"No, it's not and I was looking at her legs. Stop it, Sophia. You know I look, but I don't touch."

"You better not, boy. Why don't you go wait for me at the bar? I need to call my sister. I have no idea why she's bothering me down here. Then we can head over to your brother's house."

There must have been a break in the traffic because the couple's voices faded away as they walked over towards the hotel. Karyn snuck a peek over her shoulder and saw that it was Harry and his woman. He was dressed in khakis and a light blue shirt while Sophia had on shorts and a sleeveless red blouse. Karyn found herself looking down and asking, "Was he looking at my legs? I think they look pretty good today."

When she saw the two going into the hotel, she went across the street and back to the bar by way of the gate. She perched up on a barstool on the corner of the bar that afforded her a view of the back door from the hotel that led out to here and the entire swimming pool area. A bartender wearing the smallest of bikinis over her ample assets came and asked her what she wanted. Karyn ordered a margarita on the rocks without salt. As she waited for the girl to prepare it, she saw Harry come outside. Karyn turned sideways so that the corner post of the bar holding up the palm roof would partially block her. Harry sat down three stools to the right of her. At the moment, his attention was on the girl behind the bar.

When the bartender brought her drink over, Karyn idly wondered if the girl's boobs were real. They were pretty spectacular one way or the other. Miss Bikini continued down the bar to take Harry's order. He asked for a vodka and cranberry juice. The girl giggled and asked if he wanted it on ice. When Harry answered he would take it any way she wanted to give it to him, she laughed again. When the young woman set Harry's drink in front of him, Karyn decided it was time to do this.

She took a gulp of her drink, closed her eyes for a second, and then got up and walked down to Harry. He was taking a pull on his glass when she said, "Don't you get enough of the beach at the Hamptons?"

Harry almost choked when he saw Agent Karyn Dudek of the FBI in front of him. Karyn thought that for the first time since she met Harry, he had nothing to say. She watched several emotions cross his face until he blurted out, "What the fuck are you doing here? This is harassment. You want me to call your boss

284

and ask him why I have to see your face a thousand miles from New York?"

"He knows I'm here, Mr. Strickland."

"Did he send you?"

"No, I sent myself."

Harry gave her a hard look. Then he let out a smile and said, "Then why are you here? The airport would tell you that I'll be back on Tuesday. I'm taking a long weekend."

"I wanted to come here to give you some news. Ozzie Marcos is dead."

It took a few seconds for this news to sink in. Karyn watched Harry's smile fade. Darkness came over his features and his eyes narrowed. That was about all of the reaction that Karyn got. She had been hoping for something more theatrical. The only other move Harry made was to down the rest of his drink. He put the glass back down on the bar firmly, but not in anger. Looking Karyn in the eye, he quietly asked, "How?"

"There was an anonymous tip last night called into the Rockville Centre Police. When they investigated, they found your friend cut up pretty badly and burned. The preliminary coroner's report I saw when I landed said Ozzie may have endured large amounts of electricity. They haven't determined exactly what killed him."

"Where?"

"Some cold storage facility in an industrial section of town."

"Who?"

"No idea. That's why I wanted to tell you personally. Any insight?"

Harry stared off at the pool. Karyn could almost see his mind working. He said, "I don't believe in coincidences probably any more than you do, Agent Dudek. This is too much like what happened to Spanky."

"That occurred to me too. You've probably guessed that I've been interested in you about the jewel thefts that seemed to originate at the airport. I will also tell you that I've made you a person of interest in a ransom case and a kidnapping. You know if I had solid proof, I'd have you in cuffs right now. What I can't figure out is how any of those crimes would lead to this. Can you enlighten me?"

"Agent Dudek, I have no idea what you're talking about. I told you before that I don't know anything about those jewel thefts, and I certainly don't know what the fuck you're talking about with those other crimes." Harry continued looking at Karyn as he said this while he beckoned the bartender to make him another drink.

"But you knew the two people who were tortured and murdered."

Harry blinked a little when she said this. Recovering, he said, "I know a lot of people in that neck of the woods. It's not my job to keep tabs on everyone. Ozzie was a good friend and I knew Spanky. I'm very upset by everything that you told me. But if you think I had something to do with this, you're crazier than I gave you credit for."

"No, Mr. Strickland, I don't think you had anything to do with what happened to them, but I'm trying to find out if you have any idea why they were killed. Was either of them involved with anything that would get somebody this furious with them?"

Harry shook his head. Karyn didn't believe him, but she let it go for now. He did ask, "How bad did Ozzie look?"

She hesitated. "I know he was a friend. I'm not sure if you're up for pictures, Mr. Strickland."

"I told you before to call me Harry. Show me. Please."

Karyn pulled out her phone and went to her email. She found the one she wanted and brought up the photos. She passed the phone over to Harry, who scrolled through the pictures. With each one, she saw that his face was getting tighter and tighter. He got to the last one and gave her back her phone. Through clenched teeth, he said, "Whoever did that deserves to die."

Karyn felt a wave of compassion go through her. "I don't disagree with that. Somebody is on the warpath and I don't know why. Nobody knows why. I want to put these bastards in jail forever."

"They don't deserve jail!" spat out Harry.

"I'm a federal officer. As much as there have been times in my career that I wanted to make like Bruce Willis in the *Die Hard* movies, I can't go around shooting people." She added in a much harder voice, "Neither can I look the other way if somebody ever did that. You understand me?"

Harry glared at her and softened his look. "I'm not asking you to, Agent Dudek. Right now, I feel mad, upset…dammit, I don't know what I'm feeling. The whole reason I wanted to escape down here for a couple days was to wash the taste of Spanky's funeral out of my mouth. The man led a righteous life. He didn't deserve to die; certainly not like that." He looked down at his feet. "Neither did poor Ozzie," he added quietly.

"Harry, you know I've been following you. You're definitely in my viewfinder for those crimes I told you about." She reached back into her purse and pulled out her card. "If you're in any danger and need help, call me. My cell is on there as well as the office number." When he went to take the card, she wouldn't let go until he looked at her. When Karyn was sure she had his attention, she finished with, "Remember, anything can be worked out. As my boss told me last night, murder trumps everything. I saw in person how these sick fucks left Ozzie. Every cop who was there wants to wipe the scum who did this off the street. I certainly do."

Harry nodded and took the card. "I have to process this, Agent Dudek. I have to admit, I'm in a bit of shock here."

"Don't blame you for that. And call me, Karyn. My flight isn't until tomorrow afternoon. I imagine you'll be heading north right away. Frankly, I'm too exhausted to even look for an earlier flight. If you need to talk, I'll be back in the office by tomorrow night."

Harry was just about to say something when they heard, "What the fuck is she doing here?"

They looked up to see Sophia behind Harry glaring at the FBI agent. For a fleeting second, Karyn felt like she was caught in a compromising position. She shook that off as stupid. She was doing her job. She looked at Sophia and said, "I'm here on government business, but I'm done for now." She reached into her pocketbook and threw some money on the bar for her drink. She looked at Harry. "I'm really sorry." Glancing over at Sophia, she said, "I'm sure you have stuff to talk about."

Karyn turned away from them and went back around the bar to exit by the gate. As she hit the sidewalk, she heard Sophia screech, "Ozzie, noooooooo!"

Chapter 30

HARRY LOOKED OUT AT the Atlantic. He usually marveled at how this was the same ocean he swam in up north. Out on the beaches of Long Island, the surf was usually rough and dark. Down here, it usually seemed as calm as a lake and you could see the bottom, even if you were standing in five feet of water. He leaned back on his elbows and thought back to some diving trips that he took off the Florida Keys. It was like swimming in an aquarium.

He looked at the moon rising in the distance in the twilight. Right now, he wished he could be swimming underwater and not ever have to come up. Ozzie was dead! He still couldn't get his head around that one. He was completely taken aback by seeing Karyn Dudek at his hotel's bar, but her news practically shut his mind down. He knew she made this trip to get a reaction out of him. He hoped he totally disappointed her.

The fight with Sophia didn't go well. They went back to their room after Harry explained what happened to Ozzie. Once there, she hit his chest with both fists and said, "This had something to do with that shit you and Ozzie and John are always doing, doesn't it Harry Strickland? Damn you, damn you, damn you!" He knew when she used his full name that he was on the losing end.

Whenever Harry tried to say something, she shut him off. Lying on the bed crying, she said, "Get the fuck out of here. Don't come back here tonight. I'll make my own way home." Harry stood in the middle of the room at a complete loss. He never saw Sophia so angry. Since he needed to think anyway, he threw his things in his bag. He left her airline ticket there and told her to use it or exchange it. He left and found a room in another hotel a block away. He wanted to sort things out before returning home.

Harry Hid It

The first thing he did was call his brother and explain that they wouldn't be coming over tonight. He truthfully said that a friend died and they were shook up by it. He explained that he and Sophia were going to find a flight to get back home. Both his brothers knew he had been wild when he was younger, but they thought Harry had settled down when he secured the job at Kennedy. Harry accepted his brother's condolences and hung up.

His next call was to John. The phone went so quiet when he broke the news that Harry thought he lost the connection. Then John said, "Fat Tony?"

"It's got to be."

John said, "When we were at Spanky's funeral it occurred to me that Ozzie borrowed his truck for that night at the club. I didn't want to jinx anything by saying it aloud, so I kept it to myself. It seemed a little too far-fetched."

"I thought that way too," responded Harry. "It's my fault they're dead. If I weren't so hell bent on revenge, they'd still be alive."

"Don't start that shit, Harry. Hindsight is 20/20. I'm not blaming Ozzie, God rest his soul, but if he stole a truck instead of borrowing Spanky's, they'd both be alive. That boy was never the brightest star in the sky."

"I know. And you're right; I can't waste time thinking that way."

"You think Ozzie gave us up to Fat Tony?" asked John.

"We have to assume he did," said Harry. "I saw the photos of what they did to him. Any of us would've talked."

"How did you see photos?"

"The FBI chick showed me."

"Huh?"

Harry explained about Agent Karyn Dudek showing up in Miami today. When he finished, John said, "This is some serious shit. The feds are looking at us and now Fat Tony is too. This is that between a rock and a hard place you hear about."

290

"It's a clusterfuck," agreed Harry.

"Any ideas?"

"Avoid the feds and kill Fat Tony before he kills us."

"Harry, we've been in fights, but neither of us has ever killed someone, especially in cold blood."

"We have money. Maybe we can hire someone to do it."

John lapsed into more silence. Finally he said, "That's an idea. How much time do you think we have?"

"Probably not a lot. It would be great to get some intel on all of this. I'm not coming home until tomorrow. Can you contact Cowboy? Tell him I'll double what I paid him before."

"Sure. I'll arrange a meeting tonight. I have to move Julia somewhere. I want to keep her safe. How's Sophia?"

"Doesn't want to talk to me. She thinks I had something to do with Ozzie dying. I'm sure she put Spanky in that equation by now."

"Not helping your guilt trip at all."

"Things have been strained with us for the past few weeks. This may have been the final nail in the coffin."

"Poor choice of words, Harry."

"True. Sorry."

"I'm going to get moving on this end. I have to tell Julia. It won't be pretty. Once she's safe, I'll set up a meet with Cowboy. I'd rather talk in person with him."

"I'll call you when I get back up there. Watch your back."

"You too."

Harry looked around the room and felt very claustrophobic in it. He put on his bathing trucks, threw on a cut-off T-shirt, grabbed a towel out of the bathroom, and headed to the beach. The sun was setting and the beach was sparsely populated. He put the towel down and ripped off his shirt. Kicking off his sneakers, he ran into the ocean and swam for about a quarter of a mile, staying parallel to the beach. He returned to where he started doing a quick backstroke. Harry needed to burn off some of the anxiety of learning about Ozzie and fighting with Sophia. Swimming seemed like the fastest cure.

Now he was leaning back in the sand and trying to remember past diving trips. Harry knew that giving his brain a rest and coming back to a problem gave him new insight on how to solve a problem. That didn't happen this time. He was still no closer to figuring out what to do about Fat Tony other than to hit him with a truck. Maybe hiring someone to take care of him was the way to go.

Harry didn't think of himself as a millionaire, but he realized that is what he was. He could certainly use some of Tony's money against the fat bastard. Not for the first time, Harry tried to figure out if Fat Tony would be this mad if they had only stolen a hundred grand or if his idiot son didn't run in front of the gun. Probably! After knowing what the sick son of a bitch did to Spanky and Ozzie, Harry thought he must be psychotic. Harry also knew that if he had that knowledge ahead of time, he still would've carried out his revenge caper.

That was the crux of it for Harry. It was his plan to take on Fat Tony that night. It all led to Ozzie's death. Harry knew he had to do something or he'd be looking over his shoulder for the rest of his life. Moreover, he would like that life to be as long as possible. He could just split up the money and gems with John now and they could both run and hide. That might be the smartest thing to do.

As Harry stood up and brushed the sand off, he knew that he wasn't one to run away from a fight. He'd certainly give John that option and would talk to him about that when he went home tomorrow. He certainly wouldn't think less of John. He had Julia to think of.

Back in his hotel, Harry stood with a towel wrapped around his waist after showering off the sand and the ocean. He was hungry, he needed a drink, and he didn't feel like staying in his room all night. He wanted to be out with people, even if it was watching others have a good time from a distance. Ozzie's death still didn't seem real and Harry wondered when it was really going to hit him. He and Ozzie were pals since middle school. Harry seemed to always be pulling Ozzie out of one scrape after another. He wasn't able to do it this time.

He looked over at the nightstand and saw everything he pulled out of his pants' pockets. On top of his wallet and money was Agent Karyn Dudek's card. Harry sat on the bed and looked at it. On impulse, he grabbed his phone and dialed her cell number. He was about to give up after five rings, but then a very groggy woman answered with, "Yeah?"

"Agent Dudek…Karyn, this is Harry Strickland. What are you doing for dinner?"

He heard movement on the other end and then, "Harry? Dinner? Where are you?"

"Still here in Florida. I'm heading back tomorrow. I need to eat and I thought company, even an FBI agent, was preferable."

"Don't you have a brother down here?"

"Sure, but I wouldn't be great company for him. Besides, I really don't want to talk to him about anything right now. Mind you, I probably won't be great company for you, but what the hell."

"Where's your girlfriend?"

Harry noted with amusement the way she said "girlfriend." It sounded like it was with a bit of derision in her voice. "Let's just say she isn't happy with me right now. For all I know, she's on an airplane going north right now."

"She took Ozzie's death hard?"

"Yeah, we all hung out. Anyway, we're in South Beach and you're the only person I know around here. You want to eat?"

"Sure. I have to get ready, but can meet you somewhere in an hour."

Harry thought for a minute. "There's a great Cuban place here. It's called Larios on the Beach and it's nearby on Ocean Drive. Think you can find it?"

"Hang on," said Karyn. He heard some clicking and then she said, "I see it on my iPad. It's only a couple blocks from where I'm staying. I can find it."

"See you in an hour then." Harry clicked off. He laughed aloud, which felt good in itself. His life was getting very dangerous and he was having dinner with the FBI agent who was trying to nail him for the jewel thefts. "Oh well," he said to the empty room, "you only live once. And she's a looker. Beats the hell out of drinking by myself tonight."

He put his khakis back on, but this time with a black buttondown short-sleeved shirt and loafers. Leaving the hotel, Harry walked around the streets to kill some time. As much as he tried to shut it off, he couldn't get those pictures Karyn showed him of Ozzie out of his mind. This would be slightly easier to deal with if Tony ended Oz's life with a quick bullet to the head. Torture was the sign of a very sick mind.

Giving up on the walking, Harry went to the restaurant. From the outside, it looked like a place you could find in Havana. The inside was beautifully decorated with a great deal of wood and soft colors. Harry went up to the hostess and gave his name to secure a table for two. Then he made his way to the bar and ordered a drink while he was waiting. He watched the various customers making their way to tables or hanging out in the bar area.

Just as he ordered another cocktail, he saw Karyn enter. She wore a simple black dress that flattered her figure and had more than one male looking her way. Harry put up his arm and waved. Karyn saw it, smiled, and headed toward him. He admired her walk and the confidence in which she moved. It was a quality he didn't find in too many women and one that he liked. The fact that she wanted to put him in jail almost added to the allure. This should be an interesting evening.

Harry stood as she came up and held the adjoining seat out for her. He said, "We have about ten more minutes until our table is ready. Would you like a drink?"

She seemed to appraise him and he had the feeling she approved of what he wore. She said, "As you pointed out on the phone, we are in South Beach. Tomorrow, we get back to reality."

"Sweetheart, you gave me as much reality as I can handle today. How about we call a truce tonight? I don't want to spend the evening verbally sparring."

She put out her hand. "Deal." As Harry shook it, she continued, "I was thinking along the same lines. I meant what I said when I left you before. I'm sorry for your loss. It's tough losing a friend, especially in such a violent manner. As for me, my brain is cooked. You woke me with your phone call."

"You wouldn't know it by looking at you," commented Harry. "You look great."

The FBI agent blushed. "Thanks. Let me see that drink menu." Harry handed it to her and Karyn ordered a chocolate martini. When Harry raised an eyebrow at the order, she said, "I usually drink whiskey neat, so give me a break. I'm a girl and I'm craving chocolate today."

They clinked glasses when Karyn's drink arrived. At that moment, the hostess came up to Harry and told him their table was ready. She escorted them to a table in the back corner of the dining room and laid menus down in front of them. As she picked hers up, Karyn said, "I was impressed when you mentioned this place. When I lived in Miami, I always wanted to eat here."

"When did you live here?" asked Harry.

"It was several years ago. My first assignment for the FBI was working out of the Miami field office. Then I went out west."

"What's a nice girl like you doing in the FBI?"

"My dad was a cop in Colorado. I graduated with a degree in criminal justice from Colorado State University. I thought I was going to become a lawyer when I took the FBI test for the hell of it. Apparently, I passed with flying colors and before I knew it, I was going through training at Quantico. I could already shoot, and they taught me everything else I needed to know. I became an official government ass kicker!" She smiled and sipped from her drink.

"What do you mean by saying you could always shoot?" inquired Harry.

"I grew up on a ranch. My father had me shooting a single-shot .22 rifle when I was six. In high school, my friends were cheerleaders or played soccer. I was on the shooting team. I was captain my senior year."

"You sound like you were a regular Annie Oakley."

"Not to brag, but I could shoot pretty good from a moving horse. We don't do much horseback riding in the FBI."

"Do you miss the west?"

Karyn opened her menu and thought for a moment. "I do. I love the wide-open spaces and the mountains. What you call mountains out here in the east are molehills. Being sent to New York City was actually a step back for me."

"How come?" asked Harry.

Karyn was horrified she just said that. She also was intrigued that Harry seemed genuinely interested in the answer. She meant to say to him that she didn't want to talk about it, but before she knew it, she told him the entire story. How she lost men under her, her jerk of a boyfriend, and how it led to her exile to a demoted position in New York. She finished with, "My boss seems to believe in me, so that's something at least."

A waiter came over and took their order. Harry realized that this woman was good at her job. He kind of guessed that when she started to focus on him in her investigations. He didn't know if inviting her to dinner made him the fox in the chicken coop or if he were one of the chickens. He smiled to himself a little as he thought, "Well, she's sort of foxy looking."

"What are you smiling at?" asked Karyn. Damn, that woman noticed everything.

"I don't know. How you shocked the shit out of me by showing up this afternoon and now we are at dinner together."

Harry Hid It

"Believe me, the irony isn't lost on me."

"You do look radiant tonight," said Harry. "Is the little black dress standard FBI issue?"

"I always travel with it. Doesn't take up much room in the suitcase and it's good for any number of occasions. Even having dinner with a potential suspect."

Harry toasted her with his glass. "For whatever reason, I'm glad you accepted the invitation."

"Harry, I don't know what's going to happen, but you aren't a jerk. I've taken down many scumbags in my time, but you don't fit in that category. Hell, I may be barking up the wrong tree with you. I've been wrong before. Anyway, enough of that. I don't want to break our truce. Let's talk about something else. How long have you been with Sophia?"

"You mean not counting today," said Harry ruefully. "I'd rather talk about the crimes you think I was involved in."

"I'm sorry. I wasn't thinking."

"Nah, that's fine. We've been together for four years now."

"You love her?"

"God, you're direct!" exclaimed Harry. "Why don't we just philosophize on what love is. Then we'll get drunk and never make it back home tomorrow."

"I don't like hangovers," said Karyn. "I've had a few lately."

"Drinking too much?" asked Harry.

"We're talking about you now. What is it between you and Sophia?"

Harry blew out some air and looked at Karyn. "You know, I've been asking myself that a lot lately. We have a great time together and all. I love her family. It's fun being a part of that and it means a lot to me, but this has been an odd summer. It doesn't seem to be as easy being together. So how's your love life?

Karyn snorted. "There is none. Except for drunk guys who hit on me at bars, there's been nothing since I got to the city. No real desire either."

"Been spending a lot of time in bars?"

"I was. I think I was feeling sorry for myself." It was Karyn's turn to toast Harry. "Thanks for giving me something to work towards."

"Glad you feel that way, even if you're so wrong. But you seem good at your job. You'll get it figured out."

"I'm damn good at my job. How about you? How did you end up at the airport?"

"I've always been good with mechanical things. I went to college for a year to be an engineer and got…uh, distracted. Things happened and I bummed around from garage to garage working on cars. My brothers work for airlines or airports and said I would make much better money working in that industry. I applied for a position and got in. I like it, but it's not what I want to do the rest of my life."

"What would you rather be doing?"

"Living down here in the perpetual warmth, buy a boat, and take people out on fishing or diving trips."

"I like the sound of that. You have things better planned out than I do."

"Is the FBI going to be your career?"

"I don't know," said Karyn truthfully. "For the hours I put in and the money I earn, I make less than a cashier at Walgreens."

Their food came. Harry said, "You're smart. You'll figure it out. Let's eat. I just realized how hungry I am."

They dug in and continued talking about their lives and likes and dislikes. They both kept their conversation on the surface, only venturing into the depths of any subject very sparingly. Harry liked the FBI agent. He realized the first time he saw her that she was attractive, and he enjoyed getting to know her now. They cruised through dinner and dessert and before they knew it, they were back on the sidewalk strolling on the beach side of the street.

As they came to the corner near Harry's hotel, he said, "I feel like I should walk you back to your place."

Harry Hid It

Karyn smiled. "Harry, thank you for being a gentleman, but I have a gun in my pocketbook. It's only two blocks away. I'll be fine." She held out her hand. "This was nice. It was fun getting to know you."

Harry took her hand and squeezed slightly. He asked, "Is this like the Christmas Truce of 1914?'

"What's that?" asked Karyn.

"During the first World War, the British and Germans were fighting each other from trenches. The ground in between the two armies was known as 'No Man's Land.' The week before Christmas of 1914, the two armies started an unofficial truce. They walked into No Man's Land, shook hands, and wished each other a happy Christmas. It's said a soccer game between the two armies broke out. When it was over, they want back to their respective sides and proceeded to blast the hell out of each other."

Karyn looked thoughtful as she pondered the analogy. As she turned to head to her hotel, she said, "It's up to you, Harry. I'm not sure what's going on back home, but I'll find out. Secrets will come out with all the shit going on, especially with Ozzie. Have a good night, Harry. You have my number. You can always call again if you need anyone to discuss things with."

Harry stood there for a few minutes watching Karyn's hips sway until she was lost in the crowd. Tonight ended up being a nice distraction. Now, he had to go back into the fire.

Chapter 31

KARYN ALREADY MISSED FLORIDA. Even on a Sunday, she had to battle traffic and people to get to the office. A storm settled over Miami for most of the day on Saturday and delayed her flight home. She ended up using her seat in a quiet part of the terminal as her headquarters. From there she called for reports from her agents and communicated several times with the assistant director. The autopsy did determine that Ozzie had electricity shot through him several times. Death was from heart failure. Whether it was from blood loss or electrocution, the coroner couldn't determine.

The body had been released to Ozzie's mother and a quick funeral had already been arranged for Monday. It struck Karyn that it was exactly a week since Spanky's funeral. She needed to get to the bottom of this before there were more of them.

The police accepted the FBI's offer for help and the Bureau's resources descended on the location of Ozzie's death. They combed through the entire building. All law enforcement personnel were out interviewing anyone they could find in the industrial park. Nobody noticed anything.

Agent Wills tracked down Ozzie's truck. It was parked at a commuter lot and the only reason he found it is that he tried Karyn's idea of looking at the stolen car report for that day. He went to five different places where cars were stolen until he arrived at one where a Ford Escape went missing. He went through Ozzie's truck but didn't find anything that helped. The Escape had yet to be found. He told Karyn that either someone picked Ozzie up there or he stole the Ford and went somewhere. Chuck Wills' money was on the stolen car scenario.

Harry Hid It

Karyn agreed with that idea and asked that all the local police units step up their search for the Escape. Chuck told her that he'd already done that, but nobody had seen it yet. She had no idea if it would offer up any clues, but when you don't have much, you tried to check out everything possible.

She did have an interesting conversation with Gonzales. "I looked closely at the photos of the crime scene, Agent Dudek. When the police first got there, the victim's wallet was lying right next to him. Whoever did this is very good at hiding their identity, but they wanted to make sure we knew who they killed."

"I didn't think of that," said Karyn.

"I worked organized crime for a couple years," continued Gonzales. "There were two types of murders. One was where you rarely even found the victim. He'd just disappear. The other kind was when the killers didn't want to leave any doubt about who the victim was. They wanted to let their allies and enemies know that they'd taken care of some kind of business. It's the modern equivalent of putting your enemy's head on a stake and planting it outside the village. Ozzie was a message. We have to figure out what it means."

"Yeah, that's the crux of the problem, isn't it," said Karyn quietly.

"You told me yesterday that Strickland didn't show much of a reaction when you told him the news."

"I definitely surprised him with it. If I were expecting him to confess all his deep, dark secrets to me, it didn't happen. Unless he's an Academy Award winning actor, I'll swear that the first he heard of Ozzie's death was from me."

"Did he head back up here last night?"

"He was doing that today. I didn't look what flight. For all I know, he's here at the airport waiting for his delayed flight too."

"How do you know he didn't change his mind?"

Karyn realized saying she was at dinner with Harry wouldn't fly. She simply said, "I kept him under surveillance through the evening. He walked around and went to dinner. I think he was in shock."

"If he knows anything, it would help if he spilled to us. Maybe we should bring him in for official questioning."

"He won't budge. Let's see what else we can find out. I think Harry Strickland is the type that may be more willing to talk if we present him with some facts, instead of speculation."

"Your call, Agent Dudek. I'm heading home before my family forgets who I am. Hope your plane leaves soon."

"I have at least another hour. I won't get in until tonight. I'll come into the office tomorrow."

"I don't plan on being here," said Gonzales, "but you can always call. I'll see you Monday."

Karyn did as much as she could via phone and iPad. It was eight at night before she dragged herself into her apartment. Finding nothing to eat in her kitchen, she ordered a pizza and went to bed early.

Now it was Sunday and she was struck by the silence as she stepped off the elevator. She saw a couple agents scattered about the office, but it was definitely low key compared to the hustle and bustle during the week. She was surprised to see Agent Susan Burroughs hunched over her computer terminal. Susan had red hair pulled back in a ponytail and wire-framed glasses. A former track athlete in college, Susan had been with the FBI for two years and could outrun anyone in the office. Karyn asked, "What are you working on?'

Burroughs gave such a start that she had to keep her glasses from flying off her face. "Shit, you scared me. I never heard you." She gestured to her monitor. "I guess I was kind of lost in this."

"Which is?" Karyn asked.

"Chuck is out looking for the car stolen from the lot where he found Ozzie's car. He's getting frustrated. Barry is shadowing Frank, Spanky's partner, but nothing is happening there. You asked me to see what connections I could find between the two murders. Other than common friends and stuff like that, I found nothing. Ozzie seems to be nothing more than a small-time hood. Spanky was a good businessman and someone who did a lot in his community. Other than knowing each other, and Ozzie working for his company for a very short time a couple years ago, there was nothing. Then I had an idea."

"A good one, I hope."

"I think so." Agent Burroughs attacked her keyboard. She tilted the monitor up so that Karyn could see it.

"What am I looking at?" asked Karyn.

"For whatever reason, it hit me to look into the buildings where the two murders occurred. I started a search for ownership. I didn't expect it to be neat and clean, but I had to go through several layers of holding companies and dummy corporations before I got to the owner of the buildings. It appears that an Anthony Russo owns both of them. That's his picture there on the screen."

"That's a big stretch of a coincidence," mumbled Karyn. She bent forward to look at the screen. Burroughs brought up a newspaper story from the *New York Post*. It talked about businessman Anthony Russo, who was entering court on charges of fraud and blackmail. Karyn looked at the date and saw it was from two years ago. "So, what happened in court?"

"Apparently, he had a good lawyer. He got a slap on the wrist and paid a large fine."

"Where is he now?"

"I just found all of this out when you scared the crap out of me. I was about to yell 'Eureka" when you startled me. You agree it's worth investigating?"

"Damn straight. Great work, Susan. Let's see what we can find on this guy."

They spent the next several hours pulling up data. There was information in the FBI files, but it talked about suspicious activities without any real evidence against Russo. Karyn knew from experience that she needed to dig up some people who could shed some light on the written reports. This wasn't an easy task on a Sunday afternoon, but she found someone she could talk to who currently worked in organized crime. It wasn't an easy conversation since Agent Doug Hunt was in the concourse of the New York Giants stadium at halftime of a football game.

"I'll pull up my personal information on Fat Tony when I get to the office tomorrow for you. Basically, he thinks he's a much bigger fish in this large pond of ours than he really is. As near as we've been able to tell, every time he tries to get a big piece of the action in prostitution or the protection racket, the sharks in the water push him away. It seems like he's been trying to increase his presence in the drug trade recently. What's your interest?"

"You remember that ugly torture and murder a week ago? There was another. Both happened in buildings owned by this Mr. Russo."

Karyn heard the agent whistle. "That's interesting," said Hunt.

"Why? Do you see him doing something like that?"

"The information I get tells me he isn't wrapped too tight. Could he go the torture and murder route to prove he was a tough guy? Definitely."

"Anything else that may be of help?" asked Karyn.

"We don't spend a lot of time on him in OC. He's like a gnat on the ass of an elephant. When I get home from this game with my son, I'll make a few calls and let you know tomorrow if I find out anything. I seem to remember that something happened in the summer to Fat Tony, but it was more like a rumor. I'll call or stop up to see you, Agent Dudek."

"Thanks. Enjoy the game."

Karyn printed out a photo of Fat Tony and put it up on her corkboard. Now she had a minor league crime lord wannabe owning the two buildings where the police discovered the two murder victims. This put a spin on the situation that made some of the puzzle pieces come into focus. Whenever Karyn worked a case, she always had a mental picture of a jigsaw puzzle in her mind. She could actually see pieces fitting together as she uncovered clues and more evidence came to light. Even a good solid theory helped form a picture. The problem with this puzzle is that she was missing some key pieces. The entire center was missing and she thought that Harry Strickland held the key. If she could bring a little more substance to the conversation, maybe she could get Harry to sit down and talk.

With the violence that erupted and taking the lives of two men, Karyn suddenly felt like she was in a race. Her gut told her more people would die if she didn't figure this out soon. She looked at Fat Tony. He certainly looked like a grumpy, ugly man. Was he that stupid or that rash to use his own buildings for Ozzie and Spanky's deaths? Whichever it was, Karyn found that people like that tended to be the most dangerous. She hoped that she could bring him down.

***

Out at the Ocean Club, Fat Tony Russo was talking to Sean Riley. Actually, it was more like talking at him. A football game droned on in the background from the big screen television mounted to the office wall. Tony was in a foul mood and venting to his lieutenant.

"Jesus Christ, what do you mean you don't know who John and Harry are? Why the fuck didn't you get a last name out of that asshole before he died?"

Riley had to tread lightly here. "Boss, I told you that last bolt of electricity would kill him. It took us three hours to get him to confess that he was in on the job where he helped rip you off and Tony Junior died. He was a tough fucker."

"Are you saying that it's my fault we didn't get the information?" Tony started touching the gun that sat out on his desk. "You better watch how you phrase things, Riley. You can be replaced."

"No, no, boss. That's not what I'm saying at all. After what we put him through, he wasn't going to last much longer. He just happened to kick off when you threw the switch."

"Hmmmm," said Fat Tony, momentarily pacified. "It felt good to finally find one of those assholes and kill him. Did you get the word out that we're taking care of those who decided to mess with me? I want people to know that I'm someone they have to be careful around. I will not tolerate any more lack of respect."

Riley felt like rubbing his temples as he tried to think of how to answer Mr. Russo. He had a constant headache for three days now. The torture and killing didn't bother him. It was listening to the ridiculous monologues his boss went off on. As Ozzie's life was bleeding out of him a few days ago, Fat Tony droned on and on about how nobody would fuck with him again and how dare this piece of shit steal from him and kill his son. Sean considered that Fat Tony seemed to be slowly losing his marbles. If he went down, then Riley would go down with him. If Riley tried to leave, his severance pay would probably be a bullet to the skull. Not a great choice!

Focusing back on the question Tony asked, Riley said, "Yeah, we're slowly getting the word out. It's a fine line between letting people know and having the cops come down on our heads. We left his wallet in plain sight so that they'd know who died. I'm a little worried about using buildings you own. They may trace them back to you. It would seem a little odd for the cops that two men were left for dead in your real estate."

"Screw them!" shouted Fat Tony. "I pay good money for lawyers. They tell them that it's merely circumstantial and someone is trying to frame me. You worry too much! Now, how are you going to find out who this John and Harry are?"

"I'm going to Ozzie's funeral tomorrow," said Riley. "I'll pretend to be an acquaintance and ask around. If these guys were close, they should be at the funeral. At the least, somebody there will know something."

Tony looked surprised. "That's a good idea. You have a week to find and clean up these last two scum."

Harry Hid It

"Just out of curiosity," asked Riley, "why a week?"

"Because I had to move up the timetable for delivery. The shipment of meth will be here a week from tomorrow night. I'm in the middle of negotiating for buyers to show up that night so that I don't sit on that stuff. I want to get it here and sell it immediately. With the money I get that night, I'll firm up our operations all the way around. I had a couple of buyers on the fence, but when I told them yesterday that I was taking care of the problem we had in the summer, they started coming around. Power equals respect, which gives us customers."

"You need this done before the deal?" asked Riley.

"It will encourage more buyers to work with me. With more customers, I can raise the price of the goods and make more money. It's simple capitalistic principle."

"I'll do my best, boss."

"You damn well better," said Fat Tony, idly toying with the gun again. "I want their deaths big and loud. It will be a long time before anyone decides to come up against me again."

"Are you going to need my help with the shipment coming in?"

"If you have this mess cleaned up by next Monday, sure I will, Riley."

Riley asked, "How's all this product coming in, boss?"

Fat Tony picked up a paper on his desk and skimmed it. "That's still being negotiated. Right now, it looks like the seller will be using a boat. They won't give me all their details, of course, but the last stage of transport will be on the water. Whether they're coming from Baltimore, Jersey, or somewhere else, I don't know. It will be on a fishing boat. As soon as they finalize their details, they'll tell me where to pick it up. I may ask them to deliver it here."

This made Riley shake his head. Tony saw it and said, "What?"

Taking a deep breath, Sean Riley explained his thinking. "First of all, the last time you did a drug deal here, all hell broke loose.

That may turn off your potential customers. Second, and this is a bigger problem, the club property is a bottleneck. There's only one way in and out of the parking lot, and it's a long driveway from the road. It would be easy for a few people to seal the place off. Tactically, it's not a good idea."

Fat Tony's face turned red, but then he calmed down. He wanted to show people that he was in total control of everything, but what Riley said made sense. He asked, "What, are you worried about cops? I'll get a heads-up if any raid is planned."

"We have to worry about them or someone who wants to take the drugs or the money for their own operation. If you want a suggestion, when the sellers tell you where the delivery is, keep it to yourself. Maybe tell your buyers the general area, but call or text them about thirty minutes before the shipment arrives. We're stretched pretty thin, boss. Especially if I'm tracking down the two remaining dickheads who ripped you off for the rest of the week."

"Good advice, Riley. You keep this up and I'll give you a bigger piece of the action. You'll move up with me as we slowly take over Long Island."

Riley wasn't sure how much longer he wanted to be tied to Fat Tony, but he knew he had to put up with him for at least another week. After Monday night, he could evaluate how things were going and make a decision. He simply said, "Sounds good, boss. Everything will go smoothly this week. People will know that you're someone they have to reckon with when doing business out here."

"You bet your ass. Is that geek of mine in today?"

"You mean Kevin? No, you gave him today off. What do you need him for?"

"I want him to start preparing the logistics for all the money we're going to take in next week. I don't want any slipups. I may take him with me to act as my bookkeeper. Wall Street will be jealous at the amounts of money changing hands when the stuff gets here."

"Want me to call him in?"

"Not necessary, Riley. It can wait until tomorrow." Fat Tony leaned back and folded his hands on his ample paunch. "Very soon, we're going to be on top of the world. Happy hunting at the funeral."

Chapter 32

Two funerals within a week were two too many for Harry. He was standing in a different cemetery than he did last Monday, and the pain he was feeling was more intense. At Spanky's funeral, he had a sneaking suspicion dancing around the fringes of his mind that he was indirectly responsible for his death. Today, he knew with a certainty that he was the reason Ozzie was being lowered into the ground. He looked over the crowd and saw John. His face resembled what Harry was feeling – sorry, fearful, and not sure what to do next.

Sophia stood near Harry but wasn't holding his hand or anything. She'd barely spoken three words to him all morning. Harry found that he didn't really mind it all that much. For whatever reason, he discovered he'd like to talk to Agent Dudek again. Even though they'd danced around why she was in Florida while at dinner, he found that he enjoyed the time together. He'd welcomed the slight mental break that the evening afforded him. He wished there were some way that he could steer her to Fat Tony without compromising himself and John.

The graveside part of the service was over. He and Sophia headed back to the car. As John caught up with them, Sophia asked him, "Where's Julia?"

"She's working on a huge case for the past couple weeks. In fact, she's staying with a friend in the city until it's over. We figured it would be easier for her that way."

Harry opened the door for Sophia and said, "I need to talk with John for a bit. Then we'll head over to the luncheon."

She got in without a word and Harry steered John to the back of the car. John said, "Ozzie's mother is a mess. I'm surprised she was able to arrange all of this so quickly."

310

Harry Hid It

"Oz's sister flew in from Colorado as soon as she heard. With the condition his body was in and the circumstances, she thought the faster they buried him the better. Last night at the funeral home, I gave her money to pay for it. I told her Ozzie had done some work for me and I was getting ready to pay him this week. I'm going to arrange for his mother to get some money from what we've squirreled away."

"Any thoughts on how to stay alive in the meantime?" asked John.

"I've been working on it, but nothing is jelling. I hired Cowboy to see what he can find out from Fat Tony's camp. I feel like I'm going into a dark room blind. Are you carrying?"

John patted the pocket of his jacket. "Yup. It's like the Boy Scout motto, 'Be Prepared.'"

Harry said, "Unfortunately, we aren't dealing with any Boy Scouts. Watch your back and we'll talk later."

John nodded and walked off. As he got in the car, Sophia said, "It's a damn shame. Did you see Ozzie's mother? She's a total wreck."

"I know, Sophia. I'm not happy about it either."

"Especially if you had something to do with it, Harry. And don't start denying it again," she said as he started to say something. "Why else would an FBI agent come all the way down to Florida to break the news? I'm not an idiot, no matter what you think."

"Sophia, I never thought you were an idiot," was all Harry managed to say.

She held up her hand. "I don't want to hear it. Why didn't you get home until Saturday night from Florida? I found a flight Friday night."

"I needed to do some thinking," Harry said honestly. "Then there was bad weather on Saturday and I didn't get out of there until the evening. What do you care? You're barely talking to me anyway."

Harry Hid It

"I'm mad at you, Harry. I really want you to promise me that you're done doing anything that even smacks of criminal behavior. If you can't do that, then we can't be together. I know when you're lying. You think you're good at it, but not with me. You know why Ozzie was killed in such a gruesome manner, so that means it was probably something you were involved in together."

Harry thought about denying everything she said, but then decided it was best to quietly drive. Finally, he said, "I can tell you that I'm done with any activities that you don't approve of."

"I certainly hope so," stated Sophia. "What did you do in Florida after you left me? Did that FBI woman bother you anymore?"

"No, she didn't bother me. And technically, I didn't leave you. You told me to get out. I got a room, went for a long swim, and then walked around and grabbed dinner. I booked a flight in the morning, but I spent most of Saturday cooling my heels at the airport. That was my exciting time."

"After lunch, I want you to take me home. I still need some time to cool off. Plus, I'm really sad about Ozzie. I'm going to miss the big lug. His girlfriend Donna looked very sad today."

This comment made Harry wonder if Ozzie's family was safe. If Ozzie talked, how much did he say? Fat Tony seemed to be a total nutcase and it wouldn't surprise Harry if he reached out to hurt anyone connected to Ozzie. He looked sideways at Sophia. If his name were mentioned during Ozzie's torture, was she safe? Harry realized he needed to stop this mess somehow because he didn't have the resources to protect everybody. Maybe he should just take his gun and plug Fat Tony. Then it would all be done and over with.

They arrived at the restaurant where the post-funeral repast was being held. It was a family-run Italian place and Harry knew the food was good. He realized he was hungry. His last good meal was with Karyn at the Cuban place on Saturday night. Going inside, Sophia excused herself to head to the bathroom and Harry ran into Frank.

"What the fuck is going on, Harry?" he asked. "First Spanky and now Ozzie. Both of their deaths were unspeakable. Why would someone do this?"

"I'm not sure, Frank. You haven't noticed anyone hanging around the construction office or following you, have you?"

"No, not at all." Frank's eyes widened. "You think someone might be after me too?"

"All I'm saying is that you need to be vigilant, Frank." Harry thought that if anyone were after Frank, he'd be oblivious to it all. Even if the guy was dressed in a red cape and wore clown makeup.

"I'll be careful, Harry. It's just a terrible thing. Terrible."

Frank drifted away. Sophia came back out and they sat down. Harry managed to get through the time without Sophia attacking him over anything and without having to talk with anyone else. It was with a feeling of relief that he dropped her off at her parents' home and drove back to his house. He closed the door behind him and braced himself for the inevitable pouncing by Max. He wasn't disappointed and hugged the big mutt when he jumped on him.

Harry fetched a beer out of his refrigerator and sat down in his favorite chair. Max put his head on Harry's lap. As he scratched behind the dog's ears, Harry tried to get his thoughts in order. He'd been wrestling with the Fat Tony problem all weekend and was no closer to a solution. The one thing Harry knew was that this was a "him or me" situation. It didn't seem there was any way he could feel safe as long as Fat Tony was around. Harry would always be waiting for someone to come at him with a gun or worse. He shivered. He didn't want to end up like Ozzie or Spanky.

"Fuck that," said Harry to Max. "That's not going to happen to me and I'm not going to run scared. I'm going to have to end this one way or the other."

The dog turned his head as Harry talked. Having said that, he wished Max had some good ideas, because he had nothing right now. As he was contemplating his next move, his phone buzzed with a text message. It was from Cowboy. He asked Harry if he could meet around seven. Harry told him to go to Art's and they could talk there. Cowboy signed off with, "I'll be there. Keep your eyes open."

"Just what I need," thought Harry, "more reminders that life sucks right now.

Suddenly, Max raised his head and made a moaning noise. A second later, Harry's doorbell rang. He pushed Max away and pulled his gun from his belt. He went to a window where he could see his front door and saw Karyn Dudek standing there. Sighing, he put his gun back and made sure his shirt hung over it. He realized that if anybody were trying to take him out, they wouldn't bother ringing the bell.

He opened the door and said, "I'd say this was an unexpected surprise, but I had a feeling I'd be seeing more of you."

"Disappointed?" asked Karyn.

"Under other circumstances, no," replied Harry. "I don't think this is an extension of our social get-together from Friday night."

"You got that right. May I come in?"

Harry backed out of the doorway and gestured inside. She took two steps in and stopped as Max sat right in front of her, blocking her way. She reached down with a clenched fist and allowed Max to sniff her. He did and then he stood up with his tail wagging. Karyn went down on one knee and rubbed her hand down Max's head and neck. The dog whimpered happily and took another step forward, barreling into Karyn. To prevent being knocked on her butt, Karyn wrapped both arms around the dog and hugged him. Soon Max was kissing the FBI agent's face and enjoying Karyn petting and scratching him all over.

Harry smiled, looking down at the woman. "He likes you. It usually takes a little more time for him to warm up to someone."

"I've always loved animals." Karyn stood up and looked at

Harry Hid It

Harry. "I told you I grew up on a ranch. Dogs and animals were a part of life. I admit that I miss having a dog. It's one of the things that drives me crazy about my job." She gave Harry a quizzical look. "What did you do with him when you were in Florida?"

"His name is Max. Jeannie, the waitress from Art's, watches and walks him whenever I'm out of town."

"He's a beautiful dog. He's definitely the type of dog I imagined you with."

"We're close. I've had him for three years, and he still thinks he's a puppy. Now that you've met my family, such as it is here, what can I do for you?"

"Before I get to that, how did the funeral go?"

Harry shrugged. "It was a funeral. There was shock and sadness and it was something you just get through. Ozzie is safely buried and is wherever we go after we die."

"Since I saw you on Friday, I found out a great deal. I want to bounce some ideas off you."

Harry picked up his beer bottle and said, "Let's go into the kitchen. We can sit at the table and talk."

Karyn followed him inside and liked what she saw. Harry obviously kept his home neat and clean, but not in the sense of an OCD person. It certainly had a lived-in look. The furniture all looked comfortable and there was a certain degree of style. Everything looked like it belonged here. As they went into the kitchen, she saw a long room off to the side. It was obviously added on to the original structure and didn't have a floor over it. Sun streamed through the skylights and she saw there was little furniture in there. She saw a small desk and bookcase in one corner, but the great majority of the room contained only paintings mounted to the wall or displayed on easels.

Going into the kitchen, Harry asked, "Can I get you anything? Beer, soda, coffee, tea?"

Karyn said, "Tea would be great. It's been a long couple of days."

As Harry put water in the kettle and set it on a burner, he said, "Since this isn't a social call, we can get to it. What's up?"

"You know I originally ran into you because of those jewel thefts. Don't think I'm done with that, or a few other situations I believe you might be involved in. However, my priority shifted to your friends' murders. With Spanky and Ozzie dying as they did, I'm concerned that more people are going to end up dead. Nobody wants that, so my boss wants me to get to the bottom of it and stop things before it gets worse."

Harry gave a noncommittal nod, pulled out a mug, and put a tea bag in it. "Have you found out anything?"

"Actually, I have. Does the name Fat Tony Russo mean anything to you?"

Pouring hot water into the mug, Harry said, "I've heard of him. Some kind of hood in the city, isn't he?"

"Hood, yes, but he seems to have aspirations to being a big deal out here on the Island. He's been pretty small potatoes, but he keeps trying to grow his business."

"How does he tie into this?" asked Harry.

"It took some good digging on the part of one of my agents, but Fat Tony is the owner of the buildings where both Spanky and Ozzie bought it." She took the tea and poured in some milk Harry took out of the refrigerator. She looked at Harry's face as she talked. So far, there was no reaction. Karyn made a mental note never to get into a poker game with this man.

"Does he own many places?" asked Harry. "Could be a coincidence."

"I thought we already determined the other day that neither of us believes in those too much. Regardless of that possibility, this led to my team doing more digging into him. I don't have a full picture of him yet, but I had a good talk with a colleague who specializes in organized crime. I asked him to track down some rumors he'd been hearing about Fat Tony's organization."

Harry Hid It

Taking a seat across from her, Harry took a swallow from his beer bottle. "What were these rumors about?"

"The word on the street is that someone interrupted a drug deal Tony had going in the middle of the summer. A few people showed up and took his money just as he sold a big shipment of drugs. The details are fuzzy, but Tony had a son who was killed. Whether the ones who robbed him did the shooting or something else happened isn't clear. What this agent did know is that Fat Tony started to go a little crazy after this. Not that he was wrapped too tight to begin with, apparently. Part of the story is that he shot one of his own bodyguards for some reason."

"Fat Tony certainly sounds dangerous," commented Harry.

"I think that's an understatement. You want to know my theory?"

Harry smiled. "I have a feeling that's why you came here and that you can't wait to tell me."

"Am I that transparent?" asked Karyn. Putting her mug down, she said, "This is what I think. I believe that you and Ozzie and perhaps one of your other friends put on your own little raid on Fat Tony. Somehow, you knew the drug deal was going down and you put the hit on. While you were doing this, something happened where Tony's son got shot. Whether it was your doing or an accident, I don't really give a shit. But I think that somehow Fat Tony or some of his minions finally tracked down who did it, and that's why Ozzie and Spanky are dead. What do you think?"

Harry took a deep breath and thought about what to say. With everything going down, he could certainly use Agent Dudek as an ally. The problem was he wasn't sure how much he could walk the tightrope. He wasn't going to rat on anyone, certainly not himself. Might as well throw out a few things and see where they landed.

"There's a certain amount of logic there. If your theory is indeed fact, what would happen to those that stole money from Fat Tony? I mean, if they didn't have anything to do with killing anyone."

Harry Hid It

Karyn gave him a long, cool look over her tea. "I don't think there's any law governing thieves taking from thieves. I'm not worried about that. I can certainly talk to my boss about any information or help we get in putting Fat Tony away." She put her mug down with a sharp bang on the table. Looking earnestly at Harry, she said, "Harry, I hate what he did to your friend. You know how it goes. Once someone like Fat Tony gets a taste of blood like this, not only do they not stop, but they also get worse. This man is a menace. I've put drug kings and gangbangers away, but someone like Fat Tony is an entirely different level of bad."

"Why can't you just go in and pick him up?"

Karyn looked dejected. "We don't have anything solid. We need real evidence. Someone to turn on him or proof he was there. If we went in now, a decent lawyer would have him back on the streets in two hours."

"How do you think I can help?"

"If you were there that night, you can tell me what happened. That may help us to get into his organization somehow and get out some hard evidence. You know the hangers-on to people like that. We get one of his associates; he won't be too hard to flip. So, can you help me?"

Harry walked back out of the kitchen. "Come with me."

Curious, Karyn scrambled to her feet and followed. Harry led her into the room she saw when walking into the kitchen. She looked at the neatly arranged desk and bookcase. A few books were piled on the corner of the desk since the bookcase was jammed pack. She looked at the variety of titles. One was *Scuba Diving The Wrecks and Shores of Long Island* by David Rosenthal. Another title she saw was *Subway Madness: Exploring the Hidden Spaces and Underground Culture of the NYC Subways*. A guidebook on hiking trails of New Jersey and Pennsylvania was leaning on those books. Next to that was an old USA Geological Survey. Peering at the yellowed pages, she saw the name Cornwall on it. She looked up when Harry cleared his throat.

318

Harry Hid It

"Sorry, I love books. I never get a chance to read for fun anymore since I started working for the FBI. You certainly have eclectic tastes."

"I like learning about different things." Harry's smile lit up his face. "I'd certainly be much better in school now than when I was in high school."

She thought that she liked when he smiled as he continued, "But my reading habits aren't why I brought you in here." He swept his arm around the room.

She looked in amazement at the paintings. As she moved further into the room, she saw a series of landscapes done on the beach. One was painted when the sun was rising or setting, and another one showed the anger and power of an approaching storm. In the lower right hand corner of each painting was an "H" and an "S" done with a flourish. She looked at Harry. "These are yours?"

"Yes, they are, but I have a feeling you know I paint."

Karyn slightly blushed and said, "I did, but I hadn't seen any of your work. These are terrific."

"Thanks. I like to come in here to think sometimes. I certainly have to think through some of this stuff you just hit me with."

"I'm sure." Karyn looked at another landscape. It looked like it was done in a slightly mountainous area as a river carved a path through the rocks. "This is beautiful. Where did you do this one?"

"I was in the Delaware Water Gap on the Jersey side. I was tired of doing the beach. I keep trying to stretch myself."

Karyn looked at the one next to it. It was another river scene. "What else do you do?"

"I've been puttering around with stills. Over on this wall is your basic bowl of fruit."

Karyn admired the detail and color. She looked up, and next to one of the river pictures, saw a partial painting of a penny. "That's different."

"I figured Andy Warhol made a fortune painting a can of soup, so I practiced with a penny. When I got to that point, I kind of liked the concept of it being a work in progress. There was something about the penny not quite being done. So I hung it up. I may still go back to it later."

Karyn did think it was pretty cool how he painted it. The man had talent. Turning, she saw another painting that made her suck in her breath. It was a painting of a woman with her naked back to the artist, but she turned in a way that showed a slight profile. One arm was above her head, hanging on to a pole. Flowing curtains made up the background. The woman was very curvy and Harry had made her sensual and beautiful all at once. With a small smile, Karyn knew that she was looking at the lovely rear of Vicki Light. "That's excellent, Harry."

"I appreciate that. It's the first person I ever did. Well, except for Lincoln on the penny. I'm not ready to do faces yet, I guess."

Without thinking, Karyn said, "If I ever want a nude done of me, I know who to contact. That's simply beautiful."

Harry gave a chuckle. "I can't say that I'd mind doing that."

Karyn's phone beeped and she looked at it. "Harry, I have to go. Thank you for the hospitality and I'm flattered you showed me your paintings."

He took her back through the house to his front door. "I'll be back in touch with you. As I said, I have some things to ponder here."

"You ponder away, Harry, but don't take too long. If I'm right, you may be on borrowed time."

Harry made a face that seemed to say, "Like I don't know that." Aloud to Karyn he said, "I won't take long."

"I'll leave you with the words that Doug Hunt, the organized crime agent, told me about Fat Tony."

"What's that?" asked Harry.

"It was a very technical term. He said Fat Tony is a bat shit crazy motherfucker."

Chapter 33

AT 6:45, HARRY HOOKED up Max to his leash and they started their walk toward Art's. He was still mulling over everything Karyn told him. He was a bit surprised that she had such a good idea of why Fat Tony was on the warpath and how it came about. While Harry knew that the resources of the FBI were vast and they had contacts all over the city, he was still amazed what she discovered in a relatively short amount of time. Harry cursed out loud at himself for using the airport computer one too many times for his jobs, and at Ozzie for borrowing Spanky's truck. As far as he knew, those two events were the reason he was in such a shitty position.

Going into Art's, Harry waved to the proprietor and headed over to an open table he saw in the corner. Jeannie came over to take his order. "Max was so good for me when you were gone, Harry. I'm sorry you had to come back early because of your friend."

"Thanks, darling. I'm meeting someone here in a few minutes. I'm not really hungry, but if you can bring me a drink and Max a burger, we'll be good for now."

Sensing Harry's somber mood, she simply nodded and went to fill the order. After she brought it over, Harry was feeding bits of burger to Max when Cowboy walked in. He headed over to the table and sat next to Harry. When Jeannie came to the table, he ordered a beer and absentmindedly started to rub Max's snout when the dog stood up to say hello. He looked at Harry and said, "How you holding up?"

"I've been better. I'm starting to feel like I have a big target on my back when I'm walking around. Other than that, I'm doing terrific."

321

Cowboy thanked Jeannie for the beer when she delivered it and took a long drink. Setting it down, he said, "You aren't too far off about the target. The good news is that it isn't quite there yet. The bad news is that I don't know how much longer you have."

"You want to explain that to me?"

"John contacted me Friday night. He told me what's going on and gave me the full story of what happened the night you three went into the club to rob Tony. I'd heard some rumblings after it happened and figured that you acted on the info I gave you back then. Anyway, I went into full investigator mode when he explained what happened to your friend. Nobody should go out that way."

Harry tilted his drink toward Cowboy. "You got that right. I'm sure John told you I'm good for your fee."

"No worries, Harry. I know you're a stand-up guy or I wouldn't be doing this. Anyway, I started snooping around. I actually took this girl I've been seeing to the Ocean Club on Saturday night. I'm more into country line dancing, but I figured it might be a way to strike up a conversation with a few employees. The good thing is that Fat Tony's organization has more leaks in it than the White House."

"It's always helpful when people blab," said Harry. "What did you find out?"

"I talked to a few of the security muscle heads over there. One of them pulled additional duty for Fat Tony at times and gave me some insight. He says the old man hasn't been the same since his kid died. Granted, he told me that Fat Tony was never very stable, but he's been really out of control lately. He has one of his head goons looking for the guys who robbed him."

"Did your new friend help this person in his search?"

"No, apparently Tony had him go outside of the organization for additional help. Fat Tony isn't so far gone that he doesn't realize that he has some internal security issues."

"Did you get a name of the person Tony is using as his main man on this?"

"Not that night, but yesterday I did. It's Sean Riley. He's a big fucking Irishman with red hair who seems to be good at his job."

"Do you have anything else on him so I might recognize him in a dark alley?" asked Harry.

"Better – here's a photo." Cowboy took out his phone and went through a few pictures before he showed the screen to Harry. "I'll send that to your phone and beam it over to John."

Harry looked closely at it. "He doesn't look very comfortable in a suit."

"I'm thinking between that and the funeral where I took this photo, he was a bit nervous."

Looking up sharply, Harry whispered, "What funeral?"

"Your friend's. I was there this morning. So was Riley."

"I didn't see you there," exclaimed Harry.

"You weren't supposed to." Cowboy allowed himself a small smile. "I'm good at what I do. From everything I gathered from people who heard stuff from a friend who heard it from a friend, your buddy talked when they were doing their shit to him. He didn't give up everything. He seemed to give some names, but not the entire name. When I heard that, I tried to think how this asshole Riley would react. If I were in his position and trying to clean this up in a hurry, I'd go to the funeral and see who showed up. Then I'd try to put some faces to names and see if I could figure out who Ozzie hung with. That's what he did, and that's how I got these pictures."

"Is that what you meant by I had a target on my back, but maybe not all the way yet?"

"Yup. I don't know what this clown picked up at the funeral. He may or may not have put the finger on you and John. After I leave you, I'm going to put out some more feelers."

Harry leaned back and placed the cold glass against his forehead. "I'm fucked, Cowboy. It's only a matter of time before he finds either John or myself. I've heard from some people too. Fat Tony sounds like he should be fit for an extra-large straitjacket."

"That's what the guy at the club told me. He asked me if I knew anyone who was hiring because he wanted to change employers. He said he heard some big shit was going down and he thought it would be a good idea to leave before it did."

"What kind of big shit?" asked Harry.

"I have no idea yet. Part of what I hope to discover tonight."

Harry looked Cowboy in the eye. "I need to do something to get rid of Fat Tony. He wants revenge. Somebody gets that bug up his ass and he doesn't stop." He snorted with a short laugh. "I should know. That's how I got into this mess."

"What do you mean?" asked Cowboy.

Harry told him what happened in that club with young Tony the first time he went there. After that incident with him and Sophia, Harry wanted to get back at him. "When you told me about the drug deal going down, it seemed like the perfect opportunity. Ripping off Fat Tony in his son's club seemed justified. I didn't know the little shit was going to get in the way of a bullet."

"You said that you heard about Fat Tony from somebody else. Mind if I ask your source?"

"The feds."

That took Cowboy by surprise. "Really! How do you have a contact with them?"

"It isn't so much of a contact as a situation where I'm a person of interest in some crimes. That's taken a back seat to the murders for now. Murder and torture make cops nervous, no matter their jurisdiction. They seem to think I know what's going on with all of this. I do, obviously, but I don't know how to make it work to my advantage."

"The government could protect you…and John too, for that matter. It depends on what they want you to say and what kind of deal you can work out."

"Don't think I haven't thought about it," said Harry, "but it leaves a bad taste in my mouth."

"So does a bullet," said Cowboy.

"They teach you to be that direct where you grew up?" asked Harry.

"I was a fucking Texas Ranger, not a diplomat. You want fancy words, get a lawyer." Cowboy drank more of his beer. "Harry, here's a piece of advice from someone who worked law enforcement. Making a deal with the cops or feds is just like any deal making. You have to go in from a position of power. The more that you can give them, the better your bargaining position. You have to realize, the way the bureaucracy works on that level is that you're a success if you bring a bunch of bad guys down. It doesn't have to be all the bad guys, but it has to be enough to impress the bosses. If you can give them Fat Tony or more, whatever you did may be reduced to a slap on the wrists. It's all politics, man."

"I see what you're saying. If I can do something and keep John out of it, maybe I will. One way or the other, I have to talk to him about it first."

"These things where you're a person of interest, do they have anything they can nail you on?"

"Nope, purely circumstantial."

"Then don't give anything up you don't have to. John hasn't told me any details, but I know you guys were doing things. I certainly don't want to know about them, but if nobody got hurt and they have no evidence, don't give them a damn thing. Make Fat Tony the prize for everyone involved."

"I don't know if him in jail will make me sleep all that well," said Harry. "You hear stories how guys in prison make things happen from behind bars."

"That's the big cheeses who know what they're doing," said Cowboy. "They have power and an organization – family or otherwise. From everything I've discovered so far, if the feds or other law enforcement officials put Fat Tony away, anyone who works for him will abandon him faster than rats off a sinking ship. I don't think there's all that much loyalty there."

"That's your impression?" asked Harry.

"More like fact, from what I've been finding out. What you did in the summer knocked Fat Tony for a loop. He lost business, a great deal of it. That probably helped loosen a few more screws in his head. He doesn't have a lot of money on hand. I don't know what this big project he has going on is, but I'd think it's his last-ditch effort to make good somehow. There should be a lot of chatter out there on it. That's why I feel pretty good that I'll find something out in the next day or two."

"You're the man, Cowboy." Harry took out an envelope from his pocket and slid it across the table. "There's a payment for you and some extra. Keep it or use it to spread around for information. Whatever you think best."

"I appreciate it, Harry. I'll text you as soon as I have any information at all. My biggest fear is that I don't know if you and John are in the crosshairs of these assholes yet. That's my first priority to find out."

The two men stood and shook hands. "I can find some guys to watch your back for you if you want, Harry."

"Tempting, but I'm not quite ready for that. Cowboy, one more thing."

"What is it, Harry?"

"If you can find out exactly who did the work on Spanky and Ozzie, I'd greatly appreciate it. If it were this Riley character or others or Fat Tony himself, I really want to know."

"I'll work on that, Harry. All I need is one good stool pigeon to ply with liquor and money. The sooner I can nail someone like that, the more we'll know. Watch your back, man."

"Constantly," Harry said to Cowboy's back as he left Art's.

Harry attached the leash back to Max's collar. "Listen, pal, it's time to earn your keep. If anything bigger than a squirrel comes near the house tonight, you better bark your ever-loving heart out." Harry left some money on the table. He waved to Art and Jeannie as he left. Not ready to go home yet, he and Max walked several miles through the neighborhood. Harry felt like all his senses were on high alert as he tried to stroll along at a normal pace.

***

At the Ocean Club, Sean Riley waited outside Fat Tony's office. The man was inside shouting on the phone. It sounded like another potential buyer for his meth was wimping out. Riley had some good news, but he knew Tony's mood was toxic. To say the man was unstable was like saying the Grand Canyon was a big hole in the ground. Riley worked with people like this ever since dropping out of high school, but he never saw anyone deteriorate like this mentally and emotionally before. Fat Tony probably needs a first-rate shrink, if he could manage not to shoot the poor bastard when he tried to treat Tony.

When he heard the phone crash down on the desk in disgust, Sean lightly knocked on the door. Tony yelled out, "Get the fuck in here, whoever you are."

Opening the door, Riley said, "It's me, boss."

"I'm having a bad day, Riley. You better have some good news for me. Do you know how many people have disrespected me today by saying they weren't going to buy from me? I have all that shit coming here in a week and I need more buyers. I need to show these fuckers not to fucking fuck with me!"

"Yeah, boss, I know. Listen, I think I got a line on who John and Harry are."

"That's the best news I've heard so far. Tell me more."

"I went to the funeral, like I said I would. I thought I'd hit up the women in case I accidently ran into the two douchebags we want. I met the sister of the deceased. Nice woman who flew here from Colorado for her brother's funeral. She said Harry and John were her brother's best friends. In fact, Harry had given her some money to pay for the funeral."

Fat Tony's face became so red that Riley thought he was going to have a heart attack. "He's giving her *my* money to pay for that shithead we killed! I want him dead. More than dead. I want you to put up a cross and crucify the son of a bitch. How dare he do that to me! You see, Riley, everyone is disrespecting me." He glared at Riley. "You don't disrespect me, Riley?"

"Of course not, Mr. Russo. I'm here for you. Anyway, she also pointed out John to me. I got last names for them and I did a little more asking around. Harry is some kind of mechanic and John is a big time motorcycle guy. They don't sound like people who could've masterminded the hit on you here."

"That's probably why it took us so long to find them," said Fat Tony. "They thought they could fly under the radar. But they can't hide from me, can they, Riley?"

Riley thought that it didn't seem like a good time to tell Fat Tony that it was a lucky find on the geek's part that he got a line on the getaway truck and that he'd done all the legwork on this. Instead, Riley just gave a noncommittal grunt.

Tony started up again. "So why aren't they dead yet, Riley? Why the fuck are you here? I gave you a job to do? Do I have to get someone else to kill them?"

"No, boss, I have good people with me. Nobody from here is involved. I stopped by to find out if you want them first. I know you wanted to be there the last time. Do you want to watch them die?"

Fat Tony sat back, calm again. He reached out, picked up a mug on the desk, and drank. "You know, Riley, that was damn thoughtful of you. Sorry I flew off the handle there. The pressure has been tremendous lately. No, I don't have to be there. Snuff out their lives and we can move on. When it's done, I want you to get the word out why they died. I need people to see once and for all that I'm someone they need to fear and respect. I hope when you get this finished that these pussies who are afraid to deal with me will change their tune."

"I'm sure it'll help you a great deal, Mr. Russo. Uh, I do have to ask. I need some cash to pay the men helping me."

Harry Hid It

Tony looked at Riley and sighed. Heaving himself up, he went over to a cabinet and opened it. There was a small safe built into it with an electronic keypad. Tony pressed the buttons and the door popped out. Riley watched his face flash with concern as he felt around inside. He pulled out two stacks of bills and tossed them to Sean. "Tell your help that there will be more if they successfully kill these bastards. There will be a big bonus after next Monday."

Riley looked at the stacks he caught. It was sufficient for now, but barely. Was the old man that cash poor? "Sure, boss, they'd be real happy to hear that."

"You need to wrap this up, Riley. I want you there with me Monday night. This deal is too big to screw up. I want you in charge of my security."

"That's a big honor, Mr. Russo." Riley knew he was lying through his teeth. He wanted to leverage the work he was doing now into some other outfit that was saner than Fat Tony's operation. Until that time, he had to continue kissing this guy's ass. "I'll be there. As we get closer, we should talk how we're going to make that night go smooth. As for this Harry and John, we'll finish them off tomorrow."

"Good, Riley, I look forward to this being over."

As he left the office, Riley thought to himself, "You and me both."

Chapter 34

ON TUESDAY MORNING, HARRY called into work and took the rest of the week off. He had the time and it didn't sit well with him being stuck in one place for too long at the moment. It seemed much better if he could be on the move. Cowboy had given him some things to think about. Harry hoped his friend could unearth some solid information on Fat Tony that he could take to the FBI. At the moment, he wasn't in much of a bargaining position. He sensed that Karyn Dudek liked him, but not enough that she wouldn't want something in return. He wasn't about to admit to his involvement in any of the crimes she thought he did.

What would be a good idea, though, was to keep the lines of communication open between him and her. That way it would be easier to decide on a course of action if and when the situation presented itself. With that thought in mind, he gave her a call. She answered with, "Harry?"

"You got that right. I didn't wake you, did I?"

She laughed sarcastically. "It's 8:30 in the morning and I've been here over an hour already. You headed into work?"

"I took the rest of the week off. Wouldn't be safe for the aircraft I work on. They wouldn't have my entire attention."

"I can understand that," said Karyn. "What can I do for you?"

"Any chance of getting together today and talking?"

"What about?"

"I did some thinking in regard to our conversation last night. I thought if we could help each other that it would be worth exploring."

"You have something that will take Fat Tony off the streets?"

Harry hesitated. "Not really, but I heard some rumors and I'm trying to get a handle on them. I figured it doesn't hurt to explore my options."

It was Karyn's turn to be quiet for a minute. "I have an operations meeting I need to be at this afternoon. I'm in the city right now. Can you come in here?"

"Nothing personal, but I'd rather not meet at the FBI office. Why don't we split the difference? I know a good coffee shop in Queens. It's not far from Citi Field."

"That's doable. I can meet you at eleven."

"Here's the place and address." Harry gave it to her. "Thank you, Agent Dudek, I'll see you soon."

After hanging up, Harry took Max for a long walk and came home to shower. So far, he hadn't seen anyone hanging around the house or following him. He tried to imagine how Fat Tony's men would come for him. Break into his house and kill him? Do it out on the street? Or maybe grab him and bring him in front of fatso himself to do the deed? None of the choices did much for Harry. He'd much rather be on the offensive than playing defense. He'd have to give that some thought and figure out how to attack Fat Tony.

Trying to put it out of his mind, Harry brought the Camaro to life and headed for the rendezvous with Karyn. He hadn't heard from Cowboy yet today and hoped the ex-Texas Ranger would feed him some information that would help. He'd love to go into this meeting with something concrete, but if not, he was prepared to wing it.

The day was cloudy and had the look of rain in the sky. Harry tried to pay attention to the cars around him, but the traffic was heavy. He hoped that he'd notice any vehicle that stuck with him. Maybe he should reconsider Cowboy's offer of having somebody watching his back. It would be easier to focus on what he needed to do rather than trying to be aware of everything around him.

After thirty minutes, Harry pulled into the parking lot of the place where he was meeting Karyn. As he shut his car off, his phone's buzzing told him that he had a text message. He pulled out his phone as he stepped from the Camaro. Slowly walking to the entrance of the coffee shop, he saw that it was a message from Cowboy. In all caps, it said, "THEY KNOW WHO YOU ARE. I SUGGEST LYING LOW. CONTACT ME WHEN YOU CAN."

"Shit!" Harry said aloud. He was hoping he had another day or two. Now he wasn't even sure that he could go back to his house. Maybe he could call Art and ask him and Jeannie to go get Max and watch him for a few days.

He looked up as he heard a car horn. It was Karyn pulling into the parking lot. Harry watched her stop in an empty spot not far from his car. She waved as she got out of her vehicle and came over to him. "You look serious. You okay?"

They started walking to the entrance of the coffee shop together. "Not really. I just found out..." Harry didn't get any further than that. A black Ford Ram pickup truck that had been parked on the street peeled rubber as it shot forward and pulled into the driveway in front of Harry and Karyn. It screeched to a halt and two men came out of either side of the truck. Harry grabbed Karyn's wrist and said, "Run!"

He made a beeline for the back corner of the coffee shop. He pivoted around the side of the building and yanked Karyn after him. Bullets thudded into the pavement and into the brick façade of the building. Harry pulled out his gun and took two quick blind shots around the corner in the direction of the truck. At the same time, he heard another vehicle accelerating to cut them off from the other side of the building. There was a narrow alley there and if it got here in the next few seconds, he'd be dead.

Karyn had pulled her gun from her pocketbook and screamed out, "FBI! Back off!"

A bullet whizzed by as a response. Harry said, "We're going to be outgunned in a second. I hope you have your running shoes on." He saw the front end of a car entering the alley they were in. "We need to go now. Follow me."

Harry Hid It

Harry grabbed her elbow and ran across the alley alongside an apartment building. The car slid to a stop and they heard more shots ring out. Bullets went past them or struck the structure, but thankfully, none of them found their mark. As they sprinted out past the front of the building, Harry bore to the left with Karyn on his heels.

She said, "Damn it, Harry, I'm a federal agent."

Harry ran into the parking lot of a small shopping center. They heard footsteps behind them. Harry saw a bread truck parked along the side of the store and headed that way. Rounding the corner between the building and the truck, Harry threw Karyn against the wall and then flattened himself against the wall. "And you're going to be a dead agent if we're not careful."

They heard someone pounding towards them and it sounded like he was speaking into a cell phone or radio. He said between deep breaths of air, "I got them. They ran behind the supermarket. I'm right behind them. Bring the cars arou…ugh!"

The last part was because as he came around the corner, Harry swung the butt of his gun with all his might. He caught their pursuer in the temple and his feet came out from under him. He fell flat on his back, leading with his head. There was a loud "thwack" as his skull met the pavement. A cell phone went skidding under the truck and the gun came to a rest at Karyn's feet. Harry didn't recognize the man he just clobbered. He was in jeans, an old sweater, ratty sneakers, and hadn't shaved in about three days. He was out cold. Karyn reached down, put the downed man's gun in her pocketbook, and cuffed him to an electrical conduit that stuck out of the building. She looked up as she heard the squealing of tires and racing engines entering the parking lot.

"Now what, Harry? There's a ten-foot fence behind the store. I haven't tried pole vaulting since high school. We defend ourselves here? Cops should be on their way with all these guns going off."

"We might be dead before they get here." He peered around the corner and saw the truck coming towards their hiding spot and an old Chevy Caprice blocking one of the two driveways into the parking lot. Then he got an idea. "Into the truck."

He pushed Karyn to the passenger door of the bread truck. He entered first and scrambled across to the driver's seat. He saw the keys still in the ignition. The driver must be in the store finishing a delivery. The engine roared to life as he saw in the side mirror the truck stopping behind him. Fortunately, the driver pulled forward so that the bed of the pickup was blocking the truck and not its cab. He saw a brawny guy getting out of the passenger side holding a semiautomatic machine pistol. Yup, he and Karyn were certainly outgunned.

"They don't know we're in here," said Harry. "Hang on to your ass."

With that, he threw the bread truck in reverse and stamped on the gas pedal. The truck's tires spun for a moment, grabbed the pavement, and shot backward into the pickup. Harry hung on as the impact rocked the truck. He kept pressure on the gas and kept the truck going backwards. He saw Karyn coolly waiting with her pistol in both hands. The force of the bread truck pivoted the pickup around on its front tires. The man with the machine pistol was trying to get out of the way so he could get a clear shot. As Harry turned his truck free, Karyn kicked open the passenger door and took a bead on the man with the gun. He started to randomly fire and the shells tore into the side of the truck making its way up to the cab. Karyn fired twice. As Harry struggled to get the truck going forward, he saw the guy fall. "You're good with that thing!" he shouted.

"Told ya. Can we stop now?"

"I have no idea if there's more. Let's get out of here, but feel free to call in the cavalry."

Harry had the truck facing forward and he put the transmission in drive and gunned the engine again. He was surprised at how quickly the truck accelerated and he aimed the truck for the open driveway. The Caprice saw what he was doing and moved forward to try to block him. Harry cut the wheel, went over the sidewalk and the curb, and caught the Caprice's trunk as he maneuvered the truck into the street. Trays of bread fell all around behind them as Harry struggled to straighten out the truck. It stopped skidding and moved forward. Karyn said, "The black truck is coming after us."

Harry set his jaw and flew down the road. Karyn had her phone out and was calling 911. Waiting for it to connect, she looked up at the corner sign to see what street they were on. Her eyes widened. "Harry, you're on a one-way street."

"I'm only going one way," he shouted.

"No, you...oh shit!" she braced herself in her seat as a UPS van turned the corner coming at them. She had time to register the terror on the driver's face as Harry deftly pulled his truck to the right and drove up on the sidewalk. After sending three garbage cans flying, he pulled back onto the street. He made a right turn at the first intersection. Taking a second to look in the mirror, he saw the pickup still behind him.

Karyn was yelling into the phone. "This is FBI agent Karyn Dudek. I'm in a bread truck being followed by a black pickup. The people in pursuit are heavily armed. I need backup now." She listened for a second. "Yes, I'm in a bread truck." She looked up at a sign they were going under. "We're pulling onto Grand Central Parkway heading south. Request help."

She shut off the phone and looked at Harry. "They're scrambling the troops. Help is on the way."

"Never thought I'd be so happy to see the cops," said Harry. He could still see the truck behind him. He looked past Karyn at the passenger mirror and saw that either he'd knocked it off or it had been shot off. "I can't see on your side. Is anything there?"

Karyn was just angling her head when the Caprice hit the truck directly behind the passenger door. Karyn yelped as Harry cursed and fought with the wheel. The Chevy kept pushing, trying to direct them into the concrete divider. Karyn struggled to roll down the window. When she had it halfway down, she stuck out her gun to fire at the car. Just then, the bread truck sideswiped the cement barrier and the pickup plowed into the back. Karyn lost her grip and her gun tumbled harmlessly onto the highway. Harry heard her curse a blue streak.

"They're trying to squeeze us," said Harry. He pulled the wheel as hard as he could to the right, but he couldn't push the car out of the way. He looked behind the truck and saw the pickup back away. "Must be gearing up for another ramming job," thought Harry.

Instinctively, he stomped down on the brakes. "Brace yourself," he shouted. The truck slowed abruptly and the pickup banged into the rear. The Caprice scraped down the side of the truck and suddenly drifted into the front of the bread truck. Harry accelerated and pulled to the right. He glanced off the trunk of the Caprice, forcing it into the concrete divider. In the mirror, he saw the pickup also hit the car, which spun around several times in the road. Traffic had backed away from the three vehicles and the Chevy stopped in the middle of the road.

Harry continued to the right and zipped up an exit. He ignored a traffic light at the end of the ramp. Horns blared as Harry concentrated on keeping the truck between cars. Behind him, he saw the pickup not being as considerate as it knocked a minivan to the side and roared after them. Karyn yelled out, "Anyone with a brain would've quit a long time ago. You must have one hell of a price on your head."

"Either that or they don't have a brain." He saw Karyn checking the gun she took from the guy he knocked out in the parking lot. "You lost your gun?"

"Yeah, and I'm pissed. It was expensive and I'll have to buy a new one." She examined the clip and shoved it back into the pistol. "Hope this damn thing doesn't blow up in my hand," she muttered. Louder, she said, "What's your plan?"

"We either isolate this truck and you take down the driver, or we lead him into the arms of the police. I'm open to suggestions."

"Let's get off the road. We can't let people get hurt by these assholes."

Harry looked ahead and gave a wolfish grin. "Just what the lady ordered," he said.

Karyn watched as he pulled off the road and headed to what looked like a mall under construction. There were work trucks ahead near the main building, but Harry steered towards the parking deck that looked finished. "Are you nuts?" asked Karyn.

"It's been mentioned before," said Harry. "He's got more horsepower than us and I can't beat him on an open road. In there, we'll be equal. Can you get the marines to head in this direction?"

Karyn got back on the phone as Harry aimed the truck at the parking deck's entrance. As he saw the height requirement, he wondered if the truck was too high. As they bounced off the speed bump, the top of the truck scraped the roof. Harry kept the truck to the center of the garage. Like most parking decks, the driver had to keep the wheel turned to keep ascending higher.

Karyn turned to him. "What are you going to do when you get to the top?"

"Where are the cops?"

"They should be here any minute."

"This garage is one way. I keep seeing exit signs. Once we get to the top, we'll head back down. Hopefully, the cops will be there to intercept this asshole."

Suddenly, their truck emerged into cloudy sunlight. The pickup accelerated and banged into the rear of the bread truck as Harry aimed for the exit ramp. Karyn yelled out, "This has gone on long enough." She climbed between the seats and climbed over the mounds of bread that fell on the floor. She found the clasp for the door and released it. She sat down and put her legs against the door, while she held the pistol in a two-handed grip. Pushing out, the doors flew open and Karyn pulled the trigger twice to let off two quick shots before they banged shut again.

Harry yelled back, "That got him off our ass a bit."

Karyn felt the truck tilt forward as they started down the deck's ramp. She scrambled back up to the front. "I don't have any way to keep the doors open; otherwise, I'd empty my gun into him."

Looking out toward the driveway as the view flashed by, Harry didn't see any police cars yet. He wasn't sure if he could do another turn of follow the leader through the garage, but the truck would nail him if he headed back to the highway. He could feel the engine of his truck starting to labor. He said to Karyn, "You need to make him back off again. I want to do something, but we need a few seconds."

Karyn didn't ask why. She just groaned and went to the back. This time she let off a few shots that shattered the front of the pickup's window. As her truck's doors started to close, she grabbed trays of bread that were scattered around her and started throwing them out the back. Like a dog digging into the dirt, she pushed everything she could find behind her so it slid out of the back and into the path of the black truck.

Harry could see everything through the mirror. The shattering of the window slowed down the truck considerably and it tried to avoid the loads of bread coming out of the back. As Harry made another turn to go down another level, he saw the truck glance off one of the walls. It must've knocked the driver off course because for the first time since they entered the parking deck, Harry lost sight of the truck.

"Karyn, get up here. We have one shot at this."

She came up and got in her seat. She saw they were on level two and heading to the bottom floor. "What are you going to do?"

As an answer, Harry turned the wheel and slammed on the brakes. The car skidded down the rest of the ramp and stopped just as it was about to enter the ground floor. Harry managed to block the ramp right at the last bend on the slope. He shoved open his door and dragged Karyn after him. He pulled her behind one of the support pillars and they crouched down. They heard the pickup accelerating off the second floor as it came down the last part of the ramp. Too late, the driver hit the brakes. Harry and Karyn heard the truck trying to stop as it plowed into the bread truck. The force of the pickup pushed their ride forward and out of the way. The pickup spun in a 360-degree circle until it smacked into the wall and came to a stop.

Karyn approached the truck at a dead run. "Don't fucking move," she shouted as she approached the driver's door. She yanked it open and watched as he fell to the ground in front of her. She could see that he was breathing, but his eyes were glassy and he appeared stunned.

Cop cars started pouring in as Harry came up behind her. She asked him, "Where the hell did you learn to drive?"

"Misspent youth. Nice job back there. I can see you shooting from a horse."

For the first time this morning, she smiled. "Is life always this exciting with you, Harry Strickland?"

Harry could feel himself starting to calm down as the adrenaline began to leave his system. He managed to smile. "I have my moments."

Karyn had her FBI credentials out and her gun still pointing at the driver on the ground. "Let me do the talking. I don't want to confuse the cops."

"I'm going to hold you to doing all the talking…to everyone," Harry emphasized.

"What do you mean?" asked Karyn.

"Look at the bread truck. I'm not going to explain that to the owner."

Karyn turned her head and saw their ride. What used to be your basic box truck now resembled an accordion.

She blew out a puff of air. "Sure. I'll take care of that too."

Chapter 35

As Harry and Karyn were sorting out what was going on with the cops, John was talking on the phone. He said, "You warned Harry, then?"

"Yeah, I sent him a text," said Cowboy. "I'm trying to track down some more leads and I hope to hook up with him later."

"How did you find out that they identified me and Harry?" John asked.

"It's really weird shit. It seems that Fat Tony went out of house to hire his hit men. That means the word is out on the street about what's going on and nobody has any reason to keep his mouth shut. One of the guys who rides in that motorcycle gang we joined with a few times out of Brooklyn told me about a bar where you can find dirtbags to do just about anything. He used to be a cop and knew about it. I went there and asked around."

"Somebody told you Fat Tony knew it was us?"

"He was pretty shitfaced when I talked to him. A person who sounds like this Sean Riley I told you about was in last night recruiting people. He mentioned your names and said he was looking for two crews to go after you both today. There's an extra ten thousand dollars for whoever actually kills you."

"Only ten thousand," said John. "That's insulting!" The truth was that he was scared, but he was trying to figure out what to do.

"Where are you?" asked Cowboy.

"I'm home."

"Get out of there, John. That's probably where they're going to start looking. Where's Julia?"

"She's over in lower Manhattan. I told her what was going on and she's staying with a friend."

"How did that go over when you told her?"

340

Harry Hid It

"I'm still alive, but she wasn't happy."

"Well, you aren't going to be alive much longer if you don't get out of there. Head over to the clubhouse. We can keep you safe there."

The clubhouse was a motorcycle repair shop on the Queens/Nassau County border. The back of the shop was a very large garage that became the headquarters for John's motorcycle gang.

"Sounds like a good idea," said John. "I'm going to grab a few things and head over."

"I'll be out and about. Hang tight there with the other guys until I get there. Watch your back!"

As he clicked off, John gathered up a backpack he'd put a change of clothes in and headed toward the back door. Stopping at the kitchen table, he picked up a present that a friend left him last night. Technically, it was a lupara. Most people who used it called it a lupo, which means wolf in Italian. It was the ultimate traditional Sicilian close-quarters combat weapon. It was a double-barreled, sawed-off shotgun. While shepherds and goat herders used it to kill wolves and bandits, it became popular among Sicilian assassins. It was powerful and he didn't have to worry too much about his aim.

He and Julia lived in a small, two-story house. There was enough room in the back that John built a small garage for his motorcycles. As he stepped out the back door and put his helmet on, he heard someone smash in the front door. Without looking back, he ran to the other building and threw open the door. Jumping onto his Harley, he stuck the lupo in a saddlebag, kicked over the machine, and roared out onto the street. Looking behind him, he saw a car and a truck that he didn't recognize sitting in front of the house. He saw somebody in sunglasses looking at him with his mouth open.

John hunched over his bike as he poured on the power. Glancing in his mirror, he saw two motorcycles chasing him. John figured they knew he was a biker and had a couple of people with motorcycles just in case. John had been riding motorcycles since he was fifteen. He started to go faster and figured he'd find out quick enough how good these two were.

Every nook and cranny of his neighborhood was familiar to John. He drifted over to the left side of the road, before making a hard left and taking off up a side street. Making a right, John found himself in an area of small warehouses. He quickly went up a ramp that small trucks would use to enter the warehouse to load or unload. As soon as he was inside, he whipped his bike around and throttled down. He saw the two motorcyclists pass by, roaring in the direction he'd been going. Edging his bike to the door, he looked outside and saw the two pursuers slow down at the intersection. They made hand motions to each other and one went left while the other went right.

John felt like he'd been holding his breath since he left his house. He took a few big gulps of air into his lungs and he started out again. He coasted down the ramp and headed back the way he came. As he turned onto the street that would take him to the highway, John had to swerve out of the way as a red Toyota almost careened into him. Glancing to the right, he saw the driver trying to aim a gun at him. John put on the brakes and the car shot ahead of him as he cut behind it and roared down a side street. He braked at the stop sign and took his time to look around. He wasn't sure where to go. He knew if he could make it to the highway, he had a chance to get to the clubhouse.

He heard a car skidding around the corner and picking up speed. He felt something zip past his helmet and realized it was a bullet. They were shooting at him! John's front tire rose off the street as he fed gas to the engine. He went off like a shot, leaving the smell of burnt rubber in the air. In front of him, an old brown dump truck pulled out into the street and stopped. He realized this was one of the vehicles he saw in front of his house. "Christ, how many of them are there?" he shouted. "Fuck it."

He poured on the power and drove his bike behind a bus stop

pavilion and onto the sidewalk. People jumped and scattered out of his way as he shot past the truck. A motorcycle appeared on the sidewalk in front of him and raced toward John. Instead of slowing down, John went even faster. This was the ultimate game of chicken. He counted on his skill to get him out of this one. As they closed in on each other, John quickly shifted his backpack off his shoulders and into his left hand. At the last second, he pulled his bike to the right of his attacker and hit him as hard as he could in the face with the backpack. The force of the blow knocked the rider sideways and he and his bike smashed through the display window of a shoe store.

John swayed back onto the street and tried to see who was around him. He saw the other cyclist a block away, but the red Toyota was up ahead and the dump truck was lumbering behind. Right now, John would give anything for a cop car to show up. Why were they only ever around when you didn't want them?

Speeding up, John swerved his bike back and forth as he headed to the Toyota. He had a better view of the driver now. He was a large man with red hair wearing sunglasses. It looked like he was shouting instructions into a radio. He saw the passenger side door open and a man getting out holding a gun. Instead of speeding up, John sharply braked his bike and stopped behind the car. The man with the gun wasn't expecting this and was out of position to turn his gun on John. For his part, John pulled out the lupo and pulled the trigger. The first barrel of the sawed-off shotgun went off and blew away the man with the gun as well as part of the rear window of the car. As he heard the other motorcycle coming behind him, John turned and shot the other barrel into the rider's helmet. It disintegrated as glass, helmet, and brains mingled together in a spout of red blood.

As he revved up his engine and was about to take off, the red Toyota shot backwards and rammed into John. He felt his left leg break under the impact. The bike fell on top of him as he saw the wheels of the dump truck go by his head. He felt hands pick him up and throw him and his bike into the dump truck. He saw the driver of the Toyota get into the truck with him and felt the vehicle moving forward. Finally, John heard sirens in the distance, but he had a sinking feeling that it was too late.

As John tried to maneuver out from under his motorcycle, the big redhead crawled next to him and pulled out a gun. "Don't move." John stopped as the man brought out handcuffs and put them around John's wrists in such a way that he was bonded to his motorcycle. When he was sure John was secure, he put the gun away and searched John and the bike and took anything that might make a weapon. Then he sat back against the side of the truck. The big man said, "You certainly made this hard. You're lucky I didn't have enough money to get some really good people. You wasted a couple of idiots. It sucks that this is what I have to work with."

John grunted out, "Why are you doing this? Let me go and I'll go away."

"Not that simple, Ace. You weren't very nice to Mr. Russo. He still pays me." When he heard his phone ring, he said, "I have to take this."

Riley answered the phone and was quiet for a few minutes. Finally, he said, "What happened after you broke down on the highway?" He listened again and ended with, "You better be smart enough to avoid the cops. If they get you, you'll be a dead man." He looked down at his phone with a look of disgust.

John watched him bang his fist on the bed of the truck. "Damn it. What a bunch of fucking idiots." Looking over at John, he said, "Your asshole friend appears luckier than you. I'll get him too and be done with this." Picking up the phone, he made a call. "I got the one I went after, Mr. Russo. Nailed him on his motorcycle." Riley grimaced as he listened. "No, a couple are dead. Don't worry; nothing can be traced back to you. What do you want me to do with him?" His eyes widened as he heard the answer. "OK, I'll take care of it."

Harry Hid It

Sean Riley looked at John blankly for a minute. "Sorry, pal, you picked on the wrong guy." He stood up and banged on the roof of the truck's cab. It slowed down and pulled over. John watched the man vault over the side and heard a door open and close. Immediately, the truck started up again and picked up speed.

The pain in his leg brought tears to his eyes. John wrestled the motorcycle off his body and looked around for a way to slip the handcuffs off the bike at least, but the big goon had wrapped them around the main support strut. He was in a fix. Somebody had to see them throw him in the truck, so where were the cops? Trying to stand himself and the bike up, John cried out as his leg gave way. He felt in his pocket for his cell phone but couldn't find it. Had they taken it or had it fallen out of his pocket? It didn't matter much now. He realized that all he wanted to do was talk to Julia one last time.

The surface the truck traveled over changed from asphalt to dirt filled with many ruts. Dust flew up and John saw flattened cars piled on top of each other. Where the hell were they? Some kind of salvage yard, he reckoned. He also guessed they'd be stopping soon. It sounded like they didn't get Harry yet. Whatever happened, he hoped his friend would get these bastards somehow. The truck lurched to a stop and then backed up. John saw some type of machine looming above the dump truck. He was trying to figure out what it was when the bed of the truck started to tip up and the gate of the bed opened. John tried to brace himself, but he wasn't going to win the battle against gravity. Soon, he and the motorcycle tumbled down the bed of the truck and onto something made of steel.

As much as he tried to spin out of the way, the Harley landed on top of John, crushing the wind from his lungs. It felt like he broke a couple of ribs. Some sharp edge on the metal he landed on was cutting into his side. John forced his eyes open and saw that there were walls of metal around him. He heard the sound of hydraulics and watched a curved metal top coming down and sealing the top, shutting out all of the light. John felt like they closed him in a huge metal coffin.

He was trying to figure out what this was when he heard another whine of hydraulics and the sound of a machine coming alive. He heard things start to move. Terrified, John realized where he was. It was a car-crushing machine in a salvage yard.

Outside at the controls, Riley couldn't hear John screaming over the sound the machine made. In less time than it took to microwave a hot dog, the crushing stopped and the top of the apparatus opened up. Riley signaled to the man sitting in the crane and he maneuvered forward. The claw on the end of the crane's arm descended and grabbed hold of what was in the machine. It slowly rose and pulled up a compressed cube of metal that used to be a BMW, a Harley, and John. The claw swung around and deposited the block into a different dump truck than the one Riley used to get here. That one was in the corner of the yard having its license plate and markings changed.

Approaching the driver, Riley gave him a sheet of paper and an envelope. "Here's the address. After it gets dark, take this thing there and dump it in front. Stick the envelope on it so people can find it. Make sure you don't get caught and put on gloves right now so you don't get your fingerprints all over it. Mr. Russo will want to hear that you did a good job."

The driver took out a pair of latex gloves and put them on. He took the envelope and address and slowly drove away. Riley looked around. Seeing he was now alone, he let loose and shouted out every curse he knew and leveled them at Fat Tony Russo. The cheap motherfucker had only given him enough money to hire the bottom of the tough guy barrel.

Calming down, Riley realized that in any kind of business, you get exactly what you pay for. Other than himself and the dump truck driver, everyone he had used today was a hired hand. The results certainly showed. Two men were killed on his team and he wasn't sure about the one who went through the plate glass window of the shoe store. These men didn't know who he was or that Fat Tony was bankrolling the operation…not that he shelled out much money to begin with. Riley began to suspect Tony would've had trouble coming up with the ten thousand dollar bonus he promised to anyone who actually did the killing. Then Riley's ass would've been in a wringer with these hired scumbags.

The problem was that when he talked to a couple of good gun hands that he knew, he was forced to give a little more information about what the job was about and why Fat Tony was involved. When one man heard Fat Tony was behind it, he picked up his drink without a word and went to sit on the other side of the bar where they met. The second one started laughing as if it was the best joke he ever heard in his life.

At least there might be only one more jerkoff to deal with. Riley knew he had to figure out what kind of damage control he had to deal with regarding that fiasco. Maybe the truck driver did nail Harry and he could put this mess behind him. Riley pulled out the burner cell phone from a back pocket and looked to see if he missed a call. If anyone killed Strickland, they'd be calling to claim their prize.

Nobody called except the driver who apparently wrecked himself out on the highway chasing Harry. Riley was about to put the phone away when it chimed. He quickly said, "Yeah?

He slumped against the controls of the machine as he listened. Then he said, "I don't give a fuck that you're in jail. That's your problem. You should've used your phone call for an attorney, because I'm done. Now I have to destroy this phone, asshole." The man on the other end yelled something in the phone. Riley looked surprised but said, "If you were any good, you stupid son of a bitch, you wouldn't have been caught. Rot away."

Riley took the phone, found a piece of pipe lying nearby, and pulverized the phone into dust. It was overkill, but he needed to beat on something. When he was done, his breath was coming in short gasps and his red face broke out into a sweat. He started walking back to his car, which was near the front of the salvage yard. He was thinking about how to handle this new information.

Remembering how his predecessor as Tony's right-hand man lost his job, Riley decided to call Fat Tony with the news. Depending on his reaction, Riley figured Tony would calm down by the time he saw him again or Sean would pack up and go find another line of work today, preferably in a different state. Taking out his regular cell, he called Tony. He heard, "You better have good news for me."

"Uh, I have both actually. John is finished and will be delivered tonight like you asked."

"I take it that's the good news. What's the bad?"

"There was an FBI agent with Strickland when they tried to take him down. The feds may be on to you."

"Did your people get both of them?" asked Fat Tony.

Lamely, Riley said, "I don't know. I'm still trying to find out."

All Riley heard was "stupid motherfu…" when the call went dead. He had a feeling Tony threw another cell phone against the wall. Riley got into his car and headed out to find out if Harry Strickland was alive or dead.

Chapter 36

HARRY WAS EATING A slice of pizza at a place down the street from the FBI's Manhattan office. He was starved. Anybody watching him would see him periodically shake his head as if in amazement. They'd be right. Harry was constantly playing out in his head his escape earlier in the day. There was no way he and Karyn should be alive. Whether it was luck or skill on their part, or a piss-poor hit team, Harry didn't care. It was nice to be here munching on pizza.

Thinking it through, Harry thought that he must've had the truck or car they tangled with on his tail since leaving his house in the morning. He had no clue why they just didn't kill him in his driveway. Maybe the one watching was waiting for backup. Regardless, he didn't know if he'd be that fortunate again. He had people go up against him in the past for some small bullshit, but nothing like he experienced today.

When he was in the parking deck waiting off to the side while Agent Dudek dealt with the police, Harry called Art. "I need a couple of favors," he said when the big man answered the tavern's phone.

Art heard something in his friend's voice. "Are you okay, Harry? I never saw you look as serious as you did yesterday."

"I'm fine, but a lot of shit is going down. I need you and Jeannie to do a few things for me."

"What do you need?"

"I have some bad people after me. However, I just finished with a few that I've been tangling with for the last hour. Since they were all chasing me, I'm going to assume there's no reason anyone is at my house. Can you two go there? Jeannie knows where the key is. In my bedroom, you'll see a big nylon bag on

349

the floor. Throw a bunch of clothes and underwear and shit in there for a few days. There's a black bag in the bathroom I keep packed. Take that too. Grab a coat and my hiking boots from near the back door."

Harry could tell Art was writing it down. "No problem. Anything else you need?"

"Yeah, you'll find a set of car keys on a hook near the door. Drive my Chevy over to your place and stick it in your lot. It's a lot less conspicuous than my Camaro."

"I can do that. Jeannie can drive it over here."

"I owe you, Art. Can you put Jeannie on the phone for me?" Art yelled over to her and then he heard some mumbled conversation between the two of them. When the waitress got on the line, Harry asked, "Can you take Max for a few days for me?"

"Harry, I love Max, but my apartment is only slightly bigger than the booths here at the bar. It's going to be tight."

"I can appreciate that, sweetheart, but I don't trust Max with just anyone. I'll pay you for your time. More than that cheap bastard you work for."

She laughed. "He treats me fine. Why do you think I've been here so long? He said somebody is after you?"

"Yeah, I just stopped a few of them. I can operate much better knowing Max is safe."

"I'll take care of the big mutt, Harry. I better go. Art already has his jacket on and is giving me the hurry-up motion. That's interesting. He's taking the gun he keeps under the register with him. What the fuck, Harry?'

"That sums it up. It's fucked up. You'll be safe with Art. Grab the dog food and leash and anything else you may think you'll need for Max. I'll be in touch."

"You take care of yourself."

Harry put his phone away and watched Karyn dealing with the cops. She impressed him. He had never worked with a woman in the context of any of his "side jobs" as he liked to call them.

Harry Hid It

Other than not realizing right away the severity of the situation they'd been in, she was a cool cookie under fire. When she had the chance, she showed no hesitation in shooting back at the assholes they dealt with. He wondered what happened to the two they left in the parking lot and the guy who finally broke down on the highway.

Looking over at the broken bread truck, he figured the owners had insurance. He smiled to himself as he imagined an insurance adjuster reading that report. Harry knew he was still in deep shit with Fat Tony, but he felt a little better knowing that Max was safe. Plus, there was something exhilarating about escaping death. It was a great high, but he was okay if he never experienced it again. He'd get pumped when jumping from a plane or diving into the depths of the ocean, but it paled to how he was feeling right now.

Soon, Karyn had everything straightened out with the local cops. There had been a little shouting, but between her conversational skills, looks, and FBI credentials, everybody seemed to be getting along. Eventually, she beckoned him over and they got a ride back to the coffee shop in one of the unmarked cars that showed up on the scene.

They didn't talk at all on the ride back. After they got out and the police car took off, she looked at Harry. "Do you know how much bloody paperwork I have to go back to the office and do? Not only are we lucky that we aren't dead, but nobody else is either. Well, except for the loony tune with the machine pistol that I shot. Out of the four people after us, two are in custody, one is dead, and the bozo on the highway ran away."

"Don't you people keep score with how many arrests you make and how many people you shoot?" Harry asked.

"Jesus Christ, Harry, it's not funny! Do you know how many FBI agents go through their entire career without discharging their weapon? Most of them! But one morning with you and I shoot to the top ten percent." She stepped up to Harry with a serious look on her face. "Look, Harry, I'm grateful we're alive. That was some badass driving you did. But I need to know if it was worth it. Without going into details, nailing Fat Tony would be a big deal to my boss and me. Since he's trying to shoot your ass, can you deliver?"

"Look, Karyn, I didn't know this was going to happen. I only found out that I had people after me the other day. By the way, you were great today. You can ride shotgun with me anytime."

"Dammit, I don't want to make a steady routine out of this. We can discuss it later. I want you to come into the city with me. I have to go report to my boss."

Harry immediately went on the defensive. "I told you before, I'm not going to go into the FBI office with you. To do that, you have to arrest me."

"Stop the bullshit. We both know that I don't have anything to arrest you on…yet. You know what you did, I think I know what you did, but I have no evidence or anyone talking to me. No, Harry, this is just to make things easier. I need to talk with my supervisor, and then we need to see how we can work together to put Tony Russo away before he does more damage. You can even follow me in your car and hang out somewhere nearby until I'm done. I don't want to get caught up in another Hollywood chase scene just to talk to you. I've been straight with you and you owe me after taking me on your little thrill ride."

In spite of the situation, Harry liked how her eyes flashed when she was angry. There was a lot to this woman, unlike any he had ever met. Bringing himself back to the matter at hand, he thought about what she said. The closest to anything concrete she had was Harry's vague acknowledgement that he may have been there when Fat Tony was robbed and his son killed. He knew that if one piece of evidence surfaced connecting him to the other jobs, she'd have cuffs on him faster than a politician telling a lie. Maybe the FBI didn't care too much if crooks robbed from each other. The other possibility is that they looked at him as a small fish that might help them catch a bigger fish.

Seeing Karyn as the best possibility to neutralize Fat Tony without sustaining a murder rap, Harry said, "I'll follow you in. We can talk when you're done." He pursed his lips as he thought. "I really have no place to be right now. I originally wanted to meet you this morning to help me think about a few things. After what we just went through, I obviously have a lot more thinking to do." He saluted. "Lead on."

"Geez, Harry, you can be such an ass sometimes." She went to get in her car.

"I've been told that too," Harry said as he opened the door to the Camaro. He followed Karyn through the maze of traffic until they were in Lower Manhattan. The FBI had their city headquarters at Federal Plaza, which wasn't too far from City Hall. He followed Karyn into a parking garage. She stopped at a security guard who waved her through. When Harry pulled up, he said, "Go over there to the left. You'll see spots for visitors. There should be a couple openings."

Harry did as instructed and found a space for the Camaro. Karyn met him as he stepped out of his car and said, "There's a door over there that leads out to the street. Keep your phone handy and I'll give you a call when I'm done. This may take a while. I never shot up the streets in New York before."

"I'll be waiting. While you're in there, I'll see if I can find out anything from my few contacts."

Karyn simply nodded and went over to a bank of elevators. Harry made his way outside and walked a couple blocks. He actually felt safe here for the moment. Fat Tony and his minions had no idea he was in Manhattan. In fact, they'd have to scramble around to find him again. He realized the knot in his stomach for the past couple days was actually gone for the time being. That helped him realize he was very hungry, and with that he found the pizza shop.

After finishing off his slice and thinking about having a second, his phone rang. It was Cowboy and he picked it up. "What's going on?"

"You're still alive," said Cowboy. "Good deal. Anybody try to whack you today?"

"As a matter of fact, four came after me."

"Holy shit, how did you get out of that?"

"Kind of a long story. I was meeting up with that FBI agent I mentioned when they hit us. She was a big help, and we were able to run away and stole a bread truck. The final tally is two in jail, one dead, and one got away."

"Why did you steal a bread truck?"

"It seemed like a good idea at the time. I told you it's a long story."

"What happened to you coincides with what I've been finding out."

"What's that?" asked Harry.

"For some reason, Fat Tony's trust meter within his own organization is down to zero. That Riley guy seems to be his main lieutenant, but for some reason he's looking for outsiders to do the dirty work. I'm thinking Tony is paranoid and subcontracting work. On the other hand, maybe he doesn't have too many men left. I'm trying to get more of a handle on that."

"Have you heard from John?"

He heard Cowboy clear his throat. "I talked to him earlier, right before noon. I told him he was definitely a target and to head to the clubhouse."

"That's the place your gang hangs out, isn't it? Big garage behind some cycle shop?"

"Yeah, I sent a couple boys over there loaded for bear. I'm hoping to get a call soon that he arrived. I'll keep in touch."

Harry sat there for a minute thinking about what Cowboy shared. He wondered if any of the people he tangled with a couple hours ago were Fat Tony's men or just hired help. One way or the other, when Fat Tony heard the news about today, it would be another wound to his sorry ass. Harry wanted the man to bleed until he was dead. He felt himself starting to get furious again as he thought about what he did to Ozzie and Spanky. At this moment, he felt like nothing would stop him until he brought the bastard down. Harry realized the fury that he felt now was stronger than the hate he felt for Tony Junior when he gave him and Sophia a hard time. "What a fucking loser family," Harry thought.

Still holding his phone, he called John. The phone went right to voice mail. Harry said, "Had a hell of a day so far. Hope yours has been better. Call me."

As soon as he clicked off, the phone rang again. It was Art. "How did you make out?" asked Harry by way of greeting.

"You keep everything nice there," said Art. "If I were like that, my wife wouldn't constantly be on my case."

"It's an extension of my work," said Harry. "I've always liked keeping my tools in order. It kind of carried over into everything."

"It made it easy to find what you wanted. It took ten minutes to pull everything together and get out of there with Max."

"Where is he now?"

"Sitting at the corner of the bar like he's fucking royalty. I may have to hire him. He's very popular with the customers. Everybody has been coming up to talk to him and pet him."

"Jeannie said you took a gun with you?"

"Better safe than sorry. You know why I was so good at professional football?"

"Because you blot out the sun with your size?"

"That, and I always prepared for every possibility before the game started. Better to be ready for what can happen, since we rarely know exactly what will happen. The gun seemed like a good idea."

"Thanks, Art, I really appreciate what you and Jeannie are doing. I'll be by today or tomorrow for my stuff."

"Sure, Harry, anything I can do?"

"Nah, you already have. I doubt it'll happen, but if somebody comes in there looking for me that you don't recognize, try to take a photo or take down a description.

"You got it. I'm here if you need me."

They said good-bye and Harry realized Art and Jeannie were almost like family to him. He and Max spent a lot of time there when he wasn't hanging around with Sophia and her family. The thought of Sophia gave him pause. He knew he should probably call her, but he didn't feel like going through the third degree. She was still pretty mad at the funeral. Keeping his distance might not be a bad idea for another day or two.

Deciding he didn't want any more pizza, Harry paid his tab and went outside. Looking up, he saw a mixture of blue sky and clouds. It had been that way all day. He realized it was starting to get cool out as they were heading closer to autumn. As he started to walk, he thought back over the past couple months. Was it only three months ago that he stole his last car for somebody else when he decided to move on to bigger things? A hell of a lot had happened since then and he wished he had a crystal ball to see how it was going to play out. For the most part, everything had gone about as well as it could. Yeah, there were a couple screwups that put him where he was now, but Harry wasn't sure if anyone else could plan things as well as he did. They did a handful of jobs in quick succession, made a lot of money, and nobody really got hurt.

"Oh, Ozzie, why couldn't you just steal a fucking truck that night," Harry said to himself. He knew he screwed up using the computer at work, but he was pretty sure if this shit with Fat Tony didn't start happening, Agent Dudek would've faded away by now. He also realized he'd have been a little disappointed if she weren't around.

Thinking about everything he planned and executed through the summer gave Harry a certain amount of confidence with dealing with Fat Tony. He always knew he was smart in figuring out how to do things, whether it was putting an engine together or planning a job. What he needed to do now was apply that same skill to getting rid of Fat Tony once and for all. He didn't have enough information yet to figure something out, but he had faith in Cowboy.

Harry was definitely scared. He remembered hearing once that having courage didn't mean you weren't afraid; it just meant you could move forward in spite of the fear. He felt like their close escape gave him some additional confidence. Harry knew he wasn't bulletproof. He also understood it was easy to hide in plain sight here in lower Manhattan and it would be different when he went up against Fat Tony.

It was then that Harry received a text from Karyn. She asked if he could meet her at a bar not far from her office in an hour. He told her that he'd be there.

As he continued walking, Harry knew he was going to beat Fat Tony and that motherfucker who did his killing. He was smart enough to realize he couldn't do this on his own. As much as it went against his grain, he realized he'd need Karyn and the resources of the FBI to pull this off. One way or the other, this would soon be over. He just hoped that it wouldn't be over his dead body.

Chapter 37

THE PLACE KARYN TOLD him to go was the Lamp Light. As he went in, Harry saw a large bar against the left wall. The remainder of the space was devoted to tall tables that were haphazardly placed around the room. He decided against the bar and went to a table in the corner. Its position allowed him to observe everyone coming in and out. It wasn't quite happy hour yet, so the tavern only had a few patrons. He figured that due to its proximity to the FBI building, this was probably a place where agents hung out.

A middle-aged waitress came over and took his order. Harry was halfway done with his first drink when Karyn Dudek walked through the door. She quickly spied Harry and came over. She sat down and waved the waitress over.

"Millie, I'll have a double Jack over ice. It might be a good idea to just bring over two of them now and save a trip."

As the woman hustled off, Harry raised an eyebrow and said, "You do knock them back, don't you?"

"Getting shot at, driving around with a maniac in a bread truck, and then having my ass chewed out gives me a good reason."

Harry looked down at Karyn's chair. "Your ass still looks pretty good from here."

Two heavy glasses being put in front of her silenced Karyn's retort. She picked up one and downed all the contents in one gulp. Placing the glass back on the table, she said, "That certainly helped. I don't know what it was. I was sitting at my desk and all of a sudden I got the shakes. It scared me. That never happened before."

Harry knocked back the rest of his drink. "That's common when you think you're going to die and you don't. It has something to do with all the adrenaline you have shooting through your body when you go through stuff like we just did. Then when the fear of death goes away, so does the adrenaline. I'm certainly no doctor, but it can certainly lead to where your entire body feels on fire or you start shaking. When I started skydiving that's exactly the rush I had the first couple of times. It's still a high for me, but I have so many jumps under my belt, it's not as intense." He signaled for a refill. "If it's any consolation, I was feeling the same way walking around before."

"I'm surprised," said Karyn. "I thought you were cool as a cucumber out there."

"And I could say the same about you. So why did you get your ass chewed when you went to your office?"

"What we did wasn't exactly by the book."

"Next time we'll give the shooters a script to follow. Will that help?"

"Shut up, Harry. I'm not mad at you...exactly. And my boss is being pretty cool about it. I had to tell him the story twice. I don't think he likes being in the office all the time. He misses the street."

"Then what's the problem?"

Karyn started on her second drink. This one she sipped. "I know this will come as a surprise to you, but there's a lot of crime in New York." She looked at him over the glass. "I'm pretty sure you've contributed to that. Anyway, there's been pressure on us from Washington to show some results. People think we have plenty of people here, but the truth is that we're undermanned for the metropolitan area. Hell, we should have an office full of agents strictly devoted to Wall Street with all the crime that goes on there."

"How did you almost getting killed lead to being yelled at?"

"Because an FBI agent was involved in something that caused havoc on the roads, shots were fired, and people thought there was a terrorism event at a mall under construction. I guess this was the day for traumatic events around the area. I heard something about another chase and bullets flying around where somebody drove through the window of a store. Fortunately for the Bureau, no FBI agent was there. From what I heard, neither were the cops because nobody was arrested in whatever that mess was."

"Are you in trouble?"

"The reason I'm in New York in the first place is because I'm in trouble," huffed Karyn. "This doesn't help my case. What happened to your friends has the place spooked. Murder and torture on our watch doesn't sit well. If we can do something about solving that or more, then we'll get an "Attaboy" and the heat will be off us."

"I'll be honest with you," said Harry. "The cops haven't exactly been my friend in the past, but I didn't know you had all that bureaucratic bullshit."

"I work for a government agency. Those two words together should bring up a vision of endless red tape. I wasn't kidding about all the reports I have to fill out. I thought I had everything together in one file so that maybe I can get some of them done tomorrow when I remembered I lost my gun. That pretty much doubled the file." She tossed back the remainder of her second drink. She held up her glass to indicate that she needed another.

"You girls from the west like your booze, I see," said Harry. "Are you going to be able to drive home?"

"No, I take the subway. Harry, here's the deal. I talked about you to my boss. The fact that Fat Tony killed your friends and is after you kind of proves that you robbed the man." As Harry started to say something, she held up her hand. "Wait, let me finish or I'm not going to get this all out."

Resignedly, Harry said, "Go for it."

"You know I started to talk to you because of those jewel thefts. I also found a few other crimes that I believe I can tie to you. Granted, I have no hard evidence right now, but give me time and I can find the dots I need to connect…at least for one of them, I'm sure. That would be enough for you to go away for many long years."

Harry Hid It

Harry felt himself getting pissed off. He thought of several things to say, but instead said through gritted teeth, "Is there a point to this?"

Karyn's third drink came to her and she drank half of it in one swallow. She looked around, lowered her voice, and hunched forward. "I see a couple of my colleagues came in from the office. This isn't for public knowledge. You help us get Fat Tony, accept a small token charge, we'll forget about everything else, my boss will put in a good word for you, and you'll be out in a year or two."

He couldn't believe what he was hearing. "How's this a good deal for me? Besides, I didn't do those other things you're talking about."

"Maybe...maybe not. However, if we nail Fat Tony and any of his men and they tell us how they figured out it was you who robbed him, that's going to set you up for years of hell, Harry. The district attorney around here or justice department will be all over your ass. They're the ones that keep score on convictions. Depending who goes after you, that's all some of those people care about. They don't give a fuck about justice or right and wrong. They want to close cases in their favor and move up the power ladder."

Harry knew this was the truth. He had seen more than one acquaintance get brought down from a relentless prosecutor. He knew a few who were even forced to plea bargain for something they didn't do because of the way the deck was stacked against them. He was beginning to feel a little less decisive, but he wasn't happy about being pushed into a corner.

Karyn looked intently at Harry. He thought she looked pretty clear-eyed for drinking five shots of Jack Daniels in twenty minutes and about to consume her sixth. "I'm good at my job, Harry. Regardless of the politics and other bullshit I have to put up with in the FBI, I really do want to do what's best. First and foremost, it's getting rid of Fat Tony and his ilk. If I have to spend more time putting a thief away for a long time, I'll do it." She looked away and her voice grew even softer. "I won't like it or really want to do it, but I will." She looked up at him again with a rueful smile. "I'm OK with not spending all those hours trying to bring you down. I can do this so you go away for a year or so."

For some reason, that made Harry chuckle. The woman was intense, but he appreciated the straightforwardness. He said, "You're not asking for me to make a decision tonight, are you?"

"No, as my supervisor said, this was an unofficial feeling out of the situation."

Harry asked, "They have any food in this place? I had a slice of pizza while waiting for you earlier." It was his turn to smile. "I think you should have something in your stomach to absorb the booze."

"You're a smart man, Harry Strickland. I've noticed that about you. I'd much rather work with you than go up against you. But in answer to your question, yeah, they have some good burgers here." She called over to Millie for a couple menus. They both ordered cheeseburgers and fries.

While waiting for the food, Harry asked, "Agent Dudek, if I agree to this arrangement, how do I know it'll go through like you say? I trust you well enough, but there are too many people above you who can say, 'Hey…just kidding!'"

"You don't, Harry. You'll have to trust me."

Thinking of John, Harry added, "Hypothetically, say there was someone else involved with all of this. I'd want him kept out of it."

"How about if he got the same deal?"

"Nope. I want him completely absolved or immune or what-ever you call it." He hesitated and then said, "Even if I had to take on another year."

Karyn looked at him wide-eyed. "Wow, Harry, that's loyalty. Is it that guy Frank?"

Harry doubled over in laughter. It took him a minute to get

control of himself. Wiping his eyes with his napkin, he exclaimed, "No! Let's not do the name game now. If you can get back to me on that, I'll consider telling you who. You okay with that?"

She nodded as their food was set in front of them. "I'll think about how best to do this. You do realize that we may need to use you as bait."

"It occurred to me. We'll see how it plays out. Let's eat and talk about something else for a while. So, what do you like to do for fun?"

The two of them effectively shut down any more shoptalk while they ate and talked about other things. Something changed for Harry and Karyn that day. It was similar to what military people feel when they go to battle together. The two of them faced death and lived to tell about it. They also knew that they were alive due to the effort of the other person. When Harry thought about it, he wasn't totally sure how he felt toward Karyn. He knew he liked her, but more importantly at this point, he respected her. That meant a lot in his book.

Karyn had two beers with dinner. When the check came over, Harry reached into his pocket, but Karyn waved him off. "This is on the FBI. What the hell, they bought a bread truck today; I guess they can pay for our dinner." As she pulled a credit card out of her pocketbook, Harry noticed that she was finally slurring some of her words. He knew men who would be under the table with what she drank in the short time they were there.

After paying, she stood up and put her hand on the table to keep from swaying. "O...K, guess I may have had a little too much. Sorry, Harry, I guess I get like this after being shot at and chased." She closed her eyes and seemed to will herself to stand straight. "Where are you staying tonight? I would imagine your house might not be safe." She put her hand to her mouth. "Oh, what about that gorgeous dog of yours?"

"I took care of that while you were dealing with the cops at the parking garage. I figured since everybody was after us, the house would be clear. My dog walker went and took Max. She can keep him for a few days until the air clears. As for me, I'll grab a room somewhere. I need a good night's sleep."

"Screw that. You can sleep on my couch. Your car will be fine in the garage." When Harry raised an eyebrow at this suggestion, she blurted out, "Don't get any ideas, pal. You'll be safe for the evening and I wouldn't mind you escorting me home tonight. I'm exhausted and had maybe one or two more drinks than I should have. Besides, I have my gun."

"No, you don't. You dropped it on the Grand Central Parkway."

"Fuck you, Harry Strickland. I have a spare. Now, be a gentleman and let's get out of here."

***

Cowboy cut his engine and glided his motorcycle to a stop outside the clubhouse. He hadn't worked like this since his Texas Ranger days. He tracked leads from one borough of New York to another. In the afternoon, he traded in his truck for his bike because it was a little easier to get around in traffic. He needed to sit down and put all his notes together. He also craved a beer. Stopping at the clubhouse tonight would give him a chance to do both with a little peace and quiet. People would leave him be if he asked. There shouldn't be that many there now anyway. It was pushing eleven and contrary to most people's impressions of motorcycle gangs, most folks that gathered at the clubhouse had jobs to get to in the morning.

He walked in and nodded at three men playing cards. Their women were at another table quietly talking. Cowboy waved a hand at them and went over to one of the well-stocked refrigerators in the place. Choosing a Lone Star beer from the case that he kept here, he went over to an out of the way table and turned on a nearby floor lamp. He brought out his pad of notes and his phone.

Harry Hid It

He tore off the pages that were full of his scribblings and sorted them. Starting with a clean sheet, he started to arrange everything he learned so far into some kind of order.

He was grateful as a whole that crooks had big mouths. At least the bad ones did. Spreading around some of the money Harry gave him helped too. Fat Tony was doing some bad shit. Cowboy had the feeling that the man was so careless that the police would track him down sooner rather than later. However, John and Harry might be dead by then and who knew how many other people. Harry certainly had his own adventure today and it was fortunate a bystander didn't get hurt in what went down.

As it was, Cowboy was worried about John. He never showed up here today. Cowboy was holding out hope that he'd find him when he arrived tonight, but there was nothing yet. Maybe he couldn't get here and took off somewhere else. Cowboy wished he had Julia's phone number to give her a call and see if she heard anything. He texted Harry at ten, but the reply was that he hadn't heard anything either.

Cowboy learned a long time ago how to compartmentalize his tasks. For the time being, he put John out of his mind and concentrated on pulling together everything he learned. He had almost enough to put a timeline together of what had gone on since Fat Tony's son bought it in the robbery to now. He had a meeting with some minor drug runner tomorrow that sounded encouraging about filling in some of the blanks.

At about midnight, the three couples said good night. He heard their motorcycles rev up and then fade off into the distance. Cowboy helped himself to another beer and continued working. After another half hour, he leaned his head on his arms to rest his eyes. At 1:30, he awoke with a start. He heard a loud thud out in front of the clubhouse and then a truck engine rumbling away. Pulling out his gun, he ran over to a side door and slipped out. He cautiously looked around the corner toward the main door. He saw a square shape sitting there. Looking beyond it, he saw the taillights of some big vehicle pulling away down the road.

Cowboy cautiously approached the object. It didn't look like any bomb he ever saw, but you could never be sure these days. As he got closer, it looked like a cube of metal under the building's outdoor lights. Some type of paper was attached to the cube with copious amounts of duct tape. He carefully examined everything the best he could. There seemed to be something red sticking to spots on the cube.

He saw that the paper was actually an envelope. Seeing no wires attached, he pulled out his penknife and carefully cut away the tape. He slit open the envelope and pulled out a single piece of paper. There was writing on it. Cowboy couldn't quite make it out and went over to the front door so he was directly under a light. He sucked in his breath and felt faint as he read it.

"Your friend and his motorcycle are in here. The BMW is a bonus. Don't fuck with us."

Chapter 38

IT WAS SEVEN A.M. when Harry's phone rang. Fumbling on the coffee table where he left it, he looked at the display and saw it was Cowboy. He answered with, "What is it?"

"We need to talk," Cowboy tersely said. "Where are you?"

"I'm in the city. What happened?"

There was nothing for a second and then Cowboy said, "Fuck it. I can't sugarcoat it. John bought it. He's dead."

Harry felt the living room spin for a moment. He concentrated on breathing and making the merry-go-round stop. "How? When?"

"I need to tell you that in person. It happened yesterday. I found out last night. I almost called you then, but I needed to make sure."

"You needed to make sure?"

"Harry, I'll explain when I see you. I haven't slept and spent the last six hours with the cops. When and where can we get together?"

Looking at his watch, Harry made some mental calculations. "Meet me at Art's at ten. He's not open yet, but he'll be there getting ready for the lunch crowd. He picked up some of my stuff and I need to get it anyway."

"You didn't go back to your house, huh? That was probably a good move. They might have some bastard hanging out there waiting for you to come home. If I went by there, I might just blow his fucking head clean off."

Harry said quietly, "He's really dead then?"

"Yeah, man. It hurts. I didn't know your other friends, but John and I were tight. I know enough not to go off half-cocked right now, but it's not easy. I'll see you at ten."

367

Harry Hid It

Harry looked stupidly at his disconnected phone. He felt totally empty inside. John was the one guy he could depend on in any situation. Harry also respected his opinion. John reined him back in a few situations when things could've gone bad. He was a good friend. Harry didn't have that many people in that category to lose.

He stood up and walked over to the kitchen sink to splash water on his face. It wasn't a far walk. Karyn's place could fit in his living room at home. And Harry didn't have a big house. The living room and kitchen were really one room, with a small breakfast bar marking the boundary between the two. When Harry helped Karyn onto her bed, he saw the bedroom was just big enough for a full size mattress. As for the bathroom, you had to leave it to have enough room to change your mind.

By the time they took the subway and reached Karyn's place last night, the alcohol she consumed had reached her head. Fortunately, she didn't get sick, but she was feeling no pain when they arrived. Harry laid her on the bed, took off her shoes, and then bedded down on the couch. There was an afghan draped over the back of it that he used for a blanket. The stress of the last few days caught up with him, as he had no trouble falling into a dreamless slumber. Funny how well you can sleep when you aren't worrying about people crashing through your door to put a bullet in your head.

He dried his face with a paper towel when he heard the bedroom door open. Turning, he saw Karyn slowly enter the room. Her face was screwed up in pain. At some point in the night, she woke up and undressed because she only wore an oversized T-shirt. Harry absently wondered if she had panties on. She did. He knew because when she reached above the sink to fish an aspirin bottle out of the cabinet, the shirt rode up. She had on rather brief blue ones.

She shook out several tablets and poured herself a large glass of water. She drained it as she washed down the aspirin. Looking at Harry, she said, "Been ages since I had a man over not wearing his shirt. Technically, that hasn't happened since I lived out west. Thank God you have pants on." As Harry went over to slip on his shirt, she asked, "Did I hear you talking to someone?"

"Yeah. John's dead." She looked at him uncomprehendingly. "My other friend whose name I didn't give you last night."

Her hand flew up to her mouth. "Oh, Harry, I'm so sorry."

"Me too." He was going to say something else but changed his mind. Instead, he asked, "How are you feeling?"

"Not bad. The headache will fade soon. It was self-inflicted, but I needed to do that last night. Yesterday was a bit much."

"That's an understatement. I guess John didn't make out as well as we did."

"What happened?"

"Not sure yet. I'm going to get filled in soon. I need to go and get my car and head back to my neck of the woods."

"You watch yourself."

"I got my gun."

"Is that thing legal?" asked Karyn.

"Actually, it is. I have the permit and everything."

Harry went back to the sink and picked up a glass. It was his turn to fill it up and down it. He was conscious of the warmth emulating from Karyn's body, as he stood right next to her. Looking down at her, he said, "That stuff we talked about last night?" She nodded. "I'm not making any deal with the feds, but I'll make a deal with you. It's not like I have to worry about ratting out on a friend anymore." Harry felt his eyes get wet. "You understand the difference?"

She quietly nodded.

He continued, "While me and some other people would love to kill Fat Tony now, that's not my style. I want this dirtbag to rot forever."

"You know you'll be going to jail yourself for a year or so."

"Yeah, but I need the vacation. Maybe you can talk your boss into making it one of those federal country clubs I hear about. I can catch up on my reading and get some painting in." He started to walk to the door but turned and asked, "Part of this is that you'll stop hounding me for things that you think I did?"

She simply nodded.

"Good. I've lost people this week. I'd rather have you as a friend than an enemy. There are too damn many enemies I have to clean up." Almost to himself he added, "When Sophia hears about this, that'll be it for that too. I'll miss her family. I liked them."

Karyn was at a loss for words. The hammer banging away in her brain didn't help. She never saw Harry Strickland look…she searched for the word…vulnerable. Then with a strength of will, he seemed to shake it off and straightened up. He gave her his boyish smile and said, "I know you have a lot to do today. Keep in touch and I'll do the same."

As he opened the door and started out, Karyn exclaimed, "Harry!" When he turned, she said, "Thanks for being a gentleman last night." He bowed and closed the door behind him.

Karyn looked down at how she was dressed. "Oh! I must really trust that crook. I'd never come out here in a shirt and underwear for just anyone." She stripped off the T-shirt and panties as she walked to the bathroom. She needed to stand in her telephone booth of a shower for as long as she could stand it to clear away all the cobwebs before she went to the office. She doubted there would be any kind of downtime for the next few days.

***

Harry negotiated the subway back to FBI headquarters. He grabbed coffee and a muffin to take with him in his car. He found the Camaro where he left it and started on the journey back to Art's. This time of the day, the commuter traffic was heading into the city, so his path was fairly clear of vehicles.

Harry Hid It

As he arrived back in his neighborhood, he thought about driving by his house and seeing who had it staked out. Realizing it would be a stupid thing to do by himself, he started to get the germ of an idea. It was well past time to go on the offensive. He thought about the lesson you learn at the age of five in the schoolyard. The best way to deal with a bully was to punch him in the nose. When you came down to it, Fat Tony was a bully. Granted, he was a psychotic bully, but still a bully. "Time to bloody some noses," said Harry.

He still had a half hour to go before meeting Cowboy. Harry had texted Art from the city to make sure he'd be at his place by ten. He drove his car about a mile away from the tavern and parked it in a small strip mall on the highway. His car would be safe enough here and Harry didn't want to do anything to attract attention to any other friends. Tony's hoods knew the Camaro and he didn't want to park it near Art's. He made sure he had everything he needed from the car, locked it up, and walked to the tavern.

When he went through the back door, he heard a whine and Max leaped on top of him. Not expecting it, the dog's weight and exuberance threw Harry against the doorjamb. Recovering, he went down on one knee and hugged and wrestled with his four-legged friend. Finally, Harry pushed Max back and stood up. He saw Art looking at him from the kitchen.

"When you told me you were coming this morning, I went over to Jeannie's and grabbed Max. I woke her, but I figured it might do both of you some good to see each other."

Harry put out his hand and shook that of the ex-football player. "Thanks, Art. You're a prince."

"Tell that to my wife when you see her. She may beg to differ. Anyway, I whipped up a breakfast for you and your friend. You have the bar area all to yourself." The tone in his voice changed. "What you texted me about John is true then?" Harry nodded his head. "Damn shame. He was a good man."

371

"You got that right, Art. And thanks for the breakfast. You didn't have to do that."

"No biggie. Go ahead in."

"I am. I texted Cowboy to come in the back way."

"No problem. I'll bring him in when he gets here."

Harry went into the bar. He stopped in surprise at Art's "no biggie." A large table was laid out with carafes of coffee, a pitcher of orange juice, eggs, pancakes, home fries, bacon, sausage, and toast. He contemplated what to start on when Art brought Cowboy in. His face looked drawn and exhausted. His eyes widened when he saw the table.

"My God, I just realized I'm famished." He turned to Art. "You, sir, are a gentleman and a scholar."

"I'm going to leave you two to your business. All these compliments this early in the day are going to give me a swelled head. If you guys need me for anything…and I mean anything…let me know." Art gave them a knowing look and retreated to the kitchen. Max passed him on his way out to be with Harry or to be around all the food. Harry wasn't sure.

The two men sat down. Cowboy poured himself a large orange juice and sucked it down. He then started on the coffee. Harry threw a sausage to Max, who snatched it cleanly out of the air. Harry waited until Cowboy got some food into him before he said, "Okay, give it to me. What happened?"

Cowboy carefully explained how he found the hunk of metal in front of the clubhouse last night. "I wanted to throw up when I read the note. Then the old training kicked in. I decided not to jump to conclusions and that maybe this was just a sick joke. I called the cops and they came in. I explained what happened and that John had some bad people after him recently. When they asked for more details, I told them I didn't have any. It was something John had only mentioned to me the other day."

"You don't want to show all of your cards?" asked Harry.

"Damn right. The coroner was able to ascertain that there

were human remains in there. It's going to take some work to extract them from that compressed metal. They'll have to make the match using DNA. I hate to say it, but I'm fine with the cops telling Julia. I didn't want to do it."

"You and me both," said Harry.

He got very quiet and Cowboy could see the anger and frustration pass over Harry's face. Cowboy said, "Go ahead and ask it. I did."

Harry took a long drink of coffee. Then, "Was John alive when they threw him in the compactor?"

"I'll give you the answer I received. They don't know. The coroner may be able to figure it out, but that's not guaranteed."

"Jesus Christ, what's with these people? They're downright sadistic."

"I need to get my head back in the game, but what I found out yesterday is that Fat Tony is a paper tiger. You put a big hurt on him back in the summer. He's been on a steady spiral downward since then. At first, I just thought it was financially, but it sounds like he's losing it. I don't know if he had all his marbles before, but he's delusional, paranoid, violent, and probably has mother issues. At least, that's the stuff I remember when I got my psych degree."

Harry stopped with a forkful of pancakes halfway to his mouth. "You have a psychology degree?"

"Just a bachelor's. That was enough schooling for me."

"If he's hurting financially, why is he spending so much money on personnel to kill people?"

"The easy answer to that is he's nuts. The other thing is that he's not renting top of the line talent out there. I found out that no one who's any good wants anything to do with Fat Tony. Besides, he won't pay their rates. That may be one reason you're still alive. You basically had assholes after you. You have to fill me in with the details from yesterday, but you might not have been so lucky with someone else."

"You're probably right. They had to begin following me when I left my house. I'm not sure why they didn't try to kill me when I went to my car. Don't get me wrong. I'm glad if I went up against the "B" team."

Cowboy said, "John wasn't so lucky. I'd like to get my hands on the police reports, but there was a lot of action in John's neighborhood yesterday. Two people were shot at close range with a shotgun and a motorcyclist got very cut up going through a plate glass window. Don't ask me why, but none of the fucking cops got there until after it was over. They didn't see a damn thing, but they must have witness statements by now."

Harry remembered Karyn saying something yesterday about someone going through a window. "I think I may be able to get my hands on those reports if you think they'll help."

"Definitely. I'm interested in descriptions of any of the people involved."

"Why?" asked Harry.

"Since you didn't mention a big redheaded Irishman chasing you, I want to find out if he might've been after John. He seems to be the only direct link I have to Fat Tony. This is the guy trying to hire people to help him with tracking you down. I have a hunch he may be the one who's been at the murders of all three of your friends. If he took down John, I'm going to fucking kill him."

Harry thought about this. "If you know this for sure, isn't there enough for the cops to go on? Why are they still walking around?"

"Harry, one of the frustrating things when I was with the Rangers was proof. You needed solid evidence to bring anyone in. The bigger the crime, the better your proof had to be. Otherwise, court and everything else turned into one big circle jerk. The bad guy either got away scot-free or had such a joke of sentence that he was back on the street quicker than a prairie dog jumping into his den. The alternative is dealing with it yourself. It happened, but you put your career at risk doing it."

"What are our alternatives?"

Harry Hid It

"Figuring out a way to put Fat Tony and his people away for good without question. The other choice is turning vigilante on them. I'll take either one right now. It's still early so I don't think any of the boys at the clubhouse know about John yet. They all loved the guy. They're going to go apeshit when they hear this."

"I know the feeling. Look, Cowboy, keep them from doing anything rash. We may have an unlikely ally on our side."

"Who's that?"

"The FBI."

"Oh, yeah, we talked a little about that the other night. Did you make a deal?"

"Not with the feds directly, but with one of the agents."

"What did you give up?"

"Maybe a year of my life, but no future harassment on anything they may have an interest in me for."

Cowboy put jelly on a slice of toast as he thought about it. "You don't have to confess to anything or give anything back?" He stuffed the bread in his mouth.

"It wasn't mentioned."

"If they stick with that, Harry, it's not bad at all."

"I trust who I'm dealing with. Guess I'll find out how good their word is." Changing the subject, Harry said, "With what you were telling me before, are you saying John took out three of theirs when they were chasing him?"

"Certainly sounds that way," responded Cowboy.

Harry raised his orange juice glass. "To John. I'm glad he stuck it to those sons of bitches to the very end." Cowboy picked his up and they touched glasses and then drank. After they were silent for a couple minutes, Harry asked, "What are you going to do now?"

"Continue working the case like I was. There's something in the air about Fat Tony working some big deal to make himself right with the criminal world again. From what the state of his affairs sounds like, it's got to be the equivalent of trying to throw an eighty-yard pass in the last seconds of a football game to win it. I don't know what he has planned. It might be all bullshit rumors. As the politicians say, knowledge is power. The more we know, the better we can come up with something to bring him down. I wouldn't mind if he dies when we get to him, but I like to stay flexible that way."

"Would it help to interrogate someone who might be involved? I mean, it may be one of these bargain basement thugs Fat Tony and his man are hiring, but it could help."

"I'd love to get my hands on someone like that," Cowboy said with serious menace in his voice.

"If we did it, do you know somewhere we could take him to quietly question him?"

Cowboy gave it a long thought. Then he said, "I think I can. Who do you have in mind?"

Harry stood up and threw another sausage at Max who again engulfed it in midair. "They're still looking for me. As far as I know, there are only two places they could stake out to find me. One is work and the other is my house. It doesn't sound like they have the manpower to try and follow any people I know. Even if they have a computer hacker, anything I've paid for in the last several days has been with cash. They can't track me that way."

Standing up, Cowboy checked his gun. "I'm thinking you want to take a drive by and see how things are at the house?"

"Yup. It's time to take the fight to these bastards. More importantly, I want them to know we're taking the fight to them."

Chapter 39

"Nice neighborhood," said Cowboy.

"I like it," said Harry. "I think the neighborhood watch committee would frown on hit men hanging out in the street."

"Then I consider it a public service to clean them out," said Cowboy. He was driving his truck and they were still a block away from Harry's home. In the passenger seat, Harry was swimming in the hoodie Art lent him to keep him concealed as much of possible. He had on sunglasses, a Brooklyn Nets baseball cap pulled low, and the hood over the hat. Slouched down, somebody that knew Harry wouldn't have recognized him from outside the truck. Cowboy drove slowly while Harry looked for strange cars parked on the street.

He straightened up a little in his seat. "That blue Mazda on the left doesn't belong here. Let's see if anyone is sitting in it."

Since it was on Cowboy's side, he gave a sidelong glance as they drove past. "Caucasian male, scruffy, maybe thirty-five years old, and he's so focused on your house he didn't even look at us go by."

"Damn, I hate when you sound like a cop. Keep going down the street after the intersection and let's check out the area for a couple blocks. Maybe we can see if he's alone or if he has any backup around here."

Cowboy did just that. Since it was the middle of a workday, cars parked out on the curb were few. Nobody was sitting in any of them and after repeating the circuit, Harry and Cowboy felt sure that the Mazda was it. Cowboy pulled to a stop around the block from Harry's street.

Harry asked, "You only saw the one guy?"

"Could've been somebody napping in the back."

"Would you only send one guy?"

"I wouldn't," said Cowboy, "but I know what I'm doing. Remember what I told you. Fat Tony is in a rage and wants to kill you, but he's doing it on a budget. Now that I think of it, here's a piece of advice. The sooner we squash this the better. If Russo does pull off something for big bucks, he'll be able to hire better people and raise the bounty on your head."

"What's that going for now?" asked Harry.

"Ten grand."

"On top of everything else, now I'm pissed for being treated like some discount item in a dollar store."

Cowboy smiled. "The other reason that there may be one guy here is that you and John took out six or seven of his people yesterday. It depends if the guy you left on the highway ever showed back up. He may have cut his losses and moved on." Cowboy pulled out his gun and placed it on his lap. "How do you want to play this?"

"We go back around so that we come up from behind him. The way he's parked, the driver's side is next to the sidewalk. You let me off on the corner and I'll casually stroll down to him. When you see me about two car lengths behind his car, drive up next to him and signal that you need him to lower the passenger window as if you're asking for directions. While he's distracted, I'll open his door and whack him in the head. Then we'll take him to wherever you have in mind and ask him a few questions."

"Simple, but effective," said Cowboy. He leaned over and opened the glove compartment. He took out a set of handcuffs and gave them to Harry. "These will reduce any flight issues we might have with him. Try not to smack him too hard. We can't wait all day for him to wake up."

"Gotcha," said Harry. "Let's roll."

Cowboy stopped at the intersection and watched Harry get out and walk down the sidewalk towards the Mazda. Still wrapped in the too big sweatshirt, he strolled as if he didn't have a care in the world. When he was about fifty feet away from the car, Cowboy eased the truck forward and rolled to a stop so he was even with the car. He leaned out of his truck and made the universal sign for rolling down the window. The driver of the Mazda made a face but engaged the passenger side window. Throwing on his Texas accent, Cowboy said, "I'm new to these parts. I'm looking for the nearby elementary school to go pick up my little girl."

On "girl," Harry opened the driver's door, reached in, and yanked the driver sideways by the collar of his jacket. In one smooth motion, his other arm arched downward holding his gun in reverse. There was a resounding "thwack" as Harry made solid contact with the man's skull. Harry reached in and took out the keys from the ignition. He popped the trunk with the key fob, dragged his victim around to it, and threw him in. He patted the guy down and found a gun in the belt, one on the ankle, and a nasty looking knife. He snapped the handcuffs around the wrists and closed the trunk lid. Cowboy looked at his watch and saw that the entire episode lasted for thirteen seconds.

As Harry came around to the driver's side of the truck, Cowboy asked, "I thought we were going to throw him in mine?"

"Change of plan. If anybody comes around to relieve or check on him, it'll look like he drove away. I'll follow you. I hate Mazdas, but it'll do for now. Where we going anyway?"

"You're following me to the town of Babylon. I did some security work for a client. I advised on alarm equipment for a small office building he has there. It's empty for another two weeks and I know for a fact he's in Aruba this week. It's nice and quiet."

"Lead on. I'll be right behind you."

Harry followed Cowboy up to the Long Island Expressway and they headed east. It wasn't long before they entered Suffolk County and drove south again until they entered Babylon. It was a typical Long Island community with a combination of stores, apartments, and homes. Cowboy drove down Sunrise Highway for about a mile before turning into an industrial area made up of small office buildings and warehouses. He pulled into the driveway of a brick building that had an entrance in front with the parking lot along the side. Harry followed him through the empty parking lot and around to the back of the building. Cowboy went past a rear door and stopped. He left Harry enough room to pull up so that the Mazda's trunk was even with the door.

Cowboy went over to the door and unlocked it. He stepped inside and entered the code on the alarm panel to disarm the system. Harry was waiting near the rear of the Mazda and Cowboy explained. "I put a key pad at both the front entrance and back here. That way you can get in using either door. Nobody is able to see us back here. There's a utility room right across the hallway where we can do this. He can scream his head off and nobody will hear him."

Harry looked around. A fence went across the back boundary of the property sealing off any view of this area. Satisfied, he opened the trunk and dragged their prize out by the arm. He was now conscious and tried to get his feet under him as he hit the ground. Harry threw him through the door so that his face smacked the opposite wall. Blood spurted from his nose.

Shaking his head, Cowboy said, "Dammit, Harry, wait until we get in the utility room. He can bleed all he wants in there. There are drains in the floor and we can hose blood down them. I have to clean up any mess we leave out here."

"Sorry, I wasn't thinking. I'm finding myself getting more pissed off by the minute with this asshole."

The said "asshole" had slid down the floor and was looking back at his two abductors with a wild look of fear in his eyes. Blood dripped down the front of his shirt and a few drops hit the floor. Cowboy said, "Drag his ass in the room. I have to clean this up."

Harry grabbed the man by his hair and dragged him to the door Cowboy pointed out. The man yelped until Harry opened the door and threw him inside. Following him in, Harry found the light and turned it on. It was a cement room painted gray. It contained the building's heat and hot water system. There was a shelf in the back with a variety of supplies and tools on it and a sink in the corner. Harry could see what Cowboy meant. Drains were built into the concrete floor. Probably in case there was a problem with the hot water heater and it needed to be emptied.

There was a whimper at his feet and Harry kicked hard at the body to flip him over on his back. He saw a folding chair near the shelf, brought it into the middle of the floor, and opened it. Reaching down, Harry effortlessly plucked up the man and sat him down. He said, "Look at me. Do you know who I am?" Harry took off his hat and sunglasses.

The man tried to focus his eyes while sniffling. He sucked blood back up his nose, causing him to go into a spasm of coughing. Finally, he stopped and looked at Harry again. It took about thirty seconds and his eyes widened. "You're the Harry guy that I'm supposed to…supposed to…" He stopped talking. His mouth kept moving, making him look like a beached fish gasping for air.

"Kill me," shouted Harry about two inches from his face. He stepped back and then threw all of his weight into one punch that caught the man flush in the face below his left eye. He went flying backwards over the rear of the chair and did a somersault before the heater halted his momentum. Harry set the chair back up and threw his would-be killer back on it. His eyes glazed over and he tried to lean on the back of the chair so he wouldn't slide to the floor.

Harry went over to the sink and ran cold water over his hand. It felt good to punch the bastard, but he wouldn't be able to use his hand tomorrow if he did this for any length of time. Cowboy came in and looked at the chair. "Thought I heard a few thumps in here," he said. "Learn anything yet?"

"Nope, just getting to the preliminaries. He did sort of admit to wanting to kill me."

"Sort of?" asked Cowboy.

Harry Hid It

"I may not have given him a chance to get all the words out."

Cowboy walked over to the chair. He struck out with his boot and kicked the chair from under the man, who fell on his ass. Cowboy picked him up and threw him with all his strength into the empty wall next to the sink. He smacked against it with his back and air came out of his lungs with a whoosh. Making a fist, Cowboy drove it into his stomach. The man doubled over. Like a huge tree that sustained the last blow of an axe, he slowly toppled over and fell on his battered face. With his hands still handcuffed behind him, he lay motionless.

Looking at Harry, Cowboy said, "You don't hurt your hand that way." This time he was the one to straighten out the chair and throw the carcass back on it. He filled up a bucket at the sink and dumped it on the head of their victim. He coughed and spluttered but slowly got his wits about him.

Harry crouched down in front of his face. "You know those movies where you have the good cop and the bad cop? Well, we're both the bad cops. Your people killed our friends. Unless you want to end up the same way, you might want to answer our questions. I don't give a shit what happens to you. Understand?"

He nodded.

"What's your name?"

Through cracked lips, he stuttered, "T...t...they call me Pistol."

"Why? Because you killed before?"

Pistol hunched over silently. Harry stood up abruptly and drove his left knee into Pistol's face. His entire body rocked upwards and he flipped over the back of the chair again. Harry grabbed him by the ear and pulled him up. "We're not going to wait for you to decide what you're going to answer or not answer." Harry was yelling so loud in his face that his spit mixed with Pistol's blood. He let go and Pistol fell to the floor like a sack of potatoes.

Turning to Cowboy, he said, "Let's just shoot the fucker. That's

382

one more jerkoff we don't have to worry about. If Fat Tony wants a war of attrition, we'll give it to him."

From the floor, they heard mumbling. Cowboy went over and turned him over with his foot. "We can't hear you. What did you say?"

Pistol spit out a tooth. "Fat Tony don't even know who the fuck I am. One of his men hired me."

"Again," said Harry, "are you Pistol because you kill for a living?"

The misshapen face shook his head no. "I thought it would make me sound tough and get me some work."

"How many men have you killed?" interjected Cowboy.

Pistol mumbled.

"How many?" Cowboy bellowed.

"None. I told him I did, but I never killed anybody."

Harry and Cowboy looked at each other. It was Harry who asked, "How much did you get paid?"

"I got a couple hundred and then I'd get ten thousand dollars for...for..." He broke it off and looked at Harry in fear.

"Yeah, I know, for killing me," finished Harry. "Who hired you?"

"Said his name was Riley. Big, redheaded man. I'd seen him around, but never did no work for him before. He said he worked for Fat Tony."

"Where did he find your sorry ass?" asked Cowboy.

"I was hanging down at a hole-in-the-wall bar. He came in there the other day."

"Were you involved in chasing anyone on a motorcycle yesterday?"

"No. He didn't actually hire me until last night. He didn't want me the first time around."

"There's a surprise," said Harry. "You had no problem going up to a perfect stranger and blasting him?"

Pistol looked unsure. "When I was sitting there in the car, I was having second thoughts. I don't know what would've happened if I saw you."

Harry looked at him closely. "I think you're telling the truth on that one. You may want to rethink your line of work. Why were you sitting in the car?"

"Riley told me a bunch of guys fucked up trying to nail you. He didn't know where you were and gave me your address. I knocked at your door, but there was no answer."

"My God," said Cowboy, "what a fucking moron. What else can you tell us? You spill everything you remember and you might get out of here alive."

They could see Pistol doing his best to think. Neither of them thought this was his strong point. Finally, he said, "He did say that if I pulled this job off, he might be able to use me on another big job on Monday night."

"Did he say what it was?" asked Harry.

"No, he didn't."

"Anything else?"

This time Pistol started to slowly shake his head. Then he stopped and said, "Yeah. Riley said Harry...you...were getting off easy because he slowly killed everybody else. You'd go quickly. I don't know what he meant by that."

"We do," said Cowboy through clenched teeth. "That son of a bitch is a dead man walking."

Harry nodded in agreement. They looked at each other in silence thinking about how the others died. Shaking himself from those thoughts, Harry asked, "How were you going to tell Riley I was dead?"

"I have a phone number. It's in my shoe." Pistol was already kicking off his shoe and propelled it in the direction of Cowboy.

He took out a slip of paper and stuffed it in his pocket. "Probably a burner phone, but it might come in handy. Let's step out into the hall for a minute."

Harry Hid It

He and Harry left the utility room. "What do you think?" he asked Harry.

"I wouldn't have that asshole knock over a candy store. I think he's been straight with us. One way or the other, Riley is going to go down for what he did."

"You got that right," agreed Cowboy. "Apparently, Fat Tony does have something going on and it's happening on Monday. That means we only have a few days to find out what that is. If he gets the money to bring in the first team, it might be harder to keep you from getting killed."

"Now that you have the day, it should be easy to use your detective skills and find out what's happening on Monday." Harry clapped Cowboy on the shoulder.

"It actually does help a little. I was going to work on that today anyway. What do we do with sack of shit in there?"

"Throw him back in the trunk, drive the car someplace, and then tell him he can come out in ten minutes. He's not going to go back and report to Riley. If he really is that dumb, we'll tell him that Riley will probably just shoot him. His best bet is to go far away from here."

"Hope the stupid son of bitch listens," said Cowboy. "I'm going to go take off his cuffs and tell him to clean up the room first. I'm not going to do it."

That's exactly what they did. A very contrite Pistol stiffly walked around the utility room with rags and cleaned up all of his blood. Harry gave him the riot act of what would happen to him if he ever went back to Riley. Pistol nodded and said he never wanted to see any of them ever again.

Harry opened the trunk of the Mazda and Pistol climbed in. Harry took off with Cowboy following. Seeing a Wal-Mart, Harry drove into the parking lot and stopped at a remote parking slot. Cowboy pulled behind him. Getting out, he went to the back of the car and said to the trunk, "Pistol, I'm going to pop the trunk. You hang onto it and count to a thousand before you open it.

You'll find the keys on the front seat. You get your ass out of here. I never, ever want to see you again. Got it?"

Pistol grunted affirmation. Harry did as he said and then hopped in Cowboy's truck. They quickly left Wal-Mart and Cowboy started back for Art's. He asked Harry, "Do you think he can count to a thousand?"

"Good point. He might be in there until midnight. I'd have been pissed if I let a derelict like that shoot me."

"What are you going to do now?" asked Cowboy.

"I want you to stop at my house for a minute. We'll make sure it's still clear, but I want to use the opportunity to run in and get a few things I'll need. Then I have a few people to visit. As much as I want to go shoot this Riley and Fat Tony or help you with what you're doing, we don't know enough yet. I'd only cramp your style as you try to find out more. For all I know, my face is on milk cartons with the ten thousand dollar bounty plastered all over it."

"If we can be sure to nail Fat Tony and Riley somewhere, you don't want to go in and take them down? I know a lot of the boys from the clubhouse will want to help when I tell them about John."

"It may come down to that," said Harry, "but let's find out more first. It would be nice to do this so we aren't looking over our shoulders for cops or other lowlifes for the rest of our days. I already fucked up one attempt at revenge. I'm not going to do that again."

You're right," said Cowboy, "but it looks like we only have until Monday. The clock is ticking."

Chapter 40

"HARRY, STAY THE HELL away from me. If I find any of your stuff around, I'll see that you get it back. Jesus Christ, first Spanky, then Ozzie, and now John." Sophia broke down into huge, gasping sobs. She tried to say more but couldn't get past her crying, which led to a fit of coughing. She was hunched over Harry's Chevy Cruze outside her house. Finally getting ahold of herself, she wailed, "I know it's all because of you. Maybe next it'll be me or one of my family." With that, she managed to pick herself up off the car and run back into the house. The door closed with a seismic bang behind her.

Looking at the house quietly for a few minutes, Harry slowly walked around and climbed into his car. Starting it up, he knew he wouldn't be back here again. Part of him knew it was for the best and another part realized a bunch of his years were wrapped up with Sophia and her family. He'd miss it a lot.

It was Saturday and he decided to come here and tell Sophia in person about John. He felt he owed her that rather than hear about it from someone else. It went about as he expected it would. He half thought that she'd smack him in the face, but that never materialized. She did hit him with a wail of grief and fury. He quietly took it and watched her go. While he didn't go into detail about how John died, there were no words to cushion the blow or defend himself. Regardless of what Cowboy said, Harry knew John and the others would be alive if it weren't for him.

Once again, Harry exerted his tremendous willpower to file that haunting fact to the back of his brain. It wasn't going to help him with what he had to do to stop Fat Tony. While a small part of him held onto the fear of what happened to his friends, Harry also liked the freedom he felt from deciding to bring down Fat Tony one way or the other. Feeling as if he had nothing to lose gave him a sense of exhilaration. He was banking on the bit of fear to help him exercise caution.

He smiled grimly when he ran "nothing to lose" through his mind. He was a millionaire. If he went to jail for a year or so like he worked out with Karyn Dudek, he'd still have all that money. That was one more thing he needed to do this weekend. He needed to get to his cache and make sure it was secure. He also wanted to tap into some of the cash from Big Tony. He wanted to give some to Julia to at least pay for the memorial service she was planning for Tuesday. He had found her at her friend's in lower Manhattan the night before. When she saw Harry, she hugged him and cried her eyes out.

As she finally finished with the tears, she said, "Harry, I don't know what led to this and I don't want to. John looked at you as his best friend. I know you two had your...uh, let's call them projects. I loved the big lug. And I'll miss him terribly. He was a big boy. Whatever he got into, I'm not going to blame anyone else for."

Harry dumbly nodded. He didn't know what to say.

Julia continued, "You know I'm a lawyer and I'm supposed to uphold the law and all that. But, Harry," she grabbed the front of his shirt and pulled him down to her height, "if you can get the son of a bitch who did this, do it!" Tears started down her cheeks again. She kissed Harry on the cheek and turned away. Harry left.

Geez, there was such a difference in women! Then there was Karyn. He made a deal with her that could actually put him in jail for a spell. Part of it was self-interest. He wanted Fat Tony put down for what he did to his friends and so Harry wouldn't spend a lifetime looking over his shoulder. Harry also knew his motivation was because he really liked the woman. He'd known many girls in his time, but Karyn was the first one that seemed to be the female counterpart of him. Maybe they swung from different sides of the plate as far as the law was concerned, but she seemed to match him in brains, guile, and grace under pressure. She was also pretty damn cute and sexy. To Harry, that was a combination to continue exploring.

He decided to head to Art's. The owner had put a cot in his office and Harry slept there the previous night. As he was deciding what his next step would be, Cowboy called. Harry answered, "Hey, learn anything new?"

"Putting more pieces together. How you holding up?"

"Just broke up with my longtime girlfriend."

"Life's a bitch, and then you die," said Cowboy.

"Damn, don't go into relationship counseling," said Harry.

"Never crossed my mind. You doing anything?"

"Driving. What do you need?"

"What do you think about going into the lion's den? Or at least on the outskirts."

"Care to explain?"

"I need a set of eyes on Fat Tony's operation. I have a few people running around some leads for me, but I don't have enough people. As near as I can put together, Fat Tony makes his headquarters at the Ocean Club. He used to work out of the back room of a bar he owns in Queens but moved there ever since Tony Junior met his maker. I know you're familiar with the club."

"That's an understatement. What do you want me to do?"

"Keep an eye on him and anybody who comes to meet him. Apparently, he's become something of a recluse since his son died. Which is so weird because from every report I have, he thought his kid was an idiot."

"Blood is thicker than water," said Harry.

"I guess. I scoped out the place yesterday. I know a fence surrounds the property, but the land next to it contains a boat dealership that's out of business. There's a nice little grove of trees on the edge of the boat lot that goes right up to the fence of the club. You can set up there and nobody can see you. Do you have a camera with a telephoto lens?"

"I can get one," said Harry. "You want me to take photos of people that come in? That's going to be hard when the club opens."

"Just for the rest of the day. You can pack up and leave when the club activity starts."

"I know you have a good reason for this, but do you want to share?"

Cowboy chuckled, "Sorry, I'm ahead of myself here. I've been trying to put together what's going on. Something is definitely happening Monday night. It sounds like Fat Tony is making a drug buy and then trying to sell them as quickly as possible. I'm receiving mixed messages from the street, but I'm trying to solidify it. I figure that if you get some photos and run them by your FBI friend, we might be able to get a handle on what's going on through the people he's associating with. I'm doing the same by following Riley around."

"Sounds reasonable. Did you think about grabbing Riley and asking him until he talks?"

"Oh, God, yes, but I'm taking the long view. That may make Fat Tony run to ground. If Riley disappears, we may lose any chance to end this. As it is, the boys in the motorcycle gang would like to get a hold of Riley, put a chain around each limb, and pull in opposite directions with their bikes. They want blood. I told them they'll get it, but they have to wait a couple days."

"I'll get right on it," said Harry. "Art drove by my house this morning. Two cars of assholes are watching my place. I'm probably safer outside his club."

"You're right. As far as I can tell, nobody knows that we're on the offensive against him. Let's use that to our advantage for as long as we can."

They disconnected and Harry changed direction to a Best Buy. Hurrying inside the store, he bought a Canon camera, several different size telephoto lenses, a tripod, and an extra battery for the camera. His purchase was identical to equipment he already owned, but he didn't think the people watching his home would let him stop by to pick up a few things. At least he already knew how the camera operated.

Harry passed the Ocean Club and pulled into the abandoned boat lot. The place still had red, white, and blue streamers stretched from poles to the one-story brick building with the huge glass windows. At one time, a couple of boats were set up inside the building so customers could see them when they pulled up. Now all Harry could see were a few desks and chairs scattered around.

Pulling around behind the building, Harry parked the Cruze there. Opening his trunk, he rooted around and took out a green jacket and hat. They both had the patch of the New Jersey Forest Service on them. Harry had on black jeans and sweatshirt, but he figured wearing green in the trees wouldn't hurt. Besides, the jacket and hat helped him to move around freely in his travels before and were sort of a good luck charm. He didn't think anybody would be watching, but he wasn't going to take a chance at this point.

He set up the equipment and positioned it to make sure no sunlight would reflect from the lens. After he made sure he could zoom onto the entrance of the club, he made himself comfortable and kept watch on any cars coming in or people coming out of the club. He had his binoculars with him and used them to keep an eye on things. Whenever the occasional car pulled up, he'd man the camera and take as many photos as he could of the occupants.

After five hours, all he had to show for his efforts were three carloads of visitors. It seemed no one who showed up could drive. They all had a driver and at least a bodyguard or two. Harry took photos of a Hispanic male, a black man, and to his surprise, a female Asian. They all had their supposedly armed entourage around them. Whatever Fat Tony was up to, he was obviously an equal opportunity criminal.

It was closing on 5:30. Harry thought he'd shut down and get out of here. It would be getting crowded soon with staff and early customers for the club. He'd break down the equipment and run the photos to Karyn. He had called her and told her what he was doing when he first arrived. She thought there was nothing to lose by doing the observation. She and her counterpart from the organized crime unit were working all day at the office and had their agents beating the bushes to find out what Fat Tony had planned. To Harry, it sounded like Cowboy was winning the battle in obtaining intelligence. He knew more than the FBI. Harry decided to keep it that way for now and told Karyn that he'd see her later.

As he detached the camera from the tripod, a white Cadillac Escalade pulled up. A driver alighted from the vehicle and opened the door. Nobody got out, but there was movement at the club entrance. Focusing his binoculars, Harry saw Fat Tony waddling out. This was a surprise. According to Cowboy, Tony rarely left the club. Harry wondered what was so important to make fatso leave. Then he decided it wouldn't hurt to find out.

He made sure he had all his new equipment and ran back to the car with it. He threw everything into the trunk except for the camera, which he placed on the passenger seat next to him. Harry drove around the building and made his way to the road as he saw the Escalade pull out of the club driveway and head in the opposite direction. Harry allowed a couple of cars to get in between him and the bigger vehicle and started following. Traffic was light and it wasn't difficult to follow from a leisurely distance.

Harry soon found himself heading into Manhattan. At first, Harry thought the Cadillac was drifting down to lower Manhattan. "Good," he muttered to himself, "he's going to the FBI and turning himself in. He feels bad for everything he did and is going to throw himself on the mercy of the court." This wasn't the case, of course, and Fat Tony's chariot navigated to the West End. It pulled up outside of a restaurant called One if by Land, Two if by Sea. Fat Tony left the car accompanied by a big goon and walked up to the entrance.

Harry Hid It

This place was supposedly a great restaurant known for its Beef Wellington. Harry also knew it was built in an old carriage house once owned by Aaron Burr. He smiled briefly. Maybe he should just challenge Fat Tony to a duel and be done with this bullshit once and for all. Driving by the restaurant, Harry saw a small antique store closed for the day. He pulled into the owner's parking spot at the rear of the shop. Going back into his trunk, he pulled out a sport coat and blue shirt. He stripped off his sweatshirt, put on the nicer shirt, and completed his outfit with the jacket. Slinging the camera over his shoulder, he strolled quickly to the eatery. "Maybe they'll think I'm some hip, world-traveling photographer in this outfit," Harry thought.

He cautiously entered the restaurant and looked around. A piano tinkled in the distance. Candles adorned the tables and reflected off a great deal of glassware. Chandeliers hung from the ceiling. Harry would have to remember this place if he were ever going on a special date. That thought made him grab his phone and dial Karyn. His eyes never stopped moving as he waited for her to pick up. Just as she answered, he saw Fat Tony sitting at a table in the back corner of the dining room. He was there alone and seemed to be waiting. Harry saw his bodyguard leaning against a back wall watching Tony. "If he were any good," Harry muttered into the phone, "he'd be watching the people coming in, not Tony."

"What, Harry?" asked Karyn.

Harry started. He had been so intent taking in the scene that he didn't hear Karyn answer. He maneuvered over to the small bar by the piano and took a seat. "Sorry. Do you want to meet me? I'm at a place called One if by Land, Two if by Sea."

"Nice place from what I hear," said Karyn. "We have too much to do for a date, Harry."

"Who said anything about a date? I'm here watching Fat Tony. For whatever reason, he left his lair. Since it sounds like he doesn't do that much, I followed. I want to see who he meets.

Care to join me?"

"Sounds like fun. It's not far from here. I'll grab a cab. See you in a few."

As Harry put away his phone, the bartender came and asked for his order. Harry gave it and looked around. Only the first wave of diners was coming in, so it wasn't too crowded yet. He saw that a table very close to Fat Tony's wasn't yet occupied. A crazy idea entered Harry's head. He assumed that Fat Tony and his men had some kind of photo of him, but he wondered how good it could be. Besides, he hadn't shaved all week and his scruff was turning into a respectable beard. He thought he looked like a globe-trotting photographer, so he might as well go for broke. Harry gave a little wave of his hand and the maître d' saw it and came over.

"Yes, sir, what can I do for you?"

Harry said, "Do you have any tables available?"

"I'm sorry sir, but we're booked solid tonight."

Looking up with what he hoped looked like pleading eyes, Harry said, "I just got into town from Europe kind of unexpectedly. I'm having my girl come over. Our first date was here and we had a great time. I was hoping we could get the exact table we had on that occasion. I plan to propose to her this evening."

The maître d' smiled with a trace of pity. "I wish I could help, but my hands are tied."

Harry palmed two bills in his hand and slipped them to the man. Before putting them into his pocket, the maître d' could see they were two hundreds. His smile became bigger as he said, "I'll see what I can do. What table would you like to entertain your guest?"

"It's that one along the wall over there. It's right next to where that large gentleman is sitting."

"If you give me a second, sir, I'll be right with you."

As Harry picked up his drink and took some, the maître d' came back and escorted him to the table. Harry took the chair so his back was to Fat Tony. He gave another hundred to his new friend, described Karyn to him, and asked that he bring her back here. As the man was leaving, Fat Tony called out to him, "Is there any way not to sit other people near me?"

The maître d' had been very warm toward Harry, but his voice took on the quality of ice water as he answered Tony. "Sir, while I'm sure that's what you prefer, this establishment doesn't take kindly to those requests. If you wish to dine alone, I'm sure there are several hot dog wagons in this vicinity. Besides, Mr. Bailey reserved this table and this is where he prefers to sit." Turning away, he returned to his station at the front of the restaurant, but not before Harry thought he heard the man mutter, "shithead" under his breath.

Harry silently toasted his new friend for his impeccable perception of character. At least he now had a name. He wondered who Mr. Bailey was and when he'd be arriving. He didn't dare look behind him, but he could feel the impatience of Fat Tony rising from the fidgeting and little noises he was making.

Ignoring Fat Tony for a minute, he shot off a text to Karyn explaining the cover story so she didn't blow it when she came in. The only response he received said, "Proposal? You haven't even kissed me yet, you big jerk!"

That almost made him laugh aloud. A man in a well-tailored suit coming his way distracted him from doing so. He looked to be in his seventies, but a very youthful seventy. There was a spring in his step and he had a full head of gray hair brushed back. He had a serious look on his face, but Harry could see that it probably didn't take much to make him smile. He had that air about him that could only be produced by wealth.

"Mr. Russo," he said with a slight remnant of an Irish accent, "I hope you weren't waiting long."

"I'm glad that you finally arrived," Fat Tony said with a trace of arrogance in his voice.

Bailey sat down. Harry strained to listen as the newcomer said in a low voice, "Mr. Russo, if you can't keep a civil tongue in your head, I'll have you escorted out of here, and I'll enjoy my dinner in peace. I'm doing you a favor, got it?"

There was silence, and Fat Tony finally agreed by saying, "I understand and I appreciate you seeing me on such short notice."

A waiter came over with menus and their conversation stopped. Then Harry saw the maître d' leading Karyn over. She wore a lavender knit top that accented all her curves, gray slacks, and she carried a matching gray jacket. When she got to the table, Harry stood up and she threw herself into his arms. "Clyde, why didn't you tell me you were coming back from Europe early? I barely had time to find something to wear and run over here when you called."

"I missed you, baby," Harry said as he embraced her. He had to admit that after his last couple of days, it felt good to pull Karyn into him. They pulled apart and the maître d' signaled to a woman, who came over with an ice bucket that held a bottle of champagne. She deftly opened it and poured each of them a glass. The maître d' smiled when Harry looked at him. "My compliments, sir. It's the least I could do."

Harry acknowledged with a semi-salute and they were soon alone at the table. They toasted and Harry said in a low voice and a raised eyebrow, "Clyde?"

"Best I could do on the spur of the moment," said Karyn with a twinkle in her eye.

"That makes it worse," said Harry.

She took another sip of champagne. "Good stuff," she said in approval. Then, looking serious, she asked, "How do you feel being this close to him?"

"I figured I could shoot him four times in his fat face and walk out of here before anyone stopped me. While it had its merits, I didn't think it was the best thing to do."

"Good man," said Karyn. "Hear anything?"

"I know the man he's with is a Mr. Bailey. He's the one who invited Fat Tony here. Apparently, he's doing Tony a favor by doing this meeting. That's it to this point. Since you can see them, you'll be able to tell when they seem to be talking about something more than the weather. Then I'll try to hear their conversation."

"Right now, they're looking at the menu. Shall we do the same?"

They did. When their waiter came over, they both ordered the Beef Wellington. "I guess we'll find out if this place is all hype or not," said Harry. He reached over and took her hand. When she looked at him, he said, "Just playing a part here. Remember, we're lovers."

"Did you bring a ring? I mean if you're going to be a method actor with this charade, I'd expect you to have all the props."

"Funny girl. As you put it, that was the best I could come up with at the spur of the moment."

"Sophia isn't going to be happy you're proposing to someone else – even for pretend. I think she'd scratch my eyes out on a whim."

Harry snorted. "Not an issue anymore. Let's leave it at that for now."

Karyn looked at him closely and then glanced over Harry's shoulder. "They finished ordering. They seem to be getting into a deep discussion.

Harry leaned back a bit in his chair. He tried to make as if he were focusing on Karyn and not trying to hear. Bailey was speaking, "This is highly unusual, Mr. Russo. Why are you moving on this so quickly?"

Fat Tony was almost inaudible. It sounded like he was hemming and hawing about something. Finally, Mr. Bailey said, "You're a liar and from what I hear, not very good at what you do. Didn't you have something similar go bad for you in the summer? Something about getting ripped off in the middle of a transaction?"

Harry could hear Tony say, "That was unfortunate. This deal will put me back in the forefront around here. You have the only facility that will make this all work smoothly and fast."

Harry Hid It

The waiter bringing over salads interrupted them. Harry leaned forward and filled Karyn in on what he heard so far. "It would certainly be helpful to know who Mr. Bailey is." Karyn looked around the room and smiled. "Have to powder my nose. Be right back." She quickly got up and moved away. Their salads came while she was gone. The two men behind him had started talking again. For now, they were talking so low that Harry couldn't hear them well enough to make out much. It didn't help that they were eating while talking. Didn't they know you shouldn't talk with your mouth full?

Karyn returned in five minutes. She took a bite of her salad, said "Yummy," and went to work on her phone.

"What are you doing?" asked Harry.

"The route to the ladies' room gave me a clear view of our Mr. Bailey. I took a couple pictures when I was coming back. I'm sending them to my office to see what anyone can dig up on him."

"You're good," said Harry.

She looked up at him with a wicked grin. "You have no idea, Harry Strickland."

"Why the feisty mood?" asked Harry.

"Because I finally feel like I'm getting close to bringing something to an end since I got to this city," explained Karyn. "I like to win and if we put that fat idiot behind you away, we did good."

Harry nodded in agreement. They proceeded to eat their meal. Every now and then, he'd lean back to see if he could hear anything, but the increasing din in the restaurant was making it difficult. In between his efforts, he decided to enjoy the time with Karyn.

They both agreed the Beef Wellington more than lived up to its reputation. Harry had never had the dish before, but the pastry and meat seemed to melt in his mouth. He filled Karyn in on what he saw at Tony's club earlier in the day and said he'd give her the photos when they got out of here tonight.

She asked, "Do we follow them when they leave?"

Harry Hid It

"Perhaps Mr. Bailey needs following when he goes. Fat Tony will most likely hightail it back to the club."

Karyn looked around at the beautiful dining room and pulled her phone out again. She sent off a text message and waited for a response. When it came in, her face beamed. She looked at Harry and said, "I have two agents coming over. They'll pick Bailey up and see where he goes."

"Why did you do that?" asked Harry.

"Because when a handsome man invites me out to an elegant restaurant, I'm ordering dessert."

Harry shook his head, but then he held up his hand. He could finally hear them saying something behind him again. Bailey was saying, "Very well, Mr. Russo, it'll be number 34 or 56. I'll let you know on Monday. Do you have an exact time?"

Harry wasn't sure, but he thought Fat Tony said he'd let Bailey know when he heard from him on Monday. Then Bailey said, "I'll do this for thirty percent of the take."

Karyn asked, "What happened? Fat Tony looks like someone is going to have to perform CPR on him. He got all red in the face."

"I think Bailey is asking for more that what Fat Tony wants to give for whatever they're talking about."

Karyn's phone beeped. She said, "They're in position outside. We can hang here when they leave."

They ordered dessert and ten minutes later, Bailey and Russo left and made their way out of the restaurant. Harry said, "First, this cake you ordered is delicious. Second, we have to figure out what we overheard."

"Maybe it will clear up some things when we find out more about Bailey." She delicately wiped her lips with the napkin. "Harry, that was the best meal I've had in ages. Thank you for asking me to help you with this. There's only one thing left to do," she said.

"What's that?" asked Harry.

Harry Hid It

She bolted up from her seat. As she descended onto Harry's lap, she squealed loudly, "Oh darling, of course I'll marry you!" She locked her lips on his.

To the sound of applause around them, Harry kissed her back.

Chapter 41

DAWN ON SUNDAY BROKE bright and cool. With the sun in his rear-view mirror, Harry headed out with Max sitting in the passenger seat. The dog had his head on his owner's thigh and Harry gently scratched him around the ears. He didn't know when, but Harry knew things were heading toward some inevitable climax with Fat Tony. That could mean that Harry would be in jail soon or dead. Because of that, he had to start making some arrangements. He wanted someone to watch his house, and more importantly, take care of Max.

As if sensing his concern, Max sat up and started licking Harry's face. He hugged the big mutt and then gave him a shove back to his seat. This wasn't the time to get into an accident. He had way too much to do.

Finally, Harry parked. Max jumped out of the car and ran over to do his business in the bushes. Popping the trunk, Harry shrugged into the jacket and hat he wore taking photos yesterday. It was definitely getting closer to autumn and the chill was still here in the air. The elevation probably added to it, not that it was very high. Picking up a backpack and some tools, he whistled for Max and they started hiking together. After a time, they stopped. Harry saw that the area looked fine. He got to work and soon dragged out a couple waterproof containers. He studied the containers with a mixture of satisfaction and regret. He and the boys made a lot of money with a few well-planned jobs, but he lost the boys in the process.

For Harry, the money was a means to an end. He never had a lust of money for the sake of having more. It was simply to help him lead a simpler life where he could do what he liked. He knew that John had felt the same way. Harry smiled sadly when he realized that Ozzie would've blown his share in a year and would've been back to stealing cars or acting as muscle for some jerk like Fat Tony. Sighing, he quickly counted some stacks from the cash they took from the Ocean Club and stuffed them in the backpack. It took him a little longer to put everything back the way he found it. Looking at his work, Harry thought he had an eye to be a set designer for a movie or play. Not that anybody looking would know anything was out of place, even if they were right on top of it.

He double secured the iron gate. Max sat like a sentry at the junction of the path. He'd have given Harry plenty of warning if an early morning walker were coming in this direction. Max's sheer size would've deterred anybody from getting closer. They wouldn't know that Max would only want to play with a newcomer. Harry often marveled at how his dog epitomized being a "gentle giant."

When they got back to the car, Harry looked around. He had been looking forward to painting this area when they were deep into autumn. He thought the foliage on the trees with the water in the background would be beautiful. He looked at his watch and then at Max and said a bit wistfully, "What's another hour or two. I'm probably not going to get back here for a year or so."

He placed the backpack in the trunk and took out an easel, an empty canvas, and his painting supplies. Looking around, he spied a rock that looked to be a good vantage point. He set up and looked at the scene he wanted to capture. Taking a piece of charcoal out, he started sketching. He put all his concentration into his work. Harry was partially aware of Max running around and chasing squirrels and chipmunks.

It didn't take long until he finished putting in his last dab of color onto his painting. Standing back, he compared his work to the real thing and liked the result. He sighed and started packing back up. If nothing else, he hoped he'd get a chance to do some painting if he went away for a year. He figured that at the least he'd be able to draw.

Harry Hid It

As he was carefully placing his new painting into the Cruze, Harry thought for the thousandth time about skipping out on the deal with Karyn. He could go back, get all the loot from the jobs he masterminded, and drive off into the sunset. However, he realized he couldn't turn his back on Cowboy, who was working his ass off to bring down Fat Tony. He also knew that if he split now, Karyn would hound him to the gates of hell until she found him. Then she'd probably find all of the evidence from his crime spree and he'd never see the light of day. No, it was better to stick with the deal. It was ironic that to get his "get out of jail free" card, he actually had to go to jail. Better a year or so than ten to twenty!

He opened the passenger door and Max jumped in. As they started the trip home, Harry flashed back to last night. He smiled at the kiss in the restaurant. Karyn knew her job and was certainly cool when people were shooting at her, but she did have a playful side. Harry acknowledged the clapping of the other diners around them with a smile and a wave. He and Karyn left One if by Land, Two if by Sea hand in hand. Once on the street, Karyn broke out into fits of laughter. "God, Harry, if you could see your face when I said I accepted your proposal. I wish I had been able to take a photo of that!"

"I didn't expect it. And for the record, I never asked you anything."

"I'm not holding you to it." She held up her left hand and indicated her ring finger. "Besides, you didn't put a ring on it. I'm an old-fashioned girl that way."

"So no sex until the honeymoon?" Harry asked with a twinkle in his eye.

Karyn blushed. "Hey, I'm not that old-fashioned. Unfortunately, I have work to do now. I need to find out who this Mr. Bailey is. I better grab a cab back to the office."

"My car is right up the street. I'll drop you off."

"Sure you won't break into hives being that close to the FBI?"

"If I can park in your building, I can certainly drop you off in front of it. Now, shut up and get in."

Her hand traced over the trunk of the car as she walked to the passenger door. "Where's the Camaro?"

"This is my stealth car. It makes following people easier."

He dropped her at the office and gave her the card from his camera so that she could download the photos of the people who visited the Ocean Club. On the way to Art's, Harry gave Cowboy a quick call to tell him what he discovered today. Cowboy didn't know who Bailey was either and they agreed to meet the following afternoon. That's when Harry figured that he'd use Sunday morning to pull out some cash.

Now the morning was turning into Sunday afternoon as Harry pulled into Art's. He went inside and the owner greeted him with, "I have to tell you, they're persistent. You still have two carloads of douchebags watching your place. I took a cruise over there about an hour ago.

"Hopefully, this nightmare will be over soon. I can't thank you enough for what you're doing."

"You want some lunch, Harry?"

At that moment, he realized he had yet to eat today. "Sure. Can your guy throw together one of those Buffalo chicken wraps for me while I clean up?"

"I'll let him know."

Jeannie came out of the kitchen with a tray. She dropped two plates of food off at a table and came over to Harry. She said, "Harry, I love Max and will keep watching him as long as you need, but I think we're both getting claustrophobic at my place."

Impulsively, Harry put his arm out and hugged Jeannie to him. "I appreciate everything that you're doing. It won't be for much longer, I promise."

She looked up at him. "For a tough guy, you can be such a mush at times." She hugged Harry back and went over to one of her tables to take the customers' orders.

Harry Hid It

Harry left the bar area and went back to Art's office. He had folded up his cot in the morning and tried to keep the place neat. He grabbed clothes and a towel from a bag and went into the adjoining bathroom. The previous owner had installed it complete with a shower. Harry allowed himself a full ten minutes enjoying the water pounding on his body. He changed into fresh jeans, a T-shirt, and swapped out his hiking boots for sneakers. He put on a button-down shirt that he left open to hide the gun at his back. Feeling refreshed, he wolfed down his lunch and was back in his car, driving to Manhattan.

He had called Julia and she agreed to meet him at a friend's apartment. She wasn't ready to go back to her house yet. When she gave Harry a hug as he entered, he could see that she had been crying some more. "How you doing?" he asked.

"Hanging in there. Sophia called me last night. You two aren't together anymore?"

"Looks that way." Harry blew out some air from his lungs. "Sometimes life just sucks."

"Yeah, but you're still alive. That's something," said Julia. "Whoever did this to John hasn't been able to find you?"

"Oh, they found me OK," said Harry. "It didn't end well for them though. I won that battle. Julia, I'm doing my best to win the war. Hopefully, this will be over in another day or two."

"Like I told you, Harry, I don't need to know the details, but if you do end this, please tell me. That will help a little."

"Sure thing. I brought you this." He handed Julia an envelope. "There's twenty grand in there. Use it for the memorial service or whatever."

She made a gesture as if waving it off but then reached out and took it. "Thank you, Harry. I really appreciate it."

"What are you going to do next?" he asked.

"You mean after I bury John, or what's left of him?" This started a tear running down her cheek again. Harry nodded. "I really don't know. There's been a firm in California after me for

405

several months now. Maybe it's time to just get the hell out of here."

"I can understand that. I need to go. You take care."

"Don't die, Harry."

"Hey, I'm trying my best." They hugged and Harry made his way back outside and to his car. He received a text message from Karyn just as he switched on the ignition. It said, "Found out some things about Bailey and your other photos. Where are you? Can we meet?"

He texted back that he wasn't that far away from her in Manhattan and they settled on meeting at a Panera Bread near her office. It didn't take long for Harry to zip over there, and he was waiting in a booth with a cup of coffee when Karyn walked in. She waved to him and stopped at the counter to get a tea. Today she wore jeans and a black sweater. As she came over to the booth, Harry thought she looked terrific but tired. When she sat down he asked, "I take it you had second thoughts to my marriage proposal?"

She smiled weakly. "I don't seem to remember any proposal, big boy."

"Figured you needed a laugh. You look exhausted," said Harry.

"I am. Got home at two in the morning and came back in at seven." She reached into her large pocketbook and pulled out a manila folder. "When this is over, I'm taking some time off. Let's get through this before I fall asleep in front of you." She slid the folder to Harry. He opened it up and took out four photos. The first three were of the three people who showed up at the Ocean Club yesterday afternoon. The other was one that Karyn took of the infamous Mr. Bailey at the restaurant.

"You've identified these people, I assume."

"Yeah, they were all in the database to some extent. My people followed Bailey to a luxury apartment building on Central Park after he left us last night. You know the type where it takes a small fortune to own one of the condos. Anyway, the address helped us find him quickly. The FBI has been trying to nail him for years, but no luck. He owns a ton of legitimate businesses, but his foundation is based on being a service provider to criminals. He doesn't run any prostitution, drugs, or gambling, but he provides the locations and security to do so."

Harry looked thoughtful. "Based on that, Fat Tony probably came to him for help with whatever this deal is he's working on."

"That would be my bet. Have you found out what that's all about yet?"

"No, but I'm meeting up with someone later. I hope he has more light to shed on the topic. He's been busting his ass on this like you are."

"What's his motivation?" asked Karyn. "Money?"

"No, John was a good friend. He's got this old west ideal of justice. He wants to help bring it about."

"I hope he doesn't go off half-cocked," said Karyn. "We have to do this right. The more people we bring down, the easier it'll be to shelve those other investigations I'm doing as unsolved. You know what I mean, Harry?"

"I do know, sweetheart. The guy helping me would like to shoot the entire lot of them. However, he also realizes everything you just said. He wants this to go down the right way."

"Good. I can only deal with so many problems at once. Now, you said last night that Bailey said it would be at either number 34 or 56, correct?"

"That's what he said. Do you know what it means?"

Karyn pulled out a piece of paper. "It could mean any number of things. Some of the services that Jacob Bailey, that's his full name by the way, provides are warehouses, trucks, docking space, and boats. Those numbers could signify a particular location or vehicle. Much of his legit business revolves around transportation and storage, but so does his alternative enterprises. You want a shipment of girls from China for your massage parlors; he can do that. Store your collection of stolen luxury cars and he's the man."

"OK, that gives us an idea of what he's doing for Fat Tony. I have a hunch this revolves around drugs. That's how Fat Tony was trying to build his empire in the summer. Drugs don't need as much of an infrastructure as hookers or gambling. It's the quickest way to make a bunch of money."

"I'd say your hunch is correct." Karyn gestured to the other three photos. "Those people are all known drug distributors. You have in front of you some of the leading drug pushers for the Hispanic, Asian, and Afro-American communities. They'll gladly sell to anyone, of course, but they do target their own ethnic group or race. A lot of crime is divided along those lines."

"And Jacob Bailey works with everyone?" asked Harry.

"Seems to be an equal opportunist on that score. He started out in what we used to refer to as the Irish mafia and moved up to where he is now. We have a great deal of information on him but scant evidence. That's the story of the FBI more often than not."

"It certainly looks like drugs are the deal then. You said these three are mainly into distribution on the streets?"

"You got that right. Those three have their local networks, but in the world of drugs, they aren't the main players. If you look at this in a business context, they're the retail stores. It seems that Fat Tony is trying to play wholesaler for those stores while the actual producer of the narcotics is somewhere above him. Jacob Bailey is the logistics partner."

Harry sat back. "If you look closely, you'll see that the light bulb just went off above my head. I think I know what Fat Tony is trying to do. He needs cash and he needs a lot of it quickly. He has aspirations of being the Godfather of Long Island. Forget for a moment that he isn't bright enough for that title. I think he has a shipment of drugs coming in and he wants to move it as quickly as he can. He's gun shy because of what happened in the summer, so he doesn't want to sit on it and take a chance of something bad happening." Harry shook his head in amusement. "I wouldn't put it past him to bring this shit in and sell it to the retail stores, as you call it, immediately."

"You mean provider, seller, and buyers will all be there at the same time?"

"We know Fat Tony isn't smart enough to be subtle. I'd say that's a very good possibility."

"Oh my God, Harry, do you know what a coup that would be?"

"You mean for you to take them all down? I'd say that you'd be the golden girl of the FBI. It would be quite an accomplishment."

She looked at Harry closely. "You aren't having second thoughts about aiding in their demise?"

He smiled. "Fancy words, Agent Dudek. No, I'm following through on this. For one thing, I'm no fan of drugs. I've seen too many of my friends get fucked up on them. Two, you know I need to see Fat Tony go down. There's lots of satisfaction in making that happen. And three, you said you're an old-fashioned girl. Well, I'm an old-fashioned guy. My word means something to me. I promised I'd do this and I will."

She leaned over the table and tenderly kissed Harry. When she backed up, she said, "I keep my word too. Now let's go find out if we can put the details of this together and stop Fat Tony."

Chapter 42

AN ACCIDENT SOMEWHERE IN front of him had Harry driving at a snail's pace as he tried to get out of Manhattan. He saw that he had missed a message from Cowboy asking him to come to the clubhouse at eight that night. Harry called to tell him that he'd be there and to share what he learned from the FBI. When the call went directly to voice mail, he just said that he'd see Cowboy at the planned time.

Harry had some time to kill and he wanted to put it to some productive use. On an impulse, he aimed his car at the first exit ramp he came to. Disengaging himself from the traffic going nowhere, Harry negotiated a bunch of side streets. It took about half an hour, but he was soon pulling up to Tommy Petrillo's place of business. In some ways, it was stealing those two cars for Tommy a few months back that catapulted Harry into much larger crimes. Harry upped his game when he weighed the risk versus reward of stealing vehicles. Tommy had got him started as a kid and maybe he could give him some insight now.

He went up to the door on the side of the building and entered. He was in a small room facing another door. He looked up at the camera in the corner and said, "It's Harry. Is Tommy around?" He knew somebody was watching and listening. It was part of Tommy's security.

It took a minute, but the door opened and a guy Harry thought was named Hal beckoned him inside. In a gruff voice, the man said, "Tommy's in his office. He said you knew where it was."

"Thanks, I know the way." Harry went through the car area and admired a jet black Lamborghini that two technicians were working on.

Entering Tommy's office, Harry saw the older man get up

and approach him with his hand out. When Harry went to shake, Tommy pulled him in and embraced him. When they broke, he said, "So the prodigal son returns. Looking for a gig?"

"No, I told you that I retired from lifting wheels," said Harry. "Came by for a little advice."

"Have a seat, Harry," said Tommy indicating a chair. Settling behind his desk, he asked, "What's going on?"

Driving here, Harry considered how much to tell Tommy. He said, "I got on the bad side of someone who considers himself a big deal. This guy is after me hard. He already killed Ozzie and John and someone else. I wanted to see if you know him or knew of him and had any suggestions how to deal with him."

Tommy's face wrinkled in concern. "Holy shit, Harry, that's bad stuff. Who did you piss off?"

"Tony Russo."

"That fat fuck! Jesus, Harry, he's a nut job. For the last twenty years, he's always tried to make himself be a major player around here. At one point, he wanted to process a couple cars through me. It was the most screwed-up deal ever and I told him never to call me again. Why did you pick on him?"

"It had to do with his kid. It escalated to the father."

"Wait a minute," said Tommy holding up his hand. "Did you have anything to do with his son getting knocked off? I heard something about that."

"We were there. We didn't touch the kid, but Fat Tony blames us and that's why I'm in the spot I'm in. What can you tell me?"

"Steal a Mack truck and run over the fat son of a bitch. After you do that, back it up over him again to make sure he's dead. I truly believe he's psychotic. You certainly can't reason with someone like that."

"When you told him you wouldn't work with him again, how did he react?" asked Harry.

Tommy thought for a moment. "This was going on ten years ago or so. He wouldn't let up. He kept badgering me about how working with him would be the greatest partnership ever. I finally sent a couple guys over, had them take a Cadillac he had at the time, and drove it through his office window. He finally got the message."

"Man doesn't listen, does he?"

"You know how guys are, Harry. You have the smart ones who can take 'no' for an answer or who listen to reason. There are others that you have to tap on the arm to get their attention. Then there are those you have to smack with a baseball bat to wake them up. That's Fat Tony."

"I wish your guys ran him over with his car," said Harry.

"I'm sure you do," said Tommy. "However, take the lesson I learned dealing with that pompous asshole. The only thing that he understands is if you hit him hard. No half measures are going to work. Don't be a pansy when you go after him. I know that's not you anyway, Harry, but Fat Tony is a cockroach. You have to keep stamping on him to make him stop. Capiche?"

"I got it, Tommy. I knew that. I guess it helps to hear it from someone like you."

"Something else to remember, Harry. No matter how good the plan is, you always have to be ready for the unexpected."

"I know that. Sort of why I'm in this mess." Harry stood and the two men shook.

As he headed out the door, Tommy said, "One more suggestion for you." Harry stopped and turned. "With someone like Russo, don't feel like you have to go it alone. Make sure you have backup. Hell, try to have a whole fucking army with you."

"I'll keep that in mind. I'm heading out now to see about recruiting an army."

Driving to the clubhouse, Harry felt a little better talking to Tommy. It told him two things. One was that Tommy reconfirmed for him that he needed to take down Fat Tony completely and thoroughly. The second was that either Fat Tony wasn't publicizing this vendetta he was on against Harry and his men, or nobody really cared what he said. One reason Harry visited Tommy was to see if he heard anything. The man had his ear to the underworld pipeline, but he didn't know Harry was a target.

Harry wasn't sure if that meant anything or not. It did show that he was dealing with a man who thought he was a big shot, but the rest of the criminal world didn't think much of him. It might not make him more dangerous than he already was, but it certainly made him delusional. Harry had often seen people believing they were something they were not. He saw it a great deal with criminals, but it was in all walks of life. It happened with employees at the airport, people he bumped into at bars, and just about anywhere else he could think of. "If everybody could just take an honest look at themselves in the mirror," Harry thought, "half the bullshit in this world would go away."

As he approached the clubhouse, Harry could see motorcycles of all types parked around it. He had been here with John a few times, but never with this many bikes. He skirted the motorcycles until he found a clear spot to slide the Chevy in. As he left his car, he could hear some voices in the building. Maybe they were having a club meeting or something.

As he went through the door, all the chatter stopped. Harry stood still and saw all the men and women inside turn their heads towards him as one. Glancing from side to side, he estimated there must've been close to a hundred people there. They were sitting or standing. Most of the men had bottles of beer, but bottles of wine and booze with various glasses and plastic cups were all over the room. For once in his life, Harry wasn't sure what to do. Then one person in the room started clapping slowly. Somebody else joined in just as slowly, and then another, and another. The tempo and sound picked up and soon the entire building was applauding and cheering. Harry saw Cowboy emerge from a side room and hurry over to him.

"What the hell is this?" asked Harry, still off balance from the reception.

"They know the people who killed John are after you and you did away with a few of them," Cowboy shouted over the noise. "They also know you're going to bring down Fat Tony. It's their way of showing respect and support."

Harry breathed easier and acknowledged the crowd with a smile and a wave. Somebody brought him a beer and there were pats on the back and words of encouragement. A woman came up to him and said, "I talked to Julia earlier today. She told me what you did for her. My man and I have your back, Harry. Nail the bastard!"

Cowboy helped guide Harry through the crowd of well-wishers and led him to the room he vacated a moment ago. Closing the door muffled the noise, but it was still pretty loud. "I'm still not sure that was warranted. I mean, if it weren't for me…"

"Cut that shit right now, Harry," said Cowboy. "The people out there understand that stuff happens. They all miss John and I've been spending time that I don't have keeping some of the boys from doing something stupid. Now, we have to talk and we have twenty-four hours to put something together to do in Fat Tony. I'll explain why, but we're going to get one chance at this and we have to make it good. Sorry I missed your call earlier. Tell me what you found."

Harry explained the reports he received from the FBI. Cowboy nodded in satisfaction when Harry told him about the three people visiting Fat Tony at the club being drug dealers. His face positively lit up at hearing the role Mr. Jacob Bailey played when helping people like Tony.

When Harry finished, Cowboy said, "You helped confirm all the bits and pieces I've been finding out the past few days. Fat Tony is truly a piece of work. Nobody wants to work with him, but he's bringing in a huge shipment of meth tomorrow night. The price he's offering is so low that the major dealers all want a piece of it. He's setting up a time tomorrow where he hopes to bring the drugs in and distribute them in an hour." Cowboy paused and looked at Harry. "What are you smiling about?"

Harry Hid It

"You just confirmed for me what I said earlier this afternoon. Fat Tony is determined to make his mark and pull in as much cash as he possibly can. I think when you heard what Jacob Bailey does that it made the entire picture as clear for you as it did for me. Tony couldn't make this work on his own. He needed someone with the resources like Bailey to provide a location to bring the drugs in and the room to distribute them all at one time."

Cowboy said, "It seems that the shipment is coming in via the water. Nobody knows the location yet, though. A message will go out tomorrow to the dealers where to meet so they can buy what they want. The word is that it will all go down around ten at night."

"How did you find out about this?" asked Harry.

"It wasn't easy at first. As Fat Tony and that Riley jerkoff went about trying to solicit customers, I started finding out a little more. My big payoff came about five this afternoon. I watched Riley go into some dive bar and talk to some little guy. I went inside and sat back in a corner. I could tell Riley was getting steamed. He even made as if to hit the man, but the bartender threatened Riley. They talked a little more and I could see the man putting some information into his phone that Riley gave him. When Riley left, I went over to him. He looked broken and I asked what was wrong."

Harry asked, "Did he tell you?"

"Surprisingly, yes. I expected him to tell me to take a hike. I bought the guy a beer and he told me his life story. He said he had been a dealer, but he was trying to give up the business. He lost a nephew to drugs a month ago and now he found out his wife has cancer. He had no stomach for it any more. The poor bastard thought he had finally pulled the plug on his business three days ago when Riley popped in. Riley reminded him that Fat Tony had done a favor for him a year ago and it was time to pay it back by taking some of the product. This man had heard what Fat Tony had been doing to people who crossed him lately, so he agreed."

"Not exactly a happy customer then," said Harry.

"Not at all, but then I had an idea. First of all, Harry, do you have five thousand dollars?"

"Of course," exclaimed Harry. "I told you, Cowboy, whatever you need."

"Great, but it's not for me. I told this man, his name is Sammy, that I'd give him five thousand for the information on what was happening tomorrow night. I explained that it would work out great for him because he wouldn't have to show up. When he worried about what Fat Tony would do to him, I assured him that this was going to be Fat Tony's last sale. He seemed to like that."

"So he's going to feed us the information about where to go tomorrow night when everybody is going to be in one spot."

"Yeah, the problem is that we'll only have an hour to get there. Riley was taking Simon's email address. Apparently, an email will go out in the afternoon telling all interested parties the general location of the exchange. Then an hour before the drugs arrive, another mailing will go out detailing the specific location."

"Is Fat Tony nuts?" asked Harry. "It's going to be like when the stores open their doors to customers on Black Friday. How's he going to control this?"

"I have no clue. Maybe that's where Bailey comes in."

"I don't know if he gets that hands-on. It sounds like he provides facilities and transportation. The feds probably never got their hands on him because he keeps an arm's length away. I bet you anything he's watching television in his condo when this goes down tomorrow."

"I wouldn't take that bet," said Cowboy. "I agree."

"Then it's going to be confusion. That's going to help the FBI take this group down."

Cowboy's face looked like he had eaten something bad. "Uh, Harry, we do have a little problem with that."

"What do you mean?"

Harry Hid It

"The boys out there want blood. They want to be in on this. They want to hurt Riley bad. He was the one who did in John. A friend sent me the police report of when these assholes chased John around town. The cops pieced together what happened. John sent one motorcyclist into a window. He blew away another with a sawed-off shotgun he had and also used it to kill the other guy in the car chasing him. That car backed into him though and put him down. A dump truck came by and John and his bike were thrown in the back. Three different witnesses said the driver of the car seemed to be in charge. The descriptions were similar. He was a big man with red hair. Since Riley is the only man in Fat Tony's orbit who fits that description, it must be him."

"I have a feeling he was involved with the other murders too," said Harry. "Let me think on this. I know exactly how your friends out there feel. It would help if we knew the lay of the land where this is happening. I'd have a better idea how to keep everyone happy if I knew what we were running into."

"You said Bailey gave Tony an idea how he'd help him?"

"I couldn't hear that part, but I did hear Bailey say it would be number 34 or 56. My FBI contact speculated that could be a designation for a warehouse or a truck or a boat. Apparently, Bailey has all of those."

"Plausible. I guess when we get the first call we might be able to narrow down the potential locations better. Any idea how to do this?" asked Cowboy.

"I think I'm good at tactics," explained Harry, "but I never choreographed a full-blown assault before. I'll figure out a way to make this work so they have a shot at Riley. Then the FBI can come in and pick up the rest of the scumbags. They're drooling at the prospect of picking up so many drug criminals at one time."

"I'm sure they are. Somehow we need to keep anyone on a motorcycle from getting caught or killed."

Harry asked, "I don't suppose there's anyway to nail Riley before the big deal goes down?"

"Probably not. Plus, as I told you earlier, Fat Tony may get spooked enough to pull the plug if Riley suddenly goes missing."

"Yeah," said Harry, but Cowboy could tell that his mind was somewhere else. Suddenly, he turned to Cowboy and said, "We can't have fifty motorcycles descending on wherever we end up. Even if I can convince the FBI to look the other way when bikers are around, if there are too many, nobody can guarantee anything. When I work, I like a small group and the idea is to get in hard and fast. When the objective is met, it's time to leave."

"I think you're selling yourself short, Harry. When I was in the military, I don't think I ever heard the concept of a plan explained that concisely. Why don't you give me a few minutes and I'll see if I can organize the rabble into a fighting unit."

Cowboy left the room and Harry heard the crowd outside quiet down. Periodically he heard groans and even a little booing. Then Harry heard Cowboy call out names. When that was done, he could hear Cowboy saying something else and then everyone cheered. As that noise was dying down, Cowboy came back in the room with eight men.

"Here you go, Harry. I'll give you the details later, but here are the best of the volunteers. And almost everyone out there volunteered. We have here five combat veterans from Iraq and Afghanistan, one who spent ten years in Korea, and two cops who worked in Newark. There you have it – Harry's Heroes waiting for your command!"

Chapter 43

"KARYN, COWBOY. COWBOY, KARYN." Harry made the introductions in the clubhouse. They were back in the space where he and Cowboy discussed plans last night. Harry began to think of it as the War Room. It had the look of such a place. A large map of the city and Long Island stretched out on the table. Various rifles and weapons sat on a small table in the corner. Karyn was dressed in black fatigues. Cowboy had a revolver at his waist and a Beretta automatic in a shoulder holster. Harry's Heroes were waiting in the other room wearing various pieces of uniform from their military and cop days.

Cowboy said while shaking hands with Karyn, "Now I see why Harry kept you under wraps. If we had people that looked like you when I was a Texas Ranger, I'd still be on the force. Thanks for listening to what we want to do."

Red tinged Karyn's cheeks at the compliment. "I want to thank you for the work you did. We didn't have the time and connections to pull out the intel you did. That's one of the reasons I'm going along with this cockamamie partnership."

Harry said, "How did you get this by your boss?"

Karyn looked hesitant. "Uh, I didn't exactly tell him. This was one of those cases where I'm going to be asking for forgiveness rather than permission. You know how cops are at every level. You get to a certain point and you want to say it was your operation that won the day. I just want to bring down Fat Tony and all of the scum he's selling to."

"This is going to be quite a collar for you," said Cowboy.

"Either that or I'll be sending out my resume tomorrow," said Karyn. "I don't think there is any in-between. So what did you geniuses figure out for tonight?"

419

"Harry can fill you in on that. He put together the plan."

"Of course he did," said Karyn with a small smile.

Harry picked up a pencil and indicated the map. "Thanks to our man, Sammy, we know that the general activity is going to happen here near Baldwin Harbor. Karyn's team was able to dig out the fact that Jacob Bailey owns several commercial docks in that area. They aren't that big and are mainly leased out to commercial fisherman. However, it's the right size for any boat bringing in the meth. It's not like they have to dock the *Queen Mary* or anything like that."

"How reliable is this Sammy?" asked Karyn.

"I'd say that he's giving us the honest word on things," said Cowboy. "Especially after the way Harry treated him."

"And what did Harry do?" asked Karyn, looking at him.

Before he could answer, Cowboy said, "My deal with Sammy was five thousand dollars. When Harry heard the guy's wife was recently diagnosed with cancer, he gave him ten thousand for working with us."

Karyn raised her eyebrows. "Just full of money, aren't you?" she said to Harry.

"Yeah, well…as I was saying, tonight is going to happen somewhere in here. Specifically one of these two docks." Harry circled two areas on a photo he had printed out from Google Earth. "Those are piers 34 and 56 as designated by Bailey's company."

"It fries my ass that we aren't going to be able to nail Bailey tonight," said Karyn. She looked closely at the two areas. "I can see these aren't that far apart. It won't be difficult moving my people in place when we get the word on the exact location. They both look like they have small warehouses or garages near them. I guess that would be ideal for Fat Tony to transact business."

"That's what we were thinking," said Harry. "Fat Tony, being the shrewd character he is, has decided to set up shop tonight in what you western folk would call a box canyon. Whatever pier he uses only has one road into the area. When everything is in place and the meth delivered, Cowboy and Harry's Heroes are going to go in and zero in on Riley. This does two things. It neutralizes Fat Tony's most competent lieutenant. It will also give the guys here some satisfaction in avenging John."

"That sounds good," said Karyn. "Who the hell are Harry's Heroes?"

Cowboy chimed in, "I named them that. Harry didn't want a parade of bikers descending on the action tonight, so we picked the best for a small squad. All they want is Riley."

"What happens to him after you get him?" asked Karyn.

Cowboy gave a noncommittal shrug. "Guess it depends if Mr. Riley goes down hard or easy."

"Uh-huh," was all Karyn said. She looked like she had the inmates running the asylum. "It would be nice if we could do this without a lot of bloodshed."

This time Harry spoke. "That would be great, Karyn. The problem is Fat Tony is off his rocker. Whatever you and your people do, remind them you aren't dealing with someone whose elevator goes to the top floor. A sane man, when faced with overwhelming odds, will surrender. This guy may think he can blast his way out of anything."

"I know. Cowboy, are you going to be with Harry's Heroes?" She broke out in a smile when saying the name.

"Yup. I hope to keep them in some kind of order."

"Here's the deal then. When I first see the motorcycles in the area, you have five minutes. Get in there, stir up the pot, get this murdering asshole Riley, and then get out. My crew will be rolling at that five-minute mark. I'll tell them to let the bikers go, but if a firefight starts…well, you know what happens in battle."

"Copy that. I do. I can see in your eyes that you do too."

"Where are you going to be, Harry?" she asked.

"One of the Heroes has a van and I'll be with him following the bikers. Once in the center of the action, I'm getting out and going after Fat Tony."

"Harry, why don't you let the professionals do that?"

"Because if this goes right, you're going to have your hands full. I want to make sure the tubby son of a bitch doesn't get out of this one. I promise not to hurt him too much."

"I must be out of my fucking mind to agree to this," said Karyn, looking up to the heavens and shaking her head. "This isn't by the book."

"Karyn, I know you're no fan of the book. This is the only way to make this work. Do you have enough people deployed?"

"Not as many as I like, but it should be sufficient. I'm going to brief them after I leave here." She looked closely at the picture of the docks. "They're both similar in layout and buildings so we can adapt easy enough. I have the Coast Guard ready to come in once the boat delivers the drugs. I want them too and they'll seal off any escape by the water. It would be nice to know the time frame. Is Fat Tony going to wait until he has the meth before calling in his buyers? Just getting Fat Tony and his crew will be a major coup. Scoffing up everyone else would be the cherry on top."

Harry said, "I've been thinking about that. We're not dealing with a rocket scientist here. My guess is that Tony wants to make a big splash in the minds of people. I'm not up on the etiquette of drug dealers, but I don't think it's usually done this way. A businessman will secure and check his product, whatever it is. Then he'll package it as he sees fits. Russo wants to come across as the master criminal, which means lots of flash. He probably has his buyers coming at the same time as the boat to say, 'See what I can do!'"

"I agree with Harry," said Cowboy. "I'm sure you've seen this too, Karyn. The difficult crooks to catch are those who do their best to stay below the radar. The ego-driven ones are easier to nab."

Gazing at Harry, Karyn said, "Yeah, I certainly have seen that. Anything else I need to know?"

Harry Hid It

Harry and Cowboy looked at each other and each gave a short shake of his head. "No," said Harry, "I think that's it. It isn't complicated, but simple plans have less moving parts to worry about. Do you have anything for us?"

"No, our mission is straightforward. Swarm in and apprehend the bad guys. For God's sake, make sure all of your people are clear, Cowboy. I don't want to be filling out paperwork for the next three weeks."

"Aye," he said with a salute. "I'm going to go discuss this with the Heroes and make sure everybody is on the same page." He left the room.

Harry and Karyn looked at each other. She was the first to speak. "You want to wear a vest. It might be a good idea."

"You have one without FBI plastered on it?"

"No," she said. "You afraid of breaking out in hives again?" She tried to smile.

"I lose all my street cred if I go down wearing anything that says FBI on it. It just wouldn't be right."

"You're a silly man, Harry Strickland."

"Believe me, I've been called worse. How's this all going to work when we're done?"

"On top of everything else I've been doing the last few days, I've been researching this. I'm going to arrest you on a weapons charge. I have to take you in tonight. Can you afford a good lawyer?"

Harry just looked at her.

"Sorry, lost my head there," said Karyn. "Of course you can. He can have you out by the morning on bail. That way you have a couple days to tie up loose ends. I can arrange it so that you can plead quickly to the gun charge and you can get started on your sentence. With you in jail, anything you may or may not have been involved in will just go into our thousands of unsolved cases. When you get out, you pick your life back up."

"Will you be there when I get out?" Harry asked.

"If you're good, I plan on visiting you and keeping you company before you get out. I mean, if that's OK with you."

"More than OK. Shouldn't we make this deal official somehow?"

"What do you mean?" asked Karyn. "You insisted that I not go through channels with this, even though I could have. It's not like we can write this out on paper. It wouldn't hold up in court and I'd be out on the streets or in jail. And we wouldn't be sharing a cell."

"Then we do it like this." Harry took two steps over and took Karyn in his arms. His lips found hers and they kissed for a long time.

Breaking apart, she looked at him and said, "Don't die, Harry."

"You know, I'd feel better if people stopped saying that to me."

***

It was closing in on 9:30 at night. There was a definite chill in the air this evening as the crescent moon barely illuminated eight motorcycles. They formed a cluster behind an abandoned service station two miles from the Baldwin Harbor area with a dark van parked behind them. The group had been here an hour now. Restlessness started to set in as everyone constantly checked the time. They were waiting for Sammy's call. Once that came in, they still had approximately an hour to wait. Arriving early had been a precaution in case the clock moved up. It was difficult to be in a keyed-up state for that long. All the men were ready for action and they felt like jumping out of their skin by now.

"This is just like the Army, man," said one of the bikers. "Hurry up and fucking wait."

Cowboy said, "It should be soon."

When Karyn left the clubhouse, Harry and Cowboy went in Harry's car to scope out the two possible locations. Dusk was starting to settle in, but there was plenty of light to see by. Piers

34 and 56 were practically mirror images of each other. With pier 34, you entered from the left side of the pier through an open gate in the fence and pulled into the parking lot. A building that resembled a small airplane hangar sat above the pier. The dock itself had slips for about eight good size boats. Currently, a fishing boat was tied up at the end of the dock. Pier 56 was the same setup, except you entered from the right of the dock. This location had a fishing boat and what looked like a big cabin cruiser or a small yacht tied up to it. Harry snapped plenty of photos with his phone and sent them off to Karyn.

Watching Harry take photos, Cowboy said, "She's probably already been here. She seems like a sharp cookie."

"She is that. Saved my ass when Fatso's men were after us the other day."

"How do you like working with the feds?" asked Cowboy.

"Technically, I'm not working with the feds. I'm working with Karyn. I learned long ago that I don't have all the answers. Without her, your information would've been incomplete and vice-versa."

"Situations like this make strange bedfellows. No pun intended."

Harry laughed. "No worries. It hasn't happened. And it probably won't for a year or so, if ever. I'm going to jail for a bit after this. It was part of our deal."

"What do you get out of it?" asked Cowboy.

"Unofficial immunity from the FBI being a pain in my ass."

Cowboy considered this. "She gets Fat Tony and whatever else tonight's net brings in?"

"That's right. According to her, the FBI's reputation in this area is hurting. She's banking that the haul tonight will give her some leverage with her bosses. I don't play the politics game, so I'm taking her word for it."

Nodding, Cowboy said, "I can see what she's doing. Crime fighting really isn't as black and white as it's made out to be on

TV. It's often gray, and usually downright murky. One of the reasons I got out is I was getting sick of all the bullshit."

"Well, you've gone above and beyond the call of duty on this one," said Harry.

Cowboy simply said, "John was a good friend."

They both considered that for a few minutes in silence. Harry took a close look at the area again and took two more photos. "I'm good. Let's get ready."

Back at the clubhouse, Cowboy assembled Harry's Heroes and told them the plan, such as it was. Harry was impressed with their quiet and thoughtful questions and a few suggestions that came from the group. Cowboy chose his people well. Harry was afraid he'd be dealing with a bunch of drunken bikers when Cowboy first told him the group wanted in on the action. Watching them now, he safely dispelled that notion.

At eight o'clock, they'd mounted up and made their way to behind this service station. He and Cowboy had discovered it on their reconnaissance drive. They thought it was about as central a point between the two piers as they could get. The plan was to cycle out to a vantage point over the target. They found places near each pier. From here, they'd descend on the appropriate dock at the right time.

Now in the dark, Harry received a text from Karyn. "Any word yet?"

Harry texted back that they were still waiting. Then he had a thought. He sent, "Can you contact the cops near where I live after this is over? Two cars of goons are sitting there waiting to take me out." Harry had heard from Art a half hour ago that they were still there.

"Will do," she sent back.

Right then, Cowboy's phone buzzed. "Yeah?" he answered. After listening, he said, "Number 34. You're sure…OK, Sammy, you take care of yourself…No, you won't have to worry about Fat Tony Russo anymore." Looking at Harry, he said, "It's pier 34 in an hour. Tell the cavalry."

Harry Hid It

Harry immediately texted Karyn. She replied with, "Good hunting."

"Sounds like everybody is locked and loaded," said Harry. "I have an idea. Let's go down to 34's observation point twenty minutes before zero hour. I want to make my way closer and see what's going on. I wouldn't want to hit them prematurely. We'd look pretty silly riding around with nobody out in the open."

Cowboy looked at Harry, who was dressed in black and had his ski mask tucked in his belt. "That works for me. We can see from where we park, but if you can see and hear things by being closer, it will be better. Just don't bump into any FBI guys. They may be around too. Friendly fire can kill you just as well as the bad guys."

"No shit," said Harry. "I'm pretty good at this. It will maximize our advantage."

They agreed and the group continued waiting. Finally, it was time to move. The engines started up. For Harleys, they were pretty quiet. Then Harry realized that Cowboy had the men find the quietest bikes among the clubhouse gang. He figured those who weren't on the mission felt a sense of pride by lending their bike to a member of the Heroes. It would make them feel like they were part of the mission.

All seven bikes coasted into the area they spied earlier, with Harry in the van following. From here, Harry could see a white Escalade parked next to the building. Three men were under the light where the pier first jutted out over the water. Harry had his binoculars around his neck. He got out of the van and focused on the waterfront. "That's Fat Tony and his people over there. The big guy with him might be Riley. He could have red hair, but hard to see from here. The other man looks like a geeky type. I'm going to slip down closer for a look-see. When you get a call from me, don't bother answering. Just ride."

"See you on the flipside," said Cowboy. "Watch yourself."

Without another word, Harry melted into the shadows. It was

interesting being part of such a big operation, but he liked being on his own again, even if it was only for a short time. Using what natural cover he could find, he advanced on the marina. Crouching behind a few trees growing across from the entrance, he saw two men on either side of the opening in the fence leading into the small parking lot. He looked around. Maybe he could go to the outer corner and scale the fence. As he considered this, a small pickup truck pulled up to the gate. One of the guards came over and said, "Place is closed."

The driver was a man and Harry heard him say, "Fat Tony said to come here. I'm Brucie. There's product to pick up."

A flashlight flickered on and the guard studied a paper. "OK. Go in and park next to the building. Stay in your vehicle until called."

Without giving it much thought, Harry covered the distance to the back of the truck in five steps. He lightly vaulted into the back and lay face down in the bed of the truck. He felt it move and in five seconds, he was in. As the truck slowed to a stop, Harry was already out and running to a corner of the building. He went around it and flattened himself against the wall. He waited, but when nobody shouted out, his breathing went back to normal.

Moving along the back of the building, Harry stopped and crouched down. Covering the light from his phone, Harry texted Cowboy, "Am in. Two guards at the gate. Move on my call."

Chapter 44

TAKING A DEEP BREATH, Harry continued to the far back corner of the building and worked his way around to the front of the hangar-like structure. He now had the building between him and the parking lot with a clear view of the water. He focused on the group under the light with his binoculars. It was Fat Tony, Riley, and some geeky kid. Harry heard another car coming into the parking lot as he took a close look at the geek. He looked to be in his twenties, had glasses and unruly hair, and had an iPad in his hand. He looked extremely nervous and continuously glanced between Fat Tony, the water, and back at the building.

Harry heard vehicle doors opening and closing from the parking lot. Riley moved away from Fat Tony and started for the parking lot. He yelled out, "Stay in the cars until we tell you. It won't be long now."

Now Harry heard grumbling and doors re-slamming. The wind blew off the water and Harry could hear part of the conversation wafting over from Fat Tony. "Kevin, I need you to record all the sales on that thing of yours. I want to make sure nothing gets lost between the cracks."

Kevin nervously responded, "Yes. Mr. Russo, but someone could've written it all down and I could've updated the records back at the office."

"Christ, Kevin, that's double the work. Everyone talks about a paperless society. Besides, I don't trust any of these idiots I have working for me to write their own names. Hot damn!" His voice became more excited. "Here it comes. Finally!"

Harry wasn't sure what he meant, but then he heard it. A motor cut through the water towards the dock. Soon, Harry could see a Boston Whaler approaching the end of the pier and coming up along its left side. It came around the fishing boat still tied up on the end and angled into the dock. Two men on the boat lightly jumped to the wooden dock with ropes in their hands. They made the lines fast and secured the craft to the pier. They jumped back on and soon came to the side wheeling two huge containers.

Harry heard some talking and then heard Fat Tony say, "What do you mean you won't lend me the wagons? How am I supposed to get this shit up to the building?"

"That's your problem, mate. We only deliver."

"I'm paying you a lot of money…"

"Fuck you, asshole." Harry heard the definite sound of guns being cocked. "We'll take this back with us. What's it going to be?"

"Do you know who I am?" said Fat Tony.

Harry gasped in amazement. The idiot was going to screw up this entire night with his stupidity.

"You're going to be a dead fat man in a second," said one of the men on the boat.

Harry then heard Kevin's pleading voice. "C'mon, Mr. Russo. We need this stuff or you're ruined."

Fat Tony reluctantly said, "Drop it there on the dock."

The men did and Fat Tony turned to Riley. "We need to get this up there."

In the dim light, Harry thought Riley looked frustrated. "We didn't bring that many men, Mr. Russo. You said you didn't trust anyone."

"Oh, this is my fault now!" His voice rose. "Go get some of those parasites who are buying this stuff from me. They want it. They can help carry it up to the building."

Riley eyed his boss, a quizzical look on his face. Then he turned and went up to the parking lot. His face now looked resigned, Harry thought. It wasn't like he had much of a choice.

In two minutes, Riley started walking back to the pier with seven people behind him. Harry realized this was about as good as it got. He pressed a button to call Cowboy's phone. On the second ring, he heard the herd of motorcycles come to life. Everybody heard the noise and looked out to the road. There was nothing to see. Harry realized that Cowboy ordered his crew not to turn on their lights. As they were about to enter the gate, they lit up their bikes.

Harry ran out in front to get a better view and to help where he could. He saw two bikes brake at the gate and the riders jump the two guards. One motorcycle veered off to the parking lot. A rider with a pump shotgun methodically started to blow out the tires on the vehicles parked there. Harry saw someone jump from a car and level his gun at the rider. Harry pulled his and shot him.

Turning, he looked at the chaos in front of him. Most of the people that came to buy were on the ground. One person was trying to bring out a gun when Cowboy ran into him and then ran over the fallen body. His victim screamed. Cowboy rode over to someone on the ground who was trying to aim a gun and kicked it out of his hand. When the man went to say something, he received a mouthful of cowboy boot.

Riley was trying to steady his pistol. A biker took a baseball bat out of a holster he rigged to the bike and swung it at Riley as he zipped by. There was the resounding sound of a bone breaking as the rider connected with Riley's arm. Riley screamed out in pain and held the broken limb. Another cyclist shot forward, spinning something above his head. As he let it go, Harry realized it was a lasso. The loop went over Riley's head and fell down his body. As it arrived near his ankles, the biker poured on the speed and pulled the rope tight. Riley's legs jerked out from under him and the biker dragged him behind the motorcycle. Harry watched in fascination as the rider made a sharp turn, and Riley's momentum caused him to slide right into the lamppost with a sickening crash. The bike then quickly zipped up the parking lot still dragging Riley. He pulled up to the van that quietly followed the motor- cycles. The driver leaped out, took the loose end of the lasso from the biker, and hog-tied Riley. He then effortlessly picked up the big man and threw him in the back of the van. He slammed the doors shut, and that was the last time Harry saw Sean Riley. With a burst of gravel shooting out from its tires, the van accelerated out of the parking lot. This seemed to be the signal as the other cyclists followed.

A rainbow of lights and sirens zooming into the marina immediately replaced Harry's Heroes. Looking around, Harry saw the kid with the iPad standing with his arms in the air. He looked like he was going to cry. Harry looked past him and saw a lumbering figure heading to the fishing boat parked out on the pier.

Harry took off. As he quickly gained, he heard Fat Tony shouting, "Start it up. Somebody's after me."

Too late, Harry realized Fat Tony wasn't totally stupid. He had that boat tied up since earlier today as his ticket out of here. A light from the boat blinded him and he heard, "Stop and drop it or you're dead right there."

Harry pulled up. He was only ten feet from the boat and Fat Tony. He reluctantly dropped his gun. Fat Tony turned. Harry saw his face was red and he sounded like he was going to have a heart attack from the physical exertion. When his eyes focused on Harry, they widened in surprise and he said, "You! You're the motherfucker that did all of this. Again! At least I get to kill you this time."

He had a gun in his hand and quickly brought it up. From somewhere behind him, Harry heard two quick shots. The spotlight shining on him exploded and half a second later, he felt a bullet pass by his ear. He fell to the dock and found his dropped gun. Someone on the deck of the boat started shooting at where he had been standing. Lying on his side, Harry took careful aim and fired a single shot. The shooting stopped and all was silence on the water.

Harry stayed motionless for a full minute. Crawling over to the boat, he unhooked the flashlight on his belt. When he got to Fat Tony, he switched it on and looked. There was a perfect round hole in the middle of his forehead. He didn't want to see what kind of mess the back of his head was. Crawling over the gunwale of the boat, Harry cautiously looked around. The man he shot was on the deck holding his stomach and curled in a fetal position. He was still alive. Harry found the gun the man had been using and put it in his belt. He quickly searched the rest of the boat and found it empty.

As he stepped back out on the dock, he saw a figure coming toward him with a rifle balanced on a shoulder. Drawing closer, Harry saw it was Karyn.

"Are you OK?" asked Karyn.

"You really are Annie Oakley," Harry said in amazement. "The one shot came kind of close to my ear though."

"It was the only way to nail him," said Karyn, gesturing at the deceased Fat Tony. "In another half a second he would've dropped you. I couldn't let that happen." She put her arm around his waist and said, "Besides, who am I going to put away for illegal firearms?"

Harry stepped away and held up his gun. "I have a permit for this."

"How about the one in your belt?" asked Karen.

His hand went down and he felt the gun he just pulled from the man on the boat. "Damn. By the way, the guy on the boat is alive. This is his gun."

Karyn talked into her microphone and soon a paramedic with two cops following thundered down the pier. She directed them onto the boat and they leaped on. She started to walk back toward land. Harry gave a quick jog to catch up. "How did things go on your end?"

"About as perfect as it could. You and Cowboy and Harry's Heroes," she said the title with a lilt in her voice, "really softened up everything. We caught two people trying to run away. Everyone else was either incapacitated or in shock. Funny thing, though, there's no sign of the Riley guy."

Harry shrugged his shoulders. "I don't know what happened

to him. I was concentrating on Fat Tony."

As they hit land, Harry surveyed the area. FBI vehicles and cop cars were all around. All types of lights were flashing and illuminating the area. A large group of people sat on the ground with their hands behind their backs. Cops were starting to take them to squad cars to go up to their station. He said to Karyn, "The cops have their work cut out for them tonight."

"That's someone else not too happy with me tonight. I called them when I heard the first motorcycle start up. I didn't want them here to screw up an already fucked-up raid." She looked up to the road. "They're still coming."

Harry saw two more cars with their lights on and sirens wailing pulling up to the marina. "That reminds me," he said, "can you call the cops or state police to go clean up in front of my house?"

"Oh, right. The state police would be better if they're a hit squad." She turned away and brought out her phone.

Looking at everybody running around, Harry almost started laughing. He realized he was free. Fat Tony was gone. There wasn't anyone to shoot at him anymore. Then he sobered up when he thought of Spanky, Ozzie, and John. Ozzie and John knew the possible consequences of what they did, but poor Spanky was a total innocent. Harry knew their deaths were something he was going to carry with him for the rest of his life.

Karyn came back to him. "That's taken care of. They'll be out of there tonight."

"Are you going to arrest me?"

She sighed. "Don't I look like I have enough to do tonight? If I could figure out how, I'd do this later." She reached into a back pocket and pulled out cuffs. "Put your hands behind your back and I won't make them too tight. You're going to have to wait here with me though. I need to take you in after this mess is cleared up. If someone else takes you in, it might get all fucked up." She looked into Harry's eyes. "A deal is a deal and I'm going to make sure this goes the way we agreed. You aren't the only one whose word means something."

Harry gave a small smile as he brought his hands behind him. "I can wait. My lawyer is waiting for my call and he said he'll stay by the phone all night."

As she secured the cuffs, Karyn said, "Funny how this would've given me great pleasure a month ago. I'm not happy about it now."

Harry turned back around and said, "Ugh, is it OK if I take the arresting agent out on Saturday night after I make bail?"

Karyn looked around at the chaos surrounding her. "I should have this mess under control by then." She sighed. "I hope."

***

Harry opened the door to his Camaro for Karyn and they went into his house. She hugged and petted Max as he ran around them. Harry thought she looked very pretty in a royal blue dress. Jeannie at Art's said they made a great-looking couple. She complimented Harry on actually wearing a suit, even if he didn't bother with a tie.

Harry started them out there. He wanted to introduce Karyn to Art and Jeannie. Then he had taken her into Brooklyn to a great steak place that he knew. Cocktails at a club followed that, and the two even danced together a few times. Harry knew Karyn was having a good time, but she looked exhausted. Her car was at his house and he headed back there.

Once inside, Harry asked, "Do you want tea or coffee or another drink?"

"Tea would be great."

He asked, "Since we avoided talking about the rest of your week all night, how was your week?"

"It was interesting," answered Karyn. "Kevin is that nerd we captured in the raid. He's been singing his little heart out. He told our people how to find all the evidence they need about Fat

Tony's operation on his computer at the club. He's also going to testify how Sean Riley orchestrated all the murders."

"Any sign of Riley?"

"Nope. Cowboy and the rest of the Heroes have no clue. I asked them because I had to and then walked away."

"Riley killed their friend. It's not complicated."

"I know, and I want to stay on their good side. Let's see, what else can I tell you? We broke up at least a half a dozen drug networks by capturing the buyers who were there. And the Coast Guard nailed the boat running the drugs right outside the harbor. Those idiots skimmed some of the drugs off the shipment and the Guard found them on the boat. They're being held and charged."

"You really scored then," said Harry. "Is your boss happy? What kind of promotion are you going to get?"

"That's a little complicated right now. I had to endure a half hour of my boss bawling me out. Loudly. He wanted to make sure the entire floor and half of Manhattan heard him. When he got done, he shook my hand and quietly said that he'd have done the same thing. He said he'd smooth over any of the rough edges with the higher-ups."

"What rough edges?"

"You know, the help of a motorcycle gang, exactly how I came by all my information, and you."

"How much did you tell him about our deal?"

"When I started to vaguely mention some things, he put his fingers in his ears and walked away. It was his way of telling me to do it without specifically approving it. As for a promotion, I don't care about that right now. I feel like this will erase the one black mark on my record from out west."

"Are you going to be staying around this area then?"

Max came up and plopped his head in Karyn's lap. She giggled and started scratching behind his ears. Max whined in contentment. "Yeah, I'm going to be hanging out here for a time. There's a ton of follow-up to be done with Fat Tony's records. He wasn't the most accomplished criminal around here, but he was into many things. It will keep me busy. Plus, there's always three or four new crimes that pop up every week that finds its way to the FBI."

Karyn drank some of the tea Harry put in front of her and said, "Have you done what you need to do?"

"Pretty much. I was out on bail by early Tuesday morning. I was able to make the memorial service for John that afternoon. I went to that and then headed back to the clubhouse. I have to admit that I think it all hit me then. I drank too much, but I think I had a good time. I needed to blow off steam. The last few days I've been getting my affairs in order."

"Harry, if you died, I estimate there would've been a small fortune lost somewhere. Am I right?"

"That's only if I did any of those things you think I did. You know about what happened with Fat Tony. Anything we took from him I made sure John at least could figure out where it was."

"And how would he do that?" asked Karyn with a twinkle in her eyes.

Harry gave her a big smile. "You know, for the time I've spent on the wrong side of the tracks, as some would say, my favorite books as a kid were the Sherlock Holmes mysteries. I'll answer that the way Holmes did once. 'You know my methods, Watson, now apply them.' It really isn't complicated. Other than that, this part of the conversation is now ended." Harry was still smiling and saluted her with his mug of tea.

Karyn shook her head at the audacity of the man. She'd really have hated putting him in jail for a long time. He was a good guy. Maybe just a little misguided at times. She looked down at Max as she continued petting him. "Who's going to take care of this beautiful animal while you're gone?"

She looked up sharply as the sound of metal clinked in front of her. Following the sound, she saw a key still vibrating where it landed. She picked it up and looked at Harry with a questioning look on her face. He said, "I want you to move in here. You don't deserve to live in that shoebox of an apartment. You and Max like each other. I'll feel a lot better if you were here. One reason I took you to meet Art and Jeannie is that they're like my family around here. If you run into trouble or you have to travel for work, they can help with looking after the house and Max. Art swears he makes more money when Max is holding court at the bar. What do you say?"

It had been a long time since Karyn was overwhelmed. She'd love to get out of her apartment. This would be a wonderful break. She almost felt like a real person again. She said, "What happens when you get out?"

"We'll figure it out then. There are two bedrooms. Maybe we'll be roommates. One thing at a time."

She'd tell the office she found a house to rent. They didn't have to know the circumstances. "Harry, consider your home in good hands."

He stood up and took her hand. "Would you like to go see your bedroom, or are you too old-fashioned?"

She stood. "I'm not that old-fashioned."

Epilogue

KARYN OPENED THE DOOR from the garage. Max bounded up to her and then looked behind her and whined. Going down on her knees, Karyn hugged the dog to her. "I know, boy, I miss him too." Then she started crying.

It was her second cry today. Before that, she couldn't remember the last time she cried. Harry and his lawyer came into the office around ten this Monday morning. It had been a week since the takedown at the dock. She did the formal processing for Harry. Gonzales had made arrangements for Harry to be brought before a judge in the afternoon so that he could get to where he was going as quickly as possible. In fact, Enrico Gonzales came into the room when Karyn was filling out the paperwork. He asked if he could have a few minutes with the prisoner. Harry said it was fine and Karyn and his lawyer left the room.

Ten minutes later when Gonzales left and Karyn went back in, Harry had a big shit-eating grin on his face. She'd have to ask Gonzales about that later. When two officers came to escort Harry away, Karyn shook hands with his lawyer, went to the bathroom, and cried her eyes out in one of the stalls. Maybe everything had hit Harry last Tuesday after John's service, but now it was her turn. When she stopped and cleaned up her face, she decided to go in and ask for a few days off.

She knocked on Gonzales' open door. He waved her in and indicated she should shut the door behind her. He looked as tired as she felt. Before she said anything, he said, "Get out of here. I don't want to see you until next Monday. You look like shit."

"Just what every woman wants to hear," said Karyn. "Thank you, I need it. You look like you could too."

"I do…and I will. I have to go down to Washington for a few

439

days. They want to parade me around as someone who can make a difference on crime."

"Are these the same people who threatened you a month ago?"

"That would be them. Sometimes I wish I worked for the Park Service and had a mountain to watch or something. I don't think bears bother with politics."

"Sir, I have a question. What did you say to Harry Strickland?"

That brought a grin from Gonzales. "I told him I'd give him a medal if I could. I told him the irony shouldn't be lost on any of us that he saved the reputation of this FBI office. He found that as hilarious as I did. I also thanked him for watching out for one of my best agents."

Karyn felt tears starting again. She quickly rubbed her eyes. She didn't expect that.

"Now get out of here, Agent Dudek. See you next week."

"Thank you, sir." Karyn straightened out her desk and left.

Max followed her up the stairs. He watched as she changed into jeans and a sweatshirt. She had put her suitcase in the guest bedroom. Karyn couldn't quite make herself move into Harry's room. She looked over at his room with a knowing smile.

Downstairs, she made herself some tea and started to explore the house more. She didn't have much in her apartment, but she could get somebody to move her stuff this week now that she had the time off. She spent some time looking at Harry's painting room. He really was a man of many talents. Coming back into the living room, she sat in Harry's chair. Maybe tonight she'd walk over to Art's with Max and eat. It would give her a chance to get to know Art and Jeannie.

As she sat there in his chair, she thought about Harry. She'd visit him as often as she could. She hoped the year would fly by. Harry would be sentenced for three years, but if he didn't get into any trouble, he'd be paroled well short of that. She gave up trying to reconcile that he was a good man and a crook. One didn't necessarily negate the other.

Harry Hid It

When she did the math, she realized he had five million dollars or so out there somewhere. She said aloud, "Harry, where the hell would you hide it?" Then she remembered the quote from Sherlock Holmes: "You know my methods, Watson, apply them." Was Harry telling her that she had information to figure out the riddle herself?

She let out a laugh loud enough that Max leaped to attention from the rug where he lay. He came over and looked at her. She looked back and said, "That son of a bitch is challenging me." She hugged Max. "He wants to see if I can figure out where it is!"

Harry Strickland will return in June 2017

The Contest

I hope you enjoyed *Harry Hid It*. As you know, Harry stashed away something near $5 million that he accumulated from the heists in the story. Where is it?

That's where you come in.

From March 1, 2017 to the contest deadline of June 15, 2017, you can submit your solution to the puzzle. There is only one entry allowed per person, so make sure you give it your best shot. We want to give people plenty of time to pick up the book, comb through the story, and submit their answer.

Starting March 1, 2017, you can go to www.harryhidit.com and enter electronically. You will be asked for the location of the hidden money and the clues you found in the book that led you to your solution. For those needing to mail the entry in the traditional way, instructions are on the next page as well as on the website. In fact, everything you need to know is at www.harryhidit.com

Yes...this is very real! It may not be the millions of dollars Harry and his gang get their hands on, but the prize pool begins at $5000 and increases by $25,000 with every 10,000 books sold. It can rise as high as $500,000!!

If there is a tie, all winners will receive a proportionate share of the prize pool. For instance, if the prize money is up to $100,000 and there are two winners, they each receive $50,000. Since the beginning of this endeavor, I said that if I do a great job on this part of the book, two or three people would split a lot of money. If I do a poor job, we will be sending out many $25 checks!!!

How the prize pool accumulates and the official rules are at the very end of the book. A third party experienced in running contests (Alliance Sweepstakes Services Inc.) is in charge of that aspect of *Harry Hid It* to ensure its integrity and compliance.

Best of luck unraveling the location of Harry's hiding place!

JJ McKeever

Author - *Harry Hid It*

Mailing in Your Entry

While we encourage everyone to enter through the online entry form that will be on www.harryhidit.com on March 1, 2017, we recognize that some people will need to mail in their solution. Follow these simple rules to be part of the contest:

You MUST have your name and address, as well as a telephone contact number (if you have one) on your submission. Please type or print. Only one entry per person is allowed or all your entries will be disqualified.

You Must clearly state where you believe Harry hid the money and jewels.

You Must list the clues that led you to that conclusion and the chapters in which you found each clue. These will be the tie-breaker for the contest so be thorough!

Mail your entry in by June 15, 2017 to:

BT Enterprise of Long Island

PO Box 109

Rockville Centre, NY 11571-0109

"Where Did Harry Hide It?" Contest

Official Rules

NO PURCHASE NECESSARY TO ENTER OR WIN. A PURCHASE WILL NOT INCREASE YOUR CHANCES OF WINNING. ALL FEDERAL, STATE, LOCAL, AND MUNICIPAL LAWS AND REGULATIONS APPLY. VOID WHERE PROHIBITED.

Participation constitutes entrant's full and unconditional agreement to and acceptance of these contest rules ("Official Rules"). The "Where did Harry hide it?" Contest begins at 12:00 a.m., Eastern Time ("ET") on March 1st, 2017 and ends at 11:59 a.m., ("ET") on June 15, 2017 ("Contest Period"). Contest is sponsored by BT Enterprise of Long Island, LLC ("Sponsor"), PO Box 109 Rockville Centre, New York, 11571-0109.

ELIGIBILITY: The "Where did Harry hide it?" Contest (the "Contest") is open to all legal residents of the fifty (50) United States and the District of Columbia, who have attained the age of majority in his or her state or territory of residence as of the Contest start date. Employees, officers and representatives of the Sponsor, the Sponsor's parent, affiliates, subsidiaries, agents, advertising and promotion agencies, and Alliance Sweepstakes Services Inc. (the "Administrator") (collectively, "Released Parties") and members of the immediate family (mother, father, sons, daughters and spouse, regardless of where they reside) and household members of each such employee, whether or not related, are not eligible to participate in the Contest. Participation constitutes entrant's full and unconditional agreement to and acceptance of these official rules. Void in Puerto Rico and where prohibited by law.

HOW TO ENTER: During the Contest Period eligible participants may enter one of two ways: (1) By visiting the Sponsor's promotional website at www.harryhidit.com and follow the directions to the contest page where they must fill out all the required fields on the entry form, or (2) they may enter by mail by using the pre-printed entry form found in the back of the book or by hand printing or typing their name, date of birth, address (including zip code), telephone number and e-mail address (if applicable), answering the question explained below and mailing their entry in a business size envelope to: BT Enterprise of Long Island, LLC PO Box 109 Rockville Centre, NY 11571-0109.

All participants, regardless of the method of entry must answer the following question: Where did Harry Strickland hide the money, gems and diamonds that he and his crew stole during their five capers detailed in the *"Harry Hid It"* book? (the "Question"). Each entrant must also submit a narrative (300 words maximum) written by the entrant that lists all the clues that they followed to derive at the answer to the mystery. Each properly completed and received entry will receive one (1) Submission to the Contest.

Only one (1) Submission per person is allowed. Duplicate submissions from the same email address will not be accepted via the online entry form. If a person enters more than once, they will be disqualified. Once submitted, a Submission cannot be deleted, canceled, or modified. Incomplete Submissions, or those containing incorrect information or those which do not follow the Official Rules will be voided. Proof of sending a Submission will not be deemed to be proof of receipt by Sponsor. By participating in this Contest, entrants agree to be bound by these Official Rules and the decisions of the Sponsor which are final and binding in all matters relating to the Contest. Any personally identifiable information collected by the Sponsor during an entrant's participation in this Contest may be used by Sponsor, its respective affiliates, agents and marketers for purposes of the proper administration and fulfillment of the Contest as described in these Official Rules.

SUBMISSION GUIDELINES: Each Submission must be received by June 15, 2017 and contain a narrative written by the entrant that lists all the clues that they followed to derive at the answer to the mystery in the "*Harry Hid It*" book (the "Book"). Each Submission must not exceed 300 words. Submissions must be the original work of the person who entered. Entrant must be the sole owner of the copyright of any submission he or she submits. By entering a Submission, each entrant guarantees that he or she is the author and copyright holder of the Submission. Sponsor will not assist any entrant with the development or production of a Submission. Each entrant represents and warrants that Submission does not infringe any other person's or entity's intellectual property rights. Entrant represents and warrants that he or she will not have and will not acquire any trademark rights, copyrights, or any other rights in or to Sponsor's trademarks, trade names, logos or other intellectual property. Sponsor specifically reserves all its rights to protect its intellectual property against any infringement or other illegal or improper use.

The Sponsor, in its sole discretion, may remove a Submission and disqualify any entrant from the Contest if it believes that the Submission fails to conform to the Submission Guidelines contained in these Official Rules. Submissions which include any content that may be deemed inappropriate, indecent, obscene, or disparaging of the Sponsor, as determined by Sponsor in its sole discretion, will be disqualified.

Sponsor shall have the right to edit, adapt and publish any or all of the Submissions and may use them for any proper purpose, including, without limitation, for Sponsor's advertising/promotional purposes or in any media in association with the Contest without attribution or compensation to the entrant, his/her successors or assigns, or any other entity unless prohibited by law. Sponsor is not responsible for lost, late, incomplete, invalid, unintelligible, illegible, or misdirected Submissions, which are void.

JUDGING: Each entrant who meets the eligibility requirements as outlined in these Official Rules will move on to the Judging phase. A panel of qualified judges (the "Judges"), determined solely by the Sponsor, will then review all eligible Submissions throughout the Contest Period. At the end of the Contest Period they will choose a Grand Prize winner based on the following judging criteria: Correct answer to the Question, 25%; finding all the clues, percentage pro-rated based on the number of correct clues (maximum 50% for finding all of them, 0% for finding none); and quality of submission, 25%. The decision of the Judges will be final.

GRAND PRIZE: One Grand Prize (the "Grand Prize") will be awarded based on the total number of Books sold from the first sale of the Book up until May 31, 2017. This Contest has the potential of accumulating up to a $500,000 total prize pool. A guaranteed minimum prize pool of $5,000 will be awarded and the prize pool will grow based on total book sales as outlined in the chart below:

# OF BOOKS SOLD	PRIZE		# OF BOOKS SOLD	PRIZE
under 10,000	$ 5,000			
10,000	$ 25,000		110,000	$ 275,000
20,000	$ 50,000		120,000	$ 300,000
30,000	$ 75,000		130,000	$ 325,000
40,000	$ 100,000		140,000	$ 350,000
50,000	$ 125,000		150,000	$ 375,000
60,000	$ 150,000		160,000	$ 400,000
70,000	$ 175,000		170,000	$ 425,000
80,000	$ 200,000		180,000	$ 450,000
90,000	$ 225,000		190,000	$ 475,000
100,000	$ 250,000		200,000	$ 500,000

The Sponsor's website, www.harryhidit.com, will post a tally of the number of Books sold to date & the accumulating prize pool based on sales which will be updated monthly.

In the case of a tie in which multiple entrants have the same highest score based on the judging criteria outlined in these office rules, the prize pool will be prorated equally amongst those entrants and they will all be considered to be the grand prize winners.

PRIZE VERIFICATION & CONDITIONS: The potential Grand Prize winner(s) will be notified by the same method of how they entered, via: email, phone or regular United States Postal Mail Service.

If a prize or prize notification is returned as unclaimed or undeliverable to a potential winner, if the potential winner cannot be reached within thirty (30) calendar days from the first notification attempt, if the potential winner fails to return requisite document within the specified time period, or if a potential winner is not in compliance with these Official Rules, then such person shall be disqualified and the Submission with the next highest score (unless in the case of a tie) may be selected for the Grand Prize. The Grand Prize may not be awarded in the event an insufficient number of eligible Submissions are received that meet the minimum criteria outlined in these Official Rules. Grand Prize winner(s) will be required to sign an Affidavit of Eligibility and Liability/Publicity Release which must be returned within thirty (30) calendar days of written notification, or the Grand Prize may be forfeited. The Grand Prize winner(s) will also be required to disclose his/her social security number for the purpose of issuance of a 1099 Form for tax purposes. By accepting the Grand Prize, entrant agrees to release all Released Parties from any and all liability whatsoever for any injuries, losses, or damages of any kind caused by entering the Contest or for damages of any kind caused by any prize or resulting from acceptance, possession, or use/misuse of Grand Prize awarded. All local, state and federal taxes are solely the responsibility of winner. No substitution or transfer of Grand Prize will be permitted.

GENERAL: By accepting the Grand Prize, where permitted by law, the Grand Prize winner grants to the Sponsor, Sponsor's parent, affiliates, subsidiaries, and related companies, and those acting pursuant to the authority of Sponsor (which grant will be confirmed in writing upon Sponsor's request), the right to print, publish, broadcast and use worldwide IN ALL MEDIA without limitation at any time the Grand Prize winner's full name, portrait, picture, voice, likeness and/or biographical information for advertising, trade and promotional purposes without further payment or additional consideration, and without review, approval or notification. IN NO EVENT WILL SPONSOR, SPONSOR'S PARENT, AFFILIATES, SUBSIDIARIES, ADVERTISING AND PROMOTION AGENCIES, DEALERS, DISTRIBUTORS, SUPPLIERS, PRIZE PROVIDER AND THEIR RESPECTIVE DIRECTORS, OFFICERS, EMPLOYEES, REPRESENTATIVES AND AGENTS BE RESPONSIBLE OR LIABLE FOR ANY DAMAGES OR LOSSES OF ANY KIND (INCLUDING WITHOUT LIMITATION, DIRECT, INDIRECT, INCIDENTAL, CONSEQUENTIAL, OR PUNITIVE DAMAGES) ARISING OUT OF PARTICIPATION IN THIS CONTEST OR THE ACCEPTANCE, POSSESSION, USE, OR MISUSE OF, OR ANY HARM RESULTING FROM THE ACCEPTANCE, POSSESSION, USE OR MISUSE OF THE PRIZES. By participating, entrants release and agree to hold harmless the Sponsor, the Sponsor's parent, affiliates, subsidiaries, related companies, advertising and promotion agencies, dealers, distributors, suppliers, Grand Prize provider and their respective directors, officers, employees, representatives and agents from any and all liability for any injuries, death or losses or damages to persons or property AS WELL AS CLAIMS/ACTIONS BASED ON PUBLICITY RIGHTS, DEFAMATION, INTELLECTUAL PROPERTY INFRINGEMENT, AND INVASION OF PRIVACY that may arise from participating in this Contest or its related activities or the acceptance, possession, use or misuse of, or any harm resulting from the acceptance, possession, use or misuse of the Grand Prize. Grand Prize winner acknowledges that Sponsor have neither made nor are in any manner responsible or liable for any warranty, representation or guarantee, express or implied, in fact or in law, relative to the Grand Prize.

INTERNET LIMITATIONS OF LIABILITY: If for any reason this Contest is not capable of running as planned due to infection by computer virus, bugs, tampering, unauthorized intervention, fraud, technical failures, or any other causes beyond the reasonable control of the Sponsor which corrupt or affect the administration, security, fairness, integrity or proper conduct of the Contest, Sponsor reserves the right, at its sole discretion, to disqualify any entrant, individual, entity, etc. who tampers with the entry process, and to cancel, terminate, modify or suspend the Contest in whole or in part, at any time, without notice and award the Grand Prize using all non-suspect eligible entries received. No responsibility is assumed for any error, omission, interruption, deletion, defect, delay in operation or transmission, communications line failure, theft or destruction or unauthorized access to, or alteration of, entries, or for any problems or technical malfunction of any telephone network or telephone lines, computer on-line systems, servers, or providers, computer equipment, software, failure of any e-mail or entry to be received by Sponsor on account of technical problems, human error or traffic congestion on the Internet or at any Website, or any combination thereof, including any injury or damage to entrant's or any other person's computer relating to or resulting from participation in the Contest or downloading any materials in the Contest. CAUTION: ANY ATTEMPT TO DELIBERATELY DAMAGE ANY WEBSITE OR UNDERMINE THE LEGITIMATE OPERATION OF THE CONTEST IS A VIOLATION OF CRIMINAL AND CIVIL LAWS AND SHOULD SUCH AN ATTEMPT BE MADE, THE SPONSOR RESERVES THE RIGHT TO SEEK DAMAGES OR OTHER REMEDIES FROM ANY SUCH PERSON AND/OR ENTITY (S) RESPONSIBLE FOR THE ATTEMPT TO THE FULLEST EXTENT PERMITTED BY LAW. In the event of a dispute as to the identity of the Grand Prize winner based on an e-mail address, the winning entry will be declared made by the authorized account holder of the e-mail address submitted at time of entry. "Authorized account holder" is defined as the natural person who is assigned to an e-mail address by an Internet access provider, on-line service provider or other organization (e.g., business, educational, institution, etc.) that is responsible for assigning e-mail addresses for the domain associated with the submitted e-mail address.

USE OF DATA: Sponsor will be collecting personal data about entrants including e-mail addresses from entry forms in accordance with its Privacy Policy. Please review the Sponsor's Privacy Policy at the Sponsor's website: http://www.harryhidit.com.By participating in the Contest and providing your e-mail address, entrants hereby agree to Sponsor's collection and usage of their personal information and acknowledge that they have read and accepted Sponsor's Privacy Policy.

DISPUTES: Except where prohibited, entrant agrees that any and all disputes, claims and causes of action arising out of, or connected with, the Contest or any Grand Prize awarded shall be resolved individually, without resort to any form of class action, and exclusively by the appropriate court located in the State of New York. All issues and questions concerning the construction, validity, interpretation and enforceability of these Official Rules, entrant's rights and obligations, or the rights and obligations of Sponsor in connection with the Contest, shall be governed by, and construed in accordance with, the laws of the State of New York, without giving effect to any choice of law or conflict of law rules (whether of the State of New York or any other jurisdiction), which would cause the application of the laws of any jurisdiction other than the State of New York.

GRAND PRIZE WINNER LIST REQUESTS: To request confirmation of the name and address of the Grand Prize winner(s) please send a self-addressed, stamped business size envelope, by June 15, 2017 to: Where Did Harry Hide It? Contest c/o AS, 620 Park Ave., #332, Rochester, NY 14607.

SPONSOR: BT Enterprise of Long Island, LLC, Long, PO Box 109 Rockville Centre, New York, 11571-0109.

Abbreviated Rules for print

Must be legal resident of the 50 United States (D.C.), and age of majority in his/her state at the time of entry. Contest starts 3/1/17 and ends 6/15/17. For entry and official rules with complete eligibility, prize description, odds disclosure and other details, visit www.harryhidit.com. No purchase necessary. A purchase will not increase your chances of winning. Sponsored by BT Enterprise of Long Island, LLC. Void where prohibited.

Made in the USA
Middletown, DE
20 May 2016